PRAISE FOR

THE CITY OF GOOD DEATH

"Priyanka Champaneri beautifully explores the sacred and the afterlife in this cinematic and emotionally gripping work about living and dying with dignity. . . . *The City of Good Death* confronts family, religion, and belonging in ways that reflect Champaneri's cultural dualities. It's a novel full of compassion as Champaneri deftly navigates Pramesh's relationships with his dying patrons as he himself struggles to understand the ramifications of his cousin's death. . . . This ambitious novel offers readers a unique insight into the Hindu concepts of the afterlife and the sacred, and the universally recognizable desire for empathy and understanding."

TÉA OBREHT AND ILAN STAVANS,
FROM THE JUDGES' CITATION FOR THE 2018
RESTLESS BOOKS PRIZE IN NEW IMMIGRANT WRITING

"Throughout this epic, Champaneri remains attuned to such atmospheric details, both physical and emotional. Set in the holy city of Kashi, where Hindus travel to 'die a death that was the best one could hope for on this Earth' — one that ends the cycle of 'rebirths and miseries' — the novel pays particular attention to the topographies of mourning. . . . Champaneri subtly renders how grief lurks in mundane objects and gestures. . . . The novel remains an intimate portrait of Pramesh, and yet the other characters allow Champaneri to articulate how grief and healing are social processes. . . . Just as grief descends, sudden and sweeping, so too can wonder and joy."

SPENCER QUONG, *THE NEW YORK TIMES BOOK REVIEW*

"In intricate detail and with remarkable skill, Champaneri writes a powerful tale about the pull of the past and our aching need to understand the mysteries and misunderstandings that thwart our relationships.

An atmospheric and immersive debut with a rich cast of characters you won't soon forget."

"In Champaneri's ambitious, vivid debut, the dying come to the holy city of Kashi to die a good death that frees them from the burden of reincarnation. . . . In sharp prose, Champaneri explores the power of stories—those the characters tell themselves, those told about them, and those they believe. . . . This epic, magical story of death teems with life."

"Lush prose evokes the thick, close atmosphere of Kashi and the intricate religious practices upon which life and death depend. Rumor and superstition hold sway over even the most level-headed people, twisting what's explainable into something extraordinary—with tragic consequences. . . . *The City of Good Death* is a breathtaking, unforgettable novel about how remembering the past is just as important as moving on."

"*The City of Good Death* reads so like the book of a seasoned author, it is hard to believe it is Champaneri's first. From the opening words she pulls you in, weaves you into the threads of Kashi, a city where people flock to die and others flee to a new life. Her impeccable sentences move through you like the river at the city's heart, tides of happiness interrupted by rising storms of fear, mystery, and difficult love. It is a book where magic lies right alongside the mess and beauty of human life, a book about family, tradition, and forgiveness, about finding your way even if it means turning your back on where you are from. It's the sort of book that, as I wait for the author's next work of genius, I will not be able to resist reading again."

"I was transported to India by this debut novel, for which the author won the Restless Books Prize for New Immigrant Writing. Well-deserved, too. A recurring theme is looking back or not looking back and the consequences of both. It tells the story of cousins who are more like twin brothers, growing up with their two abusive, denigrating fathers, and the choices each makes. Don't pass this one up."

BARBARA LUBIN, WHITE BIRCH BOOKS (CONWAY, NEW HAMPSHIRE)

"*The City of Good Death* is the debut novel of Priyanka Champaneri but it has the confidence of a master storyteller. Drawing on the rich literary traditions of Salman Rushdie and Arundhati Roy, Champaneri's epic saga will satisfy armchair travelers thirsty for adventure, and sick of looking out their windows."

CHICAGO REVIEW OF BOOKS

"This contemplative debut novel, rendered with evocative prose, will make you think about life, death, and redemption, together with its cast of finely drawn characters."

SHILPI SOMAYA GOWDA, AUTHOR OF *THE SHAPE OF FAMILY*

"Brimming with characters whose lives overlap and whose stories interweave, Champaneri's exquisite debut delves into the consequences of the past, and how stories that are told can become reality even when they contain barely a shred of truth. As Pramesh discovers, the bitterness of past wounds can bring hope for redemption and life."

BRIDGET THORESON, *BOOKLIST*

"*The City of Good Death* is an extraordinary novel—beautifully written, rich in characters of great complexity and passion—a family story at once familiar and exotic. I loved this novel of life and death, of time and memory. It has the depth of feeling and particularity of scene that transports the reader from the world as we know it to the world we discover and cannot forget in the death hostel in Kashi. There is so much in these characters to love and admire. I could not put the book down."

SUSAN RICHARDS SHREVE, AUTHOR OF *MORE NEWS TOMORROW*

"What follows is an astounding mystery in which nothing cooperates as it should—not even the dead. . . . This novel could be seen as one cleaved in two, with mysteries unfolding discreetly in the realms of women and of men, and Champaneri deftly balances the weight of expectation and introspection, of skepticism and faith, and what is sought out and what is hidden. As the city stirs with gossip and intrigue, Pramesh and Shobha deal with hauntings of all kinds, their stories weaving around one another to reveal the intersection of love and grief, and perhaps even illuminating some of the mysteries of the Land of the Dead."

LUCY SHAPIRO, THE ARKANSAS INTERNATIONAL

"*The City of Good Death* is a reflection on dying and on life and love and all the complications that living and dying entail. Told in accessible, evocative prose, it takes the reader into the hearts of its characters and the dilemmas they must resolve to maintain the relationships they value. This is a beautiful book unlike any other I have read recently, and forever the images of the river Ganges and the characters—the living and the dead—that populate its banks will remain with me."

HELON HABILA, AUTHOR OF *TRAVELERS* AND *OIL ON WATER*

"Champaneri's Kashi is teeming and vivid . . . the book frequently charms, and it's as full of humor, warmth, and mystery as Kashi's own marketplace."

KIRKUS REVIEWS

"Pramesh runs the most desirable death hostel in Kashi, India, the holiest of cities alongside the Ganges River. He calmly oversees a revolving door of families with their dying loved ones as well as an assortment of priests and others needed to carry out the rituals of death. However, his respected position in the community is challenged when his estranged cousin, Sagar, dies nearby without the proper rituals and begins haunting the hostel, interfering with the peaceful deaths of others. How and why Sagar came to be near Pramesh, and how to restore the equilibrium of the hostel, forces Pramesh to face his complicated past. This character-rich, atmospheric novel, winner of the 2018 Restless Books Prize for New Immigrant Writing, is a delightful mix of humor, heartbreak, and insight."

CINDY PAULDINE, RIVER'S END BOOKSTORE (OSWEGO, NY)

"This is an expansive family saga steeped in Hindu traditions."

SIFY

"It's so, so lovely. . . . I was completely entranced by this book. I thought the writing was beautiful, and I thought the story was unlike anything that I had read before. . . . The characters were fully realized; I felt like I knew them and wanted to spend more time with them. A heck of a debut, and I loved it."

LIBERTY HARDY, ALL THE BOOKS!

"What I appreciated most as the tension built were the small, painstaking details Champaneri leaves for the reader—like a woman watching everything from her window—and the way the story rewards the close reader by building on these small details as the story develops. The work of getting to know all these characters pays off as their lives intertwine on the page. . . . As Pramesh contemplates his own childhood in the village where he grew up and all the ways in which he and his twin cousin shared their early lives together, it is a beautiful combination of nostalgia and heartbreak. I found myself too thinking about these scenes and others in the weeks after I finished the book, a sign of a poignant story and one that had gotten its hooks into me. . . . This introspection about our pasts and the way we make sense of our early lives is one of the most compelling parts of the novel and one of many ways in which *The City of Good Death* is a deep and reflective story."

LAUREN WOODS, DCTRENDING

"*The City of Good Death* . . . explores the rituals and customs of death from a non-Western perspective. . . . The final third of the novel becomes a glorious, moving testament to *moksha*, to liberating the soul from the burdens of the past. *The City of Good Death* not only showcases Champaneri's cultural background, but it also forefronts the manner in which family can both hurt and heal that is both deeply spiritual and emotionally satisfying."

IAN MOND, *LOCUS MAGAZINE*

"Characters tell tales that are folklore, myth, reminiscences, or dreams. All stories deeply alter their existence and relationships. Champaneri's descriptive prose is precise and evocative. . . . The classic cliffhanger at the end of almost every chapter isn't contrived but integral to the story and its arcs. Making full use of the mysticism and magnetism of Kashi, Champaneri immerses us in a city teeming with as much life as death."

JENNY BHATT, *MINNEAPOLIS STAR TRIBUNE*

"This is an insightful look at the Hindu traditions surrounding death and 'funerals' in the holy city of Kashi. . . . This is a remarkable cultural story but also one of common humanity. Book clubs will want to give it a look."

LINDA BOND, AUNTIE'S BOOKSTORE (SPOKANE, WA)

THE CITY OF GOOD DEATH

A Novel

PRIYANKA CHAMPANERI

RESTLESS BOOKS
BROOKLYN, NEW YORK

Copyright © 2021 Priyanka Champaneri

Originally published in hardcover and ebook by Restless Books in 2020
First trade paperback edition March 2022

Paperback ISBN: 9781632062536
Library of Congress Control Number: 2019944182

Cover design by Sarah Schneider
Cover photo by Adnan Abidi © Reuters. Used by permission.
Set in Garibaldi by Tetragon, London

Printed in the United States of America

1 3 5 7 9 10 8 6 4 2

Restless Books, Inc.
232 3rd Street, Suite A101
Brooklyn, NY 11215

www.restlessbooks.org
publisher@restlessbooks.org

For Buh
For Pop
For Bhai

CONTENTS

We all owe death a life.

SALMAN RUSHDIE, *MIDNIGHT'S CHILDREN*

The wave behind calls to the forward waves,
"I will not let you go."
No one listens to the call and no one heeds.

RABINDRANATH TAGORE,
TRANS. HUMAYUN KABIR

CHARACTERS

RESIDENTS OF SHANKARBHAVAN, A DEATH HOSTEL

PRAMESH: the hostel manager
SHOBHA: Pramesh's wife
RANI: Pramesh and Shobha's three-year-old daughter
DHARAM: Shobha's father, the former hostel manager
MOHAN: the manager's assistant
NARINDER: the head priest
LOKNATH and DEV: junior priests
SHEETAL: a teenage guest of the hostel who cares for his dying father

RESIDENTS OF KASHI

MRS. MISTRY: elderly neighbor and friend of Shobha
MRS. GUPTA: neighbor of Mrs. Mistry and Shobha
BHUT: circle officer (deputy superintendent) at Dashashwamedh Police Station
RAMAN: a lovesick boatman
MAHARAJ: resident vagrant and drunk
THAKORLAL: a metal shop owner and illegal purveyor of home brew
MRS. CHALWAH: elderly widow living across the street from the bhavan
KISHORE: a prominent ghaatiyaa (river priest)

PRAMESH'S FAMILY

SAGAR: Pramesh's cousin
KAMNA: Sagar's wife
THE ELDER PRASADS: brothers who are the fathers of Pramesh and Sagar
THE MOTHERS: Pramesh and Sagar's mothers
BUA: Pramesh and Sagar's widowed paternal aunt

PRAMESH'S HOME VILLAGE

JAYA: childhood friend of Pramesh and Sagar
CHAMPA: neighbor of Pramesh and Sagar
HARDEV: farmer and husband of Champa
DIVYA: daughter of Champa and Hardev
NATTU: goatherd

THE CITY OF GOOD DEATH

There is one place in Kashi that everyone avoids. It is easy to find: walk to Mir ghat, descend those stone steps. Push through the crowds of people and drift toward the right as you go down, down, down. Stop just as you reach the final step before the stone dips into the river, and mark the place where the ground is clean, where the stone seems newly carved next to the worn and crumbling rock surrounding it. Even better: sit some paces away and watch. See how all folk avoid stepping there, how even those in deep throes of gossip or prayer direct their feet elsewhere. The youngest children know to jump over that clean stone; men cross on tiptoe; and women take the widest circle around it, hems held in hands so that no single thread of their saris will touch that cursed spot. Most don't question why they cannot cross. They obey an internal order, the action as instinctive as turning the ear toward the sound of a new story.

But for those who do know, who never come near that place without the great God's name on their lips, the reason is absolute: a ghost wanders there. A woman swollen with child crossing that path might suddenly find her belly hollow. Men setting a wrong foot begin to weep without control. Careless children lose their smiles or the ability to speak. Old folk lose their sight or the last of their senses.

There is no pattern, no rhyme or reason to the ghost's actions—simply its thirst for malice. The only thing common to these tales of calamity is what you hear, what you see just before the spirit is upon you.

The chime of silver anklets.

A song that the wind winnows down to a sob.

And the rustle and flash of silk, of a parrot green that glows in the night.

PART I

I

When the boatmen found the body in the river, they should have thought nothing of it. There was nothing unusual in steering past floating arms and blackened buttocks, in putting an oar into the river and having to reposition it when you found a soot-streaked foot barring your way. Everyone knew the Doms were cheap folk with no respect for proper funeral rites, greedy for the few rupees they might save by snuffing a pyre before the fire had claimed an entire body, dumping the charred corpse into the river, and selling the half-burnt wood to another gullible family too grief-stricken to know the difference.

The two boatmen had been out early, before the veil of morning fog lifted from the river. They shared a boat, one man at each end, and passed a bottle between them. They steered themselves to the middle of the river, to a spot shrouded in dense fog between the holy city of Kashi and the cursed far shore called Magadha.

Their spot was well chosen. Every man in Kashi knew three basic facts: dying in the holy city promised freedom from rebirth, bathing in the Ganges washed away the sins of a lifetime, and dying on Magadha guaranteed that you would come back as one of the lowest of the low, a donkey destined to bear burdens and insults until a merciful death started the cycle anew. Here, the two boatmen hid their early morning libations from Kashi's wandering tongues even as they kept a firm hand on the oars when the boat threatened to drift over to the cursed land. They sat and passed the bottle in silence, comfortable in a cocoon of mist, and they would have remained that way for some time if not for the interloper looming quietly in the distance.

7

An empty boat emerged from the fog and floated with unhurried purpose toward them. It thudded against the side of their craft and bobbed in a gentle rise and fall against the current, as if breathing, and the two men looked at it as they continued to pass the bottle, which they soon emptied. One boatman grabbed the side of the empty vessel and hoisted himself in while his friend held their own boat steady.

"This is Raman's boat," the first said as he rummaged through the scattered belongings. He held up a packet of mango beedis, which Raman was famously partial to, a pocket knife, a ball of jute twine, a glass bottle, some plastic envelopes of chewing tobacco.

"Anything in the bottle?" his friend asked. The bottle was as empty as their own, but the beedis were excellent consolation, and the two men shared the packet, musing over Raman's negligence in allowing his boat to wander. The story currently making the rounds in Kashi through the mouths of beggars to the ears of merchants and housewives was that the young boatman spent his nights and early mornings in the dancing alleyways of Dal-Mandi to see his beloved Chandra.

Smoke curled from both men's nostrils and melted into the grayness that clotted the air. Ghostly shades of sound reached them: hollow knocks on wood, a barking dog, a bell clanging. When the beedis shrank to stubs too small to fit between their fingers, the men flicked the ashy remains into the river and readied for their return to the holy city.

The first boatman pulled at the fickle anchor that lay over one side of Raman's boat.

"Pull harder, Bhai," his companion said, laughing when the anchor refused to rise out of the water. "And perhaps limit the pakora during chai this week, nah?"

The anchor dislodged from some obstruction deep below, and the rope crawled upward, though slowly and with considerable effort. As the wet rope coiled into the open boat, what emerged from the water was not the customary iron weight, but a fist. That hand was attached to an arm, and the rope knotted around that arm was tied in a neat double knot. While his companion sputtered, the first boatman kept a firm grip on the cold arm, steadied himself, and pulled the rest of the body up and into Raman's boat.

The man's life had flown long ago, and the body that remained was dark and swollen. His mustache, made thin with water, framed his parted lips, and the hairs of his wet eyelashes clung together, the long tips reaching toward his cheekbones like thick drips of kohl. A scar split one of his eyebrows in two, and a gold chain spooled around his neck. His bare feet had hardened soles and talon-like toes, and his thick black hair released a steady stream of water onto the boat deck, as did his soaked cotton pants and shirt.

"The liquor has taken your wits—put him back!" the companion hissed. "Before anyone sees, before his ghost sticks to you—where do you expect you'll get the money to banish it?"

"Yes, but look, he is wearing clothes."

"Nothing good enough to steal, if that is the thought dancing in your idiot skull. Dump him over."

The first boatman wiped his brow and leaned back as he considered the body. "He still has his gold necklace."

"Take it if you will. I will say nothing. But you'll have to melt it down to rid its affiliation to the corpse, and that will cost just as much as the necklace itself; the goldsmiths are worse cheats than the Doms."

"His skin isn't burnt," the first boatman continued, as if his companion had said nothing. "Did you see how the rope was tied to him?" He spoke the truth in a calm and unhurried manner. The body bore none of the talismans of cremation, of funeral rites. Every other charred and singed body in the river had endured an end that the two boatmen knew as well as the final scenes of a familiar story, but this body was like a tale with no ending at all.

"Bhaiya," the first boatman said from his perch on Raman's boat. "*Think.* How did this man die?"

"Rama knows. Dump him over, I say."

"*Where* did he die?"

"Stop being foolish. He is dead."

"On land? On water? And by whose hand?" His companion refused to answer. A sigh bloomed from his lips in a white wisp that disappeared into the fog. The first boatman grabbed the oars, took his position in

Raman's boat, and directed the bow toward Kashi. "Don't be blind to what is placed before you," he said to his friend. He pumped his arms and glided back to the holy city.

As the sun broke free of the horizon like a balloon slipping from a child's grasp, the light lifted the veil of fog from Kashi and beyond. The white sands of Magadha winked with the allure of crushed pearls. Birds skated along the air above, traveling in perfect circles over the land, dipping toward a pair of dogs that snarled and fought, spiraling above a tented barge that trundled along the river on an aimless journey.

The Ganges, calm and composed in the absence of the monsoon, gathered the early morning pink over its expanse like a sari laid out to dry in the sun, the edges curling against the many carved stone steps leading up to the city. The buildings towering above the ghats gleamed iridescent in the halo of light washing over the water. The bells rang in the temples; the monkeys watched with indifferent faces from their perches atop the roofs.

Men bobbed in the water, dunking themselves once, twice, holding their noses closed with one hand while the other directed the holy river over heads, arms, bellies. Women wrung out their wet saris and crowded near each other as they changed into fresh clothing. The ghaatiye—priests who sat on snug platforms with large umbrellas fanning behind them like cobra hoods—collected coins from the bathers, passed a cracked mirror to one man, said a blessing for another, listened to the dilemma of a third. A perpetual stream of people flowed down to the river and back up the steps, hurried feet sidestepping the drunk stretched out with an earthenware pot clutched in his arms.

Funeral pyres crowded a stone platform at the bottom of the steps, flames crackling, the surrounding men looking like cotton spindles from a distance with their shaved heads and sheer white dhotis. Chants laced the air, each word crisp and new as if emerging for the first time from the lips of red-eyed priests. Black smoke spangled with the occasional swirling orange spark rose up and over the stairs, where the walls bordering the alleyways and lanes drew closer, cinching all who passed through in a concrete embrace that blocked out all light and sense of direction.

Four men shouldering a bier navigated tight corners and crowded alleys. Wrapped in coarse white fabric that rose in crisp lines over the nose, the shoulders, the knobby toes, the body had become nameless, an insect tucked and tightly wound with spider's silk. Their voices, frozen in a monotone chant, echoed in the lanes. *Rama Nam Satya Hai. Rama Nam Satya Hai.* Rama is truth. God is truth.

The chant chased after the feet of a delivery boy, an old woman walking with quick steps, a white dog trotting out of the open mouth of an alley. The dog sniffed at a discarded tobacco wrapper and paused to scratch behind its ear. It looked back and then raised its nose into the air and disappeared into the alley, its tail held upward like a sail, intent on an errand whispered by the breeze.

The news traveled quickly, and speculation trailed after to fill the holes that remained. The note found in the dead man's pocket could have pointed to suicide . . . but the rope tied around the wrist suggested an accidental drowning. And what of the two boatmen who dragged the body back, who certainly could have been murderers?

All the other boatmen at Lalita ghat stuck up for the pair except for Raman. Annoyed that his craft required exorcizing and purification by priests, who insisted that it would take an entire day and a hefty sum of rupees, Raman sat on the topmost steps of the ghat cursing his luck and smoking beedi after mango-flavored beedi. The others sat around gossiping or shouted theories as they passed each other on trips up and down the river. All focused on one detail. "They found a note, didn't they? Has anyone read it?"

"A love letter, most probably," a priest called out from the middle of the ghat as he scratched his chest. "Always a woman to blame," he added to no one in particular as he labored up the stairs.

"Debts, more likely."

"Perhaps he had a curse on his head."

"Or he was looking for Yamraj—see how close he was to Magadha?"

"Nonsense. He was drunk and fell over."

"That Raman should have secured things better. What kind of duffer leaves his boat free for anyone to take?"

"Well, he died in Kashi, so at least he will find peace."

"What fool would call that a good death, Kashi or no?"

"Someone said the man's ghost is already terrorizing that widow in the woodworker's alley."

"Is it surprising? What to expect when the wretch dies in the middle of the river? On Magadha's doorstep, no less."

Tales of what had happened, what might have happened, and what didn't happen swelled across the city, ferried from boatmen to ghaatiye, carried by rickshaw drivers and cart pullers, festering inside shops and whispered via family matriarchs, drifting to the street sweepers and even the drunks and lechers too ashamed to show themselves in the light. In the course of the telling, the truth expanded, broke into pieces, gilded itself, tripped in a puddle of filth, swabbed itself dry, and left fragments behind, until everyone in the old city knew at least some version of the story.

Everyone, that is, except for the one who mattered most.

2

The week had been busy. They were full up, whole families in each of the twelve guest rooms, some doubled up if they could manage it— space could always be found; the folding of belongings and bodies was always possible. The fitting together of personalities, however, proved more difficult. At first, the guests kept their bickering to dark looks and under-the-breath mutterings, but as the hours passed and small pockets of space became akin to acres of land—a blanket claiming a corner here, a leg stretched out farther there—tempers flared and discontent became more vocal.

"It doesn't matter, I suppose, who got here first."

"And that cements your right, does it? When we have only just arrived and you have been here with yours for days—days! And nothing, no dead to show for it. This place is for the dying, you know, not the delusional."

"Next thing we will need to put Ma in our laps; that will be the only space left."

Pramesh could not turn anyone away, and so he packed the newer arrivals into the open-air courtyard and beseeched them all to be patient. But the air grew thick with irritation and impatience, clearing only when a wail went up from room No. 5.

Secrets could not last within Shankarbhavan's walls; the rooms were fitted so tightly together that everyone heard everyone else, be it a cough, a whisper, or the final creaking breaths of one of the dying from the hostel's furthest corners. And so all eyes fixed on the manager and followed him as he picked his way along the raised walkway bordering the courtyard and entered the room only recently visited by death. He felt the men among the guests move to cluster behind him just outside the door, ready for a preview of the preparations they would have to shoulder when their own dying kin left this world. The women remained behind, but the manager heard their murmurings, their mutual curiosity turning enmity into friendship. With the dead man's expansive family spread out before him, Pramesh tried to determine whose face he should focus on.

Three grown daughters sat in a row, faces shielded from view with their sari ends, mouths open with keening cries and bodies rocking back and forth. Their husbands crouched behind them, rattling off a continuous loop of *Rama-Rama* like a trio of frogs. The women's grief was loud and affected, the husbands' mechanical. At the far side of the room, next to the concrete wall where green paint peeled away in large flakes, a youth sat with his father's head in his lap. He was slight and had an early dusting of stubble, and he was silent and intent as he bent over his father's body and touched his hands to the face, the chest, the legs and then back to the forehead, his fingers trembling.

"Rama-Rama," Pramesh murmured as he always did when someone passed. He gripped the shoulder of the nearest man in a gesture of comfort. Pramesh had been the manager at Shankarbhavan for almost a decade, and he had seen and heard death at least weekly in the hostel, had grown accustomed to the constant spectacle of corpse-laden biers and flaming funeral pyres lining the ghats.

But this time in room No. 5 something was different. He knelt close to the youth, placing a hand on his back, and he took a closer look at the father. The face was still and the skin felt cold. No breath emerged from the nose or mouth, and the gnarled hands did not respond when touched. The youth was like stone. He had said nothing, but now he whispered two syllables. "Bapa."

And there it was: the papery eyelids flickered, and then the man's eyes were open, the pupils searching, and his chest resumed a halting rise and fall under Pramesh's palms.

As if their voices had been snatched away, the sisters ceased wailing. Their husbands straightened up from their defeated positions, their eyes resuming the exasperation that Pramesh had observed in the days since they'd entered the hostel more than a week ago. The youth only stared, eyes wide. His father sought out his hand and gave it a weak squeeze.

The woman on the right, the dying man's eldest, lifted her hand and gave an impatient flick of the wrist, and one of the three men coughed and stepped toward Pramesh as if pulled by an invisible thread. His face lost its irritated expression and became businesslike. "Manager-ji," he said. "You know about death. Our father has been here for days, and still he suffers. When will it end?"

Many pairs of eyes bore into Pramesh with hopeful pressure, but the youth refused to look up. "I can only tell you my experience with these things," Pramesh said. "It could be two days or two months. Death is not easily predicted."

He knew this wasn't what they wanted to hear. The disaster of remaining alive was what all such families coming to Kashi dreaded. The bhavan had few rules, but those posted on each guest's door were resolute. At least one member of the party must be dying, preferably of the old age or natural causes that defined a good death, and that person must be accompanied by at least one family member. Lodging was free; guests were to provide for their own needs. Meals were to be simple, with little or no spice that might awaken the senses, the goal being to nourish rather than entice. And stays were limited to two weeks.

The last rule ensured all pilgrims had the same fair chance at ending their days in the holy city, lest the hostel become host to folk who lingered for months on end while others languished, waiting for a vacated place. But this was also the rule that the guests argued over the most. For the old man in No. 5, returning home meant he would miss this chance to die a death that was the best one could hope for on this Earth: the city promised it would be the last—the death to end all rebirths and miseries. But now he would suffer another birth, hopefully once again as a man, but if he had been imprudent in this life he might return as an insect, a monkey, a bullock destined to draw a wooden plow until exhaustion brought upon death and triggered the cycle anew, pulling the soul into the misery of yet another life. Who knew what path a person's karma could put them on? Who could be sure they had not committed a sin that would set them backward by five births? In Kashi, sinner and saint alike could achieve the same goal. This was the city where time did not exist, or so the scriptures said, and on most mornings Pramesh truly believed it, that here he was suspended without past or future, no story trailing behind him and none unfurling ahead, just like every other denizen of Kashi.

"Ji," another husband said. "Our father has been in this state for weeks. It has always been his wish to die in Kashi, but we cannot stay away from our farm forever."

"Is there something you wish me to do?" Pramesh felt his head begin to ache. He'd had a cup of chai that morning with his wife but now felt the need for another.

The man swallowed. "Ji, we know the rules of this place, but you have seen in these past days that we are good people, devoted to this man." He rubbed his chin, glancing at his wife and her sisters before continuing. "We would like to leave him here so he may die in peace, nah? And if you send us a note upon his death we will come running back to arrange the funeral."

"Absolutely not," Pramesh said. What kind of people left their own blood in the company of strangers to die? "The rules are clear. Someone must be with him at all times."

"But, ji—"

"I am sorry," Pramesh said. "You still have a few days. But if you choose to leave, you must take your father with you." The husbands glanced at each other, eyebrows raised; the sisters watched Pramesh through the veils of their saris. The youth remained silent and still but for the brush of his thumb against his father's hand.

One of the sisters raised her hand again to summon her husband, and Pramesh braced himself for whatever excuse was coming. The man was already straightening up to deliver his wife's message, when another voice, a welcome one, cut across the room.

"A moment, Pramesh-ji?" The hostel assistant Mohan stood just outside the doorway. He fixed Pramesh with a smile almost as wide as his stomach and held up a short piece of wood, the carved leg of a rope bed.

"Again it happened! I don't know what Balram told you, but it popped out as soon as I turned the bed over to tighten the ropes." As he talked, he slowly walked to the other side of the bhavan, drawing Pramesh along with him, and the manager stifled a smile. The assistant often used this maneuver when especially vocal families were staying at the bhavan and the manager required an interruption.

Pramesh took the bed leg from Mohan. "Guaranteed to last until I am a grandfather, he assured me."

"He's always done things by halves." Mohan's fingers pulled at his short beard in a nervous twitch. "Shall I fetch him, demand he come himself to fix it?" Pramesh hardly had time to tilt his head before Mohan took off, thin legs moving with a speed that threatened to leave his large body behind.

The door to No. 5 was now closed, a rare sight in the bhavan as folk tended to pass back and forth between the rooms freely, and Pramesh felt the briefest relief. A breeze wafted through the courtyard and ruffled the potted plants of tulsi and fragrant white jasmine squatting in each corner. Men chatted in low voices or paced across what little space they could find; a steady drip sounded from an errant tap in the corner washroom. Narinder, Shankarbhavan's most senior priest, sat in one corner of the courtyard with his legs tucked beneath him and a large volume open before him, his strong nasal voice carrying the sacred verses into each of the rooms. Pramesh stepped along the walkway and stopped at each open doorway to check on the other guests and listen to those who sought him out.

"Manager-ji, my grandfather refuses to eat; should we persuade him to take some rice in milk or do we leave him be?"

"She is quiet now, but is she in pain? And the death—will the death be painful?"

"Mother has not spoken for months. Is it still a good death if she does not say the great God's name aloud?"

None of these questions were new to Pramesh, but he forced himself to don a pilgrim's eyes with every guest. Potters, weavers, landowners, farmers, teachers; the moment they entered the bhavan they became part of a common mindset, together thinking and worrying over the same details, though they imagined themselves unique. "Try to give him something to eat, but do not force him," he said to the first man. "The words on your mother's lips are important, but what the soul holds matters most," he advised another. He counseled and consoled, all while Narinder's strong voice echoed with mantras, until the last of the men drifted away to join their families, and Pramesh headed to the respite of his office, ignoring the ache in his head.

But even here, he was not alone. The youth from No. 5 sat in the chair opposite his desk. He was slim and bony, with dark shadows blurring the skin beneath his eyes. Yet he seemed different in the absence of his family: his shoulders were squared, his back straight, his gaze at Pramesh unyielding.

"My family is determined to leave, Manager-ji," he said.

Pramesh sighed. He sat opposite the youth. "It is a hard thing," he said slowly, willing the blow to land as lightly as possible. "To come here from a great distance, and then to leave without fulfilling the purpose of that journey."

"What if we didn't leave, ji? What if we stayed?"

Pramesh shook his head. As much as he preferred this boy to the rest of his family, he could not change his answer. "I cannot have your father remain here alone. This is the rule for everyone."

The youth waved his hands in a helpless gesture, as if to ward off an insect. "Ji, I meant what if I stayed with my father? Would that be enough?" Here was a proposition that had never occurred to Pramesh. The youth continued to talk, confidence blooming in his speech with every word. "I understand if you must ask us to leave once our two weeks are complete if other guests arrive and there is no other space. But if the room remains free, and I am always there with Bapa, may we stay?"

"Will your family not miss you? Will they trust you to look after yourself here without anyone to help you?"

"They each have their farms, Manager-ji," the youth answered carefully. "None of this matters very much to them: Kashi, a good death, a bad death—they don't believe in it. But Bapa . . ."

Pramesh understood. The family saw their patriarch as already dead, but the son still saw a living and breathing father. How easy to refuse those husbands, but how difficult to refuse this skinny young man! The rules were clear: No dying person may be left alone without an accompanying family member. Yet there was no rule specifying the age or circumstances of that family member. "Your name?" Pramesh asked.

"Sheetal, ji."

"Well, Sheetal," Pramesh said, concentrating on a spot darkening the wall behind the boy's head. "You may stay with your father. And it will be as Rama wishes." The boy sat thinking before he looked up, tilted his chin in thanks, and left the room.

Only later did Pramesh realize he should have answered Sheetal with more questions. Would he be able to care for his father, bathe him, keep him comfortable? When the death occurred, would he keep his emotions in check and procure enough money to buy the necessary materials for the last rites that every soul required to be entirely free of this world? Alone, could he muster the courage to light his father's pyre, crack the skull so that the life essence could escape? Most importantly, could he walk away from the final remains of the man who had once hoisted him on his shoulders, and above all else resist the temptation to look back, because such a show of attachment would prevent the old man's soul from fully reaching moksha? Could he marshal his thoughts into a single-minded discipline during the twelve-day mourning period, thinking not of his grief and his father, but of the great God?

His thinking felt sluggish. The dull ache shadowing his thoughts had turned into a slow but persistent pounding, the blood thumping behind his right eyebrow. He concentrated on the space between the pain, willing himself to exist in that pocket that lasted seconds, less than seconds, before the next wave squeezed his brain, like a child rolling an overripe mango between her palms. He needed chai and a chat with his wife, but once in the empty kitchen he remembered that Shobha had taken Rani for a visit to Mrs. Mistry's next door. He sat on the rope bed, picked up his mother's tattered copy of the Gita and flipped through the pages, but he was unable to concentrate on the words for the pain, suddenly feeling the loneliness of the space without his daughter's smile, his wife's chatter.

"Pramesh-ji?" Dev poked his head through the partition curtain. "A moment?"

The manager steeled himself and slowly pushed off the bed. "Coming."

⚊⚊⚬⚊⚊

Mohan never meant to dawdle. Despite his unwieldy frame, he walked with a speed that often left Pramesh lagging. But no sooner would he turn into a lane than his eyes would meet a familiar pair, and he wouldn't be able to help himself.

"Ah, Dhani-ji! How is your nephew? Did he pass his exams?"

"Raju-bhai, just the man I was thinking of. I heard about a remedy for your mother-in-law's constipation; how is she faring?"

"Sonam-maasi, you must let me carry those bags for you, I insist. And your grandchildren—you haven't told me about them in some time."

Striding through the lanes with the easy confidence of one who could converse with anyone, about anything, at any time, Mohan stopped and listened and asked and commiserated with those who turned to him and those who tried to hurry past. Today, by the time he made it to Balram's shop, a dark and cavernous space piled high with wood and half-made furniture, the stool that the woodworker usually occupied was vacant.

"Missed him," Arjuna the tailor offered when he saw Mohan waiting. "And he won't be back again today."

"How do you know?"

"He had the newspaper with him," Arjuna said. Everyone knew that once worked up over this or that politician's latest debacle in the paper, the woodworker was useless, spending the rest of the day at home drinking his wife's chai and loudly haranguing the air over the idiocy of the ones who sought to lead, continuing even when his wife vacated the kitchen to take a nap.

Thus disappointed, Mohan headed back, though he stopped to buy a newspaper cone of fried mung dal, passing it out to the children who appeared by his side as if conjured, and was quick to finish munching the remains before passing through the hostel gates.

He found Pramesh walking from room to room with the slow questioning gait of an old man. "Another headache?" he asked, hurrying up to the manager. "Shall I fetch you some water?"

The manager winced, but smiled weakly.

"Bed, Pramesh-ji," Mohan insisted. He knew the signs, from the way the manager slightly moved his head every few seconds, that he should not be up and about, much less dealing with the inquisitive families of the dying. "The day is already half finished," he added, in case Pramesh wished to argue. "Nothing shall disturb you—even a death. I will take care of it." When Pramesh only blinked and moved slowly to his family quarters, Mohan knew he had been right.

He turned to the families that had settled in the courtyard, the men who had clustered around the manager moments before, but those guests scattered or turned back to their dying kin, uninterested in the assistant's guidance. Still, Mohan cycled around the bhavan, making his own inquiries: Did they have enough water? Had they found the market? Was there something specific they wanted to hear the priests read aloud?

In the middle of this, a low cry sounded, and he straightened at the familiar signal and excused himself. Sobs, muffled at first, then slowly growing louder and clearer, until the sound bloomed into a woman's full-hearted wail that filled the bhavan. Narinder emerged from the priests' quarters and followed Mohan to No. 3, where they found the family inside hunched and rocking over the tiny form of their departed matriarch, a woman who'd lifted her mouth in the slightest of smiles whenever anyone walked into the room during her stay.

"So a death today, after all," the head priest murmured to the assistant, his fingers busy on his prayer beads.

Mohan addressed the room brightly: "Your mother has passed in the holiest of places—this is a happy day!" Beside the list of rules tacked up in each room, another list hung on the door that detailed exactly what the family must do as soon as death visited them. Mohan pointed it out to the men who sat silently alongside their wailing women. "As soon as you can," the assistant urged the closest man, "while the women wash the body, someone will need to get the necessary supplies." He read through the items listed, the flowers and cremation shrouds, the bamboo for the bier and the wood for the funeral pyre, the approximate amount that the priests and the Doms and countless others would expect as their rightful tax for services provided. He was about to mention the holy basil in the courtyard, whose leaves should cover the body's mouth and ears and other orifices once bathed, when Narinder gestured with his eyes behind him. "A moment," Mohan said to the family, whose men remained listless, and he stepped outside to Dev beckoning from No. 10.

Narinder sat down in a corner and began to recite from the Garuda Purana from memory, while Mohan hurried over to the other room. "Another?" he asked. Dev followed him in, and they found the potter in No. 10 weeping, his loud choking sobs drowning out the grief of his mother and his sister.

"His grandfather," Dev said. "It must have just happened. He was fine, but as soon as the man passed he simply broke."

Mohan laid his hand on the fellow's shaking back. "Calm yourself, Bhai, calm yourself," he urged. "We know this is the best thing for your grandfather, nah? This isn't befitting, not here of all places." But the man's sobbing only increased in volume and fervor, and the sound drew other families to the room, curious to see this man who did not know or care that such grief was the privilege of women. Not a good thing, for a man to be breathless with sobs as he shouldered the corpse's bier through the lanes.

Then Loknath pushed through behind Dev.

"Another," he said. "In the courtyard." At the words, the guests parted, some wandering to No. 3, others lingering on the fringes of the walkway, others staying where Mohan was in No. 10.

"Hai Rama," Mohan said, his mood lifted. Such a lucky thing, this third death—and so close after the others. He allowed himself a laugh, remembering Pramesh's tales of how sometimes, when the bhavan was full, one death seemed to set the rest of them off, like a line of women in labor.

"Shall I fetch Pramesh-ji?" Loknath asked.

"No, no; there are four of us, aren't there? No reason to disturb him," Mohan said. The priests left to look in on the most recent death. The wailing from various corners of the bhavan echoed off the walls and floated up through the open courtyard and into the air, the man at his feet the loudest of all. The assistant turned to the door, about to get the family started on preparing the body and the cremation materials, when an agonized howl sounded and he was almost knocked off his feet.

"Gone! But too soon, too soon, and what will we do without him now?"

Weeping, the man gripped Mohan's ankles and shook his legs, while the womenfolk—silently shedding tears until then—erupted into their own wailing.

"This isn't your place, Bhaiya," Mohan said, trying to unclench the man's white-knuckled fingers. "There is still work to be done, rites you must fulfill—you are the chief mourner, nah? Think of your duties; think—"

"Ji," came a breathless voice from the door. One of the guests, a man who'd just arrived a few days ago with his uncle, pushed forward. "There is a man at the gate. He wishes to speak to someone in charge here."

Mohan could not move; the convulsing man had the iron grip of someone lost at sea who'd laid hands on a drifting piece of wood. "He will have to wait. Is he with anyone? Someone who is dying?"

"He is alone," the guest said. "He's asking to speak to the manager."

"Tell him the manager is not here," Mohan said. The sobbing man reached out and grabbed him by the arm. "Tell him to return tomorrow."

The guest ran off and Mohan turned his attention back to the sodden man, those crowding behind him murmuring to each other in disapproval. But soon enough the guest was back again. "He says he must see him, the manager," he reported.

"Is he dying?" Mohan asked, temper short. "Tell him we are here for the dying only, not the living. Tomorrow, Bhai, tell him to come back tomorrow. He will not find what he is looking for today."

Finally, the grieving man tired out and crumpled in a heap next to the body. With no other man in that family to speak to, Mohan turned to one of the guests lingering behind him and pointed to the list on the door. "When he wakes, Bhaiya, make sure he heeds the list. No good to wait about these things, not when the body must be tended to, and others are waiting their turn in the space."

Out in the courtyard, Mohan remembered the waiting man. He ventured to the gates, but no one stood there. He crossed the threshold and saw only people walking, carrying on with their business. Mrs. Chalwah's eyes pierced him from where she kept watch at her upper-story bedroom window across the street. He raised his hand in greeting as always, though she never returned the wave.

As he turned to go back in, his eyes caught on a man making long slow strides across the street. The bearing and gait were as familiar as his own, now rounding the corner, now out of sight. How did—

But that was impossible; of course Pramesh was upstairs, and it would be at least another hour before the pain subsided enough for him to venture down. *Foolishness*, Mohan thought, and he pulled the gate shut firmly and turned back to the death awaiting him inside.

3

Shobha was desperate to return to the bhavan, but the neighboring women who had gathered in a chattering circle in Mrs. Mistry's kitchen did not seem inclined to let her go. She sat with them, Rani hugging her shoulders, and she resigned herself to listening to how so-and-so's cousin's daughter had forgotten to stay silent during visits from prospective grooms, yet again revealing her persistent lisp, and what was that girl's poor mother to do?

"Fear works," Mrs. Gupta said as she pulled a loose thread from her sewing up to her mouth and bit off the excess. The half dozen women gathered in the kitchen had already traded ideas about threatening the girl with spinsterdom or coating her tongue with alum. As they chatted, they worked embroidery into a blouse sleeve or picked through rice or rolled wisps of cotton into lamp wicks. Mrs. Mistry sat before the cooking fire and wound a spoon through a pot of ground almonds, sugar, and ghee, a rare treat made in celebration of her newest grandchild's birth. "Tell her the story of the Green Parrot Girl," Mrs. Gupta continued. "That will be enough."

"Is that the same as the Weeping Woman?" Mrs. Mistry asked as she continued moving her spoon through the fragrant almond mixture. She touched the back of her hand to her sweating forehead.

"It's the girl who was always back-talking to her parents, then her husband, then she was stolen away in the middle of the night and made to marry a demon, remember? And when she refused, she was turned into a demon-spirit herself, forced into the body of a parrot."

The women murmured among themselves, comparing their friend's version of the story to the versions they knew. "The point is you must scare her into behaving," Mrs. Gupta continued, her voice rising above the others. "Tell her the tale, and that will be that. Problem solved."

Shobha spoke up without thinking. "But surely she will need to say something to the boy during the meeting, nah? Before they are married?" She regretted her words the instant they left her mouth, but too late; the women all turned to her.

"Plenty of time to speak to the boy after the wedding," they clucked.

"Besides," Mrs. Mistry said as she smiled at Rani, who peeked over Shobha's shoulder and then ducked behind again, "You will not have that same problem with this one." She said this kindly, but Shobha winced. Rani was far ahead of other children her age in many ways, but she had yet to speak a single word, a fact whispered among the housewives of Kashi.

"You don't know it now, beti," an older neighbor said as she patted Shobha's knee and tweaked Rani's elbow, "but when this one grows and all the matches come in, you will have the same worries. Every mother does."

Shobha held her tongue, focusing on the warmth she felt at being included in the classification of mother, a title long sought and lately won. Six years was a very long time to be married and without child, to endure silent looks and not-so-silent comments. Rani's delivery had been painful and prolonged, and Shobha's agonized labor had lasted for the entire day and into the night. With no living family nearby, she trusted few others to look after the child. Mrs. Mistry was a good woman who was always ready with some sweet thing or funny story for Rani whenever Shobha needed to drop the girl off. So if etiquette decreed that she sit here for a half hour and listen to her neighbor's friends, then that is what she would do, even if her goodwill was beginning to crack.

"Such pretty silken hair," the sari-seller's wife murmured as she eyed Rani's locks.

"Pretty, yes, but not as thick as my nephew's son's," Mrs. Gupta said with an appraiser's air. The other women in the room looked away, and Shobha felt the blood rush to her face. Rani was now intent on undoing her coiled bun, and she reached up to disengage the girl's hands and pull her into her lap. They all knew that Mrs. Gupta, who was childless, had taken personal affront when Shobha had refused her nephew's hand all those years ago and instead chose to marry a village nobody who'd only recently taken up residence in the bhavan.

"Well, the barfi looks to have come together nicely," Mrs. Mistry said brightly. She stopped stirring, the almond sweetmeat now ready to be scooped into shallow pans and cut into diamond shapes once set. She wiped her brow with the end of her sari. "I expect her father spoils her," she said to Shobha as she held up a piece of green mango for Rani, who pushed away from her mother immediately and went to Mrs. Mistry's side. "And she will have so many choices before her that none will be left for the other girls in Kashi."

"Who can tell what might have been," Mrs. Gupta continued before drifting off so that only Shobha could hear what came next. "If things had been different, perhaps you would have two children in your lap instead of just one."

No woman could have kept silent at that moment, even if Mrs. Gupta's words stemmed from disappointment. Shobha's anger felt like a wave churning and speeding and crashing within her, irreversible and destructive. "Well," she said, eyes flashing, "If—"

"Dadi!" a child's voice called from the door. One of Mrs. Mistry's grandsons ran into the room. "The bhavan uncle says to ask the bhavan auntie to come home." Duty done and message delivered, the boy held his hand out for a piece of jaggery and coconut, his grandmother's standard medium of reward. And that woman, thankful for the additional service the spindly child unknowingly performed, piled a double fistful into the boy's hands, which he promptly crammed into his mouth before running off to tell his siblings that their grandmother was in an especially generous mood.

Watching this, Shobha remembered that she was not in her own home and that Mrs. Mistry had always gone out of her way to show Shobha a gentle, unsmothering kindness. Today was a celebration for her neighbor: a new grandson, a new life, a time to revel in sweetness and cast aside the bitter. She exhaled and released her anger. "I will be going, then." She stood and adjusted her sari before beckoning Rani to her and taking the girl's hand. "Come now," she said to the girl, "wave to all of your aunties." The girl raised a shy and dimpled hand before burying her smile in Shobha's legs. The older women cooed over her one final time and said their goodbyes, and Mrs. Mistry made Shobha take a bit of the almond barfi in a silver dish for Pramesh.

"Let it cool first," Mrs. Mistry called after Shobha, "And remember that tomorrow I will have that lemon pickle ready for you to taste. It wants just one more day in the sun."

"I will, Maasi," Shobha called as she stepped lightly out the door, Rani at her side. She pulled the end of her sari over her head and tried not to look at Mrs. Gupta as she fled.

Awake, wary of the pain still lingering on the edges of his skull, Pramesh drank three cups of chai in quick succession. He sat on the rope bed at the edge of the kitchen and held his daughter on one knee as Shobha picked through rice for that evening's meal. He felt buoyed by the deaths he discovered once he'd come downstairs, the families all in the midst of preparing the bodies, men scurrying about to gather the cremation items while the women sat in a circle around the deceased and stroked the lifeless arms and legs. But he needed to tell his wife about Sheetal.

"So the boy will remain here alone?" she asked.

The manager tilted his head in assent. "Rama willing, the old man will go quickly, and soon. Because otherwise. . . ."

"That will come later," Shobha said. "We will help him as much as we help any of the others. For now, he will stay." And with that, the matter was concluded. Pramesh relaxed in the face of his wife's decisive nature. Their emotions often balanced in each other's presence, as if one were taking on the other's load. Shobha reached her arms out for Rani, who brought her an old glass bangle she was playing with. Shobha held the violet circlet up to the soft beam of light that slipped through the arched window, and it erupted into tiny flecks that flickered across the room, some quivering in Rani's small hands. The child curled and stretched her fingers in glee, her face strong with the likeness of Pramesh's mother—or so he liked to think. He'd been so young when she'd passed; he did not always trust his memory of her face.

"How many kisses from the light? How many blessings on your head?" Shobha murmured as she tweaked her daughter's nose, the many bangles on her slim arms chiming as she moved.

Later, the bands would arrive, ready to lead each grieving family to the ghats with the loud music of celebration that preceded the processions of weddings and funerals alike. But now this corner of the bhavan was quiet, and Pramesh allowed himself to relax and enjoy the presence of his family, to rest his eyes on Rani's face and feel his own smile bloom as he watched her reach out to grasp something she could not hold.

4

Having spotted the ghaatiyaa Kishore at his usual platform halfway down the stone stairs, Bhut quickly covered the distance and came straight to the point. "That hostel man," he asked as bathers climbed past on their way back into the city, "what do you know of him?"

Startled, Kishore let out a laugh that turned into a laborious cough, shaking the white hairs on his chest. "Bhut-sahib, you should warn a man before coming upon him like that."

The circle officer at Dashashwamedh Police Station had a reputation for approaching undetected, materializing among the men smoking in the alley or the wrestlers exercising on the ghats, unexpected as a ghost. The city folk had therefore shortened his given name of Bhudev to Bhut. He stood behind the ghaatiyaa, unmindful of the sun and the stares bearing down upon him, and waited for an answer.

"Why not ask the man himself?" Kishore said with a sideways glance as he continued to accept coins from the bathers. "The bhavan is just some lanes over."

Bhut raised an eyebrow. He was not the only one with a reputation. Daily, as Kishore tended the duties of his work—sitting sentry over the river and watching over the bathers' clothes, lending out plastic combs and razors, performing the odd religious rite—he cultivated a business of another kind. When the bathers stopped to pay him, they also stopped to gossip. Every birth, every death, every assignation behind a temple, news of all this and more came to him, and he in turn dispersed choice details to the other bathers, boatmen, ghaatiye . . . and even to the odd circle officer looking for information. "They say you were the one to install him in his position all those years ago," Bhut said. "They say he arrived in the city from no-one-knows-where, and suddenly he was the old man's assistant at the bhavan."

"They will say what they say."

"I care what *you* say," Bhut said, patience run low. "Either tell me now or tell me at the station. You may choose."

"The drunk." Kishore jerked his head toward the wide expanse of stairs behind him where a filthy man lolled on the stone. "He insists on sleeping here at night. And yet I understand vagrants are discouraged from such loitering?"

"Maharaj?" Bhut glanced at the drunk, who seemed to have just woken. The man rubbed his eyes with dirty fists and grasped for the lopsided pot he kept with him. The bathers gave him a wide berth and regarded him with narrowed eyes as they passed. "He does no harm."

"He does no good, either. Shall I tell you the hostel man's story or not?" The crowd grew thicker on the ghat, the sun's heat pressed down, and Bhut had no feeling for the drunk one way or the other. He grunted his assent; Kishore began. "Your hostel man arrived ten years ago. He came with nothing, but had some story about winning admission to the university—perhaps he told the truth, but it was easy enough to convince him in another direction. Old Dharam at the death hostel had been looking for an assistant for some time."

"You recommended a stranger?" Kishore's show of altruism sent Bhut's eyebrows high up his forehead.

"Him as well as any other," the ghaatiyaa said. He paused to bark at a man a few steps below who made a grab for a pair of sandals that were not his own.

"The great Kishore-ji is no fool. You had a reason—what did he promise you in return?"

"Nothing."

Bhut waited. Eventually, the ghaatiyaa scowled. "He looked like a newborn, that man. Like he'd never seen the river, never breathed the air, never used his legs—everything fascinated him. Another country fool, staring as if the great God made the city for his benefit alone."

"So?"

"So, a man like that—other men will talk in the presence of a man like that."

"And you were right?"

Kishore flicked his hand in disgust. "I am not the first to mistake a man's character."

The circle officer shifted his feet on the stone steps. Some paces away, a pair of women plucked marigolds from a fat basket sitting between them and strung the flowers into garlands. Bhut watched the round orange blossoms pass between deft fingers until the garland was finished and tied off. He sucked the air between his teeth. "And yet he is not such a fool from the village, is he? To have married the old housemaster's daughter just a year after arriving? And then to become the manager himself when the old man died. . . ."

"No. Not such a fool." Kishore counted the money in his hands before slipping the coins into a pouch and bouncing it in his palm. The muffled jingle sounded cheerful amid the chanting and chattering, the bickering and bartering on the ghat. Kishore looked grim; he was not a man who enjoyed doing a good deed without receiving something in return. Bhut smiled. The ghaatiyaa rarely made a mistake in the people he deigned to favor.

"Have you spoken to him recently?"

"He used to come to me for advice, to tell me the goings-on at the bhavan. Then, suddenly, he stopped, and his mouth closed like a fist." For a moment, Bhut enjoyed seeing the ghaatiyaa discomfited. Kishore kept his eyes focused on the river. "This is about the dead man they found this morning, isn't it?"

Bhut's smile vanished. "News travels quickly to your ears, Kishore-ji. Perhaps you should tell me what *you* have heard."

The ghaatiyaa straightened his back and jerked his thumb behind him. "My end of the bargain is done, Bhut-sahib. Yours is behind you."

"Rama-Rama," Bhut said as he turned and walked up the steps.

"Rama-Rama," Kishore answered, shifting the money pouch from hand to hand.

Maharaj greeted Bhut in his usual wheedling tone, and Bhut answered with an expletive.

"A moment to rest, one moment only and then I shall go, I shall go to Thakorlal-ji's," Maharaj said in his singsong voice as he drummed his fingers on his pot in a hollow, echoing tune.

Bhut was never afraid to use force when needed, though he moved slower now than he had forty years ago as a young deputy. He yanked Maharaj up by the ear and let go abruptly, bringing the man to his knees. "Now," he said. He followed as the drunk crawled up the ghats on all fours, offering a helpful kick to Maharaj's backside when he stumbled, and thinking all the way.

꜠

Bhut sat in the hostel office across from Pramesh at his desk, loosely gripping a metal tumbler of Shobha's milky chai and staring intently at the hostel manager's face, his cap balanced on one knee. Pramesh looked down at the much-abused scrap of paper on the desk before him. It had been sodden in the dead man's soaked shirt pocket, then roughly handled as it was passed and folded and unfolded throughout the day. When Pramesh picked it up, the paper sighed like something alive and the soft edges clung to his fingers. It held only a single word, twice underlined. *Shankarbhavan.*

"So this dead man meant to come here," the manager said, putting the chit on the desk between them. "A pilgrim, then? Was someone with him?"

"Who can say?" Bhut said, still staring at Pramesh's face. "But I feel he may be familiar to you."

Pramesh looked back at the circle officer, wary.

"I have seen the body. The face is exactly yours—except the dead man has a scar," Bhut said calmly. "It splits his right eyebrow in two." Pramesh froze. The circle officer released his gaze and took a slow, drawn-out sip from his cup. "And now that I have seen you, I can tell you with certainty. He is your copy."

Fear glazed Pramesh's heart. His mouth felt packed with hot ash, a taste of sickness that he remembered from years ago—a lifetime ago. A voice rose out of his memories. *You cannot leave me behind.*

"A mistake," he said, interrupting the thought.

Bhut finished his chai and stood. "Anything is possible," he said, fitting his cap to his graying head. "Best if you see for yourself. Come."

Across the street, a dusk-colored pigeon paced on a second-floor window ledge, the iridescent feathers around its throat winking like an opal necklace. The widow Mrs. Chalwah pushed the bird away with one curled hand and watched the hostel manager and the circle officer pass through the bhavan gate. She shrank out of view until she was sure both men were far enough down the lane, and then leaned forward and watched them turn toward the ghats.

She spent her days counting her prayer beads, pinching God's name out of each one, and watching families carry their dead out of Shankarbhavan. One day soon, she hoped, she would be one of them; the great God and the Mother would greet her soul and whisper the words needed to cross the hellish Vaitarani river to reach the end of all ends. Today, however, no bodies had left the bhavan. No one had died, and she felt a queer unease. Seeing the two men take fast and even strides along the packed dirt, she sighed, turned away from the window, and resumed her recitation of the great God's name.

5

In the back corner of the police station, inside the largest cell with its doors wide open, a man was stretched on a white cloth, with another draped loosely over him. Bhut remained outside while Pramesh ventured in. The other cells sat empty or held a few hunched individuals who fixed Pramesh with a desperate stare or ignored him as he passed. The two deputies and the clerk in the front of the building, who'd nudged each other and followed the manager with their eyes as he trailed Bhut, remained where they were.

He knelt and gingerly drew back the cloth and stared down into a face he had last seen nearly ten years before. The body was bloated, the skin cast with an unnatural dark tone. Dried yellow spittle clung to corners of the mouth. Unwashed, the body smelled of river water and decay, a paralyzing stench in the windowless jail cell, and Pramesh drew the front of his shirt up and over his nose and mouth. Yet despite those marks of death, he saw himself in the familiar features: the hawkish nose, the dark mustache, the long-lashed eyes shadowed with dark circles, the skinny and tall frame. Like looking at his own reflection, but for the scar splitting the right eyebrow in two. *Sagar.*

Pramesh set a palm on the cold arm. Perhaps it was a mistake; perhaps Sagar was still there, like the old man blinking to life under Sheetal's gaze. . . . His hand remained still, with no rise and fall of a breathing chest, no breath streaming from the nose to warm the skin. He lifted his hand and dragged his fingers through his hair as if to pull it out by the roots.

"In the water for hours," Bhut said from outside the cell, "yet the likeness is still there. Remarkable."

"We would play twins when we were children," Pramesh said hoarsely. He dropped the front of his shirt from his face, wiped his nose on his sleeve, and stepped outside the cell. "Sometimes even our mothers could not tell us apart. Or perhaps they were pretending, teasing us, but at the time we believed them."

"When was the last you'd heard from him?" Bhut asked.

"Almost ten years."

"And what do you suppose he was doing here?"

Pramesh tried to shake loose from the drift of his thoughts. Hot ash, the stench of sweat and sickness, and that voice: Sagar's voice. *You cannot leave me behind. . . .* "I don't know," he said.

"Any news from your village? Some event that brought him here?"

"I heard nothing."

Bhut leaned against one of the iron-barred doors, blowing impatiently through his nose. "Your family—where are they? Tell me from the beginning."

Pramesh blinked and named his village. "Two of everything, in my family. Two fathers, two mothers, two sons—my cousin and I." He felt strange, his voice giving life to those people when he had not spoken of them for so long.

"Two fathers?"

"They were brothers. They married at the same time."

"And all living together?"

Pramesh slowly rocked his chin, his eyes still fixed on Sagar. "My cousin and I were never apart. Our mothers died when we were very young. A fever that swept the village." His mouth went dry, but he continued. "I was ill as well, but I survived."

"What became of your fathers?"

"They had to sell much of our land. Their sister had been widowed and childless, so she arrived to care for us. All are now gone. Dead some years after I left for the city." Pramesh shifted his weight. "That was when I was twenty-one. I wanted him to come with me, but he was stubborn—he loved the land."

"So you came here alone. You met Kishore. Then, the death hostel,"

Bhut recited. "It's a lucky sort of life, the way things ended up for you."

"Yes," Pramesh admitted. "I hadn't been anywhere like Kashi before. And Shankarbhavan as well. I wanted to do that work."

"But dealing with the old and the dead, day after day, and you, a young man. . . ."

Pramesh raised his hand, palm upward, and let it drop to the side, eyes on Sagar. "It satisfied something within me. I cannot explain it."

Behind Bhut, a low hum began, rising in volume until it was a wail, rich with pain. The circle officer walked down the hall a few paces to the cell where the sound emanated and aimed a vicious kick at fingers clutching the barred door. The sound stopped.

"Was he upset when you left him?" he asked, returning to his original spot, expressionless. "Or when he found out what you were doing?"

Pramesh shuddered and tried to concentrate. "No. He wanted me to leave. There wasn't anything there for me in the village."

"You didn't keep in touch?"

"We did, at first. But then . . . we drifted. He had his life. I had mine."

"What did your cousin do after you left? Was he successful with the land?"

Pramesh swallowed. The stench was becoming unbearable, but he forced himself to look at the puffed face. "As I said, we parted ways. I don't know what his life became, once I left him—and he never knew mine, for that matter."

The circle officer grunted, letting the silence stretch between them. Pramesh kept his face neutral, his answers carrying the heft of truth so that all the things just beneath the surface might remain there.

Bhut scratched the back of his neck, then came to the point. "You will be responsible for the funeral?"

"Yes. Of course." Pramesh exhaled. The interrogation was coming to an end. He wanted to get Sagar away from this place, out of the filth and the darkness.

"You know the Doms are divided."

"In what regard?"

"Some will refuse to give you the wood."

A weight settled on Pramesh's chest. Those who took their own lives were never cremated. Their fate was to be floated off on a bier, bodies unpurified by fire, to be disposed of as the Ganges willed.

"One thing." Bhut stretched the words out, pausing long enough for Pramesh to look away from Sagar and focus on the circle officer. "Just one thing I neglected to mention. They found an empty bottle in the boat."

Pramesh's breath caught. "What of it?"

"An empty liquor bottle," Bhut clarified. "That boatman, Raman, claims it is not his, and we believe him. He is a fool, but not fool enough to drink on the water. A sober man slipping and falling from a boat . . . difficult to pin as an accident. But you would believe the story with a drunk man, would you not?"

Nothing but the son of a drunk. Pramesh closed his eyes.

Of course, the insatiable city would demand a story to ingest. He thought of the gossips greedy for some salacious tale of murder or revenge or mistaken identity—or, even better, all three bound together in Sagar's lifeless body. No boring, domestic tale would do—and even then, someone would find a way to change it, another would add to that, and soon it would become a story any person would be proud to repeat on the way to the market or to a neighbor stopping in for chai. But a bottle, a drunk—not that. He couldn't let it be that.

"He never drank a drop in his life," Pramesh said, struggling to convey a conviction he did not feel. "Ever. He and I—we are not that sort."

"And yet you had not seen him for how long?" Bhut tilted his head to the side. "Either he killed himself, or he was drunk and fell. Which was it?"

Both scenarios flickered through Pramesh's mind. Which story would hurt less?

"Later, you will understand," Bhut said. Pramesh looked up. The circle officer's gaze was distant. "Bad as it seems now—neither end is as bad as it could be. Though time will tell whether the story will linger or die."

He met the manager's eyes fleetingly. Pramesh recalled a tale about something that happened long ago, decades before he arrived in the city. The versions and variations had changed over the years, but the essential details remained—something about an older sister—Bhut's sister—who had died mysteriously less than a year after becoming a wife, and a husband who'd fled the city. A story that shimmered into being whenever anyone from that family passed into view, like an odor that dogged their steps in the lanes. Whatever Pramesh said now, whatever he decided, would determine whether his own family would acquire a scent that trailed them through the city.

Worse than this was the possibility of it being true. Two versions of his cousin existed: the man he'd grown up with, and the man he'd grown apart from. The former, he knew never to have touched alcohol. But might the latter, who'd bound himself to a shell of a life on a dwindling farm, to a woman he never should have married, and to a family with the worst of stories attached to their name, have been driven to drink in the years that followed? He couldn't be sure. But suicide was unimaginable. "I have not seen him in years," he said at last.

"It was an accident, then," Bhut decided. "Even if they insist it was something else, how can they know? The bottle was there; we have two witnesses for that. He meant to see you; the note makes it clear. Rama knows why he was in the middle of the river, but he fell from the boat; that I can see."

"Of course," Pramesh said bleakly, wishing he could feel grateful. But now all he could do was stare at that copy of himself, sealed and preserved in death, while he would continue to walk the streets of Kashi, powered by a life that should have been flowing through Sagar, a life that was no better than a mango stolen to satiate an unbearable hunger, bitter from first bite to last.

6

As if sensing that Pramesh's mind was already overburdened, no one at Shankarbhavan passed away the next day, the day of Sagar's funeral. Though Sheetal's father in room No. 5 and the weaver in No. 8 drew rattling breaths, though the teacher's mother in No. 9 had long ago succumbed to delirious musings and the frail woman in No. 11 endured impatient glances from her grandson; though they all should have toppled out of their bodies like overripe fruit from a tree, they held on, bound by a collective knowledge that only one dead man would command the manager's attention that day.

With the help of Mohan, Sheetal, and a spare deputy, Pramesh carried Sagar's body to the bhavan on a bier. He drew comfort from completing the journey his cousin had set out upon, bringing him to Shankarbhavan even though he knew that this body, this abandoned shell of flesh and hair and bone, was not Sagar. In the courtyard, as he washed the strong limbs and muscled torso with the buckets of holy river water that Mohan had fetched for him, wiped the smooth brown skin and black hairs on Sagar's arms and chest, slicked the hair back with a wet comb and set the part neatly, all to prepare the body for the pyre, Pramesh felt an overwhelming tenderness and sorrow threaten to engulf him. He had no right to such emotion. The soul was gone, and no amount of nostalgia could bring it back.

The body was ready, and Mohan had the other items—the flowers and cloth in hand, the wood and oil waiting at the ghats. Silence reigned outside the bhavan; a death like this was no occasion for the raucous brass bands that led every other dead body to the funeral pyre. "A moment."

Pramesh excused himself and went into his office. The thing he needed to do was best done immediately, and then forgotten.

I write with the news that Sagar-bhai—my cousin, my brother—has passed. He burns on the pyre today.

There is nothing that I want from you. I will complete all the rites; everything will be done properly.

I am writing only to let you know.

He addressed the letter to his childhood home, and then he found Shobha in the kitchen sitting in front of the hearth. "Will you take this to the post office for me?" he asked, pressing it into her hands. "As soon as we leave with the body?"

She looked at the address on the envelope and then up at him. He placed a hand briefly on her hair, and then he walked out to the courtyard, to Sagar's body, and met Loknath's questioning look. "I'm ready."

＊＊＊

Some semblance of normalcy persisted in the bhavan. The juniormost priest, Dev, sat in the courtyard, his voice rising with the rhythm of mantras that recounted the journey of the soul after death. Women filed in and out, visiting the ghats and fetching water, helping their frail family members to the washroom if they could walk. Amid the preparations, the constant motion within the hostel, and Mohan's hurried trips to the market to retrieve the implements for the cremation, Shobha remained apart. She was not one to send up a wailing cry like other women; even when her own beloved father passed she kept all feeling firmly locked within.

The vacancy in her husband's eyes as he handed her the letter made her want to place her palms on his cheeks and bring his face down to hers until the light returned. But it was hard for her to muster feeling for the body. Perhaps if she'd met him . . . but like all the other what-ifs in her life, Shobha dismissed the thought. Besides, after seeing the address on that letter, someone else entered her mind.

Kamna. The woman Pramesh's cousin had married was named Kamna. She'd learned this early in her own marriage, but she never spoke the name, even in her thoughts. Doing so was enough to conjure a whole person, enough to breathe life into this woman whom Shobha had never met. And with her very real presence came a very real fear that Shobha kept inside herself, because speaking it aloud would make it true. *A woman like that does not forget.*

Pramesh never spoke of this girl selected for him, the bride his cousin had accepted in his place. Seeing her husband's twin dead in the courtyard of her home drew out her long-hidden fear as easily as a magnet pulls iron filings from a pile of sand. She concentrated on what she knew how to do: she distracted Rani by having her pick through a bowl of uncooked lentils, kept chai perpetually boiling on the fire, and made the rounds to each of the rooms, asking the women guests if they required anything. She let the work disguise her thoughts, because while everyone else focused on the dead man, Shobha—calm, collected, rational woman—could not stop thinking of the dead man's wife.

After the hostel manager came with his bhavan men to take the body away, Bhut went straight home. He was satisfied with his day's work and did not dwell on the how and why. After all, he was a circle officer in the City of Death. Why should one police district keep an accurate account of how all those souls passed, when the important thing was the simple fact that they were dead? He had as little patience for the details of death as he did for what came after: the elaborate rites, the chanting and burning, the paying of priests, all done in a foolish attempt to stave off ghosts, which he did not believe in, despite his nickname.

The manager and the dead man slipped from Bhut's mind as he walked toward the wasps' nest that was his house. Perhaps, just once, he would find that it was his neighbors who were quarreling. But no, the words tumbling out into the street were certainly spoken by his wife and his two older sisters, the heat of their argument burning his face the closer he came. He was tempted to turn back; no one had seen him. But then his elder sister's voice rose high and shrill. Once she began she would never stop, like a fireball skimming along a trail of oil until it grew big enough to engulf an entire house. Bhut hastened to remove his shoes, groaning loudly as he bent to undo the thin laces, making as much noise as possible to announce his arrival before showing his face in the kitchen doorway. Like a douse of water, his presence extinguished the quarrel.

"Chai?" he asked his wife.

She turned to the hearth and set to smashing pieces of ginger into her steel chai pot. His sisters ignored him as he took a seat on the stool closest to the window. Those two women were like extra digits on a hand: more encumbrance than utility, a magnet for talk and embarrassment. Yet they had not always been that way. As children they had been full of jokes and mischief, and Bhut had been their foremost admirer even as they switched out his milk with rice water or filled his shoes with river stones. They had been so unlike his eldest sister, the one who always had a treat waiting when he passed his exams, who mended his pants when he ripped them before their mother found out and withheld his dinner in punishment. He did not think of her often; doing so reminded him of why the gossips had declared his other sisters unmarriageable. When his eldest sister's life had been plucked too early, the other two became like fruit that hung fast to the bough, ripening and rotting and drying up past all recognition.

"Yes, ignore us; even when you know we are right." The flame of the quarrel rose up again, one sister muttering while the other shot dark glances at Bhut's wife. His knee began to ache, and Bhut rubbed it harder than necessary, hoping the motion would distract the women.

Sometimes, one of his deputies would report a disturbance in one of the lanes or cramped apartments that was blamed on a ghost or spirit. Bhut waved his hand at them, telling them to note the matter down in the logs as a domestic issue. Now, he found himself wishing for such a supernatural appearance to halt the quarrels that rose like weeds around his sisters. But he did not believe in ghosts. A man with his past, after all, could ill afford to.

7

Women and men alike came out and stood in the doorways of their rooms, murmuring among themselves, staring at the body of a man who looked remarkably like the manager. Mohan unfolded the smooth, shimmering white piece of cloth he'd purchased in the market and let it fall in soft ripples over the body, his hands trembling, eyes darting from the face to the manager's and back again.

As Pramesh pulled one end of the milk-white cloth toward his cousin's head, he drank in the details of Sagar's features and tried to read the missing years in the lines and creases. The split eyebrow, the dark spots near the lip, scarred remains of the pox that both boys had endured at nine—Pramesh knew the stories of these as if his own face had been branded with them. But the yellowed remains of a bruise on Sagar's shoulder, the whiteness of a slash near his ear like a streak of chalk that would not rub off—what of those?

A hand rested on Pramesh's back, and he looked up to see Narinder.

"Loknath will lead the rites," the head priest said. "Then, you'll return home. Then the twelve days of mourning."

Pramesh tilted his chin. He knew the rituals that follow death as well as he knew the days of the week.

"And on the eleventh day, Narayana bali."

At this, Pramesh looked up. Narayana bali was performed only when the death had been bad, an extra measure to ensure that the soul went straight to where it was supposed to go.

The head priest gripped his shoulder, then turned and began to walk around the courtyard with his prayer beads as he always did at this time of day. *Detach*, the old priest always told the families when their grief sounded in heavy waves that washed over the bhavan. *Your duty is to detach*. Pramesh stifled a sigh, lifted the sheet, and let it glide and rest over Sagar's head.

Twelve other pyres crowded Manikarnika ghat that day. Most of the men from the bhavan followed and clustered some steps above to watch the proceedings like a cordon of resting pigeons. Mohan could not do enough; he insisted on helping carry the bier through the lanes, and his voice chanted the truth of Rama's name louder than any other. Once at the ghats, the assistant fetched a barber, and though Pramesh protested, Mohan took employee loyalty to higher reaches and had his head shaved and tonsured alongside the manager's.

"In Kashi you are my family, and when I am under your roof, your pain is mine," Mohan said. While the Doms stacked the wood and readied the pyre, manager and assistant bathed in the river and then donned the same gauzy white dhotis they'd helped guests purchase for so many years, the cloth unfamiliar to their skin, the newly shaved whiteness of their heads disquieting above their brown torsos.

It all seemed a dream to Pramesh, something he watched from a distance when a guest passed away and the family headed down to the ghats. Those pilgrims, at least, had for the most part died good deaths, deaths that came peacefully at the culmination of a long life, deaths that gently drew the soul from the body and led it to join the great God. Pramesh tried to ignore the chatter that suffused the ghats that day. No matter that Bhut had declared to the old city that Sagar's death was a drunken accident. Everyone with eyes could see that Sagar was young; he'd been ripped from his body before he could weave a completed life behind him. He had been alone, with no one to whisper the great God's name into his ears as the water rushed to fill the pockets of his lungs. Most troubling of all, Sagar had died in ambiguous territory, neither holy nor cursed, that spot where the water from Kashi's shores mingled with Magadha's. "It is certainly not a *good* death," the collective murmur seemed to say, and how could Pramesh argue?

Loknath reminded Pramesh of the procedure. "You will fetch the fire from the Doms," he said. "At my signal, walk around the pyre and touch the flame to the mouth. Five times, remember, Pramesh-ji? We will wait for the pyre to burn. At the midway point I will again signal, and that will be the time to break the skull."

Pramesh blanched, but he breathed in deeply and Loknath continued. "At the end—forgive me, Pramesh-ji, I know you are aware of all this—at the end, when you extinguish the flame, remember, you must not look back. Continue on to the bhavan and we will meet you there, but no matter what happens, do not look back."

Pramesh shut his eyes. In that darkness he saw himself imparting the very same information to each family who left the bhavan carrying a body on a bier. *The soul is gone, the body is burnt, the time is past. Do not show your attachment to someone who exists no longer and never will again. Do not look back.*

Perpetual clusters of foreigners, pilgrims, urchins, Dom children playing cricket, touts looking to squeeze some rupees from the rest, cows reclining in the mud, and various scattered ne'er-do-wells sprinkled the steps, while more leaned out of high balconies and windows to witness the day's cremations at Manikarnika. They watched out of a desire as simple and instinctive as thirst: they needed a grand finale to the dead man's story, which had festered on their lips for the last two days. When the river washed away the ashes, it would also rinse their mouths and ready them for the next tale.

Like the mythic guards of Yamraj's palace, the Doms awaited Pramesh, their arms crossed against sinewy chests, bodies glistening with sweat, eyes tinged red from the billowing smoke. Behind them, the river flowed black and glinted gold where the ripples reflected the sun. They may have been Untouchable, the only class of people to handle the dead, but their ancestry could be traced back to when the first ancient fire of cremation had been entrusted to them, a fire that was theirs to care for and keep, to dole out to all who wanted proper funeral rites for their dead.

When it came time for Pramesh to fetch the fire, he paid the asking price without argument. Numb and not a little frightened, he circled the pyre clockwise once, the first of the five revolutions, and stretched the bundle of grass, burning with that sacred flame, toward Sagar's mouth. As his hand drew close, the flame sputtered and thrilled, the river droplets on Sagar's skin sizzled and escaped with a gaseous hiss, the pyre was almost alight, the flesh was almost freed, and then—

"The pyre will not burn!"

Heads swung around to where a bandy-legged priest raised his fist, prayer beads held tight, in a gesture that was half benediction and half curse. "You will see," the old man crowed. "The great God will not allow the pyre of such a sinner to burn!" Whether because of his proclaimed clairvoyance or because of the magnificent stink wafting from his skimpy dhoti, the priest received a wide berth on the cramped ghat steps. Such an interruption, such a thing to say—Pramesh froze as the sheaf of grasses in his hand smoldered with timeless sacred fury. What if the priest was right?

Such things happened: Years ago, on this very ghat, the pyre of a prominent businessman, known for his particular tastes in philandering—"Nepali girls *only*, Bhaiya. He flies into a rage otherwise!"—had refused to burn, despite the quantities—gallons!—of ghee, the top quality sandalwood and mango timbers of the pyre, the profusion of sons that presided at his funeral, the priests said to be descended from the purest of dynasties, and the hundred thousand rupees donated from the dead man's coffers to the city orphanage. Though the eldest son circled and circled and prodded his father's body with that timeless flame, the pyre would not light, wouldn't accept a single spark. Only when the sons recruited a manservant to procure a gas lighter did the wood flare with weak enthusiasm, producing more smoke than flame, enabling the supervising Doms to push the half-smoked body off the pyre and into the river under the cover of the enshrouding black clouds.

But Sagar could not be compared to that man . . . or could he? The stork-legged priest remained in his spot with his prayer beads held aloft, and the crowd tittered like a flock of restless birds. As auspicious seconds ticked by, as people argued, as Loknath struggled to surmount the tumult of noise—"Light the pyre, Pramesh-ji. Ignore them and light the pyre!"—Pramesh was numb, unable to will his body forward or back, wasting both time and sacred flame, while Sagar's body waited. Then, through a sudden imbalance in his feet or an encouraging gust of wind or a light push from Loknath that no one saw, Pramesh's hand dipped toward Sagar's mouth, and the undying fire, which had been on the verge of sputtering out, found flesh to bite into and absolve into ash.

"It lights!" A triumphant cry burst from the crowd, and a cheer and laugh went up before being quickly stifled by the stern looks of the Doms, Mohan, and Loknath.

"No good will come of it," the stork-legged priest said, but now the crowd ignored him, and he knew enough to mount the steps and depart before the audience turned against him.

Pramesh felt his legs move, his torch-holding hand touching Sagar's mouth after each revolution, and he soon completed the five rounds. Loknath placed the fragrant powder of the rites into the manager's hands, and Pramesh flung the stuff into the air, sending showers over the pyre and sparks spiraling toward the river. The heat surprised him. He'd never been so close before, and the blazing furnace roared with such affirmative energy that it seemed more capable of bringing the body back to life than reducing it to the mundane finality of ashes. Indeed, the flame pushed the body into motion, sending legs gliding away from the torso as the flesh melted away, releasing arms from their sockets, goading a hand to drape curled fingers over the pyre's edge in a gesture that seemed plaintive from one angle and commanding from another.

He dreaded what was to come next. During the countless cremations he had observed from the topmost step of the ghat, he had always turned away as the chief mourners performed the most vital action that ensured the soul's safe passage to its final destination. To crack the skull, to strike the head he knew as well as his own, and allow the spirit to escape toward its final journey. . . . Even from many steps away the sound could be heard: the solid *thuk!* of wood cracking bone, like a cricket bat making contact or woodworkers beating a table leg into its socket.

Many men, no matter how fearless, balked at the task. They escaped with a simple ceremonial tap of the bamboo staff on the skull, and with relief they allowed the priest to deliver the final blow. But Pramesh encountered death every day, and if he could not prove himself an example to his guests, or to those Banarasis staring at the back of his head with an intensity that threatened to crack his own skull, the resulting story would be one he would never shed. And then conviction—of a sick, haunting kind, but conviction nonetheless—came to him in a gush of bile and a voice long suppressed. *You've never had the courage to do the thing that has to be done.*

Loknath locked eyes with Pramesh and gave a slight tilt of the chin. Mohan appeared at the manager's side, a thick bamboo staff pulled from the disassembled bier at the ready. Pramesh took it and pressed his hands around the smooth wood. He breathed in deep, breathed out the great God's name, swung the pole, and brought it down with a crack on Sagar's charring skull.

He felt something break and lifted a foreshortened length of bamboo. Horrified, he looked down and saw Sagar's skull, resolutely intact. He'd missed.

A distressed Mohan cried out, "The staff must have already had some break in it—another! We require another!" Another was procured, appearing like a miracle out of the crowd, but Pramesh's second swing had even less conviction than the first, and he missed again, sending sparks flying into the air and the river and even, unfortunately, into Loknath's face. As the priest rubbed his eyes, already streaming with tears from the smoke, Mohan's urgent whisper came at Pramesh's shoulder. "You must try one more time, Pramesh-ji," he said.

The manager gritted his teeth and breathed in the fumes of flesh and bone, holy powder and blackened wood. Once more he raised the staff and brought it down. Loknath shielded his eyes from the sparks, and when the air was clear he glanced at the skull. Pramesh *thought* he could see a hairline crack, or perhaps it was a trick of the light. Whatever the damage, Loknath pronounced the effort sufficient.

"The skull has been cracked!" he said. "It will do."

Mohan repeated the words in his loud and blustery way, and the verdict soon rolled through the lines of people. The flames were winding down, receding, as if, like the falsely prophetic priest, they'd had their roaring say and now accepted their lot, grumbling. Soon the ordeal would be over, the fire would die out, and all Pramesh would have to do was take up a pot of Ganges water, turn his back, and throw the pot over his shoulder and toward the pyre, walking away as the water extinguished any remaining flame. *Gagri phute, nata tute*. Pot broken, relationship finished.

In the ashes, he scraped out a 9 and a 4, Vishnu's conch and discus marking the final spot where Sagar's body had rested. Then, pot at the ready, Pramesh waited for Loknath's signal. The Doms stood nearby, waiting for the pyre to burn down, waiting to scrape the wood and ashes clean and shovel what remained of Sagar back into the river in which he'd spent his last moments. A calm settled over the crowd, and the outermost edges dwindled as people returned to the places they had come from. The story was complete, and now it was time to return to their own troubles and joys.

As people siphoned away, Pramesh felt relief. Now all that existed were the pyre, the river, himself, and Sagar. For the past day, the persistent taste of hot ash had stayed with him, but as he looked at the charred remains of Sagar, the bones and the sooty black of wood indistinguishable from flesh, he had an unexpected and intense craving. He wanted aam paana.

He was startled; he hadn't tasted aam paana in years. The green mango juice, spiked with black salt and cumin and thrilling to the tongue, had been Sagar's favorite. A treat made by their mothers, something to soothe the heat of a stifling day, cool glasses held against skin, pungent liquid slipping down the throat. Pramesh wiped the sweat from his brow, looking at the smoking pyre, trying to recognize Sagar but seeing only the bones, the skull. Again he felt bile rise to the back of his throat, and he looked at the river instead, bidding his mind to go back to aam paana, to think of something else as he waited for the Doms to pronounce the burning complete.

He had missed seeing his father burn, as well as his uncle, his old widowed aunt. He'd missed seeing his mother and Sagar's burn as well. This pyre, loaded with just one man, felt piled with all the people he'd tried not to think about since resolving to leave his old life behind. Unbidden, the memory came to him like a spark landing in his palm from one of the many spangling the air.

A golden day. The Mothers laughing, and Sagar flexing his thin arms, showing off, willing the tiny muscles to pop. The air as hot and tight as today, but tinged with a clean smell, of dirt and water and green things springing up and waving in the rare breeze.

"Help us if you can't think of anything better to do," Sagar's mother said to Pramesh, who'd been aimless, unable to finish the book his mother had given him, bored with scratching numbers in the dirt next to the peepal tree, too hot to race Sagar around the yard, wandering from front room to the kitchen, looking over his mother's shoulder and hanging about his aunt's elbow until they pulled him down to sit next to them. Sagar was still running through the house and back outside again, hands sticky with brown tamarind paste or some other thing he'd stolen from the kitchen, until his mother yelled at him to sit down. "Or I will marry you off this instant. That Jaya is quite fond of you—I'm sure she wouldn't mind." At the mention of the neighbor's visiting granddaughter, Sagar wrinkled his nose and squatted down beside them immediately.

They all sat in the yard at the back of the house, fields beyond, a fire lit and water bubbling away in a large steel pot. The day was hot and promised to get hotter, but trees provided shade, and the breezes were frequent enough to refresh them. A pile of tart unripe mangos, like smooth green stones, sat on a clean cloth between the Mothers. Sagar's mother handed the boys knives made slightly dull with age, while she and Pramesh's mother kept the sharper blades, and she showed the boys how to take one of the fruits, peel it, dice the flesh, and remove the soft pit before dropping the sunshine-colored cubes into a neat pile next to the whole fruit.

"Let's see who is fastest," Sagar said, fruit and knife poised in his hands, grinning at Pramesh.

"No need for that," Pramesh's mother said sharply. She softened her tone. "It won't taste any better for you racing each other."

Where had the Elders been? Certainly not at home. Their mothers had been laughing that day, had walked to and from the house with purposeful steps, belonging to that place and to themselves. And Pramesh and Sagar had belonged to them entirely.

The smell, tart and clean, the smooth curve of each fruit fitting perfectly in their small palms. The knives were just sharp enough to cut but required effort and concentration, and soon both boys were silent, brows furrowed, focused on their task. As they worked, Pramesh's mother began to tell a story, this time the tale of Markandeya, a boy fated to die at sixteen but who was rescued when he spent his birthday praying before a linga, out of which the great God leapt to subdue the Bearer of Death.

Halfway through the tale, Sagar dropped a fistful of cubes into the pile but kept some back, and he waited for the Mothers to look at some other thing before cramming the fruit into his mouth, his grin triumphant. And then Pramesh had to follow, and the sour burst dazzled his tongue. As Pramesh moved to shove another palmful of cubes into his mouth, his mother finished the story, tsked, and looked up at Sagar's mother. "Perhaps they think we were never like them, once?"

Sagar's mother wagged her head in agreement, earrings swaying, and fetched the carved spice box with its compartments for black salt, cumin, and chili from the house. She sprinkled the spices on a small pile of cubes set between herself and Pramesh's mother, which they snacked on while dodging the boys' outstretched hands. "You didn't share with us, did you?" Sagar's mother teased. But they relented, the Mothers feeding the cousins by hand.

Once all the cut fruit had been dropped into the bubbling pot, Sagar and Pramesh took turns peering inside, poking at the contents with a wooden spoon, running back to tell their mothers about the color of the liquid, the softness of the fruit, until one of them came over and pronounced it done. Sagar's mother added the spices with a deft hand, and Pramesh's mother mixed in water, still cool from the earthenware pot that the cousins had carried to the well and back again, and then it was ready. The boys marveled at this thing they had made, the color of light filtered through a tree's leaves, made liquid; pungent and smoky with black salt and cumin.

Pramesh remembered leaning against his mother as she'd given the mixture a final stir. She was solid and warm and smelled of chai and an unknown spice. His blanket had the same smell; he often buried his nose in the cloth before falling asleep. "Who would have thought such monkeys could be such good workers?" she said, eyebrows raised, and with one hand still swirling the liquid with her spoon she reached the other around Pramesh and tickled him in the side, in his most vulnerable spot, and Pramesh shrieked with laughter. She handed the pot over to Sagar's mother, who instructed him to hold the glasses while she poured out generous portions.

Had they tasted it? A small sip, even a drop on the tongue? He thought he remembered loud footsteps coming from the front room, and louder voices, his father and uncle come home from wherever they had been, and the Mothers getting up quickly, shooing the boys outside without their hard-earned aam paana.

They both knew that it was wiser to stay out of the way. They occupied themselves outside in the heat of the day until they thought they might venture in. Through the back door, into the kitchen, their eyes immediately turned to the tumblers, the steel pot.

All empty. Not even the dried stickiness usually left behind, clinging to the pot or the glasses.

Later, in bed, when their mothers came to smooth their brows and ask them if they'd said their nighttime prayer, Sagar kept asking, "All of it? Is it really all gone?"

"Hush," Pramesh's mother had said. "So easy to make; such a stupid thing to be upset over. Tomorrow we will try again."

"Your fathers were hot and tired," Sagar's mother said, by way of consolation. "And they are your elders; remember that."

Remember that. Their Elders, to heed and obey without question. How long had it taken for Pramesh to slough off that last piece of maternal advice? To push it away meant pushing the Mothers away as well. But to keep it close—he and Sagar knew that price.

Soon after, everything changed. Pramesh had asked for aam paana when he was sick; he recalled the awful tight thirst in his throat, his tongue like a hot coal packed inside his mouth. He waited for his mother or Sagar's to come, his body shaking and twisting on his straw mat, the sweat rolling down his temples and chest. They were still not there when he woke from the fever, many weeks later. But Sagar was. His face greeted Pramesh when he opened his eyes, reentering the world of the living. Pramesh swallowed, felt the walls of his throat burn as if he'd drunk acid. He tried to speak, saying only the simplest and most necessary thing. "Ma?" Then, exhausted, he fell asleep.

The next days followed a similar pattern, Pramesh asking for his mother, then for Sagar's. Sagar's face swimming into view, relief sometimes showing in his eyes, fear at other times, then everything going black as Pramesh succumbed to sleep. But as time went by, he was able to stay awake longer. There was always a fresh blanket across him, a clean shirt and pair of pants on his skin, though he could not remember his mother or aunt coming to dress him. He would eat what they'd left—a glass of coconut water and a bowl of broth, strong with ginger and turmeric and laden with rice, the vessels difficult to lift to his mouth. Sagar stayed at his side, hunched in a corner playing cat's cradle on a loop of string. "Where are they?" Pramesh asked when he finished eating, still hungry for the sight of his mother and aunt.

"Coming," Sagar said. His voice was strange, fear still in his eyes.

Pramesh looked down at his wasted body, and he thought he understood why. His legs were thin and unfamiliar. His breath was acrid and sour, and his nails had grown unchecked into coarse points that frightened him. The two cousins had always looked like twins, but the illness had whittled away at Pramesh so that he was a shadow of his former self, of the boy Sagar still was.

One day Pramesh woke to Sagar crying. "What's wrong?" he asked. "Are you sick as well? Shall I call for Ma?" Silence. Insects singing in the night, a breeze blowing a branch against the side of the house. In the perfect blackness of the room, Pramesh lolled his head to the side and spied a single star winking outside their window. A shivering shudder, breathless, and he heard Sagar choking down a sob. He tried to sit up but was so suddenly dizzy that he lay back down. "What is it?"

"You cannot call them."

"Yes I can—what do you need?"

"They won't come."

"Are they away? Why didn't we go with them—was I sleeping?"

"They won't come."

Pramesh's head spun; talking exhausted him and he could not think straight. *They won't come* meant they were not here; if they were not here, they were somewhere else; if they were somewhere else, they would return; when they returned, they would come. The next thing in the sequence eluded him.

"Why did they leave? When are they coming back?"

"They won't come."

The repetition enraged him. "They will; they will; why do you keep saying that?" And then, to prove Sagar wrong, Pramesh gathered his meager breath and screamed, that single, perfect syllable, the sound that had always worked before, an infallible incantation, to summon his mother.

Rustling from inside the house. Someone rising, someone walking. *See how simple it is?* But the footsteps were all wrong, the hulking darkness in the doorway all wrong, and Sagar stiffened in a way that Pramesh could feel from the other side of the room. His father, silent and still.

"Another word," the man said, "and I will pull your tongue from your throat."

He turned away.

That was when he knew. The fever had taken them, his mother and Sagar's, but had been of two minds about Pramesh, lingering so long that his father and uncle gave him up for dead. The world he returned to was like a different planet. Where once there had been two mothers, two bright points of light who laughed and consoled and seemed to know every wonder of the world, there was now Bua, an old widowed aunt, the older sister of the Elders, who brought the food and changed the linens, did her work and counted her prayer beads, but who said little, with no stories to share or games to offer when the cousins came to her with their troubles and questions.

The Elders became larger in their mothers' absence. Their voices and hands boomed loud and harsh; words and beatings carried the scent of alcohol and anger. The Mothers had once been there to say *Stop* and *Enough* and *Please*. Their aunt echoed the same pleas, but what power did a widow's voice carry? The Elders ignored her.

Sagar urged Pramesh to stand, to take slow and halting steps around their tiny room. Out the window, looking at the world he'd been absent from for many weeks, Pramesh saw strange men in the distance working their land. Fields once theirs had been lost in debts and drunkenness and ill-advised business dealings. He retreated to his mat on the floor where he'd sweated and slurred. He sank into dreams, tried to forget, and when he woke, Sagar was there, watching him with worried eyes, prodding him with hot, trembling fingers.

"Bhai? Bhaiya? Are you awake? Are you still there?"

"Here. I am here."

In his fever dreams Pramesh had asked for the Mothers, and they had not come. But Sagar had, always: Sagar looking at him through the window, fetching water, Sagar asking to see him, Sagar stealing in when all others were asleep and whispering in his cousin's ear. And always, Sagar's voice penetrating the other boy's thoughts, a voice that stood tall against the fever and refused to yield even if Pramesh wanted to. A voice that echoed in his ears now.

You cannot go without me. You cannot leave me behind.

"Pramesh-ji," Loknath said. His wheezing voice, thick with smoke and sparks, brought the manager back to himself. "The moment is here. Throw the pot." Tears streamed anew from Loknath's irritated eyes; the priest could no more see the steps in front of him than the pyre, and he gestured in the general direction of where Pramesh should walk once the deed was done.

Pramesh had almost died all those years ago, but Sagar had pulled him back to life solely with the force of his will. Yet when his own turn had come, Pramesh had left his cousin with such ease, such eagerness to start a new life in Kashi, that he had relinquished his chance to challenge the Bearer of Death the way Sagar had and snatch his cousin back. The weight returned to his chest and pressed down more fiercely than before, and he gasped.

"Pramesh-ji," Loknath said again, urgency lacing his voice.

Pramesh breathed in deep for this final step of the rites, the soot swirling in the air burning in his lungs, the heavy smell of oil and flesh and wood turning his stomach. He hefted the pot as he turned his back to the pyre. Eyes shut, he concentrated on the great God's name and pushed the pot over his shoulder. He blinked, caught a glimpse of green flying overhead and disappearing into an alcove.

The clay shattered against the pyre. An errant shard spiraled toward the manager and met the tender skin between his shoulder blades. The sting jolted him, forcing a movement before the mind could register its meaning. And then, then, *then*. . . .

Pramesh looked back.

The beginning and the end: that was all anyone ever agreed upon when they told the story. In between, the tale of the ghost on Mir ghat diverged according to the whims and memory of the teller. First, her beginning. The ghost was a woman, once. And she was remembered for three things: her eyes, her anklets, her parrot-green sari. After that. . . .

Some said that, in life, she was in love with a spirit. She danced on the stone steps every night, summoning her paramour with the rhythmic jingle of delicate silver chains slung around her light feet. Night after night, she danced, until one evening she danced so long and with such fervor that her bloodied feet gave out beneath her and she collapsed, dead, a smile on her lips.

Some said she was a changeling, her true soul sucked from her body by a demon, who then deposited it into a parrot's body every night. The demon used the parrot to do his bidding, they said, to cast the evil eye. You might hear a flutter of wings by your window as you lay in bed; you might see a flash of green as your eyes succumbed to sleep; the scratch of tiny feet on a window shutter would be enough to wake you, to keep you alert for the rest of the night.

Some said she was simply a disobedient girl, one who flouted her elders, who assumed the freedoms of a man though she bloomed with the beauty of a woman. She walked where she willed, spoke to every person she met, felt no boundary in age or gender or propriety. She loved in places where such ties were forbidden. And though her life had been wasteful, some said, her death was not: it was used as a warning for all other women, married and unmarried alike, to heed.

Some said that the truth was simpler than that. A tale of a woman drugged and pushed and abandoned on the ghats, a thousand cracks spreading across her tired and soul-weary skull. Victim of her husband, victim of her in-laws—no uncommon thing.

Go to one neighborhood, and you might hear one story with small variations. Another neighborhood, and you hear different tales for every floor in a building. Some scoffed at the idea of demons, of the supernatural. Others breathed in the great God's name at the sign of a green bird flying overhead. Children absorbed the version favored in their house, and when they grew up and left Kashi, they marveled that outsiders had never heard this story that seemed to them common knowledge, like a shared understanding of when the monsoon rains would begin.

As for the woman's end. . . .

Morning saw her alive and well and sitting by the upper-story window, watching the world wake. Night saw her sprawled on the bottommost step of the ghat, mouth agape, eyes open, hands curled, a trickle of blood tracing a delicate line down her creamy forehead, as if some painter had dipped a brush into that dark red pool beneath her head to sign his name on her skin and claim her for the city, for the great God, for the river, for the cursed land stretching out beyond like a sigh.

PART II

8

Ten days of silence. Ten days of holding his tongue in Shobha and Rani's presence, of giving a wide berth to Mohan and Narinder and the other priests just as they did to him, of keeping his eyes down and walking through the clusters of guests who still sought him out.

Ten days of making his own food on a makeshift hearth he constructed in the side alley between the bhavan and the Mistry house, of eating just a single meal each day, apart from everyone else, each time facing south with his eyes trained in the direction of the Land of the Dead.

Ten days of waking each morning to walk alone to the river, of bathing but avoiding the razor and the nail clippers, of making an offering to Sagar of a single rice ball that he molded with his hands. Ten days of going without shoes or sandals and of sleeping on the ground just outside the kitchen.

Ten days of waiting, of listening as Narinder recited from the Garuda Purana, describing the horrors of the Vaitarani river, whose crossing all souls endured before they transformed from earthbound spirit to nothing, to no one, a blessed merging with the great God. Ten days of repeating the holy name to himself until his mouth was dry and his throat parched, all while banishing Sagar's name from his lips, his heart, his mind.

Ten days with the responsibility that all chief mourners bore: To exist without human interaction, without the joys of the living, to deny the name of the dead, to expunge all memory of the relationship and the bond, to replace all emotion and feeling with an iron will, to ensure that Sagar's spirit, now wandering, now in between, would not be lured by those reminders of its previous life and decide to delay its journey onward.

And all the while Pramesh was shadowed by Sagar, whose heavy presence he felt on his shoulder as he walked from the bhavan to the river to bathe, hovering around his head as he tried to slip into the solace of dreams, sitting behind his eyebrow when another headache threatened to engulf him.

Had Sagar already done this three times—once for each of their Elders and their aunt? Had his father and uncle wandered around like dead men when their wives died, when Pramesh was imprisoned in the land of fever and wondering why neither his mother nor Sagar's would come to him? He tried to remember, caught only a glimmer of green, and then stopped himself before the memory took him further, replacing it with the great God's name repeated over and over.

Ten days of this, of such intense concentration that Pramesh felt the connection to his body and to his life and reality begin to fade, faces blurring, his feet taking him from room to room of the bhavan, the manager unable even to smile at his daughter, to remember the feel of his wife in his arms.

And then the eleventh day arrived, and Pramesh felt soap on his skin, a blade smoothing his cheeks, sandals on his feet, sunlight on his face. A child's smile, his daughter's smile, registered in his eyes and he blinked, like a man just born. That morning, he walked to the ghat with Narinder, and together they spent the day completing the Narayana bali, the priest leading Pramesh in the many steps of the ceremony that was an extra precaution after a bad death, to ensure the safe passage of Sagar's soul.

When they returned, Shobha was deep in preparations for the next day's feast, Mrs. Mistry at her side kneading dough and chatting away. On the twelfth and final day, Pramesh woke, his mind already locked in prayer from habit, and he flung the gates open to welcome the Brahmins who would come to eat Sagar's favorite foods, chickpeas served with airy bhatura, spicy potatoes, sweet pura, rice studded with vegetables. When they were finished, everyone in the bhavan, and anyone else who happened to walk in through the gates, took their turn at eating. Until finally the last grain of rice was gone, the last guest sated, the sun set, and the air was peaceful.

Narinder pronounced the period of mourning complete. "He is now released to continue the journey on his own," the priest said. "Everything was correctly done." He gripped Pramesh's shoulder in a rare gesture, as if welcoming the manager back to the world of the living.

That night, Pramesh fell into his bed exhausted, Shobha at his side, Rani's soft breaths reaching his ears and filling his heart. His mind, tightened like a fist on the holy word and mantras during that time of mourning, unclenched. His cousin's name rose in his throat; he could say it now, if he wanted to. Those two syllables, absent from his lips for years, never quite gone from his heart and mind.

Sagar. The name was just a thought, at first. He glanced at his wife, who breathed the deep slow breaths of sleep. "Sagar," he said aloud, and something within him shifted. Sagar's face—his adult face—all this time like a shadow in water, clarified in Pramesh's mind. As he registered its features, so recently burned in fire, the memories arrived in a torrential rush.

Bhaiya, you cannot leave me behind—We are pawns, Bhaiya, we always have been—Bhaiya, will you make me that promise?—You lied to me, Bhaiya; all of it was lies.

He sat up, gasping for air beneath a heavy weight that pressed like a foot on his chest. Sagar's body was gone, his spirit was off on its final journey. But the memories Pramesh had tried to forget, and the guilt dragged along with them, all arrived in full force and settled squarely within his heart.

In the morning, Shobha kept her ear trained to the gate, primed for its low squeak. When Pramesh returned from bathing in the river, she had his chai ready, as well as a portion of laapsi. She'd spent the previous day cooking the favorite foods of a man she'd never met, but the cracked wheat cooked with sugar and ghee was what Pramesh loved, and she'd mixed in extra golden raisins and bits of cashew. It was what she'd fed him on their wedding day, a bare-bones hurried ceremony made somehow luxurious because of the quiet sweetness, the richness of the ghee, the look in his eyes as he'd eaten from her hands. She meant it as a lucky start, something sweet to mark his return to normal life after the mourning period.

But if he recalled that day, that joy, as he sipped his chai and ate, he said nothing, and his silence and blank stare revealed nothing. Rani sat by her side and she handed her small bites, alternating between roti and laapsi, ignoring her daughter's obvious preference for the latter, trying to think of what to say to dissolve the silence that lingered in the air after the mourning period. "I think the door upstairs will need a new key plate soon—the rust is eating away at the edges."

Her husband gave a low murmur of agreement.

She tried again. "Will you look in on the dying this morning?" she asked. The question sounded strange, as if she'd forgotten how to communicate with her husband. And he, too, seemed to have forgotten, looking up at her, startled.

"Later," he said, putting the last bit of cracked wheat into his mouth. He licked the pads of his fingers, and this, at least, lifted Shobha's heart: he still remembered sweetness enough to value it to the last grain. He plucked another fingerful of laapsi out of the bowl in front of Shobha and leaned forward to pop it into Rani's mouth. "If Mohan is looking for me, tell him I will be in my office—I will do the rounds later."

She wanted to ask him to stay with her and Rani for just a little longer, but she held her tongue. She was being foolish: most women would be glad to have twelve days without a husband telling them what to do, always underfoot. And he hadn't even gone anywhere. But he'd seemed less like the man she had married with each day of the mourning period as he walked around with his shorn head, the look in his eyes growing steadily more distant until it acquired a frightening blankness, the hollows in his cheeks growing deeper, the constant mantras on his lips, his fingers twitching through his prayer beads, making him look more like a man gone slightly mad than one in deep meditation.

She needed to be patient. That is what Mrs. Mistry would say. So she set herself to her usual chores, cleaning up after the morning meal, thinking over what she wanted from the market, until she felt enough time had passed and she ventured to check on Pramesh, a glass of water in her hand as an excuse for her intrusion.

She found him standing at his desk, reading through a stack of letters that were yellowed and crackling. She knew what they were. Letters from his cousin, missives that once arrived weekly at the bhavan, in that first year when her husband was a stranger to the city, assisting her father with the management of Shankarbhavan.

"You haven't looked at those in years," she said.

He put down the letter he was reading and took the glass from her. "There was no point in keeping them. They serve no purpose now. But then I began to read . . . foolish, I know."

In the early days before their marriage, the postman had handed her one of these letters for Pramesh. She remembered the way his face brightened when she gave it to him, the shy smile he gave her in thanks, and how, during the rest of that day, his hand wandered to the front pocket of his shirt where he'd folded it, waiting to read it in the evening, then perhaps once more the next morning, stretching the words until the next letter came.

Once, her eyes had lingered on him too long, and he looked up from reading the same letter for at least the third time that day. *Foolish, I know*, he'd said then, sheepish. And she'd smiled back before she realized what she was doing, then covered her head with her sari and hastened to hide herself in the kitchen before the entire bhavan—or worse, her father!— saw her flushed face, heard her heart drumming in her chest.

"You were so happy to see them, once," she said. "Not so foolish." She thought perhaps he wanted to be left alone, but then his hand nudged the stack toward her, the slightest of movements. He dipped his head to the side when she looked up at him, and so she took the first letter and began to read.

Bhaiya, I never took you to be anything but a village bumpkin like myself, but look at you, the new expert on Kashi! Soon you'll—

"Pramesh-ji," Mohan said, poking his head into the office, "we have three rooms open, but five families are here and they all claim to have arrived at the same time. What should I do? How should I split the space?"

He stood at the manager's office door, glancing back and forth between the courtyard and Pramesh.

Seeming to surface from some deep place, Pramesh gathered the letters into a neat stack. Shobha reluctantly handed back the one she'd been reading and he filed them back in the cabinet. He pushed the door shut and paused, leaning his head against it. "I should burn them," he said. "It was all lies in the end." Abruptly, he turned, brushing Shobha's fingers with his as he passed, leaving her to wonder what he meant.

That evening at dinner, Shobha laid out the meal and filled everyone's thalis before preparing one additional plate. As the priests and her husband began eating, she looked to Mohan. "Will Sheetal come?"

The two-week deadline had long since passed during the mourning period for Sagar, and though the rest of the family had departed, Sheetal and his father remained. The assistant shook his head. "I tried. He refuses to impose."

Shobha tsked and handed the full thali to Mohan, who left the room with it and soon returned empty-handed. "Was he hungry?"

"He promised me he would eat. I will go in directly after I finish and check."

Shobha gave a smile of thanks and glanced at her husband, but he kept his eyes on his food and seemed to have not heard. Later that night, when they were both in bed, she brought up the subject again. "He is all alone, and it won't be for long." Her husband looked confused. "The boy. Sheetal. He has no one to cook for him, and he is so busy with his father and helping around the bhavan—did you see how he mended that stool for that family in No. 7? And I always make more than enough."

As she had suspected, he had noticed nothing. He patted her hand. "You always take care of everyone," he said.

She grasped his hand beneath the blanket.

"It felt as if I was in the Land of the Dead for twelve days," he said.

"But you weren't," Shobha said. "And you aren't." She watched his face in the dark. "Why was he here?"

"A visit, probably," Pramesh said. There was a lilt in his voice, the words a question more than a statement.

Shobha remembered something, a thing she'd wanted to ask her husband about but kept to herself during the mourning period. "The letter you wrote, informing his people in the village—no one replied," she said. What kind of people had no response to a dead son-in-law, a dead husband? After mailing it, she'd half expected to see them at her doorstep, demanding to see the place where Sagar's dead body had last lain. She, certainly, would have done the same, in their place. In Kamna's place.

"No," he agreed. "I didn't think they would."

"It doesn't surprise you?"

"I've wondered if perhaps it was more than a visit," Pramesh said. "Perhaps he meant to stay. It would be something he'd do. Pack up suddenly and decide to leave—make a decision and simply act on it, all in a few seconds."

"But his wife—" Shobha's heart tripped, but she pushed the question out before she lost her courage. "Why wouldn't he bring his wife with him?"

He didn't speak. She held her tongue, counting the seconds. He turned her hand over in his, traced the lines on her palm with his fingers. "It was a bad match. They thought they were getting me, and then they found out I was already married." Shobha tensed. "They felt the Elders had tricked them. There was a dowry. And my father and uncle spent it all—not a rupee left by the time you and I visited. So the girl's family lost the money, with no groom to show for it, no home to send their daughter to. But Sagar was there . . . and her family was quite adamant that it happen."

Understanding bloomed within Shobha. Such matches were not uncommon. One family had a girl they needed to marry off, one who most families wouldn't look at. *Running around as she does . . . you know the stories.* Another family had debt they could not settle. An alliance was agreed upon, an amount set and paid, the young people wed, both families rejoiced—and the boy and the girl were left to spend a lifetime together.

He'd never spoken of this in such detail. That he was even speaking now was a kind of miracle, and she was hesitant to ask more, lest he clamp up in silence. But she could not stop herself. "Was there something about her . . . something that made them anxious to get her married?"

"Her?" Pramesh frowned. His pause was a beat too long. "I know nothing of her."

Shobha waited, hoping for more. She tried again. "So your cousin married her. Was there no other way? Couldn't the money simply be repaid?"

Something was churning within him, and the words burst out, so forceful that Rani stirred in her corner. "He never listened," he said. "When we were children, when we became men—always, he went where he wanted, never thinking it through. And the girl was no luckier. A family like that, so eager to marry their daughter off. Any husband would do. How could such a marriage, surrounded by elders like that, succeed? I tried to get him to come back with us. I begged him."

Shobha blinked. "Something happened to make him change his mind, then," she said softly. "To make him leave the family home and come here."

"Perhaps he thought about it over the years. Perhaps he wanted to but wouldn't abandon his duty . . . perhaps something happened to push him to it," Pramesh mused. He rubbed his eyebrow, then brought his palm down over his face. "He might have had bad luck with the farm. Drought, disease—it was a hard life when we were growing up. You see how many of the guests come from such places. Sheetal's family, even. Something made him change his mind. To try for a new life."

"Do you think he was actually drunk?"

He did not say anything for a long time. "I don't know."

Shobha wondered what he wasn't telling her. Most of her questions had brewed within her for years, but she had always faced the same dilemma: in order to satisfy her curiosity, she risked plunging her husband into one of his dark moods, the periods of vacant silence that she'd endured in the months after their marriage. He became less prone to them once Rani was born. When their daughter was an infant he would sit with her, rocking her to sleep during quiet times in the bhavan, or he'd walk around with her against his chest, soothing her at the same time that he soothed the guests, the child acting as a shield against whatever dark clouds followed him. But that darkness was always on the horizon, and so Shobha had held her tongue.

"A new life," she said instead, mulling over that possibility, now never to be. Then she recognized something in her husband's tone. "You feel guilt," she said. "You feel as if you abandoned him." He tensed beside her. "But you did everything for him in death," Shobha continued. "You did what you could at the moment you could. If you had seen him in life, you would have done more. Think on that. Even if the life was bad—he will be at peace now."

Her husband gripped her hand.

Once Shobha was asleep, Pramesh let out a long breath, his throat burning with all he had been unable to say. He thought of that pot he'd thrown over his shoulder. He felt the sting of broken pottery on his back. And shards at his feet, years ago. A sharp pain beneath his right eyebrow. He rubbed the spot. Why had he looked back?

He felt the weight of another clay pot in his hands. The water within making it unwieldy, but not unmanageable. The pot hefted up and over. What if he had shifted his hands? What if he had rebalanced his weight? Again and again, he threw the pot in his mind, as if rewriting his memory in order to change reality. Until at last, he fell asleep.

Shobha woke first, blinking in the dark, aware of a building noise coming from outside the family quarters. Thunder? Had the monsoons begun? She felt pain in her bones, a chill that penetrated her hands and made it hard to curl her fingers. But the air was still stifling, with none of the veins of cool breeze that the rains brought. And the sound wasn't the steady drum of rain. More like metal on metal, like Rani banging together two steel tumblers, but louder and fuller, with a chaotic beat. She shook her husband. "Do you hear that?" She shook him again. "Something is happening downstairs." His back was slick, and Shobha realized he was trembling. A nightmare. He woke and looked at her as if he did not recognize her, but then the sound crashed over him and the glaze lifted from his eyes. "Stay here," he said as he bolted out of the bed.

With each step his ears felt assaulted, the disturbance becoming louder and more frenzied, and his feet struggled to move. He had no weapon, and even if he did, he wasn't sure he could wield it against what sounded like a whole gang of intruders raiding the kitchen and the guests' rooms and throwing things about. This was a holy place; what coward attacked a building that held only pilgrims and priests and the dying?

But the kitchen was empty. Mohan met him as the manager threw aside the privacy curtain. Dev, Loknath—they were all out, circling the walkway, calming the guests who had crowded out of their rooms, hair disheveled, eyes wide or bleary, hands in front of their mouths as they whispered among themselves. The gate was shut. Nothing else was out of place—except for the crashing, the banging, the unmitigated fury of noise coming from a dark corner of the hostel.

Mohan followed as Pramesh strode to the door of the washroom, leaned in, and immediately backed away. "What—"

"You felt it too?" Mohan asked loudly. "I tried to go in, to see what it was—some animal, I thought. But as soon as my foot crossed the threshold. . . ." He trailed off, then rubbed his arms. He looked almost green.

"A lamp, Mohan-bhai?"

The assistant ran to fetch one, and as Pramesh waited, a feeling of nausea rose within him as the sound echoed around the bhavan, hideous voices swirling into his ears. Where was Narinder? His head priest should have been on night duty, reading aloud for a few hours. He spotted an open text in the corner where the priest usually sat, while Dev and Loknath attended the families, trying to shuffle them back into their rooms, yelling to make themselves heard.

Then Mohan was back, an oil lamp thrust into the manager's hand, a shaking match igniting the wick, and he saw everyone grimacing as if their veins had been filled with icy sludge, their insides shriveling, as the sound, like snakes, wriggled into their ears. Shobha came downstairs, Rani crying and clinging to her, and she rocked the child back and forth in her arms as the blood drained out of her face.

Pramesh gripped the lamp and crossed the threshold. Louder and louder, a knife's edge grinding across metal, amplified many times. He blinked, held the light out, tried to see what was there. "Who is it?" he said into the dark washroom. "Is someone there?"

No one had followed him inside. He was alone as he turned, sweeping the light around the room. No one crouched or writhed in the space, there was no man or woman or child suffering a tantrum or convulsing from sickness.

But he did see pots. Brass water pots, usually crowding a corner of the washroom in a single line, ready for guests to carry to the river to bathe their dying in the holy liquid. Brass water pots, which had no business rolling in a jumble on the stone floor, looking like disembodied heads for the poor light sputtering from the lamp, bashing into each other, cracking against the concrete wall, the sound pouring out of their black mouths like poison.

His back was still damp from the nightmare. Pramesh felt the hairs on his arms bend up and backward, imagining—*feeling*—a host of unseen things circling him, breathing their foul desperate stench on him, sending waves of nausea through his body. The dream—what had he been dreaming about? What had sickened him so?

Pots. And now pots moving from an unseen hand, or thrown about of their own volition, or flung by something or someone who was becoming more and more furious as the manager stood there with his flickering light and his furiously beating heart, the vessels moving faster, louder, angrier, crashing about until—

"Who is it? Why are you here?" he yelled. *Foolish thing.* In the pit of his sick stomach, he knew. And he vomited up the word.

"Bhaiya?"

Brother.

And the pots were still.

73

9

In the commotion and confusion, no one noticed that a family left with their skeletal mother in the middle of the night, bundles of belongings slung over their shoulders, bound for the ghats or who knows where.

"The Sens," Mohan said to Pramesh that morning over their chai. "The ones with the wealthy uncle, who insisted on staying here instead of some high-end place. I didn't even realize they were gone until this morning, Pramesh-ji. Neither did Dev or Loknath-ji."

Pramesh sighed, then took deep breaths to clear his mind. They sat alone in the kitchen, without the usual company of Narinder. The head priest was in his room, sitting on his bed, counting his prayer beads. He was in the same position, in fact, that Pramesh had found him in after stumbling out of the washroom, heart beating wildly, ears echoing with the sudden silence that was almost as painful as the violent sound it replaced. The prayer beads were motionless in the priest's hands, the lips that usually moved constantly with the holy mantras were set in a flat line. And the man, that immovable man, was trembling.

"Put the family from Haridwar in that room—they have a week left still," the manager said now, as if such departures were commonplace. He blew on his chai, aware that neither of them spoke of the thing from last night and feeling thankful to Mohan for it. Perhaps the assistant, too, suspected the entire thing could have been a dream, or the result of a particularly bad crossing of planets.

In any other place, the soul suffered a yearlong journey as it traveled to the Land of the Dead. But in Kashi, that year shortened to two days. Just forty-eight hours to follow the servants of the Bearer of Death, to breach the Vaitarani river using the holy word to secure safe crossing— the same holy word received from the great God just before passing into shadow—to reach the end of ends, to be done not only with this world and this life, but all lives, forever. How many hours since Pramesh had set the pyre alight? And since he'd walked those twelve days as a dead man?

Standing at the doorway of the family quarters, Shobha shifted Rani from one hip to the other. Since last night, she had been unable to let the child go; she needed always to be holding her or at least touching her, her fingertips on her daughter's skin proof that Rani was safe. Such horrible thoughts had encircled her the night before, filling her head with an intense illusion once she fell asleep. It took time to pull herself out of that dream, to recall herself to reality by focusing on the dark room, the narrow bed, the curtain pulled around Rani that sometimes fluttered with the child's breaths.

So vivid, that nightmare. She'd been sitting in the kitchen listening to the chants from within the bhavan. She felt intensely alone. Abandoned. As she picked through pigeon peas, rolling each between her fingers, she heard knocking, loud and insistent, like a drum echoing through the bhavan, and footsteps. Her husband was coming. Pramesh walked through the gates, stepped lightly across the courtyard, came to the door of the kitchen, and paused to look at her and his surroundings. He slowly stepped past the threshold, and then pulled someone in with him. A flash of red, a spangle of gold, the jangle of anklets and bangles. And there she was: Kamna, dressed as a bride, brought home to the bhavan.

Holding Rani, she tried to banish that image from her head, but harder to shake was the fear that lingered. The morning work was done, and outside in the courtyard, only stares and whispers of ghosts and spirits awaited her. Rani squirmed, tired of being held, so Shobha shifted her weight again and put the girl down, keeping hold of her hand. "I think," she said, her voice overbright, "We should visit your favorite neighbor.

Shall we?" Rani's eyes widened and she pulled on Shobha's hand, leading the way with a grip so strong that Shobha had to laugh.

She felt a little better when she found Mrs. Mistry alone with her family, the usual gaggle of friends and neighbors absent. Mrs. Mistry led her up to the roof terrace, where several of her grandchildren were already playing, and when Rani ran to join them, Shobha did not clutch at her or feel the separation as she had in the bhavan. "Did you sleep well last night?" Shobha ventured to ask once her neighbor's eldest grand-daughter had brought chai and small bowls of spicy snack mix.

"Oh yes—though I did wake up a few times. The heat, you know." Her fingers worked a tiny silver hook in and out of a length of white cotton thread, an intricate length of lace unfurling slowly from her hands. "Some nights are unbearable. But when you get to my age. . . ." She trailed off, a half smile on her lips.

So the thing that had visited the bhavan hadn't touched the houses nearby. Shobha shivered, despite the heat, and blew on her chai. "Maasi," she said, after a time. "Do you believe in something bad happening because someone else desires it?"

Mrs. Mistry glanced up at her grandchildren. Her youngest grandson Mittu was leaning over the roof ledge, and she yelled at him to come away. She peered at Shobha. "What do you mean?"

The bhavan mistress sipped and watched Rani, who was pretending to braid the hair of one of the older Mistry girls. "I mean, if someone thinks badly of you, enough to wish you ill—do you think that wish can come true? Simply because of the force of their want?"

"Wish you ill? Who could possibly wish anything like that toward you?" The older woman put her hook down, about to say something else, but then Mittu again caught her eye, this time leaning so far over the ledge that one leg dangled off the ground. "That boy. . . ." She gritted her teeth and stood. "Since when did you become so completely empty-headed? Are your ears burned from the inside? How many times have I warned you?" Grabbing Mittu by the ear, Mrs. Mistry dragged her shrieking grandson to a safer corner and released him, then set him to doing fifteen squats, fingers gripping his earlobes, as punishment.

Shobha watched, laughter bubbling up in her throat. A flash of green caught her eye: a parrot alighted just behind her. It pecked at the concrete ledge, then at its neat gray feet. She had grown up hearing the story of the Green Parrot Girl, had been in rooms with women who, looking out the window, whispered *Rama-Rama* whenever that bird crossed their vision. Before having Rani, she'd always thought those women were silly, too susceptible to superstition, too easily excited—like Mrs. Gupta. She looked at it, its plumage the color of a mango just shy of the first blush of ripeness, its curious eyes glinting. A bird, she told herself, could be just that—just a bird. The parrot skittered one way, then another, and finding nothing worthwhile, it flew off, melting into the sky.

"What were you saying?" Mrs. Mistry asked when she picked up her lacework, having sentenced Mittu to sitting in the corner for ten minutes more.

Shobha shook her head. "Nothing, Maasi."

⚬

That night, after seeing that Dev had all that he needed for the first evening reading shift, the manager seated himself in the kitchen, thinking, as Shobha lay curled in bed upstairs with Rani. Pramesh had been trying to remember his dream from the previous night, the one that had sickened him, made him weak with fear in his throat, in his veins. If he could remember what had frightened him, it might be a key to what had summoned Sagar.

He didn't want to believe that his sojourn into the Land of the Dead, his attempt to walk the same steps Sagar should have been walking, had been in vain. That yet again, and at the most crucial moment, he had failed his cousin. He'd said nothing to Narinder, to Mohan, even to his wife. But he didn't need to. He could see in their eyes that they were asking the same questions.

He soon nodded off, but then he jolted awake. Beneath him, the ground trembled. A slow hum, then a faster vibration, sending his teeth rattling in his head, making the wood on the hearth shiver, shaking the

77

room from side to side until Shobha's neatly lined canisters of rice and chickpea flour tipped over and rolled to the other end of the room, the walls swayed, the pictures hanging above the rope bed rattled off their hooks.

A dream, Pramesh thought, even as the earth quaked beneath him. He tried to get up, but his limbs felt frozen, while his blood was on fire. His jaw clenched and he was unable to speak, to scream. He could only move his eyes, and he darted his glance from side to side and up and down, locked in his body, a feeling swirling around him that nauseated him and set his nerves ablaze with terror. It pressed down on him, pushing harder, and the walls all around him cinched in like a box growing ever smaller, squeezing him ever tighter. Intense sadness, intense wanting, coursed through him like a gale tearing through the branches of a tree. And then the room rumbled again, and one of the pictures at the head of the home shrine tipped over, the divine eyes looking directly into the manager's.

Rama, he thought. *Rama*. And he forced all his will into his lips and his tongue, forced all his breath into his voice. "Rama."

His paralysis, the sensation of being in a box, subsided. Bracing himself, he walked to the washroom, where, he knew in his bones, the same nausea, the shivering blood, the ghostly thoughts swirling around his skull awaited him. Yesterday, he had thought that nothing could be worse than how he'd felt as the pots wailed, the sound snaking into his ears, his blood turning cold. He was wrong.

"Bhaiya," he gasped into the night. And the cloud lifted, his head felt clear again, his blood thawed and ran free in his veins. The bhavan stilled. Upstairs, Rani cried out, and he heard Shobha try to calm her. In the courtyard, another child cried, a man breathed out a loud exclamation of the great God's name. Mohan emerged from his room, looking like a man awake from a long illness; Dev was wide-eyed, hastening to catch up with where he'd left off reading the holy word aloud before his tongue froze. And the manager knew he hadn't been the only one to feel it.

Sagar had seated himself in the bhavan, determined to be heard.

They lost two more families, both packing up so quickly and carrying their dying between them with such haste that no one had time to run after them in the street, reasoning with them to stay. Even so, four other families turned up that day. The manager could take comfort in that, at least: Ghost or no, the dying would never stop coming. Sheetal stood at the door of the room he shared with his father, watching as Pramesh and Mohan kept busy. "I can help," the boy said when Pramesh looked his way. "If you need something mended—I can do simple things. Bapa taught me how."

"Pramesh-bhai—the bed in No. 1 wobbles," Mohan said. "Another of Balram's. I think the legs are loose—easy enough to fix. I can show him where the tools are."

Pramesh tilted his head and watched Sheetal run off to follow the assistant. The day when he would have to ask the youth to leave would come soon enough, but it was far from the most urgent of the manager's problems. He and Mohan divided up the rooms and oriented the new arrivals, all while they carefully picked their way around the questions that the more seasoned guests peppered them with about the previous night.

"What was it? Will it happen again?"

"Has it anything to do with the night before?"

"Strange thing, my father did not seem to notice anything. But then perhaps he is so far gone; death must be coming any minute now, yes?"

Pramesh was settling the last of the guests when he noticed Shobha lingering just inside the kitchen, trying to catch his eye. "I need to stop at Arjuna's for your shirts," she said, her eyes on the washroom. "I don't want to leave her, but you know he doesn't like children underfoot."

"I've just finished," Pramesh said, walking inside to pick up Rani. "Has she eaten?"

"She's had a snack—we'll eat when I get back." She tweaked the girl's cheek and smiled at him before walking out the door. Pramesh settled Rani more comfortably in his arms, though she twisted as far as she could, her eyes following Shobha.

"Oh, Queen of Flowers," Pramesh sang to distract her. "Where is your horse, Little Queen?" Mohan had given her the wooden toy, her favorite. Her warmth suffused his body, and her weight was a comforting load in his arms, made precious given how long he and Shobha had waited for her to come into being. "Ah ha," he said, pointing to a spot beneath the rope bed while her eyes followed. "He was hiding from you."

He set her down next to the bed and handed her the horse. As she marched it around the edge of the bed, he gently ran his fingers through her tousled hair, combing it back into order. He wondered if she remembered what had happened the past two nights, and if the memory would dissolve or stay with her as she got older. She was only three—she would forget. But if anyone outside learned of what was happening. . . . He thought of the tale that followed Bhut and his family name no matter how high he rose in the ranks. He could already imagine what people might say on Rani's engagement day, on the eve of her wedding: *He thinks he can marry his daughter off to so and so, but do you think he told the groom's family about that* thing *from so many years ago?*

He slid off the bed to sit on the floor next to her. Each day he listened as Shobha held up random objects during the morning meal—a spoon, a cup, a small clay bird—and slowly spoke the names of each, hoping this constant repetition might induce the child to speak. While Rani knew exactly what those objects were, she persisted in her silence. "She will speak when she is ready," Pramesh maintained to his worried wife, and most days he believed this. His daughter must be the sort who would rather observe first and piece the story together in her head before participating in it herself.

But perhaps Shobha was right, and he should have been coaching his daughter all along. He took the wooden horse from her and pointed first to its nose, then his own. "Now, little Queen of Flowers," he said as he raised her hand to touch his face. "This is the nose, yes? Can you say it?" Rani smiled and reached for the horse. Pramesh tried again. "Eyes," he said. He touched her hands to his closed lids. "Say eyes, little one." Rani maintained her silence.

Her smile waned and a small furrow deepened on her forehead. Pramesh handed over the horse, but she no longer wanted it. She pushed the toy to the floor and squirmed, reaching to her back, trying to grab at something between her shoulder blades. He pulled back the top of her dress, and a mosquito wafted up from that dark pocket and settled in her hair. All that time, as she sat next to him, the insect had bitten her in several places and left behind red welts, each raised like a small angry island on the girl's skin.

The sight of the insect in his daughter's hair, engorged on her blood, made him act without thinking. He snatched the mosquito from Rani's head, ignoring the girl's cry as he took some hairs with it, and slapped it against the green concrete wall. When his hand came away, the bug was a mere outline of body and legs, like an aborted sketch. Rani's blood, expelled from the mosquito during its violent demise, was on Pramesh's hand, a crimson blotch in the center of his palm.

10

That night, two hours after midnight, the pots in the washroom of Shankarbhavan rattled and seized. Mohan, bleary-eyed and drowsy, stamped to the back of the building and shouted an admonition: "Ey, quiet! Shut up, you! There are people trying to sleep and die in this place! Go, wander somewhere else!"

The newer guests, who had come with their dying just that day, stood in the shelter of their doorways, blinking like children blinded by fireworks. The rest wedged blankets and spare cloth beneath their doors in a hopeless attempt to drown out the sound.

Dev sat on a blanket in front of the priests' quarters and read aloud from the book before him. He raised his voice and redoubled his chanting efforts just as Mohan endeavored to calm the guests between his shouts into the washroom. "It is nothing, just some monkey that likes to play in the pots, nah?"

This excuse had sufficed for the past two evenings, but the merchant from No. 2 strode forth, his bald head glinting as he crossed the courtyard, and confronted the assistant. "We are supposed to be in a house of good energy," he said. "How can my mother concentrate on Rama with such nonsense?"

"Silence!" Mohan shouted out once more to the washroom before turning to the merchant and assuming his usual ingratiating manner. "Please, ji, what can we do? Only a monkey, you see—it must be climbing from the outside and jumping from the roof. He has some attraction to those water pots. Rama knows what entices him so."

"Hai Rama, unbelievable," the merchant swore. "And you cannot throw out this monkey?"

"Ah, but in the holy city even the animals are blessed—he must hear our priests chanting every night, and that is why he returns! A creature listening to the holy word. . . . It would be disastrous to expel such an animal."

"Nonsense," the merchant said. "If you refuse to, I will see to it."

As he spoke the racket continued. The teacher's family in No. 9 stood in the doorway and whispered to each other. Across the courtyard, a young man from No. 6 stood with his nephew asleep on one shoulder, his toddler niece leaning against one of his legs and sucking her fingers as she peered into the dark. Illuminated by a flickering kerosene lantern, Mohan yawned, and stifling that yawn, bit his tongue and tainted his shouts with a temporary but debilitating lisp.

The irate merchant marched to the washroom. He had arrived with his brother and their wives that afternoon, accompanying his ailing mother, and was in a foul temper. His brother had squandered ten rupees at the market to buy mustard oil that his wife massaged into the moaning old woman's legs, a frivolous purchase if their mother died, as expected, in the next day or so.

He stopped at the doorway and peered in, but the light from Mohan's lantern did not reach into the damp recesses of this corner of the building. As the merchant clapped his palms together and stamped his feet, he squinted his eyes, looking for the monkey that would surely leap from the pots and reveal itself. No animal appeared, and the pots continued to jump and shiver. "Come now," the man bawled, adding his own voice to the din. "Beat it! Go sit at some temple instead!"

The sight of this man who stamped and clapped and yelled out suddenly brought to Mohan's mind the tales he'd heard of those infamous dancing girls at Dal-Mandi Chowk, and he stifled a snicker, biting his tongue again, as his imagination dressed the angry merchant in a shimmering turquoise blouse and sari, a twisted strand of jasmine flowers crowning the balding head.

"Is this funny?" the merchant snarled. "You should be yanking the beast out by the tail and throwing it out the window!" Mohan composed himself even as he refused, so stubborn in his belief that the animal was holy that he forgot that the monkey's existence was a story he'd invented to mask what was really going on at Shankarbhavan.

In their bickering, the men didn't notice Pramesh walking with determination across the courtyard to the washroom. At his approach the pots became more frantic, punctuated shrieks and prolonged wails of brass scraping and clattering against the wall as the vessels rolled across the concrete. The manager stopped at the doorway and said the thing. And the pots stilled.

Dev's straining voice thundered in the courtyard, and a baby, previously undisturbed by one set of loud noises, bawled in anguish at the sound of another.

"Where did the beast go?" the merchant shouted. "The monkey— where is it?"

"What does it matter?" Mohan said. "It is gone, yes? Come now, back to bed, ji. The night still has many hours to it."

Weariness overcame curiosity, and the guests who had ventured out pulled blankets and shawls closer around their bodies and packed themselves into their rooms. Even the merchant, who had grabbed Mohan's lantern and shoved past Pramesh to investigate the washroom on his own only to find it empty and so damp that sneezes took over his body, eventually accepted the call of sleep and stamped back to his room.

"Pramesh-ji, do you need anything?" Mohan asked. The manager shook his head, and after shooing the remaining ogling guests back into their rooms, Mohan turned in, hoping to salvage some sleep in the hours left to the night.

The next morning, Mohan woke with an idea, a solution so obvious that he lay in bed turning it over in his mind for flaws before feeling confident enough to tell Pramesh. He found the manager drinking chai with Dev. "The pots," he said. "Pramesh-ji, they needn't always stay in the washroom. Out in the air, out in the sun . . . there's that shed in the alley—surely there is room there?"

"Of course," Pramesh said, looking startled. A small laugh escaped him. "Foolish of me, Mohan-bhai, not to think of it myself."

Buoyed, Mohan refused help with the water pots, but he first dawdled about the bhavan, checking in on Sheetal, talking to the other guests. Proposing the idea to shift the vessels was one thing; acting upon it was another. He stood for a long time outside the washroom threshold, gazing at the things that, not so long ago, had seemed as alive as the young boy now kicking a stone around the courtyard. While mustering up his courage, he tried to push away the sinking feeling he'd had since first seeing Sagar's body.

That day, when it seemed everyone had been dying. Had he dreamed it? That man, walking away and rounding the corner, so similar to the manager. So alike to that dead body that, a day later, arrived at the bhavan, the manager wiping the limbs with a tenderness that made Mohan's heart seize. Why hadn't he been able to go to the gate? And his words—what exactly had he said to that guest acting as the go-between? And that guest—what message had he in turn delivered?

He focused on the pots, picking one up with fingers that hesitated, as if the metal might bite him. But after that first one, which felt merely like metal, like a water pot, he gathered them up three or four at a time, until soon the washroom was empty and the pots sat in neat rows inside the alley shed, no more alive than the other rubbish occupying the musty space.

"Where is Narinder?" Pramesh asked Dev once Mohan had gone to move the pots. The priest's quarters had been empty that morning.

"Out on an errand," he said, Dev offered.

Everyone knew that Narinder rarely went out on personal errands. Pramesh thought back to the look on that man's face the first night, the features frozen in something that the manager suspected was terror. Pramesh had caught him in a moment as private as if he'd seen the man unawares in the middle of his morning evacuations. Still, a ghost was no uncommon thing. He would have thought that Narinder had seen plenty in his seven decades in the city.

They busied themselves with the work of the day, with the folk who were still dying and the guests who still had questions. Glancing into the empty washroom, Pramesh felt the weight on his chest ease.

When Narinder returned, his walk was as brisk as ever, his fingers busy on his prayer beads. He entered through the gates and immediately began circling the walkway as he always did. At the door of the washroom, he paused. He looked Pramesh's way, seemed about to say something, and then continued.

Sitting cross-legged on his bed that night, prayer beads in his hands as always, Narinder tried to drive his mind back into the familiar groove of meditation. But his fingers simply pushed the beads down the string, one after another, with as little intention as a child sliding beads back and forth on an abacus. Sleep would not come, and his eyes slid over the words of whatever book he opened.

And then it happened. The location of the pots didn't matter, certainly not to a thing like that. The sound was a low whine at first, and then it built, like a powerful wind trapped in the washroom, building to an echoing rush that made his hands shake. He was overcome with nausea, the uncontrollable shivering of his body, the feeling that his mind was open to a host of things he did not understand. In the airless room, the oil lamp at his side flickered wildly. He wrapped his shawl tighter around himself and hunched inward.

He heard Pramesh striding forward, his voice calling out to the same spirit for which Narinder had performed the Narayana bali. The quiet was immediate, and the manager walked past again, his footsteps slower this time.

After the first night, the priest told himself it was simply a matter of the mind. Let the mind run you ragged, or grab those reins in your own firm grip, control it, bring it to focus in the direction you willed. He tried to think of the great God, but recalled nothing. The words were gone from his memory.

All those years of prayer: where was his focus now?

II

The need for an exorcism was not unusual, on the level of finding out, say, that the paan-wallah at the end of the fruit bazaar, who was staying with his in-laws because of money troubles, had been scaling the walls from his upper-story bedroom window to meet his neighbor's wife in secret each night. Everyone had a ghost or two living in their house or some side-alley shed. What everyone contested, often in hot arguments that drew crowds in the city's lanes, was *how* to expel the ghost, *whom* to go to, and when to allow the presence to simply stay, since a little disturbance here and there could be tolerated if it meant a few rupees saved in the pocket.

The morning after the fourth night, Narinder broke his silence to reject that last option. "It is our duty to free that soul," he said, taking pains not to mention Sagar by name. "At some point it was diverted. It forgot where it was meant to go and instead chose to stay here. It is suffering, and it is making us suffer as well. So we must remind it."

"Someone to exorcize it?" Pramesh asked, and when Narinder tilted his chin in agreement, he sat, thinking. "Who can we trust?"

"I have a man in mind," Narinder said. "He does not usually do these things, not anymore. But I spoke with him yesterday. And he—Govind-bhai—was willing to come and see for himself, and to try, if he could."

So that was who he'd gone to see. Watching the priest hold his glass with steady hands, lift it up to his mouth and blow on the liquid while never breaking his gaze, Pramesh wondered if perhaps he'd dreamed seeing Narinder frozen that first night. And then he wished, not for the first time, that he'd also dreamed the rest of it.

The white-haired man who arrived at the gate was short, his head barely reaching Pramesh's shoulder, and he carried with him only a newspaper packet and a peacock feather. Any illusion that the packet held the tools of his trade evaporated when, sitting in Pramesh's office, he unwrapped it and pulled out fingerfuls of fried mung dal, munching away while Narinder detailed the problem in the washroom.

Pramesh suppressed the impulse to ask the man to put the packet away, or at least keep it hidden from the guests. "Narinder-ji mentioned you no longer attend to such matters," he said, gesturing toward his head priest, "so we are grateful that you came."

"Old friends," Govind said. Craving satisfied at last, he rolled the top of the newspaper cone and set it on Pramesh's desk. "But it's true, I stopped doing this work years ago."

"Not enough money?" Pramesh ventured.

"Too much! Once people find out you have the talent, they don't stop coming. Then you start to see ghosts everywhere, Manager-bhai. And you realize that sometimes the problem is not the ghost, but the person wanting to exorcize it. There is no solution yet for moving people to another place if they will not go. I wanted a simpler life."

"Do you think this will be easy? Removing this ghost?"

"Let me see it first. In the washroom, you said?"

They led him to the space, where the water pots sat in neat rows once again, returned there by Mohan after moving them had proved useless. Govind walked around the space, murmuring mantras and circling the room several times in a way that reminded Pramesh of Narinder walking the perimeter of the bhavan with his prayer beads. At times he stroked or tapped the pots with the peacock feather, or he brushed the walls and the corners of the washroom. "Two hours past midnight, you said?" the man asked after his final round, when he came to a stop a few steps from the pots and stood contemplating the quiet brass.

"Yes. At least, that is how it was the last four nights."

"There is something here," Govind said. "But I'd like to see what it does. Strange—it almost feels as if there are multiple ghosts. It happens, you know. Sometimes there are three or four, and they all have different wants."

"Wants?"

"Oh yes. The thing it wanted before it died. You have to satisfy that want, somehow. It's easier that way."

"But you can always banish it regardless?" Narinder asked. It was an odd feeling, Pramesh thought, to hear his head priest ask a question rather than provide the answer.

"If you wish, but better to wait," Govind demurred. "I prefer to see what it does."

At the gate, Govind took his leave, promising to return in the evening. He looked back into the courtyard as he shoved his feet into his sandals. "A place like this, Manager-bhai—it surprises me that you haven't needed me before."

"The people who come here don't intend to linger," Pramesh said quietly. "If they show up at our gate, it is because they are ready."

"Perhaps," Govind said. "Or perhaps you were lucky, and the spirits all stayed quiet until this latest one showed up. We'll see." He raised his hand in farewell and went on his way.

***

Mohan stood outside the manager's office, lost in thought. He jumped when Pramesh came up beside him and glanced into the office. The manager picked up the paper cone, still half full of fried mung dal, and handed the packet to Mohan to dispose of.

"What did you think, Pramesh-ji?" Mohan asked.

The manager shook his head. "No thoughts anymore, Mohan-bhai," he said. "Better to stop thinking, better to set yourself to whatever Rama wills."

Later, Mohan wondered about this. How *did* one stop thinking? He was not especially contemplative, but lately his thoughts would not let him be. One particularly made him speed about the bhavan at a pace more frenzied than usual looking for something to do, some task to focus on. The familiar gait, the tall figure rounding the corner. The thought returned whenever he was still, especially these last nights when he tried to sleep but instead found his body stiff and braced as if readying for a barber to pull a tooth, unable to relax until the pots were quieted.

Having settled a newly arrived family of leatherworkers in No. 3, tended to the other guests, looked in on Sheetal, and asked the priests if they needed anything, Mohan was left with a dangerous free moment. In his room, he remembered Govind's paper cone, tossed on the metal cabinet next to his bed. He unrolled the top and smelled the spicy saltiness of the mung dal, no longer warm but still comforting. He was not especially hungry, and such a snack was forbidden in the bhavan. But his door was shut, no one would see him and be tempted, and eating was something to do. Munching away, Mohan felt the prickles of unease in his stomach subside. When the cone was empty, he crumpled and threw it away. Back in the courtyard, as he soothed an argument between two brothers over whether their father was more comfortable on his back or on his side, the taste dissipated from his tongue, as did the memory of eating it.

Guests rarely demanded admittance to the bhavan late at night, the unspoken rule being that once Mohan locked the gates for the evening, Shankarbhavan would accept no one else until the next day. The iron creaked in protest when Govind arrived, his white hair shining in the deep black night, another paper cone clutched in his hands. Shobha had cleaned up from the evening meal some hours ago but still tried to offer him food, irked that a stranger to the bhavan—and an elder, at that—had decided to bring his own, and at such a late hour.

"Next time, next time," he said, palms folded together, declining the meal. "The task comes first."

The cone held puffed rice mixed with sev, golden with spiced oil, and he held it open to all, rattling the contents when Pramesh, Narinder, and Mohan all declined. "Well," he said, eating on his own, "no point in all of you remaining awake. Two hours after midnight, you said? Shall I wake you, Manager-bhai, a few minutes before?"

"We hardly sleep around here anymore," Pramesh said, but he agreed that it was best that they all go to bed and convene again closer to the time. Govind made to lay down on the stone outside the office, but Pramesh insisted that he take the rope bed in the kitchen.

"You're sure you wouldn't rather I move it outside?" Govind asked. "It's no trouble. It's better than what I'm used to, Manager-bhai." It occurred to Pramesh that perhaps Govind had other reasons for giving up the profession—that despite his talent with the dead, his status in the world of the living demanded he walk rougher paths than those deemed above him.

"Wherever you wish," Pramesh said. "You are here as a friend of Narinder-ji. So we offer you whatever we would offer him." He left the man standing in the kitchen, staring at the bed with his brow creased with uncertainty.

Stretched out on his own bed that night, as Shobha sat next to him and worked on a dress for Rani, Pramesh traced his eyebrow with his fingers, rubbing the thick hairs back and forth. "This is the right thing, I suppose," he said. "Unseating the ghost. Moving it elsewhere."

"Yes," his wife answered without hesitation. "That soul has to continue its journey, and it cannot do so until we help it along. Once it leaves the bhavan it will have no other choice."

"So many things unfinished, unsaid," Pramesh said. "So many things left unbalanced."

Shobha did not indulge him. "You completed his final rites as best you could. And you are dealing with this new problem. You cannot keep looking back when there is nothing more to be done." She drew a needle in and out of the bright blue fabric, her fingers pushing in tucks and pleats in a way that seemed like magic to Pramesh. She was so certain, always. If the roles had been opposite and women had the task of circling the pyre and breaking the pot, Shobha would not have looked back. She would have completed the rites perfectly, without hesitation.

He continued to think long after Shobha put her sewing away and went to sleep. A few more hours, then Govind would see the problem and dispatch the ghost. *Detach*, Pramesh told himself, repeating the word to himself until he felt sleep come over him. *The body is burned; so should the memory be. Let him go. Detach.*

He woke some minutes before the hour, his body as tense as a spring in a clock. He checked on Rani, thinking it might be better to wake her himself before the sound wrenched her from her dreams, but her eyes were already open when he pulled back the curtain shielding her part of the room. Pramesh's heart twisted when he saw her skin shining with tears, her face red and her breathing hoarse. "She feels warm," he said, handing her to Shobha, now awake.

"Likely a cold," his wife said, touching the back of her hand to the girl's forehead, then wiping the wet face with the end of her sari and cradling the small head to her chest as she rocked her. "She was with the Mistry grandchildren today; perhaps one of them had it first."

The pots erupted then, silencing whatever else she might have wanted to say. It seemed louder tonight, more violent, penetrating the ancient stone of the building and making its way to the upper story of the family quarters, sending Shobha's hairpins on the side table skipping and shaking to the floor, her rolled-up sewing shivering with the vibrations. Shobha squeezed her eyes shut and tightened her grip on Rani.

Pramesh found Govind in the pitch-black of the washroom, without even the lamp that Mohan had left for him, standing in the furthest corner and watching. He seemed completely in control of himself—no green visage like Mohan's, no frozen terror, no sick unease at being so close to something so unnatural. He was so calm that Pramesh almost forgot why he was there, and only when the old man looked up, questioning, did the manager remember to say the word of silence.

The sound and motion cut out instantly, echoes ringing in the dark. Mohan, lingering outside the washroom until then, stepped into the doorway, his round frame smudged in shadow. "Some water, perhaps?" Govind asked. He moved, stiffly at first, and was slow to exit the washroom. Seated in the kitchen, he refused the glass Pramesh offered and instead bade the manager to pour the water into his cupped hands. He gulped a glass's worth, and then another, before speaking.

"Has it done this every night?"

"Yes. This is the fifth."

"It is perhaps more assertive than most," Govind allowed. "But count yourself lucky—it hasn't possessed any of you. And it obeys when you speak to it—very strange." He peered at the manager. "What was it you said again? To make it stop?"

Heat rose to Pramesh's neck. He glanced at Narinder, silent and still. Govind looked at him steadily. "There's no profit in this business if I talk about what I've seen, Manager-bhai."

"Bhaiya," Pramesh said, eyes unable to meet anyone else's. The pressure on his chest returned, a now familiar weight.

Govind showed no reaction; he merely took another sip of water.

"Can you banish it now? This instant?"

"Morning would be better," Govind said. His eyes were alert, with a new spark. He reached for his cone of puffed rice and popped a few grains, considering.

"Is anything wrong?" Pramesh asked.

"No, nothing wrong. Different, perhaps—not wrong." He chewed some more. "It's already seated itself, you know," he said. "It's an inconvenience, but you don't need to do anything just yet. All I would be doing is moving it elsewhere. Whether here or there, the hope is that it will move on eventually. As I said, it hasn't possessed anyone, and that is often the bigger difficulty." He dusted his hands, twisted the top of the cone, and shoved it away. "Are you sure you wouldn't rather wait?"

"No." Narinder spoke before Pramesh could. "Nothing can be gained from waiting. And if moving it can help it along, when it never should have been here to begin with, then it is our duty to do so." He looked to Pramesh, who swiveled his chin.

"Well. It's certainly one of the more extraordinary possessions I've seen, but not the worst. I will stay the night, if you don't mind, Manager-bhai. But, as you wish: First thing in the morning, it will be done."

"Is there anything you need?"

"A few things I must beg from your wife—cooked rice. A lemon or two. Cloves and cardamom. Oh, and another thing. If you could ask your wife to lead all the women out—to the ghats, to the market, wherever—and if they could stay away until I am finished, that would be most helpful, Manager-bhai."

"Anything," Pramesh said. "It will all be ready for you." His breaths still felt shallow, as if someone were sitting on him, but there would be an end. Everything had an end to it, both good fortune and the bitterest of trials—or so Shobha liked to tell him. This chapter of his life, too, would have an end.

12

The next morning, Shobha went around to all the rooms, speaking to the women. She wanted to take Rani with her, but the child was still warm and had spent the rest of the night coughing. "Leave her here," Govind said. "She's not yet old enough to be a distraction to the ghost like the rest of them." Shobha colored as she realized why Govind had also said nothing about moving any dying women from the bhavan. Rani was too young, and those guests were too old, but the women in between were capable of the thing that barred them from the temples and rendered them impure each month. "They are attracted to such things, ghosts are," Govind continued, oblivious to Shobha's discomfort. "They have their likes and dislikes just as the living do. Anything from a living body—blood, human leavings—it all acts like a magnet, and the ghost cannot resist."

So, reluctantly, Shobha dosed Rani with black pepper and turmeric-spiced milk sweetened with honey, tucked a light blanket over her, and left her dozing on the rope bed in the kitchen. Then she gathered the women and led them all to bathe at the river as Govind had requested. They filed out in a tidy parade, unobserved except by old Mrs. Chalwah across the street, who sat at her window, fingers doubling the speed at which they moved over her prayer beads, her nod nearly imperceptible when Shobha raised a hand in greeting.

⚬

Govind crouched over the tray Shobha had prepared and scooped palm-fuls of rice, still warm, added some water to make the mixture hold, and formed three balls. He borrowed a knife from Pramesh and set that next to the lemons. A cluster of cloves and cardamom sat in the tray's center. With his peacock feather shivering atop these things, he entered the washroom, Pramesh and Narinder following.

"Not the right thing," Dev muttered as the three walked by. "Brahmins consorting with exorcists."

"It is also not the right thing for ghosts to consort with the living, but here we are," Narinder replied from the dark room, standing beside Govind as that man set the tray down near the pots. "Have you visited each of the dying yet today?"

Dev relented, setting off to join Mohan on his rounds of the bhavan while Loknath read aloud, the younger priest wearing a sulky look that reminded Pramesh of Rani when she did not get her way.

With the women gone, the men were free to talk as loudly as they wished, with no fear of offending female sensibilities or, worse, being contradicted. While many guests stayed in their rooms, finding nothing fascinating in an impending exorcism, the rest crowded around the mouth of the washroom or sat nearby on the walkway, hoping the scene might provide some entertainment, something to break the monotony of waiting for their kin's final exit.

"Three rice balls? At home the man who does this kind of thing always has four."

"Mine uses just one! But who knows, Bhaiya—yours probably keeps the extra few to eat."

"None of these things are real; not even the thing in the washroom is real. It's probably as that assistant says—an animal, something that looks for shelter at night and ends up here."

"Yes, but what sort of animal makes you feel ill from three rooms away? And the sound? How do you explain that?"

Govind began with his peacock feather, passing rapid strokes over the pots, the ground, the walls, even reaching his short arms up to the ceiling, all the while mumbling rapid mantras whose cadence Pramesh recognized but whose exact words eluded him. Govind went on for some time, pausing only to draw a breath. When he stopped, he gave Pramesh and Narinder a meaningful look, squatted down, and grabbed a clove from the tray. He held it out toward the pots, never breaking his gaze on it. Suddenly, he howled. "Where is the son of a dog?" he cried in a voice totally unlike his own, and Pramesh felt a chill pass over him. "Here, aren't you? Land here—no, *here*! Ah, fine, wander—we both know this is your place; no son of a dog can resist, you will come to me eventually."

His arm swooped and dropped down and pulled back up, as if something were pulling his hand in many directions. He continued to curse in that unearthly voice, looking like a man trying to catch a fly with only his thumb and forefinger.

Alarmed, the manager looked at Narinder, but the priest remained in his traditional stance, motionless but for the fingers that worked on his beads, his mouth moving in silent prayer. Pramesh had seen exorcisms in his village before, had seen them even here in Kashi, and the crass language and harsh theatrics should not have surprised him. But in those other cases, with disheveled women rolling around on the ground or grunting in a lane, shouting obscenities; or with men speaking without the benefit of drawing breath, servants to a tongue they could not stop even when their faces turned red, nothing that the exorcist did seemed extreme. The aggression of the spirit controlling the person demanded an equal reply.

Perhaps what had happened in the washroom over the last five nights was just as excessive . . . but Sagar was not some malevolent spirit. Pramesh stayed, unsure of what else to do, but with every word from Govind he felt further conflicted. The spot behind his eyebrow emitted a low ache.

Meanwhile, Govind kept trying to catch the ghost, moving where the spirit seemed to go. After some time, he tired, and he set the clove down and wiped his forehead with the back of his arm. He blinked and looked at the manager, and when he spoke, his voice was his own again.

"You don't like it, I can see, Manager-bhai. But one must speak to them in that way. They don't know how to listen to anything else; believe me. And actually, I am being much milder than usual. He hasn't possessed anyone, so expelling him doesn't require the same harshness."

"So he is here?" Pramesh had been trying to feel something, to feel a whiff of Sagar, but the room felt as it always had.

"Oh yes—he can't make himself seen or felt to most people because the night is when he can be most vocal. But I know he is here. You get a feeling for them, after so many years."

Pramesh turned his eyes to the pots. *Bhaiya, what are you still doing here? Why do you linger?* He willed his cousin to listen to him, to realize his folly in staying behind. Pramesh rubbed his forehead, the old pain lingering.

Just then the exorcist let out a delighted shout, and the pots shivered in response. "I have you! Ah, I have you, didn't I say? Didn't I?" Govind cut the lemon as a small sacrifice of life, and then he stuffed the clove into one of the rice balls. He pushed the other two rice balls into the first, making a single large wad of rice, the ghost residing within. "It's done!" he said, gleeful, holding the rice ball up for the manager to see.

Pramesh felt immediate relief. The sorrow would come later, he knew—but that sorrow would be borne of his natural feeling for the cousin he'd lost, rather than guilt over failing his duty to him. "And now?"

"Straight to the ghats. I will release it there."

Pramesh wagged his chin, and Govind rushed past him toward the bhavan gate, Narinder following. "I will come by in the morning, Manager-bhai," Govind said. "But you will sleep well tonight. Believe me."

When Shobha returned from the river, the rest of the women trickling in after her with fresh skin and saris, Pramesh was with Rani, applying a cooling poultice of crushed mint leaves to his daughter's back. Shobha greeted her daughter with a kiss and looked at her husband as he smoothed on a last bit.

"The swelling won't go down—she keeps scratching."

"She just needs a distraction," Shobha said, pulling off some of her bangles and handing them to Rani, who put her hands through and tried to make them stay on her tiny arms.

"I don't know how I could have missed it happening—I was sitting right there!"

"The beginning is always the worst," Shobha said after a look at Rani's skin. "It will clear up in a few days. But as for a father who cannot even protect his daughter against a single bug. . . ." She let the words hang in the air, eyebrows raised in mock disapproval while a smile curled one end of her mouth.

"But see there—" Pramesh pointed to the wall, where the mosquito's corpse remained from days before. "It had a full drop of Rani's blood in its belly. So I wasn't so useless, in the end."

"Wah—such a hero," Shobha said, and she set about washing rice and cutting vegetables. "Perhaps the hero can clean up the remains of his brave deed?"

It had been so long since she'd teased him like this. She didn't ask about the rites, but he felt her watching him closely. He stayed with her until she'd made the afternoon chai. "Gone," he said, handing her his drained glass. Her hands paused over her sewing and then picked up again. The relief on her face was like a cool breeze on his.

That evening, he blinked in the flickering light of the kerosene lamp as Shobha puttered about, hair loose in a dark waterfall down her back. Bangles and anklets jingling, she eventually settled on the bed next to him, sitting cross-legged, and uncapped a bottle of coconut oil. She looked more like a schoolgirl than his wife of almost ten years, mother of their child, with a lightness he always felt grateful for. He wondered if Rani would grow up to look like Shobha's copy or if she would assume a face that reminded him of his mother. He had so few reminders of her.

"What would your father think of all this, I wonder?" he asked. Pramesh had assisted that meticulous manager of Shankarbhavan for almost two years, until his own good death made Pramesh his successor. The most scandalous thing that happened in that time had been the family who brought not an elder or some wizened loved one who was dying, but a beloved dog, the family matriarch insisting upon a good death for the faithful beast.

"He would think the same thing he always thought," Shobha said, pouring a small amount of oil into one palm and massaging it into her scalp. Her dark hair glinted red-orange where it caught the light as she moved. Pramesh breathed in that warm familiar scent of coconut. "That there are far more foolish men out there than you, and far less patient."

"He never had a ghost in here. He never had this kind of trouble."

"Not here, he didn't. But in the rooms where we lived, he and I and my mother, plenty of things happened in that building. There was a story at least once a week." She poured more oil into her palm, rubbing it between her hands, and smiled. "Once my mother thought that *we* had something happening. She said she could hear a knocking sound on the window shutter every evening. It would get louder and louder, but whenever she opened the shutter, nothing was there. She said she had the worst feeling each time; she wouldn't let me leave for school without circling me with black salt and chili to pull off the evil eye. She was begging my father to call someone to get rid of it. Then, my father heard the sound when he happened to be standing by the window. Five quick knocks; he pushed back the shutter, reached his hand out, and grabbed it. What do you think? A long wooden staff, and then a yell from our upstairs neighbor! She'd been knocking on the shutter all this time, trying to get my mother's attention so she could share the latest gossip she'd heard in the market."

Pramesh let out a soft laugh. It was not often that his wife told these stories. She, whom Pramesh had watched sitting by her father years before with such a glow in her face that, once married, he'd been filled with a brief irrational jealousy, now spoke of her parents rarely. She never indulged in reminiscence unless it illuminated some other point. Pramesh wished he could be the same way. To her, and to any other Banarasi, the end really was The End.

His wife's voice, her soft outline in the lamplight, the smell of the oil combined with the smell of her, enveloped him and dulled those other feelings. His eyelids drooped.

"But that was just one thing. There really was a ghost, a man possessed living two floors down from us." She continued the new tale, her words dropping in and out of Pramesh's ears. Slowly, he slipped into sleep, but not before he heard his wife cap the bottle and say, "Who would he trust in those days, if not you?"

Standing in an empty guest room, Pramesh turned, confused. Where was the family that was supposed to be here? Their things were gone, the bed stripped and pushed against the wall. The floor was clean, with not a grain of rice nor speck of dust to betray who had stayed there. The window shutters were stuck—he'd have to speak to Mohan about that. He turned in a slow circle, painted green walls meeting him as he spun. The signs on the back of the door were there, but the script was blurred—the rules and instructions illegible. He tried the handle, surprised that the door was shut. When he pulled it open, he saw the same green walls, the same bed, the same blocked window. Behind him was the space he had just been in; before him was one exactly like it. He frowned. Again he turned in a slow circle, looked at the floor, found it so clean that no mouse or insect met his gaze. He tried the door again, green walls again, an empty room, an empty bed, clean floors, no sound. Another room, and now he was angry. Where was everyone? He was alone in the building; no one would help him. He wrenched open yet another door and found only green walls, an empty room, an empty bed, clean floors, no—

He woke, sweating. There was something urgent he needed to remember, some task he needed to complete right away. But what? The dream slipped faster than a kite string sliding through his fingers on a blustery day, and Shobha was shaking him.

"Downstairs," she said, but he could barely hear her voice. A wave of sound overwhelmed him. Metal on metal, just as furious despite the pains Govind had taken during the day. Heart pounding, Pramesh forced himself out of bed and down the stairs. Still half asleep and in the grip of his dream, a question formed in his mind: how was it that Sagar, who had never wanted the city in the way Pramesh wanted it, who had laughed at Pramesh's boyhood dreams, was now the one unwilling to leave?

13

They didn't need to fetch Govind; he was waiting at the gate early that morning, already sweating from the heat, eyebrows raised in question when Mohan turned the key in the stubborn lock. He'd brought a small cloth sack, and he pulled out a chai glass when Shobha served him, insisting she let him drink out of his own vessel.

Sipping at the hot liquid, he popped the occasional peanut from the cone he'd brought, the manager, assistant, and head priest all sitting in a somber circle. "I know I had him," he said finally, startling them all in their silence. "And I know I released him on the ghat. They don't usually come back so quickly." He frowned. He didn't seem to expect a reply, and they offered none. "Still, I wonder if there is more than one in there," he mused. "Perhaps I only got one of them, and the rest were hiding. But then I would have *felt* them. . . ."

As much as Pramesh wanted to believe this, that another ghost was to blame and the disturbance wasn't solely the fault of Sagar—or his own inability to keep from looking back, to detach—he could not, and neither, it seemed, did Narinder.

"Even if there were, what you did yesterday should have banished at least one of them. And yet last night was no different from the other nights—no weaker, no less vocal."

"If anything, it felt worse," Mohan muttered.

Govind considered this. He made his way through a handful of peanuts before another thought occurred to him. "Tell me: Did he have any land?"

Pramesh looked up, frowning. "He did. He lived in our childhood home, and he farmed the fields left to him."

"And now it is yours?"

A memory slipped from a door in his mind he had tried to keep shut: Sagar kneeling close to the ground and scooping up a palmful of dirt, smelling it and sifting it through his fingers, appraising the green stretching before him, his brow furrowed in ruts, just like the ones he would plow into the fields that planting season. The memory made the manager ache. That earth—Sagar had loved it so. Pramesh had never thought of the land as his, ever.

"I ask because oftentimes the reason the ghost will not budge is because it has been treated unfairly in the life it just exited. Usually in some matter involving property. The land is yours now, isn't it?"

"They can have it," Pramesh said. "His in-laws, whoever they may be, and his wife. I will sign it over to them today." Sagar was gone, and if Pramesh could not have his cousin back, he had no desire for anything connected to the man.

He sat down at his desk, writing out the words that unequivocally severed him from any ownership of the land, and then he walked to the closest government office to have the letter witnessed and stamped. The letter was with the post office in a matter of hours.

"Is that it?" Mohan asked once the manager returned. "Will it know that we did as asked?"

Govind, still snacking on peanuts while sitting cross-legged on the walkway, poured handfuls into the palms of any children whose parents allowed them to come near him, Dev and Loknath frowning. "Better to wait for the reply," he said. "But I believe you will see the end of your problem, once they receive word. These things seem extraordinary, but they always come down to the same things, the same desires. The problems of the last life never end, not for some souls." He twisted the top of the paper cone, about to hand it to the nearest child, but withdrew his hand when the mother stalked over and grabbed her son by the ear, dragging him away.

"When you get the letter, fetch me, and we will formally present it to the ghost," Govind said. "So it knows we dealt with it fairly. And one last thing. You will still have to bear with it for some days more,

Manager-bhai. Take my advice—ignore it. Don't respond to it. Let it continue, and soon enough it will stop on its own."

"But the guests. . . ." What was he supposed to tell his guests with their dying, the ones who were preparing to leave this world and certainly didn't want a reminder of what might happen to them after they passed, Kashi or no?

"The guests will come and go, Manager-bhai. They are important, yes—but more important is allowing this thing in your bhavan to run its course." He narrowed his eyes at Pramesh as he said this, and the manager forced himself to shake his head slowly in agreement. "Narinder knows where to find me, Manager-bhai," Govind said in parting, and then he was out the gate.

But the manager was unable to hold to Govind's advice. Each night the pots rang out, rattling and seizing with enraged energy until they skipped and rolled across the wet concrete floor, and Pramesh gritted his teeth, strode to the washroom as quickly as he could, and said the only incantation that could silence it. On the second night after he'd sent the letter, he decided to make himself ready outside the door to quiet the ghost immediately. But by the fifth night, *Bhaiya* no longer worked with the same swiftness, and the pots continued to rage, the sound like a massive slithering creature sliding into his ears, squeezing him from the inside. By the ninth night, Pramesh stopped waiting by the washroom and slept in the kitchen—or tried to. Gazing at the small shrine before which Shobha lit an oil wick and incense each morning calmed him, taking away some of the sick cold, the lightning stabs of fear.

"Perhaps," Mohan ventured at one point after he'd followed a family halfway to the train station, trying to convince them to stay with the promise that the disturbance was sure to cease in just a few days, "you could speak to it. Tell it you have given it what it wanted."

So Pramesh tried that as well. On the twelfth night, he stepped into the washroom, holding back the urge to retch, feeling as if his skin were being turned inside out, and tried to explain. "I never wanted the land!" he yelled, but his voice crumbled in the face of the thunderous clamor of the pots. He didn't try again. In the deepest part of himself, he felt his explanation was wrong, simply because Sagar never would have asked it from him. Sagar knew he had no desire for the land—it had never been a secret that one of them wanted to leave, the other to stay.

In his office, he stared out the window. Why had Sagar come to the city? What was Sagar's final thought—that crucial last notion to cross the mind at the moment of passing? He pictured Sagar in the boat, bottle at his side. Lifting the bottle to his lips, emptying it. A shiver of revulsion passed through Pramesh, followed by deep pity. Once, he could predict the word about to leap off Sagar's tongue a second before his cousin said it. But that was so long ago.

Mohan's stomach grumbled. He was struck with a sudden craving for the puffed rice Govind had been snacking on a few days ago. The midday meal was still some hours away. Already the heat of the day made the air tight. Moist dark circles appeared beneath his arms and at his lower back and chest. He wanted a snack, and he wanted a moment of quiet after the tales he'd had to spin for the guests, each wanting their own personal explanation of what exactly was waking them up in the night. He had tried to tell the truth as closely as he could. "Oh, it's just a soul passing on its way. It will be gone soon."

But that wasn't enough, and a skeptical look or incredulous silence from one of the guests would send him scrambling to fill in the gaps with invented details. "From the neighbors—one spirit too many in their house, and somehow it's come over here. Not to worry; it will realize we don't have what it needs and get going." With the latest guest, Mohan had blurted out, "A cat. Likely it jumped in from the roof and made a racket. It's been going around the rooftops, stealing food where it can."

None of this was a lie if it was in service to the bhavan and hurt no one. He finished tightening the ropes on the bed in No. 10, went over the lists on the back of the door with the two sons in No. 4, who wanted to be prepared to take their mother to the ghats immediately once she passed, and then wandered outside the gates to satisfy his stomach's desires. Perhaps he'd meet Sheetal on the way, join him for a glass of sugar cane juice and walk back with the youth.

Somehow the air was more stifling outside the gates. Up at her window, Mrs. Chalwah looked damp with sweat even from Mohan's vantage point. A doctor who visited the widow regularly exited the Chalwah house and raised his hand to Mohan. Mohan raised his hand limply in return and pushed himself onward. By the time he'd come to the end of the street where the lane split in three directions, Mohan felt winded. He stopped in the shade of a building and breathed heavily, the hot air of his exhalations making him hotter still. Looking back, he could see the bhavan gate and above it Mrs. Chalwah, still watching him. He looked around and felt a chill. He now stood just where that man had been when he saw him round a corner and disappear.

No, he shouldn't think of him as *that man*. The cousin. Pramesh-ji's twin, his blood. Mohan had suspected it, and perhaps he'd been slower to recognize the truth than a sharper man would have been. But he knew for sure when he heard the manager tell Govind the word he used to silence the ghost in the washroom. Mohan had felt his stomach seize with sick horror as the realization sunk in. The last thing Pramesh's cousin had wanted before he died was to gain entrance to the bhavan. And Mohan had denied him that, so now the man's ghost lingered here, in the place he couldn't access while he was still flesh and blood.

Every night Mohan watched Pramesh drag himself to the washroom, the only man able to silence the ghost. He looked like the brick haulers who trundled the lanes, backs hunched over rusted wheelbarrows filled with stone, remaining hunched even when they had no load to push before them. Each day, the manager drooped further. How could Mohan tell him that he'd missed his cousin by mere minutes? The truth would only make the man curve inward even more. He would tell the tale after the ghost successfully exited and life in the bhavan went back to what it had been.

He looked up at the sky, then back down at the lane. Something didn't feel right about the air, which slid in a thick heavy stream into his lungs, making him feel heavier.

"What are you doing, looking back and forth like that?"

Mohan turned red under Bhut's gaze, as if the circle officer could see straight into his heart. "Thinking," he said. "I was meant to go on an errand, but the air is strange."

"It won't rain for a week," Bhut said. "It does this every year, squeezes the city until you can't even go two paces. But there's a scent in the air you must be alert for. It isn't here."

Mohan sniffed.

"See?" Bhut said. "No rain today." He looked like he was about to say more, but he turned, eyes scanning the street and tilting upward toward Mrs. Chalwah's. Abruptly, Bhut turned and sped away, calling over his shoulder that he would buy the assistant a bowl of chaat if he was wrong. "But I'm not wrong. I never am about these things."

Mohan raised a hand in farewell. He no longer felt inclined to walk through the lanes, whether for chaat or for some other snack to appease his burbling stomach. Back to the bhavan he went, the dirt crunching beneath his sandals.

14

Clouds moved overhead, first thin veils that allowed the sun to pierce through, then thicker and darker shrouds that blocked the light and sent an expectant hush over the hot city. Thunder murmured, low and grinding, the volume rising to deep grumbles, like boulders rolling across the sky.

"Is Sheetal back?" Shobha felt the air in the kitchen change, a faint metallic smell rising to her nose. Pramesh sat on the floor next to Rani.

"I can go and look for him," he offered.

"You'll want to be quick," she said. "It's coming any moment."

Pramesh welcomed the distraction. A darkness had settled on him after realizing that an entire month had passed since he'd crouched over Sagar's body in that filthy jail cell. As he reached the open courtyard, the bloated clouds gave way, bursting like an overfilled paper bag, sending the rain down so rapidly that the individual droplets formed streams in the air. A thin mist rose from the ground where the cool water hit the hot earth, and outside, water quickly pooled in the dips in the lane and the gulches alongside buildings.

Mohan ran to help the family who had set up residence in the court-yard despite his earlier pleas that they share a room to prevent the soaking that everyone knew would be coming. The guests ran for the cover of the walkway, while Pramesh helped the eldest son lift his father, a tall man who weighed much more than his bony frame suggested. They ran as best as they could with their unwieldy burden into the room, where the family who had been there all along exchanged sour looks and made a point to keep their dry belongings far away from the damp party that joined them now. As Pramesh followed Mohan out, Sheetal burst through the gate, wet and out of breath.

He was soaked through, his thin shirt showing the contours of his skinny body, sopping hair dripping rivulets of water into his eyes, his too-long pants leaving a slick trail behind him. Mohan ran to get him a dry shirt and Shobha fetched a towel, while Sheetal walked straight to Pramesh, reached into the cuff of his shirt, and pulled something out.

"I tried to keep it dry," he said, "but it started so suddenly, and I was much farther from here than I realized, ji."

It was here. Finally, the letter was in the manager's hands, sodden though it was. Shobha handed the towel to Sheetal and touched her husband's elbow. "It's too wet to open," she said, taking the letter from him with gentle fingers.

He followed her closely as she went to the kitchen, where Rani sat drawing on a slate with a piece of colored chalk. Shobha set the missive between two pieces of cloth and ran her rolling pin over that sandwich, squeezing the moisture out. Then she set her tava on the hearth where the flame burned lowest, placed the letter on the black metal, and waited for the pan to gently warm the paper, flipping it from time to time with her bare fingers as if she were making roti. Pramesh squeezed his hands together, waiting. She plucked the letter off the tava and felt it, pinching it in places with her fingertips. The paper crackled, and when she flicked it with her fingernail it made a satisfying snap, with no soft damp spots. She handed it over without a word.

Narinder had come to the door, watching, and soon Mohan peered over the priest's shoulder. "Chai?" Shobha asked, and without waiting for an answer she began to grate ginger into a pot, adding extra spice to combat the damp the rains would bring. Her heart was pounding, waiting to hear the words, but she also felt strangely calm. The low roar of water filled their ears, the sound of it hitting the ground, as well as the occasional rumble of thunder. Already, the room felt cooler. She loved the monsoon, and as she watched the water bubble and boil, her mind wandered, thinking of rainy day foods, the things Rani loved to eat during the season, crunchy fried pakoras with their soft insides, or roasted corn from the street vendor who always doused Rani's with extra lime juice. She sighed. What a gift it was to be thinking normal thoughts instead of the constant fears that reigned when you shared your residence with a ghost.

Pramesh slit the envelope. She watched him unfold the single sheet of paper, rippled but perfectly dry. The paper creaked like an old door. Her whole body tensed as he read it aloud.

We are in receipt of your letter and the signed deed. We thank you.

That was it. There was no signature, no indication of who the writer was, though when she looked over his shoulder the hand looked like a masculine one. Likely Sagar's father-in-law. No mention of Sagar, no thanks for that hurried transfer of land. No mention, either, of Pramesh's earlier note, notifying them of Sagar's death. And no mention of Sagar's wife. She tried to ignore the trembling in her hands. Pramesh handed the letter over to Narinder.

"So it is done, then."

"Are they happy?" Mohan asked. "It's what Govind-ji said was needed. It should stop now, shouldn't it?"

Narinder made a sound of agreement, Shobha watched the chai, and Rani continued to draw on the slate.

Here was the final sign of approval, proof to the ghost of the thing it most wanted done. Everyone around the manager looked relieved, their backs straighter, as if the weight in their minds had dropped and rolled away. Pramesh wanted to feel the same way. Deep within himself, he'd held a dimly lit hope: surely, the news of the death—so unexpected, so great a loss—would bring out something from these people for whom Sagar had sacrificed his future. A distraught telegram, a stream of kind words, a letter of reminiscence describing the man Sagar had been, the reasons he'd been in Kashi—any of these could have stoked a flame of hope within Pramesh's heart that one day might burn away his distrust.

But this letter did none of those things.

He took the chai his wife held out to him. Narinder declined and took his prayer beads out to the walkway; Mohan drank his quickly. "Govind said to fetch him once it arrived, Pramesh-ji," he said brightly, and he bustled out to ask Narinder how to get to the man's dwelling.

"Take something to cover yourself—don't come back soaked like Sheetal," Shobha called after him.

Pramesh knew he should return to the guests. But instead he stared out the window at the water as it plummeted from sky to street, unable to see anything after a time but the constant liquid blur that never ceased.

Despite Shobha's warning, Mohan was completely soaked when he returned with an equally wet Govind, but his spirits seemed so lifted—by the rains, by the prospect of the bhavan returning to normal—that he remained in his wet clothes, eager to help.

Govind read through the letter and swiveled his chin from side to side, satisfied that the ghost would be satisfied, and strode into the washroom, Pramesh and Narinder following. He thrust the paper at the manager. "Read it aloud."

Pramesh swallowed and did so, feeling odd speaking to a room full of static brass. Shobha had prepared another tray according to Govind's instructions, and he repeated the actions of the previous ceremony in an abbreviated form. The mantras were rushed and garbled, the hand slicing the lemon was swift. "Listen," he said loudly, his voice echoing against the washroom walls. "He's done exactly what you asked. You have nothing left here in this world. This is not the place for you. Leave, leave and be happy knowing that what you wanted is now done."

He grasped a clove. "We've dealt with you fairly," Govind bellowed. "You have a debt to us now, to move on." He waited a moment and squinted at the spice in his fingers. He waved his hand above the cloves remaining on the tray and sniffed loudly. Then he dropped the clove he was holding, surprised. "Nothing there," he said.

"He refuses to leave?"

"No, ji. There is no ghost here. Nothing on the cloves, because there is nothing here to catch. And the room feels different since I entered it.

Before the feeling was that the spirit was trying to enter every crevice of my mind—was it not that way for you? Now, nothing. I feel nothing."

Pramesh glanced at Narinder, then looked around the room. He wasn't sure what he felt. And even if he did feel something, he would have a hard time trusting that feeling. "What do we do?"

Govind laughed. "Nothing to do! I tell you, ji, it is gone. Your problem is solved. The land—didn't I say? Always, always, these things might manifest differently, but the reason is always the same." He was jovial as he picked up the tray and walked out. Pramesh glanced at the pots before following him. Perhaps they did seem more like what they were—mere objects, no more capable of feeling than the pot that Shobha brewed the chai in. Had such things—the inescapable noise, the feeling of being surrounded by sorrow and desperation—really happened? And how had he, and the rest of the bhavan, endured for an entire month? He shook his head, knowing what his wife would say. He needed to accept the entire thing as an odd wrinkle in the tapestry of his life and move on. If Sagar had moved on, it could only mean that, whatever his life had been, he was now satisfied, ready to begin his journey to the end of all ends—and Pramesh would have to be content with that, too.

Govind stood at the corner of the walkway, watching the rain pour down in sheets through the open center of the courtyard and run in neat streams to the drains set in the corners. "You're lucky," he said. "The rains are never a good time to do these things. Don't mistake me—I knew it would have to go. Once you gave it what it wanted, it had no more grip on this world than a grown man on his mother's sari. But the rains can make a thing like this more difficult than it needs to be."

"As long as he—he is where he should be," Pramesh said. "On his way, I mean."

"Yes, yes, where else would he be?"

Walking Govind to the gate, Pramesh felt lighter, but the deep ache lingered. The same ache he'd felt after the burning of the pyre, and after the twelve days of mourning.

Only after the sky grew dark and the evening meal was finished, after Pramesh did his final evening round of the rooms, did the manager realize what that ache was. It was the place that the living Sagar once occupied in his heart, and that the ghost had recently vacated. It would never entirely leave him. And along with the memories he was determined to keep at bay, it was the only thing left to him of his cousin.

Alone in his room late that night, Mohan felt his stomach burble. He was hungry again, and his hands twitched in the direction of the steel cabinet at his bedside, where he kept his small number of possessions, including the packets of glucose biscuits that Dev had grudgingly said were allowed, given that many families soaked them in milk and fed the sweet mush to their dying. He turned on his side and tried to concentrate on the priest reading aloud, but it was Loknath's turn, and his voice barely penetrated the door.

His stomach emitted a louder groan, and he curled his knees upward and tried to slow his mind. The ghost was gone, the soul of the man he'd turned away was at peace, and Mohan owed Pramesh a story about what had happened that afternoon, when he'd seen the live version of the man who would next arrive at the bhavan dead. He simply could not figure out what to say, or when to say it. His anxiety crept downward. What mattered was that the manager's cousin had reaped the benefits of a death in Kashi, not what Mohan did or didn't do.

Again, his stomach rumbled, and he sighed, rolled to the other side of the narrow bed, and reached down to open the steel cabinet. The biscuits filled his mouth with cloying sweetness, and he wiped the crumbs from the corners of his lips, the butter-paper wrapper crackling on his chest. His stomach quieted and his eyes drooped.

Two hours after midnight, nothing happened. Loknath's voice unspooled mantras in a smooth uninterrupted tone, like a sari seller unfurling a bolt of silk. The minutes ticked by, someone coughed, a child whimpered and fussed and fell back asleep. Narinder snored with his prayer beads in his hand; Sheetal slept with his fingers on his father's arm. The entire bhavan had been clenched like a fist, braced and ready, but now it relaxed, chests rising up and down, breaths expelled softly or with roaring snores, dreams stretching out in no logical sequence.

All the while, the rain pounded down through the open courtyard, drumming on the roof above the rooms, filling the air with a hint of earth and sweetness and a metallic bite, the noise loud enough to shield the guests from the sounds of their neighbors. Loud enough to mask the sound of Loknath's flagging voice, heavy with sleep. Loud enough to dampen Dev's steps as he walked over to take his turn at reading.

And loud enough—at first—to mask the sound coming from a corner of the bhavan, the slow tapping, the faster rolling, building in fury, until an intense and stricken howl broke through even the deluge of rain and awakened all of them at the same time.

15

The rain poured all night and the rain poured all day, and the dusty lanes and sparse patches of parched earth drank deeply from everything the monsoon clouds offered. Monkeys took their places in the alcoves of temple roofs, eating the blessed prasad with polite restraint. Boys ran laughing and shirtless through the torrents, their scant bare chests a promise of the wiry men they would become. The ghaatiye packed their things and moved indoors to pray and fast. The boatmen welcomed the respite and retired to their houses, coating the walls with beedi smoke as they shuffled through packs of cards and shouted to their wives to replenish the chai. To the Doms the rain made no difference. "People still die, nah? They still need wood and holy fire, yes? And where will they get it without us?"

But after these first days the rain continued to fall and folk tired of indoor life. Rickshaws struggled through the flooded streets. Umbrellas collapsed beneath the constant barrage. The swollen river expanded, swallowing most of Magadha and rising up the ghats step by step, creeping toward the city. Beggars wrapped themselves in plastic bags and took shelter beneath cardboard and corrugated tin shanties or squatted beneath worn striped awnings until shop owners sent peons to drive them away. The women cradling wide-eyed babies and defeated children scattered, but in the night they crept back to the few sheltered places in the city, moving upward as the water levels rose to their knees, and here they curled up on the concrete or the slick mud and tried to forget the rain in their dreams.

Pramesh wanted to visit Govind immediately after his failure became apparent. Narinder demurred, his faith in his friend stronger even than the terror he must have felt each night, hunched and frozen on his bed when Pramesh passed on his way to the washroom. But the manager could wait no longer. One morning, when the rains stopped for a moment that he knew would not last, he lingered outside Narinder's door and announced that he would be visiting Govind today. The older man sat thinking for a moment before offering a terse nod.

Out of the gates, Pramesh felt odd, as if he'd entered this world and this life for the very first time and did not know where or who he was. He looked up and saw Mrs. Chalwah across the street gazing at him from her upstairs window, her fingers worrying her prayer beads. He'd grown accustomed to her constant watching over the years, and most days he smiled up at her and waved, a greeting that she never returned, but now her unfettered stare unsettled him.

He and Narinder walked in silence. *Why had the rites failed? And how had he failed this time?* Some days, Pramesh passed whole hours in his office trying to understand what he had done wrong, drowning in guilt as he thought about Sagar locked in that state between death and moksha, a desperate afterlife that capped off a bad death and a life that had not been much better.

Despite the water pooling everywhere, the lanes and alleys teemed with people. Men with rolled shirtsleeves and women with hitched-up skirts passed with slow and bandy-legged steps, as if learning to walk anew. Growing up in the country, Pramesh had never paid much attention to the monsoons. The rains came and fed the fields and orchards; the earth absorbed the water like a sponge. His first year in Kashi, he'd been afraid that the rain would wash the city away. How could so much water find space among these tightly packed buildings? How could the people forge on as if nothing could slow their progress?

He breathed in deep, exhaled just as deeply, and tried to focus on the fresh rain-stirred air he inhaled, the warmth of blood moving through his limbs. After sitting still and silent for these long days, he felt mobile, *alive*—but then guilt followed closely behind, inseparable from that good feeling, because every breath and step were ones that Sagar would never again take.

Narinder veered into a narrow lane. They passed shuttered stalls and came to a residential street, close to the woodworker's alley. The priest sped up his pace, looking over his shoulder for the manager. They arrived at a narrow house with heavy wooden double doors that arched in scrolled carvings at the top. Narinder rapped lightly on the door, which a wide-eyed child eventually opened.

"Go get your Dada," Narinder said, and the floppy-haired boy ran off, leaving the door wide open. Soon Govind came, and when he saw their faces he visibly deflated, as if someone had set a load atop his head. He gestured for them to follow.

The house was similar to many in Kashi: old, with water-stained ceilings and rusting door hinges, but warm and dry and smelling of chai and fried spices. Though it looked small from the outside, Govind led them through room after room, hallways branching out or ending in staircases that snaked upward, voices chattering and footsteps running overhead. Near what seemed to be the back of the house, he led them into a sort of sitting room with low rope beds and bolsters and cushions on the floor and gestured for them to sit.

His face glum, Govind sighed. "Chai will be coming. You will partake? Even if it is from my house?"

"Of course," Pramesh said. He felt himself relax, and as he did so, more sounds of the house opened to him: chatter in an upstairs room, clanging cookware from another part of the house, a bird calling from its caged perch. "Is the entire house yours? Or do you let some of the rooms?"

"My family and mine alone," Govind said, with a hint of pride. "Ten years as an apprentice, and then forty years on my own, Manager-bhai. My wife and I saved every coin so that my children's children could run through as many rooms as they wanted to one day." The floppy-haired grandchild walked in, bearing an unwieldy tray set with bowls of sev, snack mix, and spiced puffed rice, and he set this in front of his grandfather. A teenage girl followed him with a tray of steaming chai glasses, and Govind put a large spoonful of snack mix in their hands before letting them go, watching with a soft smile as they left the room.

The three men sipped and nibbled first, as was polite, though they substituted silence for the usual chai-chatter. Sitting there, putting scant bits of snack mix in his mouth and tasting nothing, Pramesh wondered what would come next. Govind had tried twice already to move Sagar along. What would a third try accomplish?

"Failure is not easy for me to swallow, Manager-bhai," Govind said. "Especially when the task was requested from an old friend—one very dear to me. All I can ask is that you believe that I did not deceive you. I did the thing properly the first time, and the second time, I truly did not feel him in that space. He was gone. But if you don't believe me, I will understand. A man like me is often scoffed at, or worse."

The manager met Govind's eyes. Then he looked at Narinder. "Govind-bhai is no fool," the head priest said. He'd brought his prayer beads, and he stretched the strand between his fingers. "He knows how to do these things properly. And he had nothing to profit from, coming back after all these years, doing a favor simply because of our friendship."

Pramesh felt only weariness. "You said that the rains make these things more difficult. Even so, will you try once more?"

Govind stayed silent for a long moment, shaking the sev in his palm as if the crunchy gram were a pair of dice, before tipping it all gently into his mouth and chewing thoughtfully. "Rain or no, my skills are no longer useful when it comes to that ghost," he said, looking at his now empty hand.

"What else can we do? What else will work?"

"You did Narayana bali, didn't you?" Govind turned to Narinder.

"On the eleventh day. I thought it best, knowing that his death . . . knowing how he died."

"It's a difficult ceremony," Govind said after a moment, looking askance at Narinder.

"I had not done it in some time," Narinder admitted. "The only thing left to try now is tripindi shraddha. The rites to appease those who suffered a bad death." He did not meet Pramesh's hopeful gaze, focusing instead on a spot near his feet as he spoke. "But it's not something I advise doing during the rains."

Govind took a sip of his chai. "It is the logical next step—the *only* next step. Unless the ghost moves of its own will." He looked up at Pramesh. "Tell me, do you know why a soul would become a ghost in the first place, in Kashi especially?"

"The rites," Pramesh said helplessly. "I erred at every turn. With the pot breaking over the pyre, looking back, with the last day of the mourning period. I tried to keep my mind in check, to—"

"But it cannot be only because of what *you* did, Manager-bhai. It must also be because of what the ghost wanted when it was still a living being, your cousin. Those that become spirits—these souls want something. They want it so badly they bypass the natural order of things and stay long past the time they should have exited, Kashi or no, so badly that they resist the pull of the rites."

"What about the land?"

"The land may have been part of it. But it wasn't enough. It wasn't the *main* thing it wanted." He was speaking more to himself than to Narinder or the manager, but his voice became more confident, and he rocked his chin, pausing to fill his palm with snack mix. "This soul, this ghost, wanted something so desperately that it was willing to give up the thing that Kashi promises all of us," he said. "A pull like that is no weak thing. Narinder-bhai cannot simply say the great God's name a few times and send the soul on its way to moksha." He looked up, a familiar glint in his eyes. It was the same look he'd had upon first meeting the spirit in the washroom. "No. Somehow, the task that soul wanted to complete must be done. If that happens, then perhaps you won't need tripindi shraddha."

"But I don't know what this ghost wants," Pramesh interjected.

Govind frowned. "Can you truly say that? You *know* this ghost, remember?" Pramesh felt his head grow warm. "You are in a unique position, nah? So often, a ghost is unknown. There is never a way to tell *what* they want because one usually doesn't know *who* the ghost was, so how to appease them? Even if what I did worked, the best I could have done was to remove the spirit and place it elsewhere, to bother someone else.

But it lingers on, moving from house to person to thing, never finding comfort."

Pramesh looked at his chai glass, still full and hot, and watched the curled wisps of steam melt into the air. All this time, he'd told himself that if Sagar simply received a nudge from the exorcist, that would be enough to turn him toward the Land of the Dead, the path that would truly be his end. He could not fathom why Sagar *wouldn't* want it.

"Listen!" Govind said, eyes bright. He set his chai glass down on the tray roughly, and bits of sev hopped out of a bowl and onto the floor. "This needn't happen in your case. If you know what that soul wanted, it means you have a chance of fulfilling its desire so it can be released to the place it needs to go once Narinder-bhai is ready to perform the rites."

"He may have wanted to start a new life here. With me." Pramesh said. "His life . . . did not go as planned. It was not a happy one."

"And is that the only thing?"

"What else could there be?"

"*That* is your duty to seek out, Manager-bhai. Find out what he was doing here."

"But what of detachment? What of never looking back? It isn't easy, but I have been trying." He looked to Narinder, who still sat staring at his prayer beads.

Govind shook his head. "It's a bit late for that, nah? You admitted it a moment ago: you did look back. You could not let him go, and for his own reasons *he* could not let *you* go when he died. That is why you are both in this mess, he as a ghost, and you with a ghost." Govind softened his tone. "Make no mistake: you will need to move beyond your cousin eventually. But first, you will need to do this. Find out what it, what *he*, wanted so badly and finish the thing that he could not. Who knows? If you succeed, it may leave of its own accord."

Again Pramesh looked at Narinder, this time speaking his name aloud.

The priest looked up, blinking. "Three months of rains," he said. "And tripindi shraddha is no easier a ceremony than Narayana bali to perform. We must wait, regardless." Pramesh's heart sank. "There is something to what he says. And why not try? You could write to his family—"

"Nothing could be gained from that," Pramesh said flatly. The terse letter about the land, the dry thanks, still filled him with disappointment. All those years Sagar had spent with such people, people who could not express even a single line of emotion for him. What could those years have been like?

"Then *think*," Govind said. "Think about what you remember. Try to pretend to be him. Find out where he walked while he was here."

Why must you always walk where you are never meant to go? A sick thrill pricked him, like a spider running up his arm. He raised the chai glass to his mouth to hide his face and, in the guise of sipping, bit down on the edge of the glass until the memory slunk away. He could see that Narinder did not disagree. Both he and Govind meant well, but how could they know, when they simply did not have enough of the story in their hands to realize their logic was flawed? He set his cup back on the tray. "Ji. I respect your word, both of you. But my cousin belongs to the Land of the Dead now. And I am in the land of the living. I detached myself once, from my old life all those years ago—I simply must do it again. And once I let go of him, my cousin's ghost will move on. He lingers here because of me, I am sure of it."

Govind's eyebrows crouched low on his forehead, and he opened his mouth as if to say something, but thought better of it. Pramesh stood to make his goodbye, Narinder rising with him. Govind held up his broad palm.

"You have listened to me with patience, Manager-bhai. And you have treated me fairly, despite the difference in status between us two. You will forgive me if I say one more thing. You have chosen your path, and you say *you are sure of it*. I have lived more years than any of the men in my family, and I have expelled more spirits than I have known living people. There is no surety in life, Manager-bhai. The path after death is just as uncertain. Even in Kashi."

At the door, he squeezed Narinder's shoulder and raised his hand to Pramesh. Outside the house, Pramesh covered his face, pulling at the rough stubble sprouting on his cheeks. Narinder paused in the lane. "I will join you later," he said, turning in the opposite direction.

"Is anything the matter?" Pramesh called after.

"Simply a walk," the priest said over his shoulder.

The sky was bruise-colored and swollen. Pramesh began to walk. Ten paces in, the clouds shifted and burst again, and the street soon flooded. He ran through the lanes, dodging others doing the same, until he came to a corner beneath an upper-story balcony where he might wait out the shower. He heard a giggle.

Only a pair of boys, still in short pants and black rubber slippers, crouched beneath a similar overhang on the building across the narrow lane. The rain soaked the boys' shirts as one of them held an umbrella over a large brown dog napping next to a stack of boxes. They petted the dog with long and loving strokes, one boy at the head and the other near the tail. The dog dozed on, but the animal's tail twitched back and forth. The boys giggled again and tried to catch the tail as they continued to smooth the dog's matted fur.

Pramesh's thoughts darted about, drawing him first one way, then another, tempting him just as the dog's tail teased the boys. A part of him agreed with the exorcist, as he stood at the door of memory, ready to open it wide to the flood within. Wouldn't that be easier? As he grew chill in the steady rain and watched the boys and the dog before him, he remembered a different pair of boys, a different dog, and a hot summer's day in a different life entirely.

The cousins were outside on the veranda, sketching idly on identical slates with identical chalk stubs while their neighbor's granddaughter Jaya, just arrived for her annual summer visit, braided long strands of grass into a neat plait. The day was hot and thick and the air was still.

"We could climb the mango trees in the backyard?" Jaya said, twisting the plait around her fingers. Sagar and Pramesh loved climbing the trees in Jaya's grandparents' yard, spotting the mangos while they were still hard as stones, but neither one responded to the girl's proposal. Inside the house the Elders were deep in an argument, the Mothers silent but for an occasional murmur. Soon, the Elders would retire for their naps on the back veranda, but Pramesh did not want to chance his father or uncle waking up to see them sitting among the branches.

Lulled by the heat, Pramesh felt his eyes flutter.

"What's that?" Sagar said. He abandoned the slate and turned to the edge of the house. A dog slowly rounded the corner. Its steps were halting, and it came to a standstill in the shade of the peepal tree that grew before the house.

"Maybe he's hungry," Jaya said. She flung the plait toward the dog, but the grass merely floated down to rest beside her.

Sagar chanced a quick look at the door, then tore a shred from the roti his mother had left for them and threw it. It landed shy of the dog's back paws and hit the dirt. The animal did nothing, only continued to stand and stare with blank, glassy eyes.

"Something is wrong," Pramesh said.

"Nothing is wrong," Sagar answered, his voice testy. "It's just so hot. Even he feels it."

The veranda was shaded and usually received the benefit of breezes, though not on that day. Both cousins had acquired a sheen of sweat as soon as they'd woken that morning, and the hairs escaping Jaya's two thick braids clung to her neck. Pramesh wanted to get the dog some water, but he knew better than to use a bowl from the kitchen. Sagar tore off another bit of roti and threw it, this time closer to the dog's front feet. Still, it didn't move. "You will get in trouble," Pramesh warned as Sagar reached for a third try. The Elders would see the roti in the dirt and beat them both for wasting food.

"They will all be asleep soon. And he will eat it—no dog will pass up roti," Sagar said.

"Let me do it." Jaya reached for the roti in Sagar's hand, but he leapt away and tossed it, sending it far beyond the peepal tree. The dog remained where it was. "I want a turn!" Jaya said, eyes blazing.

"Fine," Sagar said. "You do the last one." He made to hand her the final piece, then shoved it at Pramesh at the last second. Pramesh threw it before he realized what he was doing, and the roti hit the dog squarely in the face.

The dog opened its mouth slowly, gently, the upper jaw rising like the lid of a box. The pink tongue rolled out. Pramesh held his breath. A gasping wheeze escaped the dog's throat, its legs crumpled, and it shuddered and shut its eyes.

"You killed it," Sagar whispered, his eyes wide with disbelief.

"I didn't," Pramesh said, but doubt cinched his heart in a vise. He felt Sagar and Jaya look at him.

"No," his cousin conceded. "You didn't."

"It isn't funny," Jaya said angrily. "You *both* killed it." Her voice carried. Someone stirred inside the house, and Sagar looked at Pramesh in a panic.

"We have to go," Pramesh said, his heart beating quickly. He could hear heavy footsteps nearing the door. Before Jaya could protest, he pulled Sagar off the veranda, and they ran around the house and to the back, plunging into the fields.

But they had to come home eventually. The Elders beat them that night after dinner, more for the wasted food than the dead dog, which they'd called to be hauled away and buried by the lame herder Nattu, who lived in a shack near the crossroads. Pramesh had claimed it was his fault; he'd thrown the last piece of roti. Sagar asked for them to beat *him*; he'd started the game. Neither boy mentioned Jaya. Both Elders took a turn at beating them equally, yelling at their wives to keep away when the women tried to intervene.

No difference between the two, they said.

The fault of one is also the fault of the other, they said.

That night, cheeks wet, both Sagar and Pramesh pretended to be asleep when their mothers came in, sitting by their sides, smoothing their brows until Pramesh could feign sleep no longer and turned toward his mother, burying his face in her lap. But Sagar stayed angry.

"Shall I continue the story?" Pramesh's mother said. She'd been telling them of Hanuman, dispatched to fetch a medicinal plant, who'd returned carrying the entire mountain on his shoulders when he could not identify the right herb.

"Don't you want to hear about Hanuman swallowing the sun?" Sagar's mother asked, running her finger beneath Sagar's lashes. He wrenched away, turning to face the wall.

"I don't want you as my mother anymore," he said. Hearing this, Pramesh clung tighter to his own mother, not wanting her to think he thought the same.

"But you are stuck with me," Sagar's mother said, stroking his hair.

"I don't want you!" Sagar said, throwing off his mother's hand with a violence that sent her bangles jangling.

"Careful," Pramesh's mother said. "What will your ma do without you? And me? And your Pramesh-bhai?" She pulled Pramesh to sit up, and he moved to crawl into her lap, head resting beneath her chin.

"I'll run away," Sagar sputtered.

"Ah. Then you should go to Kashi."

"*You* go to Kashi."

"Very well." Sagar's mother got up, straightened the end of her sari from where it had fallen off her shoulder.

Sagar turned to her, indignant. "Where are you going?"

"To Kashi, as you said. You don't want your poor ma anymore."

"What's in Kashi?" he asked. "How far away is it?"

"The city of the great God, a day's journey from here."

"So I can visit you."

"If you like. But after this life, I will be gone, as you wish."

"What?" Sagar's voice lost the anger, instead tinged with panic.

"I will go there, make it my home, become a very very old woman."

"Veena . . ." Pramesh's mother said.

Sagar's mother ignored her. "And one day, I will die, just as all of us will. And I won't come back."

"Why not?"

"No one who dies in Kashi comes back. It will be as you wish. You'll never see me again, not in this life, never in any life after that."

Sagar leapt out of bed, bolted to his mother and grabbed her around the legs. She pretended to be resolute, then let her hands fall to his head. He pulled her to the bed, made her sit down, then climbed into her lap and hugged her to him, mimicking Pramesh.

"All right," she said. "All right. I will stay. I will be your ma."

"Veena, you shouldn't say such things," Pramesh's mother chided. Pramesh continued to cling to his mother as she started the story. He didn't listen to the words so much as the sound of her voice, the vibrations from deep inside her body radiating into him as she spoke.

The pressure in Pramesh's chest loosened, but the space behind his eyebrow throbbed. His shoulders and back ached, remembering the bruises put there all those years ago. The rain came down from the sky in looser droplets, light enough to see to the other end of the lane. The two boys continued to pet the dog, but now they sat on either side of the animal, right in the filthy lane that ran brown with rainwater, and took turns holding the umbrella over it. Their mother would discover them soon enough, and the entire street would be the audience to her fury. He cast an upward glance at the sky and quickened his feet in the direction of the bhavan.

16

Outwardly, Shankarbhavan was doing well. A dying person occupied every room. The rain had slowed the traffic of pilgrims to the city, but the holy month of Shraavana was approaching, and because this was the most auspicious time for a soul to leave the body, people either dying or hoping to would soon arrive. Such a death would complete the holy trifecta: to die a good death in the holiest city at the holiest time of the year. What a dream that was, a death that a family could return home and brag about.

And yet weeks had passed since anyone had exited their body within the confines of the hostel walls. Women who were sure their last days were nigh improved at miraculous rates and began issuing orders to their daughters-in-law; men felled by strokes lingered in suspended states, neither worsening to the point of release nor resuming their function as the heads of their families. In fact, the last dead body to grace the hostel had been dead when it arrived. Sagar's was still the latest funeral that the bhavan had facilitated, and there was no sign of a succeeding corpse in any of the twelve rooms that filled and emptied and filled again with each passing week.

Pramesh had realized it some days after his visit with Govind. He kept meticulous records regarding every dying person in the bhavan. As he did his monthly accounting, his pen faltered when it came time to tally the month's deaths. He went back and looked; he checked once more. He flipped through the previous month's numbers, and then the month before, until he'd reviewed the entire preceding year. He pulled out the logbook from the year before that and flipped through it as well. And then he penned a round zero on the page for that month and closed the book, angry at himself. Why had it taken him so long to notice?

In the bhavan, families came and families departed—at least that remained the same. But the bathing of bodies in the courtyard, the procurement of flowers and wood and cloth, the construction of a bier, the gathering of money to pay the priests and the Doms, the raucous brass bands leading the way to the ghats—those things faded from bhavan life. Now, as Pramesh took a turn about the rooms, the sight of the newer guests studying the instructions on the back of their doors filled him with a sick wash of guilt.

Narinder and Pramesh may have accepted that nothing could be done until the dryer months, but Mohan was not so convinced. He found Pramesh as he was looking into the rooms and broached the topic of the pots. "Is there anything we can do to at least make it quieter?" he asked. "Or is there something I can tell the guests instead of the same story night after night?"

Pramesh's attention surfaced as if from a great depth. "The story you mention—you've been telling the guests it is a cat," Pramesh said slowly, and Mohan wobbled his head, shamefaced. "How do we know it's *not*?"

Mohan, confused, tilted his chin. "Ji?"

Pramesh sighed. "How do we know anything in this world at all?" That was all he would say. Mohan, who could no longer look at the manager without feeling the burden of the untold story—the truth—took a turn around the courtyard and then took himself out into the street, the rain now falling at a moderate pace. He could think better when surrounded by the constant hum of chatting voices and running children and the low grind of bicycle and rickshaw wheels. The wheels in his own brain turned as he walked, and he came to rest on the wet stairs of the nearest temple.

Mohan remembered the early days of the bhavan, before Rani was born, when dark moods would sometimes bury the manager. Long periods with the office door closed to visitors, Pramesh so sunk in sadness that it took many tries to get his attention and recall him to the world. Then his child was born, and the moods diminished and disappeared—but now they were back. Surely if Mohan told the story of the dead man, of his visit to the bhavan, the manager's bleak mood would only worsen.

Perhaps, he reasoned, if he could find a cat, he could transform the story he'd been telling the guests each night into truth. He could blame the ghost's exploits on a real animal, and Pramesh would feel at least some of the stress lift from his shoulders. The task was not so difficult; there seemed to be a litter of kittens in every street. Mohan passed through the bazaar lanes, keeping his eyes especially sharp around any food stalls. Intent on his mission, he waved away the many people calling out his name or approaching him with the latest bit of gossip. Rounding the corner past the wireman's stall, he saw a pair of boys tempting a skinny gray feline with a piece of fresh coconut.

"You there," he said to the older one. "Fetch me a bag from the stall back there—tell them Mohan-ji has sent you. Quickly now!" The boy ran off, and his companion meanwhile popped the coconut into his mouth. The cat sat near the wall and blinked. It was a calm little beast and did not protest when Mohan gently took it by the scruff and deposited it into the burlap bag the older boy brought him. Once in the bag, however, a plaintive mewling started up, and the bundle began to squirm. Mohan threw a couple of coins at the boys and hurried down the lane to the bhavan, his burden becoming louder and more difficult to carry with every step.

He still thanked the strange luck that had secured his position at the bhavan. Alone in the world, he had been an orphan, a street ruffian. He'd stolen to eat and survive, but, once caught, he'd so charmed the vendors with flagrant excuses and well-chosen gossip that they'd turn a blind eye to his pilfering even as their wives berated their soft hearts. In return Mohan had performed little jobs for them on the side as he grew older, his abilities as a reliable running man well known across the city.

That was how he'd ended up at the bhavan. The old and ailing manager Dharam, Shobha's father, was looking for someone to help his new son-in-law and protégé. His contacts led him to Mohan, and a few hours after the old man met with the young one for a cup of chai and a brief interview, Mohan found himself running across the city to fetch his things from the tiny room he rented in the vegetable alley, next door to a shaky shed where goats congregated around the carrot peelings and cabbage leaves. Despite the unbearable stink in hot summer months, as Mohan handed his key to the landlady and walked away with a sack of clothes on his back, he felt nostalgia even for the mangy goat that followed him down the lane as if to say goodbye.

Happy days followed—filled with hard work, death, and constant planning for funerals—but happy nonetheless. In the bhavan, he had something he'd wanted for a very long time: family. Shobha became like a sister, and Pramesh an older brother. Rani's arrival gave Mohan a niece, and he spoiled the girl as much as he would have any blood relative. They had chosen him; such a precious gift demanded a loyalty that had never been difficult to summon.

His arms strained with the writhing bag as he passed through the gates, but he felt triumphant. Pramesh was in the courtyard, speaking to a guest, surrounded by others who had some quibble or question. He looked so deflated, as if he had aged ten years. Mohan thought to wait until Pramesh had a quiet moment to talk in his office, but the bundle had other ideas. With a great wrench, the burlap twisted from Mohan's hands and released its contents. The cat tumbled out, hissing at the manager's feet, and then shot between Mohan's legs back out through the gates. "Oh, Rama," the assistant groaned. "A minute, Pramesh-ji. Just a minute, and I will fetch it directly."

Pramesh looked from the gate to the assistant and back again, his brow furrowed. The men surrounding them were unamused—they had urgent questions about their dying loved ones that only Pramesh could answer.

"The cat," Mohan reminded him. "Remember, we spoke of it earlier?"

"A cat?" Pramesh asked, his face blank. "Mohan-bhai, why on earth would we want a cat in the bhavan?" He frowned and turned back to the men in the courtyard.

The words did not wound Mohan so much as the tone. He'd never heard such irritation from the manager. That night at dinner, when Pramesh seemed once again lost in his thoughts, Mohan kept replaying it:

the look of disdain on the manager's face, the abrupt dismissal. Shobha, too, seemed to treat him differently—no doubt Pramesh had told her what happened.

That night in bed, sleep elusive and hunger gnawing at him, his cowardice and this second failure echoing in his head, his hands reached of their own accord to the steel cabinet. Quickly, he ate one, two, three packets of biscuits, unable to stop. Then he promptly fell asleep, snoring deeply until the roaring of the pots, the sick chill washing through the air, snatched him back and he got up to calm the guests.

The next day, running errands, Mohan bought more biscuits to replenish his supply. But then once again his hands reached out by themselves, snatching up other things he usually bought only for children or for Rani. Bags of roasted cashews, red with masala or speckled with black salt and lime. Gram flour fried into crunchy chips and blazing with more masala. An entire box of sweets, sticky jalebi and round ladoos, carrot halwa, almond and pistachio barfi.

Shoving his purchases deep into a jute bag, laying a newspaper on top to hide the contraband, Mohan walked home. He knew the rules. He was the one to recite the list on the back of each door in the bhavan, to issue gentle reminders for first offenses and to report further ones to Pramesh. The rule regarding outside food was just as important as the nightly curfew or the instruction to keep the mind fixed in prayer. "Someone who is dying must concentrate on the great God, on separating himself from physical attachments," Narinder would explain to an unconvinced guest. "Your father cannot sever himself from this life and this world if his mind is fixed on some desired object, much less his neighbor's dinner."

Mohan stowed the things away in his steel cabinet, pushing the door firmly shut, and continued with his day's duties. That night, he lay in bed, alone in the dark, and thought of his job, his secure place in the bhavan, his respect for Pramesh and Shobha, his inclusion in the priests' circle even though he was not their equal. He thought of the dying guests and the sacrifices their families made to bring them to this holy city. He thought of the ghost, of the manager's stress, and of his own inability to help. He had prided himself on being capable, ready to meet any challenge to ease the lives of those who dwelled in the bhavan. But he hadn't been capable enough, quick enough, to answer a stranger's call at the gate, to realize just how important that stranger was, to usher him in and alert the manager. . . .

First, he ate the cashews, alternating between spicy and sour-salty. He finished with three pieces of barfi, and only then was he able to sleep. Each succeeding night he ate more, and each day he brought more home. The saltiness, sweetness, and spicy sour, the unbridled tingle on his tongue that assailed his senses—he needed these to face the night. By the time he rose for his nightly charade against the ghost-addled pots, the wrappers were disposed of, the scent of chewed cloves covered his breath, and he held in the need to belch until all the guests and Pramesh were back in bed.

These things were within his control. Others were not.

"Mohan-bhai, you have stopped liking my food, I think," Shobha said to him one morning when he eschewed the roti from the previous night's dinner that they always ate for breakfast.

"No, no, ji," Mohan replied with a half-hearted laugh. "What person can resist your cooking? I have had stomach issues for some days now."

Shobha, who did not know how to face a problem without offering a solution, promptly dipped a spoon into a castor oil concoction and forced the assistant to take it, which so distressed him that tears ran from his eyes. "One more at midday and everything will be clear," Shobha said.

No amount of home remedies, however, could fix Mohan's problem. He'd forgotten the basic principle that anyone past the childhood years of eating green mangos could tell you: changes in diet will lead to other, inevitable, changes. In the mornings, as the priests queued outside the washroom for their morning evacuations, Mohan took his place behind them, but his need was false. Later, however, when the midnight hour bridged the old day and the new, his muscles tightened in urgent familiarity and he faced his most distressing dilemma yet.

He almost soiled himself thinking about the stories. "Never go at night, never!" the old farmer Ramu used to warn the circles of dusty children who gathered at his feet to hear his ongoing narration of the Mahabharata. "Dhoti loose," he said, "ass bare in the night, and that's when they get you." *They*, of course, were the night spirits, ghosts, souls in limbo—just like the one in the washroom. Mohan shivered at the recollection. *Anything* could happen to a person who let his bowels loose in the night hours. You could be possessed or struck dumb, forced to walk backward while singing for the rest of your life, or simply disappear. And if he ventured out beyond the bhavan gates to some narrow lane where the beggars ensconced themselves, or to the ghats that the sweepers used in the mornings? No, there was Ramu again, warning him.

"Once," the old man had said in between great bites of sugar cane, wrenching off the hard green peel with his five remaining teeth and spitting the shards a good three meters behind him, "there was someone in the village. We called him Chikku because he was always eating those fruits. He was a good fellow, but he got into trouble when he drank, and hey! That is another thing to stay away from! Well, one day he angered a sadhu who lived next to a nearby temple. This Chikku took a piss right in the spot where the sadhu would sit for his meditation, and that was it. After that, nothing ever worked properly for Chikku. Every time he sat down he'd have to get up again to take a piss, and at night his stomach gave the worst rumblings and sent him racing from his house to the field. He tried everything! He begged the sadhu's forgiveness, he did puja at the temple, he walked for days to visit every doctor he could find. Nothing. Once the curse was there, no one could take it away, not even the sadhu himself. And then one day I heard that Chikku had disappeared. No one knew what happened, but there were some boys traveling the road who stopped to sleep near a field, and they said they were woken in the night by a man who ran past them screaming, and from behind they could see his ass shining in the moonlight, covered with shit like a buffalo's! No one ever saw him again, but anyone could guess at what had happened. Ghosts like such things, nah?"

As the cramps and exertions of Mohan's intestines accelerated, he let loose the rapid breaths of a woman in labor and thought with increasing panic of the unfortunate Chikku. His options were to risk going outside where ghosts *could* be, or go to the washroom where a ghost most certainly *would* be. The danger of possession, of being cursed or seized or at the very least frightened, was enough to make him pause. But he couldn't hesitate for long. Quietly, the assistant crept from the bhavan with his water-filled brass lota in hand, slipped into the haven of a wet dark alley, and—saying the great God's name as his stomach churned and sighed—did the thing.

17

The sun had been up for some time, but Rani slept on her soft mat in the corner of the bedroom. During the night, when the pots had rumbled awake, shrieking until Pramesh said the word to quiet them, she'd had trouble returning to sleep, and Shobha had spent the intervening hours before dawn sitting at her side, rubbing her back and trying to soothe her. Her frequent chills persisted and her dreams were often restless. Shobha's vigilance with ginger-spiced chai and milk laced with turmeric sometimes brought Rani back to herself, and now her breathing was light and even.

A three-year-old who did not speak was not much of a story in this city whose attention was always pulled in many directions at once, most recently with the scandal of the groom who somehow escaped his own wedding procession as it marched with single-minded determination toward the bride's home and managed to slip into his favorite house at Dal-Mandi for a quick—*very* quick, people said—courage-inducing lay. Sometimes, however, when gossip was scant, talk turned to the child living in the hostel who had yet to utter a single word. Some blamed the environment; others sniffed over family connections; a venomous few blamed Shobha. And then there were those who pointed to something else. *Her punishment after the last life,* they whispered. *She must have been a wretched thing, using that tongue to get others into trouble, speaking out of turn, spreading poison. And now look—no tongue at all.*

Shobha rarely heard the words directly, but sometimes the odd woman in the marketplace, like Mrs. Gupta, pulled her aside to tell her what was being said in what they surely imagined was a helpful way.

136

"They are all gossips," Mrs. Mistry said when Shobha told her about the latest incident, and she waved her hands as if to banish the stories.

"Words worse than nonsense," Shobha agreed.

The older woman looked reflective as she stirred her chai. "You've tried all the home remedies, yes? And a doctor—has she seen a doctor?" Shobha felt her heart skip. They had never spoken of Rani so openly, and talking of the problem with someone other than her husband made it more real. She found she could say nothing. She merely wagged her chin and ran her finger round and round the rim of her glass. Mrs. Mistry took the glass from Shobha and refilled it. "The child is smarter than all of them; she simply hasn't spoken because she has not yet found something worthwhile to say. It is a lesson many others could learn from. She will talk when she is ready. Rama will see to it." Shobha attempted a smile and then raised the steaming glass to hide her trembling lips. "You keep too much to yourself," Mrs. Mistry said softly.

Shobha blushed. "Only what needs to be kept."

"Yes," Mrs. Mistry replied. "As we all do. It is part of the responsibility of the woman of the house, no matter how young."

"Weren't you young when you married?" Shobha said.

"I was, but I was not the woman of the house. I had my mother-in-law, and his sisters and aunts. I was the last on the list, with plenty of elders to advise and manage and see when a thing might go wrong. But you, who do you have to rely on?"

"Myself," Shobha said.

"Wrong. I am here." Mrs. Mistry grasped the younger woman's hand and pressed her fingers. "Have you forgotten?"

Wetness sprang into Shobha's eyes. No, she had not forgotten. She worked to compose her voice. "You already have so much to do. I could not ask for more when you have already done so much."

"And yet I find I can fit in one more thing," the older woman smiled. "The heart can always expand. It has an infinite number of rooms. You cannot doubt that."

Shobha thought about her own heart. The rooms were few but large, some more frequently visited than others. An airy spacious room for

Pramesh, another for Rani, another slightly smaller room in the upper stories, the door shut and rarely opened, for her mother and father. Opening that door brought back the hollow pain of loss that she knew she should have long ago relinquished, but sometimes, when she found herself in the room, drawn by a smell or sound or thought, she allowed herself to enjoy the warmth of a memory of laughter, a smile, a perfect moment with one of her parents.

There was another room, one that always remained locked. She imagined it as a dark and cramped space, hot and airless one moment, cold and damp the next. Though empty, the room ached with all that should have been there. *Have you forgotten?* She would never forget. Shobha remembered gasping aloud in pain, alone save for Mrs. Mistry, who had responded to Pramesh's desperate summons when the midwife could not be found. The feeling of not being ready, of this being wrong, all so wrong, of that child slipping out of her in tandem with her cries and the sudden conviction that if only she had held fast to her pain, then her body would have held fast to the infant within rather than delivering it prematurely into her neighbor's trembling hands.

"Let me hold it," she'd pleaded when it was over, her eyes glued to the wet bloody bundle that Mrs. Mistry held wrapped in a bit of torn cloth. One moment she had been with child; the next, she was empty, with nothing to show that she had ever had a full womb to begin with. She wanted to feel in her arms that weight she'd carried for weeks. "Let me see."

"Quiet now," Mrs. Mistry said as she wiped Shobha's drenched brow with one hand while the other held the bundle at a tantalizing distance just beyond the mother's reach. "You had me so frightened, and the midwife is never here when one needs her! Who knows what could be more important than this. . . ."

Shobha asked again, her pleas becoming desperate, her weak hands curling in the air toward the bundle.

"Really," Mrs. Mistry tsked in a tone that belied the worry wrinkling her forehead. "There is nothing to see. What could be gained from it? Come, close your eyes, get some rest and then I will return and get you cleaned."

"Maasi," Shobha begged as tears choked her voice. "You must—please! How else can I understand?" That arrow of a question found a gap in Mrs. Mistry's armor. Shobha was not the only woman to have lost a baby, nor the only one to be refused her request to see, to touch, to hold, to comprehend. At last, she handed Shobha the bundle. And then she went downstairs to tell a distraught Pramesh that he would need to call for rites for only one body and not two, as they had all feared.

The memory never left Shobha. For months she would feel as if she were holding on to her child. She felt the heft in her arms, curved her body to accommodate the phantom baby when she slept. Her breasts wept with real milk when she heard its imagined cries. Each time she looked down at her empty arms or woke from a dream and felt around the bed, the loss enveloped her anew.

That baby she'd brought into the world not yet fully formed, a child in pieces, haunted her dreams until Rani came. Here was a whole child: ten fingers, ten toes, two eyes, a nose and mouth in proper position, a full head of hair. She brought that girl forth in agonizing self-imposed silence, and only after Rani was safely in her arms did Shobha let loose a breath she felt she'd been holding her whole life. No matter that the baby rarely cried; she was a girl formed perfectly. Who cared what gossips might say? Why attach importance to a single deficit when Shobha was thankful every day that she did not have a second room, equally dark and silent, carving a hole in her heart?

Her neighbor's heart, Shobha thought, was just the same size, yet it had more rooms than the bhavan, enough space to hold her husband and children and grandchildren, her neighbors and friends, any person she'd done a good turn for. Shobha wondered, was it crowded for those who roamed the halls and channels of Mrs. Mistry's love? "Maybe some hearts have only room for a few," Shobha reflected. "Maybe some hearts are huts and others are palaces."

"Maybe," Mrs. Mistry assented. Shobha got up to leave, slipped on her sandals where she'd left them on the veranda, her neighbor following behind. Then Mrs. Mistry touched Shobha's shoulder. "Maybe some hearts are small. Maybe they are all the same size. Regardless: the rooms are there."

18

"The lock upstairs isn't working anymore—did you ever look at it?" Shobha asked as she handed Pramesh his morning chai.

He winced. Of course, he had forgotten. "You have to angle the key to one side," he said.

"I did that," Shobha said, irritated. "It's jammed even more."

Mohan bustled into the kitchen and offered up Sheetal's services. "That boy can fix anything."

But the key plate proved beyond even Sheetal's expertise. "Rusted through," he declared with regret. He removed the plate and held it out to Pramesh, who admitted to his wife that she had been right. Declining Sheetal's offer of further assistance, he set out to fetch a replacement.

Walking cleared his head. He came upon the home of Kishore the ghaatiyaa, who stood outside with his ornate walking stick waiting for his young grandson to put on his sandals. As if sensing his presence, the riverside priest looked in the manager's direction.

Long ago, on the day Pramesh arrived in the city, meaning to go to the university, this priest of the ghats had instead secured his position at the bhavan. In the first hour he'd spent stumbling about the lanes, finally ending at the ghats, Pramesh forgot all about the further pursuit of his studies. He was dazzled by the life he saw bursting from everywhere, outside shops, on verandas set high off the ground, people talking and laughing and arguing and sulking, from the barber waving his foamy brush around as he railed against his in-laws, to the uniformed school-children skipping arm in arm past him, sweet voices rising in a crude song, to the housewives easing baskets strung on ropes down out of upper-story windows to the vegetable sellers below for a knob of ginger to finish off the evening meal.

This was all so different from the endless fields and siloed family groups he knew. But it was more than just the constant hum that drew him. Walking through thin passageways that dumped him into larger lanes, he came upon lingas festooned with garlands set into alcoves, humble home temples anointed with rice and sindoor behind barred gates, holy eyes staring back at him no matter where he stumbled. He saw temples much larger and grander than anything in his village, bells ringing out at random intervals as monkeys scaled the roofs and jumped on the brass. Holy men were everywhere, popping out of dark corners or sitting in a tidy row down one lane, wearing identical orange robes, grizzled hair and beards the same iron shade of gray, all speaking a constant refrain of mantras that suffused the air and surrounded him wherever he walked.

The air here felt different, a crackle in the atmosphere that sent tingles across his skin. A feeling that there was more to life than simply living. He remembered something, and he flagged down the next man he saw. "Bhai—Manikarnika ghat?"

He walked and walked until he arrived at the cremation ghat, pyres burning and filling the air with smoke and a thick stench, mourners and priests and Doms milling about. He wandered, got turned around, asked for directions again, until he found it. The place where Vishnu had stood in the most severe meditation for 500,000 years, a slab of marble imprinted with footsteps marking the spot where the God's austerity resulted in the birth of the universe. Just as his mother had described. If only Sagar could be here with him! Even he would find it hard to laugh in such a spot.

He stared until the heavy air made breathing difficult, and then he walked in a daze to another ghat, where he stopped to rest. The sun was going down, and he realized he needed a place to stay. So he asked the next man he saw—a river priest.

"Durga Hostel is not far from here," the ghaatiyaa said, looking Pramesh up and down. "Let me take you there." So Pramesh had followed, and as they walked, the ghaatiyaa asked him questions about his age, his name, his purpose in the city. Pramesh answered freely, and when they arrived at the guesthouse, the ghaatiyaa turned to leave, then turned back. "The university, you said. Well, there are universities everywhere."

"I suppose," Pramesh said, unable to concentrate, eager to be alone so he could think about all he'd seen that day.

"There is only one Kashi, though." He smiled. "You look like you have good bones. Come back to see me at the ghat tomorrow, if you wish."

In the morning, Pramesh went to Kishore's ghat to bathe, and then watched him work, more people passing him on trips up and down the stairs in a single day than he'd seen in an entire lifetime. Some of them stopped to talk to him; others continued on their business. The priest asked him to come back again the next day, and the day after, thoughts of attending university fading from Pramesh's mind amid the overwhelming clamor of the city. After the sixth morning, the ghaatiyaa at last pronounced, "I have a place for you."

"You are very young," Shobha's father, Dharam, had said to him on his first day at the bhavan. "Not easy, for the young to be around the dead day after day."

Pramesh couldn't disagree. He missed the bustle of the ghats, the chatter enveloping him from all sides, the movement and life. But time passed, and he came to enjoy helping the families, listening to their questions, listening more intently to the old manager's answers. It was a life so different from how he'd grown up, alone in the house with the Elders and Bua, only Sagar for companionship. How Sagar would have hated it! But here, Pramesh had found something that made sense to him. At night, he sometimes wandered out to the courtyard on the pretense of doing another round of the rooms to soak in the quiet, the black night pouring in, knowing that all around him, souls would soon slip out of their bodies as easily as he slipped out of one shirt and changed into another each morning.

"You lost someone when you were a child," the manager said to him a few months into his tenure. Pramesh looked up, surprised. "It's why this place suits you. You get to see the ending you missed."

Perhaps that was it. He'd had a mother, and an aunt who was like a second mother, and then he'd blinked, opened his eyes, and they were gone. With them, death had been a disappearance, not a state of change.

But at the bhavan, the transformation fascinated him. He was comforted by the rituals around the family preparing the body, carrying it to the ghat, then the burning pyre. A body—a life—didn't just vanish. It transformed into something, was broken down into ash, while the soul went somewhere. Daily, the bhavan offered proof of this.

He visited Kishore's ghat each morning to bathe and pass along news of his progress, thinking—foolishly, he later realized—that the ghaatiyaa took interest in him, perhaps even as a father might. But soon Kishore's manner went from familiar to brusque.

"There was a family of leatherworkers who came to you yesterday, wasn't there?" the ghaatiyaa said one day.

"Yes," Pramesh replied.

The ghaatiyaa sucked his teeth, eyes on the steps below. "You didn't mention it. These are things you should tell me—who comes, who goes. How is the father, the dying man?"

"No better or worse than the others," Pramesh said, disconcerted. "What—"

"When he passes, come tell me immediately."

Back at the bhavan, Pramesh observed that family, wondering why the ghaatiyaa was so interested in them. They kept to themselves, the daughters massaging their father's feet, the sons praying, none of them saying much to the other families or to the bhavan staff. Late that night, the man passed, and the women kept vigil, touching the body to keep ghosts from occupying that shell, until morning when they quickly washed and prepared it and the sons carried it away. They were all gone before it was time for the midday meal. Pramesh stayed where he was. What he observed was a family linked to each other and to the mission of seeing their father through to a good death. It wasn't his business to report their doings to anyone.

Still, he stopped at the ghat the next day, hoping the ghaatiyaa had forgotten. Kishore hadn't. "The old man died, I heard. The leatherworker."

Pramesh gazed at the river, worrying a loose button on his shirt cuff. "He did."

"And? Gone?"

"He died a good death. His sons performed the last rites. They left yesterday." He felt the ghaatiyaa staring at him. Pramesh continued to sit, keeping his eyes resolutely ahead, feeling a resolve harden within him. He faced the ghaatiyaa and said, "What is it you wanted with them?"

Kishore held his gaze, then turned away and began berating a man below for leaving his things for too long. "Are you intending to be down there all day?" He said nothing else to Pramesh, not even raising his hand in farewell when he stood up to leave.

After that, he began to visit Kishore less frequently—and soon he stopped altogether. He took to visiting a different ghat to bathe in the morning. And when he did stumble upon Kishore in the streets, he kept his thoughts to himself, his lips pressed together in a neutral smile.

Now the ghaatiyaa held his hand out, and when Pramesh tried to bypass him, pressing his palms together and saying "Rama-Rama, Kishore-ji," Kishore stuck out his walking stick in the manager's path.

"Always so quick these days, Pramesh-bhai. Such a busy life you cannot say hello to old friends?"

The manager pressed his palms together again. "It's like that with death, Kishore-ji. All day they come, and from all places. But you know this—it's because of you that I have such a busy life. How is your family?"

Kishore grunted and pulled his shawl closer around him. In recent years, his reach across the city had become broader than ever; he was a magnet for every manner of folk, from businessmen needing the latest news on a competitor's doings to the street sweepers and beggars who'd picked up their own crumbs of information they wished to sell. "Better to be busy than occupied with other things," he said. "Other vices."

"Vices?"

"I was surprised that the Doms gave you the wood. Of course I was glad—such a shock, losing your—cousin, was it? But to lose him in *that* way . . . and then imagine not being able to properly do the rites as well!"

Pramesh spoke evenly. "I was also glad. The Doms did everything without question. I'm grateful to them. They've always dealt fairly with those who stay with us."

"Fair might be a matter of how you see it. But it all turned out well, as Rama willed." Kishore dug his walking stick into the ground, turning it one way and another, as if to screw it into the dirt. "Still, one wonders. If they gave wood for a man like that. . . ."

"Like what?" He should have stayed silent, given his salutations, and walked on, but Pramesh felt a perverse satisfaction at answering back. "What are they saying, Kishore-ji?"

The man waggled his hand, his face noncommittal. "Oh, the usual gossip. I hear it all. Separating the truth from the chaff—it's a difficult thing sometimes."

"But you manage."

"I do, I do. If it pleases Rama." He glanced at the open door of his house, rapping his stick impatiently. "Where is that child?" He looked up to find Pramesh still there, suddenly in no hurry to leave. "What they say is that he was a good-for-nothing, your cousin. A common drunk, no better than Maharaj. That if the Doms gave wood for such a man, they may as well give the fire to any wretch who passes in some filthy place, doing Rama knows what."

"And what do you say, Kishore-ji?"

A child emerged from the house at last, sandals slung on his dusty feet and with a shawl, a miniaturized version of the one his grandfather wore, draped around his shoulders. One end slipped off, and the fringe dragged in the dirt. He grasped Kishore's outstretched pinkie and pulled on it. "That is something I am still separating for myself, Pramesh-bhai. You'll excuse me now—yes, yes, we'll go as fast as my legs can take me, don't hurry an old man."

The manager watched them go, wondering if he should follow and convince the ghaatiyaa that it wasn't true. But what was the point, when he himself had no idea what kind of man Sagar had become in the last ten years? Somber, taciturn, even servant to a well-filled bottle, as Bhut and apparently others had insinuated.

"Manager-ji!" Thakorlal cried when he saw Pramesh. "Either I am about to suffer a scolding for my work, or you have a big job for me. Let me guess: the front bhavan gate, nah? So old, ji, and the joints so rusted. Surely you must want it replaced?"

"Not such a big job yet, ji." Pramesh held out a rusted key plate. "Do you have a match for this?" The metal-man took the key plate and set about rummaging through the haphazard wooden boxes stacked about his shop, humming all the while. Pramesh stood off in a corner, breathing in the heavy smell of drink enshrouding the small dark space. The metal-man was known for another, far more lucrative, business: he was the city's main purveyor of cheap home brew, stuff concocted from insecticide or rotting fermented fruit. The smell repulsed the manager, and yet he continued to take deep gulps of air.

"I may have another box upstairs—a moment, ji," Thakorlal said, excusing himself.

Bhut had said that the empty liquor bottle found in the boat must have been Sagar's, that the man's death was a drunken accident that would have left a sober man alive. This was the piece of his cousin's story that pained Pramesh the most, because if Sagar had indeed turned to drink in the intervening years, the manager had willfully done the opposite. He insisted on running most errands at Thakorlal's shop, simply to prove that he could be in the presence of such persuasive poison and still overcome the temptation.

They are not like us, the Elders said of the two cousins. He could see them, his father and uncle sitting on identical rope beds, each with a bottle and a small glass at hand, goading and laughing at one another while the young cousins hid in their room and tried to remain quiet. Even from deep inside the house the boys could smell the Elders' breath, rank and stale like the air in the metal shop. Pramesh felt the old fear return, a spiky ball inside his stomach. No, he was not like his father or his uncle, and he never would be. But Sagar? What of the life he'd led after Pramesh had left?

He reached up to trace his right eyebrow. Thakorlal returned with another box, and as he set it on his worktable, he jammed his thumb into the sharp corner of a key plate and cursed. The metal-man looked up as he stuck his thumb into his mouth, and his eyes flicked to Pramesh's fingers kneading the skin on his forehead. "Headache?" he asked in a helpful tone. "Shall I get you something?"

"It's nothing," Pramesh said.

"A glass of water, at least? Chai?"

"No, nothing—it's just a habit of childhood. I hardly know I am doing it."

The metal-man turned back to his box. "Strange, the things we leave behind and the things we keep from when we were small." He continued flicking through the box, humming to himself. "My mother says I used to sleep in the strangest way—one leg always pulled up to my chest, with my arms around it. Like a stork in a pond. And my wife says I still do it. Don't ask me why, ji. All I care is that I've had a good night's sleep." He got another box and hefted it onto the table. "Is there a story with yours?" he asked, pointing his chin in the manager's direction.

Pramesh swallowed. "An accident," he managed. "Something that happened long ago, with my cousin. I can hardly remember."

"Oh yes. Poor man. That was a terrible thing, his drowning." So buoyant earlier, the metal-man turned back to his box, lips pursed, brow wrinkled. He flipped through the plates more slowly, looking up once or twice at the manager. Then his fingers stopped altogether. "Manager-ji, forgive me," the metal-man said. "But I believe I met him. Your cousin." When Pramesh remained silent, Thakorlal continued. "Remarkable, how I missed the likeness between you two. But of course he was your blood. He even had the same style of walking as you, Manager-ji."

Pramesh attempted a neutral look even as his heart sank down, down, down. Those men who were servants to the glass somehow always knew to seek Thakorlal out, whether they hailed from the city or not. An image swam up before his eyes: Sagar, red-eyed, shuffling, limp curses dripping from his lips—but then the picture of the one man split into two, and the faces were those of the Elders. He tried to shut his ears as the metal-man went on about the ease he'd felt in talking with Sagar, his great sadness at hearing of the man's passing, which he was quite sure was a *good death*, regardless of the drowning and what those other city folk said. Pramesh felt his head might burst, thick as it was with alcohol fumes, with Sagar pounding on his ears, his heart, his mind. At last, he put his hand up. "Thakorlal-ji, I really must be going. I have taken too much of your time."

The metal-man came to an abrupt stop, offended. He turned back to the boxes and made a show of flicking through the metal pieces, his careful attention from before vanished. "As you wish," he said. "If I cannot find it in this box, I am afraid you will have to pay extra so I can send away for the correct piece." Pramesh was conscious of having insulted him, but he did not know what else to do or say. As the manager stepped to the threshold, Thakorlal spoke again, his voice tight and clipped. "He was not here for the reason you are thinking, Manager-ji."

Pramesh stopped at the door. "The man is dead," he said. "You needn't lie for him."

"Your own belief changes nothing, ji. Why would I tell a falsehood?"

"Why then was he here, of all places? What else could he possibly want from you?"

If the metal-man was twice offended, he did not show it. He stacked the boxes in front of him and pushed them to one side. "A bottle," he said. "An *empty* bottle. He was quite emphatic about that."

"Nothing more?"

"Nothing more. His instructions were simple. He needed it to be unfilled, clean, and with a tight cap. He said he had some traveling to do, and he wanted to be sure it would not leak." Thakorlal looked at Pramesh, clearly expecting him to comprehend. He pointed in the direction of the ghats, exasperated. "*To carry the river*, Manager-ji. Do you see?"

Pramesh blinked. A bottle for a draft of the holy river, a container to safely hold and transport that sacred liquid. With such easy access to the river every day since he'd come to live in Kashi, the manager had forgotten what it was to live much farther away, to feel the need of those pilgrims who filled jugs and bottles with the river for when they returned home and required it for blessings, rituals, illness, or the removal of the evil eye.

"Traveling, he said. . . . Where was he going?"

Thakorlal shook his head. "He didn't say. But he mentioned you and your hostel, Manager-ji. Again, I don't know how I missed the likeness, but so many people come and go—he must have come from afar because he looked quite worn out, but when he spoke of you he looked quite different."

"Different how?" Pramesh asked. Curiosity, a sudden hunger, swelled within him. "What did he say?"

A simple singsong voice sounded outside the shop. Maharaj was approaching, his signature earthenware pot in hand, his need evident as he sang his plaintive tune. "Ah!" Thakorlal pulled a piece of metal out of the last box, as if by magic. "I found it!" He handed over the latch, and after paying him, the manager turned to leave, careful to avoid Maharaj as the man began to plead with Thakorlal for something, just a little something.

Pramesh walked slowly until he came to a temple, and he sank to the stairs. As the great temple bells rang out behind him, a new picture of his cousin shimmered to life. He wanted to feel relieved, to believe that Sagar had not changed in *that* way, but he still could not summon a whole man from the new picture. *Not like us,* his father had said all those years ago. *They are not like us.* His fingers reached up to his eyebrow, tugging at the thick hairs. Behind him, the temple doors closed as they always did around noon, and the bells gave out a final clang, the sound echoing.

Up until the year of the family illness, the cousins were identical: two skinny children with hands and feet and heads so much larger than their spare limbs and torsos that, from a distance, their appearance was comical. The fever whittled Pramesh down further, but it was the scar that cleaved Sagar's right eyebrow in two that was the clearest indicator of which boy was which. One marked, and the other unmarred: in this way, at least, they were like the Elders, though those two men never acknowledged this connection. More often, the Elders preferred to speak about how the boys were so different from their own childhood selves.

"Look at them," Pramesh's father would say. "Not like us at all, either of them."

"Where is the spirit?" Sagar's father agreed. "Where is the spark? Eh, Bhaiya? *The spark*?" They laughed. Everyone knew the story. When the cousins did not hear it from the Elders, they heard it from some villager who still held the tale in awe, as if nothing since had surpassed the audacity of that night.

The bonfire, a controlled blaze that the farmers sometimes lit in the winter against a chilled evening, rose and bit into the air. The young Prasad brothers ventured outside and sat on the ground some feet away, the heat pleasant and comforting, the tree branches cracking and popping like muted fireworks. The brothers sat on the ground, feet bare, light flickering in their eyes. One of them scooted forward, and his brother followed, each a little closer to the fire, the heat now slightly oppressive. Then, as if obeying an inaudible signal, they moved forward again. Moisture slicked their foreheads; their eyebrows sopped up the sweat dripping down their noses. Closer still, the heat blistered; they turned aside their faces. Sparks sputtered and flew as if the fire itself sought to warn those brothers from coming closer. Yet they moved forward again.

By now, the lingering adults had noticed, and they yelled for the boys' father and moved forward to pull them away. One farmer went for Younger, one for Youngest. Both were quick, but Youngest quicker. Just as he felt himself being lifted to his feet, he thrust his hand forward and made a final grab, and the fire reached out to greet him.

The village remembered Youngest as the winner of that contest because he carried the scar to the end of his days. The entire outer edge of his left hand, extending from the tip of his littlest finger to the end of his palm, remained pink and shiny and stretched, a testament to the salutation he had dared offer Agni, God of flame.

That was how these brothers were: one always the victor, the other not far behind, their childhood spent in devising and competing in contests that increased in difficulty and danger as the years passed. "We always tested the other," they chuckled as their sons slept, or pretended to, in the next room. "We always sought to prove we could do something the other could not."

"I remember proving this more often than you, Bhaiya."

"Really? Perhaps the few you won blinded you to the total outcome. Ah, Bhaiya! Such days!"

"The frog-catching contest! Or the rice-eating contest, remember that, Bhaiya?"

"And when we were older, remember the south-facing fields? Remember how we raced to see who could plow the fastest, and when I finished you still had two lines remaining?"

"Yes, but what about the time Father asked us to rethatch the roof in the middle of summer? And you fainted dead away while I was hauling up the grasses, remember?"

Their good humor, facilitated with home brew and beedis, suffused their reminiscence. Inevitably, however, the effects wore off and the mood darkened.

"What about when you said we could make money from the deal with that Singh fellow?"

"Yes, well, what about how you swore that sway-backed water buffalo was the best we ever had, when it never gave a drop of milk despite how much it ate?"

Blame became its own contest, each brother vying to bring up a greater grievance, a more disastrous blunder. In the end, they always came to the same final point.

"One contest you cannot dispute," Pramesh's father said. "My boy is the oldest, after all. He beat yours into this world."

"And is your boy still the best?" Sagar's father said. "Isn't he stranded in bed, while mine goes out and sees the men working and already thinks of making his fortune?"

They were both right—or, as Pramesh later came to think of it, they were both wrong. In the end, they called a kind of truce. "Where is our blood in either of them?" the Elders murmured as one stumbled to bed and the other stayed seated to fall asleep where he was. "More like their mothers. Weak. Why else would the fever take them? How else could they die so easily? Not like us."

Not like us. Not like us. At first, Pramesh understood that he and Sagar were to be ashamed of that fact. They tried their own competitions in imitation of the Elders. The frogs, the rice, the races. When Jaya was visiting, they enlisted her to act as the judge—but she rarely was able to announce a clear winner. Both boys ended up laughing or getting bored and abandoning the game altogether.

One day, after the evening meal, the boys sat in the kitchen doing their sums by the light of the lamp Bua left for them, and she retired after the washing up was done as she always did. Usually the Elders spent the evening on the front veranda, working their way through whatever bottle they'd brought home with them. But on this night they walked heavily back inside, settled in the front room, and called for the boys in rough voices.

Pramesh and Sagar obeyed, knowing it was better to take a beating now than delay it. "Here." Sagar's father dragged his son down by the shirt sleeve to sit next to him. Pramesh felt a similar tug as his father yanked him over so quickly that he stumbled. The men sat across from each other, their bodies giving off the scent of sweat and beedi smoke and the ever-present stench that made Pramesh inch away as much as he could, unnoticed.

The familiar bottle was on the floor between them, along with two glasses. Pramesh watched his uncle pour a scant amount into each glass. His heartbeat quickened. He tried to catch Sagar's eye, but his cousin seemed frozen.

"You both were in the peepal today. Climbing," Pramesh's father said. "Why?"

Pramesh felt cold and damp with sweat. "A contest," he managed. "To see who could climb highest."

His father turned to Sagar's, his voice smug. "Didn't I say?"

"Get on with it, then," Sagar's father said.

Again, Pramesh tried to catch Sagar's eye, wishing that Sagar would look up, just once, so that they could decide what to do. If they ran, they always ran together. But Sagar's eyes were fixed on the glass, which his father set down roughly in front of him.

"A better contest," Pramesh's father said, and Pramesh found the other glass in front of him, the medicinal smell of the liquid, tinged with a sweet rotting, wafting up. And still, Sagar would not look at him. Instead, he picked up the glass, lifted it to his face, took a hesitant sniff.

A sharp pain erupted in Pramesh's ribs; his father followed that jab with a slap to the back of his head. "Already he's picked his up—why are you dawdling?"

"Because he's like his father—no stomach for it!" Sagar's father said, his barking laughter cacophonous in the small room.

Anger throbbed in Pramesh's veins. The Elders would not let them go until one of them drank, and Sagar was like one bewitched, unable to put the glass down, unable to lift it to his lips. He could see no other way out of this. Pramesh grabbed the glass and tipped the liquid down his throat in one go, his father giving a delighted grunt beside him. In the next instant, he gagged, spitting out most of the drink. His mouth was filled with a foul taste, his tongue and gums burning, his ears warming from the inside. He coughed, mindful of the sound of his uncle laughing as he did so, tears springing from his eyes. He chanced another look at Sagar, and now at last his cousin met his eyes, his chin quivering with fear. His drink was untouched before him.

"Not like us, Bhai," Sagar's father said. "Remember that first sip? Downed at once—and I had another one directly after."

"He took a drink though, didn't he? Not like your boy," Pramesh's father said. "Still," he added with a disdainful air, "they will never be like us."

Sagar's father began a retort, but went silent.

Bua appeared from the narrow hall. Her voice shook. "Must you? Must you also bring them into it?"

Pramesh's father said something beneath his breath. Then a gentle hand was on Pramesh's shoulder, and his aunt helped him up. She made him drink a glass of water in the kitchen, then one more, Sagar hovering nearby. Pramesh avoided his cousin and swished the water around in his mouth, trying to get rid of the taste, wishing there was also something he could take to rid himself of the sound of his uncle laughing, the dull ache from where his father had jabbed him.

Bua walked them to their room and smoothed their blankets over them.

"Bhai," Sagar called urgently in the dark once she left. "Bhaiya." Pramesh would not answer. He heard Sagar slip out of bed and pad toward him. "Bhai," he said again, staring into Pramesh's face so that he could not look away. "They are not like us, Bhai." His voice held a pleading note, and he searched Pramesh's eyes. "*They* are not like *us*."

Pramesh held Sagar's stare. He wanted to sustain his anger, to leave Sagar waiting just as his cousin had left him. But he was tired. "Not like us," he repeated. "They are not like us."

19

Each morning Shobha's body greeted her with a crick in her neck and aching limbs, weary from waking every few minutes through the night in anticipation of the pots erupting, and then being unable to fall back into proper sleep once Pramesh silenced them. As she lay awake in the dark, however, she didn't think of the ghost. A more pressing subject possessed her, an idea, conceived the day she'd seen Pramesh revisiting Sagar's letters, that curled in a corner of her mind. As the days passed, the idea grew larger, until its presence was too great to ignore, and she decided to act upon it.

She wrote a letter. She addressed the envelope to the place she had visited just once in her life, all those years ago when she was a new bride. And then she slipped the letter into one of her sari pleats. She stopped at the post office and went to the window with its iron bars that faced the street. She counted out the coins to pay the postage, money scrimped from haggling with the vegetable men. Then she pushed the letter through the iron grille, into the postman's hands.

Her stomach quivered as she turned toward the bazaar. She took in a deep breath, pulled her sari end closer around her head, and continued walking. In the market lane, Shobha filled her jute bag with ten rupees' worth of miniature squash, a kilo of potatoes, and a half kilo of onions. She passed the stalls of ready-made clothing dangling from taut lines and stopped at a small table laid with cosmetics, where she purchased two cards of red bindis and a new crayon of thick black kohl. Not until she reached the puja shop and waited for the bent old proprietor to dig out a new copper oil lamp from his dusty stacks of wares did she allow herself to think about what she'd done.

What was the fate of Kamna?

That part of the letter was quick to write. She'd lingered for many moments over whether to sign her name. In the end, she'd simply written "Shankarbhavan" at the bottom. It was a cowardly thing to do, to hide behind the bhavan. Her courage extended to writing the letter and sending it, but not to fully exposing herself or her family. *A woman like that does not forget.*

Shobha was not an impulsive woman. She always thought through the consequences before acting. Unlike some of her school friends, Shobha had a choice in whom she married. She accepted Pramesh not because her father was ill and desperate to see her settled, or because Pramesh was the only man with whom she'd spent some months in close proximity. She did it because there was something different in his eyes, something that suggested a desire for sharing with, not taking from, as she had sensed with those she'd refused. She saw a possibility for happiness with this man, rather than mere existence or all-out misery with another. And they *had* been happy. That first week of marriage, Shobha had been happier than she could remember being since before her mother had died. She'd walked around the bhavan in a dreamy haze, scalding the chai, burning the roti, unable to concentrate whenever Pramesh walked into the room.

And then her father had suggested the trip, a visit to Pramesh's childhood home. Shobha had protested, not wanting to leave him while he was ill. "If I go, I go," he'd said with his usual bluntness. "You need to meet your new family, get their blessings."

"Promise me you will stay until I return," Shobha had insisted, her voice dipping back into the pleading of a little girl, as if her father could control the moment of his death. He'd laughed.

"Yes, yes, I promise. Even if Yamraj comes with his noose I will tell him to stay, sit in the corner, wait until my daughter comes."

So she agreed. All during the wait on the train platform and the journey crammed into the packed car, Shobha allowed herself to feel the sweet thrill of being the only one commanding her husband's attention. Her husband! The word so unfamiliar and yet intimate that she had to pull her sari further over her head and across her face to hide her flushed cheeks, lest some keen-eyed auntie in the train car see and immediately begin asking questions.

The rumbling train was crowded, heavy with the smell of many bodies, folk squatting or standing in the aisle, parents setting their children down into strangers' laps, people shifting and squeezing when someone tried to walk through, and then resettling into the newly opened crevices like sand. They mostly talked to their neighbors, Pramesh to the other men on board, and Shobha to the woman sitting across from her. When they spoke to each other their voices were murmurs. Once, while seemingly deep into discussing the business of Shankarbhavan with the man across the aisle from him, Pramesh reached his hand over in a slow innocuous motion, his fingers finding Shobha's with the ease of a bee alighting on a blossom, and with his skin on hers, in that crowded train car where it seemed everything and everyone demanded their attention, Shobha felt as if only they two existed. And then the moment ended when the woman in front cleared her throat loudly and gave them both a meaningful look, and Pramesh flashed a wink at Shobha, lightning quick, before turning to the man across the aisle while she bit down on her smile.

She had rarely spoken to Pramesh in the months he'd been working at the bhavan, mindful of the eyes inside and out that were ready to home in on any impropriety. Sometimes, when she'd brought her father his tiffin, she lingered while he ate, and if Pramesh was nearby, Dharam would invite him to sit as well, and they would talk, Shobha listening behind the veil of her sari.

From those chats, she knew Pramesh's mother and aunt were dead, and that most of his memories of his mother revolved around stories she'd told in the evenings or at the midday meal, spinning out tales of the Mother, of the great God's earring falling down into Vishnu's well and forming the name of Manikarnika ghat.

Of Pramesh's father and uncle she knew only that they were farmers who had been reluctant to let Pramesh come to the city. Before this trip, she'd asked about their favorite foods, thinking she might prepare something during her stay. Pramesh had instead spoken of the aunt who'd raised him and his cousin. Perhaps she'd picked a bad moment. She asked

Mrs. Mistry what she thought, and that woman had laughed her anxiety away. "A new bride must worry only about impressing the women in her husband's family—the men are always easily won over. Pleasing words, something sweet with chai—it doesn't take much, you'll see."

She was most nervous about meeting Sagar, because she could tell her husband prized that relationship above all others. When he spoke of his cousin, when he read the letters he received from the village over and over, when her father coaxed him into sharing something about Sagar, a smile crept over his face like a secret he could not completely hide. She knew they were close in age, looked remarkably similar, and that Sagar was also a farmer. And unlike with the Elders, Pramesh readily told Shobha that his cousin's favorite indulgence was pura. That morning, she'd woken hours earlier than Pramesh, her father, even Narinder, all so she would have time to make the soft pancakes, mixing the batter and dropping ladlefuls on a flat-surfaced pan slick with ghee until each pura was golden, spongy in the middle with crisp edges. They were now packed carefully into a steel tin snug in the bottom of her bag.

Her seatmate interrupted her thoughts. "Newly married?" the woman said. She spoke it not as a question so much as a statement, and one that was flat and deflated, as if the state of marriage were akin to a disease or an irreversible sentence. "A good lesson to learn," she said when Shobha smiled, turning her attention to the window, "is that they think they are always right. And they never are. But you must not ever tell them that. Not, at least, until you have four, five children between you two."

Shobha blushed at the mention of children, but the woman didn't notice. She thought of it again hours later, once they'd left the train platform and began walking, until an old acquaintance of Pramesh's family accosted them and insisted on giving them a ride.

Bumping along in the creaking cart, alone with her thoughts as Pramesh patiently listened to the chattering farmer, she thought of a child—*her* child, hers and Pramesh's, and more children to follow—and a sweet steady desire blossomed within her. She spent the rest of the journey with a secret smile on her face, taking no notice of her surroundings until they stopped and Pramesh came around to offer her a hand.

"Are we already here?" She hurried to shake the dust from her sari, to wipe the damp away from her face and adjust the hairs that had flown away from the coiled bun at the nape of her neck.

"Not yet," Pramesh said. "A small change—Maasad suggested it," he said, motioning with his chin to the farmer, who had disembarked to stroke the bullocks that had pulled them along, talking to them in a low soothing voice. "He thought it might be best to have you stay here first. He'll take me to the house and I'll come back later, with Sagar-bhai."

"Later?" Shobha looked behind her. They were at the door of a modest house, fields spreading out behind and trees stretching upward all around. A woman came to the door.

"Champa-maasi has known my cousin and me since we were children," Pramesh said. "You would have met her anyway. You are simply meeting her now rather than later."

It seemed an odd plan to her. *They think they are always right.* She wondered, suddenly, if Pramesh was embarrassed by her. If he thought his family would be displeased with her. But the woman came bustling over, smile wide, arms outspread, and the farmer carried her bag to the door and then sat himself back on the cart and turned to Pramesh. So she said nothing, simply bent to touch the woman's feet and obtain her blessing, listened as Champa-maasi exclaimed over Pramesh and how well he looked, how beautiful his bride was, and wouldn't he come in for water, for chai, for refreshment? But the farmer said they needed to be getting on, and Pramesh made his apologies, palms folded, eyes on the farmer's wife, flickering for a second, half a second, toward his own wife. And then he was in the cart and gone, hidden behind a cloud of dust. Too late, Shobha remembered the pura, still in her bag.

Now she sat in the front room while the woman made chai, unable to help, to do anything that might keep her hands busy in this strange house, this strange village, with people who were not even her husband's blood. "What would they say, you here not even half a moment, a new bride, if I were to put you to work? Come, sit and talk to Divya; she is around your age and will have plenty more to entertain you than an old woman like me." The farmer's wife bustled off, and her daughter made small talk with Shobha, chatting away until someone's voice came at the front door and she stood up to tend to whoever it was.

Alone, Shobha sighed and stood to stretch her legs after the long and cramped ride in the cart. The journey's excitement had kept her awake, but there was nothing exciting in waiting. She stretched her arms upward, feeling the delightful jangle of her bangles—the ones that had been her mother's mixed with the new glass ones from her wedding—sliding down her arms, and she yawned.

"Oh, but you must be tired!" The daughter, Divya had returned. "So stupid of us—come, you must rest; I insist." She took Shobha's hand and led her to a back bedroom, ignoring Shobha's half-hearted insistence that she was fine, and almost pushing her down to the low rope bed. She relinquished the weight of her body to the bed, thinking she might close her eyes for just a moment, but she was soon fast asleep, such a deep and complete rest that when she woke, the sun had moved considerably along its daily arc, and she blinked several times while she recalled where she was.

She heard voices, clear but low, and as she lay there, still in a hazy half sleep, she tried to pick out Pramesh's. Surely he must have returned by now; surely his family was as eager to meet her as she was to get their blessing. Yet she could hear only women.

"The older one. She wanted him specifically. Shameless thing!"

"Who told you that?"

"I heard it from my sister, and you know she does not lie. She is barren, you know."

"Your sister? Well, I would think she was too old—"

"No no, the girl!"

"How? How do you know that?"

"Everyone knows. Running around as she does. . . . She should have been with child ten times over by now. What woman does that? Leaves her family, plays the runaway, comes back home in time for chai as if she hasn't been with—"

"Hush! Such a thing to say! How can you know it is true?"

"Oh, it is. Why do you think her family has never stayed in the same place longer than a year? They move from village to village like you and I switch from a dirty sari to a clean one. They can't stay in any place before people realize what they are, what she is. You know the stories?"

"I know what people have said."

"It's the same thing, isn't it?"

"Not always. Tell me this, though—why would they want such a girl in the family? And for their eldest?"

"You know how they were. A bet they made."

"A bet? Hai Rama. . . ."

She didn't recognize the voice of the woman telling the story. She thought the other one was Champa-maasi. Shobha listened with one ear, blinking away the veil of sleep. A beam of sunlight cut through the window on the other side of the room and landed near her stomach. She slipped off a glass bangle and idly held it up to the light, turning it this way and that, watching the light split and refract, a fascination she'd had since childhood. The gossip in the village, it seemed, was no different from the gossip in the city—and nor was the means by which it traveled. She wondered how much the truth had been diluted, how many times the story had made the rounds, and which version she was now hearing.

"Yet I feel sorry. . . ." Champa-maasi said.

"For who? For the girl? Or for the Prasad boys?"

The Prasad boys. Pramesh was a Prasad. She was one now as well, for that matter. She stirred, but her anklets let out the softest of chimes, and her bangles responded, and she forced herself to remain still. What had they said in the beginning, about the older one? About Pramesh?

"The older one was lucky to leave them all behind."

"If you can call it luck for him to spurn that girl."

"What do you mean?"

"A woman like that does not forget. You've heard what happened to that one—the one she bewitched."

"So you think she would do something?"

"Rama knows what she might do. Would he have married her, do you think? If he hadn't already married the one. . . ."

The voices lowered, and Shobha could not hear the reply. *A woman like that does not forget.* Like what? Who was this other woman who had wanted to marry Pramesh?

The talk resumed, but now it shifted to something else, something mundane. She felt more tired than when she'd first given herself over to the bed, and her skin burned. She brought her wrists up to her forehead, the cool glass and metal of her bangles soothing away the heat, jangling as they did so. The conversation in the kitchen stumbled, and she could imagine the two women looking at each other, gauging how much they thought she—the interloper, the stranger, the one who'd taken another woman's place—had heard. Waves of shame washed over her. Was this what marriage would be like? Her husband leaving her to fend for herself while he continued on his own, oblivious? The marriage priest had bound their hands together over the fire, had said that the seven rounds they made around that sacred flame had fused them into one being, two halves of a single whole. Yet barely a week later, her husband was already leaving her behind.

They think they are always right. Wait for children, the woman on the train had said. Wait for years to go by; wait to establish a position for yourself before you ever contradict your husband. She longed for her mother, the old ache of loneliness washing over her; she wished for Mrs. Mistry to tell her what to do. She could tell her father, but his understanding would go only so far. She needed an older woman.

But she was alone. No one would come to her here. And sitting in the strange room, on the strange bed, would gain her nothing. Shobha pressed her palms against her eyes, breathed in the Mother's name, and breathed out. And then she got up and went to the kitchen to help the women with their midday chores—and to think.

When Pramesh returned, he arrived on foot, and alone. None of the people at the house—the farmer and his wife, their daughters and sons and the spouses and children—said anything, though Shobha saw the farmer's wife flick a glance at her husband, saw the daughter Divya raise her eyebrows at her sister. The women served the men the evening meal in the backyard, going around with the individual dishes, and when Shobha came to Pramesh's place, she focused on the vessel in her hands, on spooning out his portion and setting it on his leaf plate, avoiding his eyes, avoiding everything about him. She took her meal in the kitchen with the other women, half listening to their talk, rousing herself to answer their questions when they turned to her, trying on a smile that hurt her face.

Everyone seemed to know without discussing it that the newlyweds would spend the night in their house, and again Shobha felt like the outsider, the one everyone else talked over and around but never to. She could hear the men talking outside as they ate, her husband telling them of his new life, of the death hostel, of her father, and he laughed and asked about old acquaintances and seemed to feel no guilt about leaving his new wife alone in a strange place for almost an entire day.

That night, the women spread out on the floor in one room, and the men in another. In the midst of the rest of the family, washing up and lighting lamps, oiling hair and laughing over some internal joke, there was no time for Shobha to be alone with Pramesh, no opportunity for her to ask what was happening, when she'd meet his family, where he'd been all day, who this other woman was that his elders had wanted him to marry. She lay down for the night on a mat alongside the other women in the family, and when the air was full of snores and the occasional word spoken in sleep, Shobha felt stifled by her own silence, because if she let loose any sound, the wall within herself would break, and she wouldn't be able to control what happened next. So she stayed still, curled on her side with one palm pillowed beneath her head, and she wondered how even now, married and in a room full of people, she could feel perched on the edge of a loneliness that extended deep within her, so black and so depthless that she squeezed her eyes shut and wished for sleep to wipe her memory clean.

When morning came, Shobha insisted on helping with the morning meal, going so far as to take the dirty chai glasses from the farmer's wife's hands and bring them outside with the other plates and vessels through the back door, where they had their own well. She drew water and washed the kitchen things, half listening to the chatter of Divya, who told her all the village gossip and asked her about the city. Shobha wondered if there was a way she could ask about the other woman without revealing what she'd heard. Halfway through the washing, Divya got up to take the clean things back into the house, and Shobha was left to herself, at least until she heard footsteps behind her. But these were steps she knew very well, having memorized their stride and beat, her heart beating faster whenever she heard him approach in the bhavan, but now the warmth of anger and hurt muddled her usual anticipation. She did not look up as she continued her task. "You shouldn't be here," she said. "It won't look right."

"How long must a man be married before he can be alone with his wife without someone commenting about it?" Pramesh asked. There was something odd in his voice, and Shobha allowed herself a sideways glance. He squatted a few paces from her and pulled at the grass beneath his feet, elbows resting on his knees, face turned so she saw only his profile. Her heart twinged. *His wife*, he'd said. Perhaps he did feel bad about leaving her for an entire day.

"Much longer than a week," she said. "A year. I suppose it depends on the rules of the place you are in."

"Then we are lost. Five years here, at the very least," Pramesh said with a thin laugh.

Her bangles clattered as she scrubbed the chai glasses with ash and rinsed them with fresh water. She waited for him to speak. All the things she wanted to say and ask rose to the back of her throat, choking her. Pramesh continued to pull at the grass, gazing off and saying nothing. She realized something very clearly: *she* had to ask him. And the way he chose to respond would tell the future of her marriage for all its years to come.

"I was asleep yesterday. In the house. And I heard something." She looked his way. His eyes were on the ground. She took a breath and continued. "Gossip, really. But they said—the woman said your elders had picked someone else out for you. Someone for you to marry." Still, he said nothing. He stopped worrying the grass. He dusted his palms and then held the fingers of one hand with the other. Fear made her heart beat wildly, and her hands trembled, but she focused on scrubbing the last dish with ash and forced out the last question. "Is that why you haven't yet taken me to meet them? Is that why you left me here for the entire day?"

The silence stretched on. She finished the last dish, rinsed it clean, set it on the cloth beside her, and looked at her husband. He stood, still looking at the ground, hands on his lower back. "It was a surprise to me as well," he said.

Shobha stood, wiping her hands on the ends of her sari. "What happened?"

Instead of answering, he took in the sun's position. "Sagar said he would come in the morning, first thing after completing some work. And he is bringing Bua—they were eager to meet you."

She tried to smile. At least his cousin wanted to meet her. She remembered the pura, still in her bag, no longer fresh. Perhaps she could make them again now, if Champa-maasi would let her. Still, her heart dipped a little. "And your father, your uncle? Are we not going to your home?"

"It isn't what you wanted, I know," Pramesh said softly. She caught the pleading in his voice, and she noticed the lines beneath his eyes that she hadn't seen last night, a pall that wasn't there the previous day when he'd brushed her hand in full view of the train's occupants. He rubbed the skin on his forehead, the fingers drifting down to trace his eyebrow. "A whole year . . . nothing changed."

What did he mean by that? She stepped closer, about to ask, but voices rose from the house and Divya came clattering out, laughing and followed by her mother.

"I didn't mean to leave you so long—oh, Pramesh-bhaiya, missing your bride already?"

Shobha bent to gather up the clean dishes, but Champa-maasi took them from her, chiding her for working and instructing her daughter to throw out the dishwater. With the tray balanced against her hip she put a hand on Pramesh's shoulder.

"Pramesh-beta, lucky you! Fresh paneer made yesterday. And laapsi—your favorite still, nah?"

"So much trouble for us," Pramesh said, his voice overbright. "And we will continue to trouble you, I'm afraid. At least one more night in your house, Maasi. And more guests for dinner—Sagar-bhai and Bua."

The woman put her arm around Pramesh's waist and walked with him back to the house. Her manner with him was relaxed and affectionate, as if he were blood. Watching them, Shobha suddenly wished that these were her in-laws, with their easy manner and generous ways. Pramesh turned to catch her eye before he was pulled into the house. Perhaps he wished for the same thing, too.

Champa-maasi readily agreed to letting Shobha make pura, even going so far as pulling Divya in to watch. "I try and try to teach her, but her mind is like a butterfly—from one thing to the next, never paying attention," the woman complained. Mother and daughter chatted away, asking Shobha about the fashions in the city, how she spent her days, what the markets had. Shobha allowed herself to be lulled as she stirred the batter and flipped the pura, pushing her anxiety to the back of her mind. Once cooked, the new puras formed a tempting stack that made Shobha forget about the ones still sitting in the steel tin at the bottom of her bag.

But then the hours passed, and there was no sign of Sagar. She watched Pramesh walk from the back of the house to the front many times, shading his eyes against the sun. Soon it was time for the midday meal, and she could tell that Champa-maasi did not know whether to serve everyone, including her husband hungry from work in the fields, or wait. "Maasi—you and Maasad should eat; there is more than enough for when Sagar-bhai comes," she said, and the older woman threw her a grateful glance and began to set out the food.

"He was always late for everything as a child," she said to Pramesh once he'd come in for a bite. "You know he is no different as an adult. But he will be here."

In the late afternoon, as Champa-maasi was making chai, Pramesh walked into the kitchen. "I'm sure he's just delayed, perhaps in the fields," he said. "If he cannot step away, at least I can bring Bua."

There was a false cheer in his voice that made Shobha uneasy. She followed him outside. "Shall I come with you?"

He waved his hand at his side, a gesture he sometimes made when declining an offer of help from her father. "It's better if you stay." From the front of the house, she watched him, with his familiar straight-backed gait, striding alone and away from her.

Inside the house, she settled herself next to Divya with some sewing she took from the mending basket despite Champa-maasi's insistence that she leave the work to the family. Working the needle in and out of the fabric, fixing a tear, putting in a new drawstring, kept her busy. She assumed her husband would be gone until evening, just like the previous day.

But Pramesh was back in an hour, startling her when he walked in the door, straight through to the back of the house and out again. She set the sewing aside and ran to dip him a glass of water from the clay pot just inside the kitchen. He quickly drank, the steel tumbler hiding his face. When he gave it back to her, his hand was trembling.

"What is it?"

"Tomorrow," Pramesh said. "We will leave first thing in the morning." His voice had an undercurrent to it, as if he were holding poison in his throat and speaking carefully so that nothing spilled out.

"What's happened? Is anyone ill? Your aunt?" He shook his head and turned away from her, and she was seized with uncertainty, her heart pounding. She realized what had been in his voice. Fury. Her hand rose to her throat. "Your father, your uncle—what did they say? When they found out you were married to me?"

His back was to her, motionless, his hands were clenched. She reached out, not bothering to check if anyone was watching. Slowly, her husband's fingers unfurled as she held them. He turned to her. "What they say . . . what they do, what they are. None of that matters. That life is finished."

And before she could respond, he walked back to the house. She followed him inside and heard him telling Champa-maasi that they would stay one more night but would leave first thing in the morning. "It was only to be a short visit," he said, his voice almost normal. But she could see a vein twitching near his temple. "Her father is alone at the bhavan; he hasn't been well. We need to return to him."

He continued to explain, the farmer's wife doing her best to convince him otherwise, and Divya echoing her mother's insistence that they must stay at least for a few more days. But Pramesh would not budge. And then they converged on Shobha, planning her next visit, talking over her to discuss what food to pack for the journey, making her feel like she was their family, even though Shobha doubted very much that she would ever see the two of them again.

That last night in the farmer's house, Shobha stared up at the thatched ceiling, unable to sleep. Pramesh had been silent most of the rest of the afternoon and during the evening meal. The anger had dissolved into sadness so quickly that she wondered if she'd imagined it, those clenched fists, the hum of fury beneath his words. There must have been an argument. Scenarios of what might have happened spooled out from her imagination. Had they fought about her? And what about his cousin, his aunt? Had Sagar-bhai really wanted to meet her, or did her husband lie about it to soften the blow?

She turned on the straw mat. Her eyes fell on her bag, stuffed into a corner of the room to make space for the other sleeping women. She'd forgotten to remove the old pura. They'd eaten the new ones with the evening meal, Champa-maasi loudly exclaiming over them and asking Divya what she'd learned from watching Shobha make them, everyone praising the food while staying silent about its intended recipient.

Four people in her new husband's family, and Shobha hadn't managed to meet a single one. *Get their blessings*, her father had instructed her. She turned again, blinking in the dark.

The next morning, Shobha made her goodbyes, coming to Champa-maasi last, bending to touch her feet for one final blessing—not the one she had come for, but the one that would have to last her for the rest of her marriage. When she stood, the older woman grasped her face between her palms and kissed her forehead. "Be happy," she said.

"Yes, Maasi."

The woman slid her arm through Shobha's and walked with her the few steps to the cart, asking her if she was sure she had everything, telling her about the pickles and vegetable dishes she had packed for them, with an extra packet of sweets for Shobha to take back to her father. At the cart, she fussed over Shobha once more, telling her to take care of herself, to come back and visit soon. Shobha kept her eyes down, shy and demure as everyone said a bride should be, but feeling a tremendous sadness well up within her.

She felt a palm on her cheek, the strange skin warming hers, the hand directing her to look up. The farmer's wife looked into her eyes. "You've married a good man."

"Yes, Maasi."

"It was best he was able to leave this place and meet you in the city. His new life with you will be good—promise me you'll make it so?"

Heart aching, Shobha swiveled her chin slowly. Still, the older woman did not take back her hand.

"Things have been difficult for her as well, you know." She said this quietly, so that none but Shobha would hear.

"For who?" Shobha searched the woman's face. For a moment, she was startled out of her sadness. The farmer's wife said nothing and instead turned to the cart and made a show of opening some of the bundles and rearranging the contents. She tied up the bundles again, set them firmly in the cart, squeezed Shobha's arm, and walked back to her family, where she waved for as long as Shobha could see her, the cart traveling back the way it had come.

She made up her mind as they neared the train station. She'd mustered her courage once, just yesterday—she had to do it again. On the train platform, she waited while Pramesh bought their tickets. But when he returned, the question was lodged in her throat. If she asked, she realized, she would not be able to keep the pain from seeping out as well. And she was too proud to cry here, on the train platform, in front of strangers. *A new bride missing her family already*, people would tsk.

"My cousin will marry her. In my place."

Her eyes sprang to his. He avoided her gaze. "The woman meant for you?"

A muscle twitched in his jaw. "Her name is Kamna."

A low whistle sounded in the distance. They both looked to the left and saw the train approaching. Once they boarded, she wouldn't have another moment alone to ask him for many hours. *The older one. She wanted him specifically.* Her mind raced. "Did she accept?"

"That sort of woman doesn't have a choice," Pramesh said bitterly.

"What sort of woman? What happened?"

He stared straight ahead. "He told me to forget this place, all those years ago. And I was foolish, and returned anyway."

She felt the shiver of the platform and gripped her bag tighter.

"Do you believe in not looking back?" He was looking at her, meeting her eyes fully. The question surprised her.

"Your elders," she faltered. "Your cousin. Those aren't ties you can simply cut. Not because of a single argument." She couldn't imagine doing the same with her father. And then she realized that Pramesh had never talked about the Elders in her presence. She knew nothing about his father and uncle. "Whatever they are . . . they are family."

He continued to look at her, the platform rumbling more urgently as the train came closer. "When we get on this train—I cannot look back." His voice faltered, filled with pleading, and she was shocked to realize that he was asking her, begging her, to say she'd do the same.

She thought of how she avoided thinking of her mother lest the pain overwhelm her, preferring to wall off the past to protect herself. Back at Champa-maasi's she'd felt bereft, a loneliness so keen that her bones ached. She would continue to feel that way if she allowed herself to think of all the questions Pramesh had not answered, all the things he had not told her. Or she could agree to do the same, shut the door on this event in their newborn marriage, and embark upon their life as if it started now.

She dipped her chin. "I won't look back."

Was he relieved? She couldn't tell. He reached over and took her bag.

When the train arrived, pushing forward a breeze that sent her sari end flying off her head and streaming behind her, she followed Pramesh, keeping close behind him. With her right foot leading she stepped onto the train, her lips whispering the great God's name for good luck on their journey, just as her father had taught her.

Her father was neither better nor worse when she returned home, but she kept the story from him, focusing instead on the food she'd eaten and her impressions of the village, things she knew he would listen to with only half an ear. Days later, however, she told Mrs. Mistry everything. "Do I ask him what happened?" she asked her neighbor.

"You can try." Mrs. Mistry said after listening in silence. "Watch him closely and pick your moment. Some men simply cannot say the things that are easy for us to say." She poured more chai for Shobha and pushed forward a plate of fenugreek mathri, still warm. "But better, I think, to leave it as he has left it. You have just started a new life together. Unless it comes up again, leave it. Leave it in the past."

She followed her neighbor's advice, and as time passed, she came to understand that Mrs. Mistry was right. Shobha picked her moments, offering nothing but the comfort of her touch when Pramesh was mired deep in that black hole within himself, going about his work but stuck in some personal sadness that would disappear the next day. And she accepted his warmth when her father died months later, and when the baby they lost buried them both in grief. When Rani was born, those episodes of sadness became less frequent. As the years unspooled, as they built a life of their own, the old fears, the old questions, no longer seemed as important to her, and soon faded away.

At least, she thought they had—until the day that her husband's cousin drowned in the river. And the fear Shobha had felt all those years but had allowed herself to forget returned. Kamna never had a say in her family's choice of groom. She had been promised a husband, and a life, in Kashi, and instead she'd remained in the village, bound to another man, and was now a widow. Indirectly, Shobha had taken something from this woman she had never met, this woman who apparently did not forget. And she knew enough of the universe to understand that one day the scales would balance and she would lose something precious in return. A response, some detail about Kamna, would at least arm Shobha with information for when that moment came.

"Three rupees," the old shopkeeper said, having emerged from the sea of brass and incense and red spangled cloth surrounding him in the puja stall. The copper lamp vibrated in his palsied palm.

"A half rupee," Shobha said without hesitation.

"A half?" the man spat. "I would not give this to my mother for a half. Two rupees."

"Half a rupee," she said again as if the shopkeeper hadn't uttered a word.

"I tell you, woman, I will be begging tomorrow if I give this to you for a half. Why not simply give it to you for free? I will go to one and one half. No lower." Shobha turned, sandals grinding into the dirt road as her body twisted in one smooth movement, and before the shopkeeper could blink, the manager's wife was halfway down the market lane. "Hey!" he yelled after her. "One! I can do one rupee! No, I will give it to you for a half! Are you listening? Half a rupee, but only because you are like a daughter!" She did not turn around. Grumbling and spitting the great God's name beneath his breath, the shopkeeper grabbed his cane and hobbled after her, the gleaming copper lamp held aloft in his hand as if to light the entire world.

20

Pramesh was exhausted; strange nightmares clouded what little sleep he'd had after silencing the pots. But there was no time to rest—one of the newer guests had another relative arriving that day, and he had asked Pramesh about having someone meet the man at the train station and walk him to the bhavan. Pramesh found no sign of Mohan in the courtyard or any of the guest rooms, and then he heard an expansive sneeze echo from a corner of the hostel. He found the man bundled in his bed, eyes bleary and throat hoarse.

"You've caught a chill," he said after laying the back of his hand against Mohan's forehead. "Honeyed milk with turmeric is what you need." He threw another blanket atop his fevered assistant. "You must have gone out without a shawl, Mohan-bhai. Come now! You've lived in this city longer than I have; surely you know better."

Mohan answered with a muffled groan, and after asking Shobha to prepare something for the assistant's ailment, Pramesh set off on the errand himself.

On most days, the train station was hot and frenzied with the sounds of passengers disembarking, relatives pushing through the crowds, porters grabbing luggage and insisting on carrying bags, beggars calling out for pity and money, children darting and crying and shrieking with laughter, and conductors bellowing out the last call before departure—but some days, quiet pockets of time existed when all was as subdued and motionless as an abandoned temple. Pramesh found the station in the latter condition. The man at the ticket window dozed, and a cat wandered through the open door and back out again. He looked for the relative's train on the arrivals board, found it, and then his gaze caught on something else: an impending departure for the stop closest to his home village.

He looked away. He'd ridden the train back to his home just once, on a trip with Shobha a week after their marriage. "The one I love the most, joined with the man I trust the most," Dharam had told Pramesh when he offered Shobha's hand. The surprise Pramesh felt was equaled by the pleasure of learning that Shobha had given her consent first. She, with her confidence, her lightness, her ease in the world that he marveled at—she wanted him. Impossible thing!

Their wedding was hasty, made urgent by the old manager's sudden decline and his wish to see his daughter settled before he left this world. There was no time even to write to the Elders and Sagar with the news. Afterward, Shobha's father insisted they travel down to Pramesh's home immediately. "You are my son now," he said. "But you were someone else's son first, and it is right that you get their blessing."

On the day of departure, he arrived early at Rama ghat to bathe. Maharaj was stretched out on the steps, half awake or half asleep with his arms around his ever-present clay pot, and as Pramesh scrubbed his scalp, working soap into his hair, two boys called out to the drunk. "Maharaj, a story, a story!" The man responded with a grunt and turned away, but the children continued to pester him until Maharaj gave in, blinked, bleary-eyed, and expelled a lengthy widemouthed yawn.

"Do you know," he said, "that no one is ever allowed to leave Kashi? We are prisoners here. The city lets visitors in, lets them out, but does not let them *back* in." He tucked his arms beneath his head and, with half-shut eyes, proceeded to explain that the divine gatekeeper of Kashi, the Lord Bhairav, did not let just *anybody* stay in the City of Light. "There are many people wanting to live here, and because they did not please Sri Bhairav they could not find any work, not even a piece of cardboard to sleep on. Remember that: those who live here do so only with Sri Bhairav's blessing. But that also means you can never leave, nah? Because if a god gives you a gift, you do not spurn it." Pramesh listened with half an ear. He'd heard the very same speech about Lord Bhairav from some graybeard when he'd first arrived in the city.

"Another thing!" Maharaj said to the now restless boys. "Many is the poor soul who, having lived his life in Kashi, one day decides to take a small trip outside the city—perhaps he has the urge to visit a family member or some far temple. Whatever the reason, no sooner does the man set one foot on the earth beyond Kashi, just *one toe* on that common soil, and hai Rama, his heart stops, a snake bites him, a stone falls from the sky and breaks his skull. Just like that. Dead! Outside of Kashi the man loses his life, and all those years of being in the city are come to naught. Next thing he knows he is born again as some faraway laborer, and Kashi is out of his grasp for another lifetime."

Pramesh finished his bath and his prayers and dried the river from his body. He laughed quietly to himself as he secured his dhoti. Shobha's father came from a long line of Banarasis. If he was willing to send his sole offspring out of the city along with his new son-in-law, then surely Lord Bhairav was not as unforgiving as Maharaj made the god out to be. He shook his head and looked over at his neighbor in the river, a scrawny man who insisted on keeping his spectacles on as he poured water over his head from a brass lota. "Sometimes the drunk man is also the wise one," the man said to no one as water streamed down his head.

"Plenty of people come and go, Bhai," Pramesh said. "Half the people in this city would be shut out of their homes if what he says were true."

"How do you know they aren't?" the man retorted. "And who are *you* to say what is and isn't true?"

Pramesh made a gesture of apology and stepped back into the water to offer his salutations to the sun one more time, as well as a prayer. He prayed that the old manager would not decline further while he and Shobha were gone, that the journey would be without incident, and that his family would give Shobha the welcome she deserved. As he opened his eyes, he saw a vulture, loose from its clambering brethren that bickered on the washed-out sands of Magadha, circle and swoop in front of him, aiming for an object floating in the middle of the river.

As he sat waiting in the train station, the familiar weight returned to his chest. He should have waited; he should have forced Sagar to join him in the city and then kept him there, away from the Elders. *Who are you?* that bathing man had asked. A day later, he'd get an answer to that question. Even now, remembering his father's voice sent the hairs on his arms standing on end: *You are nobody.* He shifted on the bench, willing those thoughts to leave him. A low rumbling came to save him; the station stirred and stretched, and everything that had previously been still came back to raucous life.

"Your bags, Sahib, your bags!"

"This way, this way, this way. . . ."

"Ah, Bhai, so many years, nah? Why so long in coming?"

"Madam, need transport, need directions, need guide?"

Pramesh watched the crowd from his bench until the train he was waiting for trundled past. He stood, and when the relative disembarked—a short and bearded man who looked terrified in the mass of people until Pramesh introduced himself—he led the way through the station, putting a hand out to give the many bodies before him a gentle nudge as they made their way to the exit. More crowds clustered around the doors, the usual group of touts vying to win over the bewildered newcomers, each man claiming that his hostel was the best in the city. Then a familiar name reached his ears.

"This way! This way to Shankarbhavan!"

He turned.

"Shankarbhavan, the holiest of lodgings in the holiest of cities! This way!"

Pramesh found the tout just outside the door, a half-chewed toothpick dangling from the corner of his mouth. The man's gaze was on the crowd, pupils moving quickly, fingers shuffling a pack of small white cards. Pramesh pushed through and the tout noticed him. The man stared back before recalling himself. "Lodging, Sahib? Just yourself? Any family, any bags?"

"Have you no shame?" Pramesh said, his voice vibrating with anger. "You men know these families have no money. They journey great lengths—must they also contend with such men as you, pretending to take them to Shankarbhavan but leading them elsewhere?"

The man kept his eyes on the crowd, a look of bored indifference plastered on his face. "And what about me, Sahib? Will Rama feed me if I sit all day at the station, calling out for alms?" He flicked the cards through his fingers, scanning the crowd. "If you change your mind, Sahib," he said, and he flicked a card at the manager before diving against the current of people and renewing his call.

Pramesh bent down for the white card, now muddied in the damp earth. *Shankarbhavan*, it read. *The premier luxe hostel of the great God's city.* The address was listed below, in a part of the city entirely untraversed by Pramesh but which he knew by reputation. He frowned and stuck the card into his pocket. He turned back to the relative who'd been waiting with a nervous smile on his face some paces away. "My apologies, ji," he said to the man, and led the way back to the real Shankarbhavan.

Only later, when he fished the card out of his pocket, did he think on what the tout had said, how he'd looked at him. He remembered his cousin's body in the airless jail cell, Bhut's wonder at the dead face exactly like the living manager's. He rubbed his eyebrow, thinking of the white slashed scar that his cousin had in that same spot. Had the tout seen Sagar?

His heart twinged, but then another voice—one he'd been practicing for many weeks now—interrupted his thoughts. *Detach.* He took the card and tossed it into one of the drawers in his desk, willing himself to forget.

21

She saw the return address first. It was written in a clear hand on the back of the envelope, while the front bore the bhavan's address in equally sure script. The old postmaster pushed the letter through the space between the metal grille and into her hands, and Shobha tried to keep her features placid as she walked down the lane, her stomach fluttering.

The vegetable sellers that day were surprised by Shobha's amiability. They knew to expect ruthless haggling, accusations of week-old greens, and even threats from the bhavan mistress to forever forsake their stall for a rival offering fresher produce—yet today, Shobha accepted what the sellers gave her without protest. When she distributed her coins among them without questioning their prices, they stared at her in surprise. As she departed, the one who sold greens rubbed his face with the end of his scarf and clucked his tongue. "Perhaps she is ill," he said to his neighbor.

Shobha's pace quickened as she neared Mrs. Mistry's to pick up Rani. "She fell earlier and scraped her knee," Mrs. Mistry explained as Shobha kept tight hold of the child's hand, lest she run back into the Mistry house to rejoin the other children. "Just a small cut, but how the blood ran, poor little one." Shobha checked over the wound and reassured her neighbor, but Mrs. Mistry continued. "Such a good child, she was so still as I bandaged it, and now she's so happy to see her Mummy, isn't she?" The older woman tweaked the girl's cheek and then launched into a story of some funny thing her grandson had just done. Shobha was almost in agony as she waited for the end of this interminable tale, which Mrs. Mistry at last concluded.

Shobha swept through the bhavan gates, exchanged sandals for house slippers, and flew past the courtyard and into the kitchen, Dev's voice following her as he read aloud. Rani pulled on Shobha's sari as her mother dropped the market bag to the floor. "I know, beti, almost time for your snack." Shobha put the child's favorite wooden horse into her waiting hands. "Your Mummy is very bad. Just a moment, I only have to run upstairs and then I promise you will get your milk." She ran to the privacy of the bedroom, the envelope already half open by the time she reached the top of the stairs.

There was only a single sheet of paper, folded thrice. Overwhelmed, her eyes could not focus on the text. She pressed the paper against her chest and forced herself to look out the window at the Mistry terrace, populated with grandchildren, as she counted to ten. Calmer, she held the letter out before her once again. The message was short. There was no greeting, and there was no signature.

> *There was a letter someone sent. A letter asking about me.*
> *I am here. I am well.*
> *But when will he be here? My husband's brother.*
> *He said he would come.*
> *We are waiting. Write soon.*

Shobha reread the lines. She had hoped for a letter from the father, or whoever else was still living in Pramesh's childhood home, but she never expected a note from the woman herself. The paper was coarse and smudged with dirt, and the handwriting was rushed but precise, different from the letter acknowledging receipt of the land. *He said he would come.* The words conveyed a promise made, a prior communication. As if a return was not just required, but expected. Why would she think he might visit?

The older one. She wanted him specifically.

The unease that had simmered quietly in her stomach since the postmaster had placed the letter in her hands rose to a boil. She unlocked one of the many drawers in her almirah and slipped the letter in among a pile of old bangles. So eager for it an hour before, she could not bear to look at the letter now.

What could Kamna possibly want Pramesh to do for her in the village? How long did she mean for him to stay there? And what of herself and Rani? Did she expect them to come or stay behind? Shobha descended the stairs and settled herself in her customary place with the market bags before her, and glanced at the other corner of the kitchen.

Rani was not there.

She turned about the room, walked out to the courtyard, and then noticed her husband's office door was open. Rani was sitting in his chair, blood running down her leg from the cut on her knee, and Pramesh was kneeling beside her, dabbing the flow with some cloth that was rapidly turning crimson. Fear gripped her heart.

"What happened?"

Her husband continued to dab, turning the cloth to a clean and dry edge until it was completely soaked through. He motioned over his shoulder, and Shobha grabbed another clean scrap from the ragbag Pramesh had upturned over his desk. "Hold it to the cut," he said, not looking at her. As Shobha pressed the cloth to her daughter's knee, Pramesh wet another clean rag and wiped away the red still clinging to Rani's skin. The girl was quiet, still hugging her wooden horse, and she smiled up at her mother when Shobha stroked a lock of hair away from her eyes.

"I found her like this," Pramesh said once the leg was clean and he dabbed peroxide on the cut while Rani whimpered. "So much blood . . . if her eyes had not been open I would have thought. . . ." He did not finish the sentence, but there was a quiver in his voice. Then Pramesh's voice was tight. "I did not know where you were."

She had never heard that tone from him before, and any explanation about being upstairs for just a moment—but had it been only a moment?—died on her lips. "She fell at the Mistry house," she managed to say. "But it was just a scratch; I don't know how it could bleed so much." The girl's knee continued to ooze small beads of blood, and Pramesh had to bind the wound with several tight wraps of cloth. He seemed about to say something else, and then they heard a voice calling Rani's name. Mohan poked his head through the door.

"The Mistry grandson insists on seeing this one," he said. Rani perked up and pushed herself off the chair before Shobha could stop her, no worse for her injury. Out in the courtyard, Mrs. Mistry's grandson presented Rani with a toy, a set of flat wooden blocks joined with thin yellow ribbon, and he showed the girl how to hold the end so that one block seemed to magically cascade down the others, as if shimmying down a ladder. Shobha felt her fear subside as Rani took the toy and repeated the trick over and over with ease, her joy evident, showing it to Mohan, to Pramesh, even running to Narinder as he walked with his prayer beads.

But that night in bed, wave after wave of shame washed over Shobha. Pramesh lay next to her, and she again heard the accusation in his voice, asking where she'd been. At the same time, the letter would not be expunged from her head. *When will he be here? He said he would come.* A low sigh escaped her lips. She raised a hand to wipe the wetness from her eyes, and felt her husband roll toward her and wrap his arm around her waist. "How can anyone doubt?" he murmured, half asleep.

She felt the warmth of his body like the familiar comfort of a blanket. For a moment, her thoughts were blissfully silent. She nestled closer and felt the strong grip of her husband's arm. "Doubt what?" she asked.

He was silent for so long that she thought he'd fallen asleep, but then he yawned and rested his chin atop her head.

"Rani," he said, his voice heavy with sleep. "Did you see her face, the happiness there? How can anyone think she is half a child?"

"I don't know," Shobha whispered. There were so many things she was unsure of, and yet this single incontrovertible moment seemed capable of eviscerating all doubt, shame, and guilt. "I don't know."

22

Rani seemed to have forgotten the desperate howling of the pots that had made her wake crying in the night: she was up before any of them. As if to make up for the frequent colds she'd suffered in the past few weeks, she now bounded about the bhavan with renewed energy, running around the courtyard, tugging at Loknath's sacred thread as he attempted to read the mantras aloud, hiding beneath the spare bed in room No. 5 as Sheetal's father eyed her indifferently. Seeing Shobha losing her temper, Pramesh scooped the child up to take her out to the ghats to run around.

At Lalita ghat, Rani joined a trio of children chasing a brown and white dog, and Pramesh sat down on the steps and watched their play. Men gossiped loudly enough for a few errant words to reach the manager's ears, a group of boatmen stood in a circle in a haze of beedi smoke, and a holy man paced the steps and muttered beneath his breath.

He found himself thinking about Govind, his conclusion that Sagar had a specific desire, that the ghost would keep wandering until that want was fulfilled. But there had been so many things denied to Sagar while he lived—how could Pramesh pick the most urgent one? A life of his own, without the influence or criticism of their toxic Elders. A true companion, a reliable woman to share the burden during life's trials. Land unmarred by mismanagement and negligence.

His eyes followed the swift currents of the river. Whenever he felt Rani was straying too far, he called after her, and the children responded by moving up the stairs to play near him. He turned back to the river, to the bobbing boats that lined the lowest ghat step in neat rows two deep.

Some men walked along the line of boats, engrossed in talk that soon grew more agitated as one of them, a young man smoking beedis with a manic speed, threw up his hands and said something that made his companions laugh unkindly. "Don't complain to us—lodge a report with Bhut," one of the men cackled.

Another turned and pointed at Pramesh with a glint in his eye. "The dead man's twin is right there. Blame him, if you must blame someone."

The manager's mood darkened as the young boatman stalked off, his laughing companions following. The last man in the group, who had neither laughed nor smiled when his friend singled out the manager, hesitated near the boats. Then he mounted the steps and sat down next to Pramesh. "You must forgive my friends, ji," he said, eyes toward the river. "Raman, you see. . . . His boat is the one your twin took out on that night. He's had trouble getting any passengers, even after exorcizing the boat. No one will trade or take it off his hands."

Pramesh nodded. "I am sorry for him," he said, and he realized that he really was.

"Was he—your cousin, I mean. . . . Was he fond of boats?"

"We were country boys, farm boys. Neither of us had any business on the water. I don't know what he was thinking, where he meant to go." He looked at the river's far shore, a stretched ribbon of white in the distance. "He could have been going to Magadha, for all I know."

Before he'd come to Kashi, he had heard about Magadha: a cursed ghost land, the most unfortunate place to die. Yet despite the warnings and superstitions, over the years he had seen the occasional boat on the far shore and people moving about that sandy beach. Walking, talking, laughing, even picnicking! The trip was a fad among young people especially, who scoffed at their elders' warnings and gathered friends for an afternoon in the sun.

The boatman looked out into the distance. "Do you think he was one of those who tried?"

"Tried what?" Pramesh glanced at the man. "Going to Magadha? At night and by himself?" The boatman raised his eyebrows and wagged his chin slowly. "That seems foolish," Pramesh said.

The boatman offered a beedi to Pramesh and then lit it for himself when the manager declined. The smell of smoke wafted up to the hostel manager like an invitation to speak, but he said nothing as he stared at the river with its swollen surface and undulating ripples, and at the desolate far shore. The boatman's beedi grew shorter until it dissolved into a stub of ash. "Never foolish, ji," he said, more to himself than to the manager. "Desperate—yes. But not foolish. Not if they mean to meet the Bearer." Pramesh fixed him with a quizzical look, and the boatman clarified. "The young, the dying. You've been in the city long enough to know—surely?"

Half-listening, Pramesh shook his head and glanced over his shoulder. Behind him, Rani sat still while another girl carefully traced an outline of her hand with chalk on the stone. The girl was patient, and his daughter seemed so at ease. He did not want to take her home just yet.

"You surprise me, not knowing the story." The boatman lit another beedi and gestured to the far shore with his chin. "It's the last chance for a man who is dying before his time. Only if he's tried everything else, mind you, and he has no other recourse."

"And the Bearer simply appears? As easily as that?"

The boatman chuckled and then sucked his teeth. "It's not a joke, ji. The divine never appear without some effort." Pramesh made no response, and the boatman took the silence as encouragement. "The man has to go alone, no matter how weak he is, and then he must walk as far as he can, until he feels he will collapse and die right there on the sand. And then, when he is at the immediate point of dying—only then will the Bearer of Death come."

In spite of himself, Pramesh looked across the river at Magadha, as if he might see that divine being from his sitting place on the ghats. A chill rolled over his shoulders and down his neck, and he straightened his back. "Impossible. This is the city of the great God. Yamraj is forbidden here."

"In Kashi, yes. But on Magadha the Bearer is welcome." The boatman flicked away the ashes of his beedi and reached for another. "It's not an easy thing. The man must really be dying—only those so close to the edge of two worlds can see the Bearer of Death. And he must be alone as well. If a healthy man whose time has not yet come hovers nearby, then neither of them will be able to see Yamraj. But if the dying man does everything correctly, if he sees the Bearer, then he has his chance to plead with Yamraj to put down the noose and snatch his soul on another day. Perhaps the Bearer will listen. But there is no way to be certain unless that man actually tries."

All of this, the boatman explained, was a great risk. The moment had to be exactly right—too late, and the man ended up passing before touching his feet to Magadha; too soon, and Yamraj would never appear. There were folk who ended up dead on the far shore, having never seen the Bearer or having been denied their request; there was no way of knowing which.

"None of our books speak of such a thing, and no dying man has ever returned from Magadha suddenly healthy—news of such a feat would spread to villages and beyond. How can you take it seriously when there is no proof?"

"Who says there is none?" the boatman asked. He looked the manager in the eyes. "There *is* proof. There is a man who did this, and he survived to come back. But the change in him. . . . He may have received a reprieve from death, but the life he received thereafter was not the same as the life he begged the Bearer to extend."

Pramesh did not bother to hide his laugh. "I suppose this is a man who lived . . . when, exactly? In your grandfather's time? And it was a story that *his* father told him, and it passed down the generations until you, yes?"

"No. *Our* time, yours and mine, ji." The boatman ignored the disbelief plain on Pramesh's face. "You never saw him as he was before—young, quick, well-liked. They expected great things of him before he became ill. There was talk of sending him to Delhi, to a grand university, a government position, an advantageous marriage."

"Where is this man? I have never heard of or met him before."

The boatman laughed. "Oh, you have, ji. All of us have, though the wiser among us avoid him just as much as others sought him out before. He has changed, as I mentioned. He went looking for an extension on his life, and instead the Bearer provided him with a different kind of life entirely. But the body, the shell, remains."

Pramesh shook his head. "His name, then?"

"No one calls him by his birth name anymore. They all use the name the city gave him long ago." The manager stared back, uncomprehending. And then his breath caught in his throat. The boatman smiled. "Didn't I say you know him? Everyone knows him, from the smallest child to the oldest graybeard. He is impossible to avoid."

Pramesh looked back at the river, at Magadha. "Maharaj." He rolled this thought around his mind until he knew it to be true. "His name is Maharaj."

With no husband to think of or child to look after, Shobha enjoyed the quiet at first. But then she replayed the morning in her head and wished she hadn't been so short with Rani. She felt restless, unable to focus. She took herself upstairs, ostensibly to organize her saris, but soon enough her hands abandoned the task, cotton and chiffon in a heap on the bed, and she instead took out Kamna's letter from her almirah and read it over again.

That woman did not *have* to write a response, especially without knowing who exactly was writing to her in the first place. But she had. More than that, she had put something quite plainly into her letter, something that Shobha had not wanted to admit the first time: sorrow, floating off the page, suffusing the ink. The woman was a widow now, after all. How had it felt to get that letter from Pramesh detailing her husband's death? To have her last memory of her husband be a hurried farewell, never guessing that he would not come back, with not even a last look at his lifeless body, the chance to bathe the limbs and pray over it before it was given to the pyre?

In one ear, the warning from that female voice in a strange kitchen all those years ago, saying Kamna was a shameless woman, a runaway who forgot nothing. In the other ear, the farmer's wife. *She's had a difficult life*. And a gentle reminder from Mrs. Mistry, her friend, that the heart could sometimes fit more than one thought it could.

Shobha took a pen from her husband's desk. The ink was drying and the nib skipped upon the page. The finished letter was messy and short, but it was done, and she sealed it and affixed the stamp before she could change her mind.

> *Kamna-behan,*
>
> *I am Shobha, the wife of your husband's cousin, the writer of that letter you received.*
>
> *I am your sister. I am your friend.*
>
> *Please. Tell me what happened.*

23

Night after night, the clanging of the pots below wrenched Pramesh from his dreams, the unbearable sound rising in high shrieks that pierced the brain and dipped to aching lows that seeped into the bones. Down the stairs he went, Shobha following to cover him with a shawl, through the kitchen to the courtyard, into the cold needles of rain, past the guests who prayed or gave out startled cries, feet in inadvertent sync with the rhythm of the mantras echoing from Dev's throat (*Om Tat Sat*), to the washroom door. The priests had taken to stuffing their ears with cotton as they loudly read from their books, and Mohan slept with a shirt wrapped around his head. The dying remained motionless but for the shallow rise and dip of their chests, as if they heard nothing at all.

But one night, something happened. As Mohan unswaddled himself and tried to calm the guests, there came a new sound amid the din.

A low wailing rose from No. 8, the weaver's room, the human sound competing with the metallic lament across the bhavan. The voices belonged to the weaver's daughters. At first Pramesh thought someone had fallen ill. It had been so long since he'd been able to record a death in his ledgers that he'd forgotten the signals. He motioned to Mohan to check the guests while he tended to the pots.

But now he was unable to silence them. "Bhaiya," he whispered. Then, louder: "Bhaiya." He then yelled out the word, and it produced no effect besides waking a baby staying within the bhavan, whose wailing cries surpassed even the pots.

Trying to think of what else he might say, Pramesh turned to see what Mohan had found. As soon as his back was turned, the pots ceased and the washroom was quiet. Guests rimmed the dry walkway, the rain falling into the courtyard blurring their figures.

He entered the room and found Mohan crouched down near the weaver's head. The assistant looked up at him; something in his face made Pramesh's heart lift. "Dead, Pramesh-ji," Mohan said.

And with that, Pramesh's life and duties returned to him. The man's features, frozen in that wash of blankness universal to every corpse, brought clarity to Pramesh's mind. "Mohan-bhai, fetch the white cloth from the office cabinet," Pramesh said before turning to Dev. "It must have happened just a short while ago. Did you see him before you retired this evening?"

"I did," Dev said. "We gave him tulsi water in the early evening as we always do, and the chanting seemed to calm him."

The weeping daughters had no male chaperone. Shobha would be the one to talk to them; she would provide the solace they needed right now just as she had done many times before. She came at once at her husband's request. There remained just one more question: he needed to know if the man had said anything before his departure, and, if he'd managed the breath for speech, it was of utmost importance that Pramesh know *what* the man had said. For if the weaver had been able to form the divine name, if he had given a verbal indication that his mind was on that higher plane at his moment of passing, during the holiest month in the holiest city, then it would be a sure sign that his death was not only good—it was, in fact, the best death possible. Such a death, despite the banging and clanging of brass in the washroom behind him, would mean. . . . What? That the ghost that was once Sagar was finally weary of its in-between existence? That it would leave of its own accord?

While Mohan soothed the guests, the priests discussed who would take charge of the funeral in the morning. Pramesh retired to the family quarters. For the first time in weeks he realized just how exhausted he was, and with great effort he kept his flickering eyes from closing completely as he waited for his wife. The privacy curtain fluttered open, and she pulled it closed behind her.

"Rama," Shobha said. "He just said it once, but they are positive. The last word was Rama."

When morning came, it was difficult for the staff to assume the neutral look of detachment that was standard when someone passed. The priests, who, excepting the unflappable Narinder, had become affected to a point of listless torpor, responded to their duties with renewed vigor. In the absence of any male relatives, Pramesh headed to the marketplace to get the things needed for the rites while Mohan went to the ghats to negotiate with the Doms.

Children clad in school uniforms walked by, their books swathed in plastic bags to keep off the rain; an old vegetable seller with his dhoti rolled to his knobby knees pulled his laden cart, wares also covered with fluttering plastic, through the soft muddy lane. Maharaj was out, going from stall to stall and begging for work, a few coins, anything. He shuffled over, clay pot held tight against his body, and held his hand out to the manager. Pramesh took a long look at Maharaj's face, the crooked mouth that hovered between smile and frown, the blank eyes, trying to find some sign of the man who once lived within that shell. He dropped a few coins into the drunk's palm, hoping that the money might be used for food instead of home brew.

He wandered about, filling the market bag Shobha had given him: a coconut, flowers both in loose bundles and strung into a thick garland to wreathe the dead weaver's neck, spindles of cotton thread and hanks of jute rope to secure the bier. He strode deeper into the marketplace until he found Arjuna the tailor, who sat cross-legged on a cushion with various pins and needles protruding from his mouth. He sat in his hole-in-the-wall shop, working tiny sesame-seed stitches into the border of some filmy purple material, but stopped and took the pins out of his mouth when Pramesh approached. "Ah," the tailor said. "At last the man whose shirts I make but whose face I never see! What lucky day is this that brings you here?"

"We had a death today—last night, actually." Arjuna, already anticipating what the manager needed, released himself from his curled position and took two steps to the opposite side of the lane. His practiced hands rummaged through the haphazard stacks of cloth until he located what Pramesh needed and then he cut up the necessary lengths of each material and folded them into crisp rectangles, using one long fingernail to press creases into the cloth. "I was afraid you bhavan people had abandoned me after all these years and were going to someone else," he said as he folded the last piece of cloth. He caught the eye of a chai-wallah and held up two fingers.

"What do you mean?" Pramesh asked.

"Your assistant is still there, yes? I see Mohan walking around the marketplace almost every day, but he has not come to see me for funeral things in so many weeks! Where has he been going, then?" Just as Pramesh was about to chide the man for being oversensitive, the chai-wallah's running boy came toward them with a metal tray and two steaming glasses, and a familiar voice arose from behind the manager and the tailor.

"I'll join you for a glass." Kishore snapped his fingers at the running boy, and Pramesh felt a low burn kindle within him. In the next breath, he doused it.

"What is this that our tailor friend was saying to you, Pramesh-bhaiya?" Kishore asked "You've stopped visiting his shop? Has some rift occurred between you two?"

"No rift," Pramesh said, hoping to avoid the details. Kishore's look, however, quite plainly said he required more information. "We all know there is no pattern to death, whether it be the season of Shraavana or of the new year. We just happened to have a drought of death that ended recently. Nothing more."

"Very strange," Kishore said, blowing on his chai. If there was one place Kishore's eyes and ears did not reach, it was the bhavan. The families were too transitory for him to get any information out of them, and the priests, of course, could not be depended upon to divulge any gossip.

"Not so strange," Pramesh said, Arjuna looking between him and Kishore. "You can never tell—some weeks, nothing. Other weeks, the entire bhavan is emptied all in one day."

"But for a whole month?" Kishore persisted. Pramesh sipped his chai and rocked his chin. His entire body was stiff with wariness. "Didn't that Govind visit you? That batty low-caste fellow—an exorcist, once, wasn't he?"

"He and Narinder-ji are old friends," Pramesh said. He tried to keep his tone light. A green parrot flew overhead and landed behind Kishore. It seemed to fix its eye on Pramesh, turning its head one way, then another, before flying off.

"But I heard—"

"Pramesh-ji, Pramesh-ji!" Mohan was running as fast as his thin legs and nervous stomach would allow, choking on his breath as he fought his way through the lane. Maharaj ceased his begging and turned to stare; other folk stood and followed the assistant with their eyes.

"What is it?" Pramesh responded, relieved that he did not have to hear what Kishore thought was "perhaps" happening.

"Not dead," Mohan panted.

For a second—less than a second, less than the thought of a second—Pramesh believed the assistant was referring to Sagar. "No," he said. "Talk reasonable, Mohan."

"No, Pramesh-ji, it is true. I saw with my own eyes. He is not dead."

"Who?" Kishore asked with impatience. "Don't bray like a donkey when Rama has given you lips to speak with! Who is not dead?"

Mohan shook his head and bent down, struggling to regain his breath; tears had sprung in the corners of his eyes from his exertions. "The weaver," he huffed. "The weaver is not dead. He is as good as you or me or Kishore-ji here. Moving, talking, breathing. Pramesh-ji, he is alive."

For some folk, those with skin as weathered as their memories, there was no Green Parrot Girl, no Weeping Woman. People of a certain age knew the ghost by a different name.

Menaka.

They remembered the place where she'd grown up, the people who were her family. They knew her not only by her death, but by her life. And if later they forgot these things, it was because such a life is dull next to scandals, to ghosts, to demons and curses and hauntings. Like a torn bit of roti sitting next to a delicate confection—necessary, but lackluster. For those who remember, who were there when it happened, Menaka's story went like this:

Like all women, she lived her life within two families: the one she was born into, and the one she joined by marriage. The first family was large and bustling. She was the eldest of four, three girls and a boy. Her father was a lawyer, her mother a beauty. Her two younger sisters were mischief-makers who raided her makeup tin. Her father was a silent man who brought home new dresses and a full set of bangles for each girl every holiday. Her mother scolded her for sitting at the window and dreaming. Her brother was the baby, and he followed her around like a living doll.

From this family, this happy first life, she entered a new one. The family she married into was smaller: her husband, his younger brother who was away at boarding school, and his mother. The wedding was large, and loud, and filled with happiness and hope. In the afternoon sun, her red sari shot through with gold, her hennaed hands clasped firmly in her husband's as they circled the sacred fire, she looked almost divine. A golden couple. The guests dispersed, bellies bursting with the wedding meal, sated with the good feeling that comes with witnessing the beginning of a happy story.

After that, Menaka disappeared.

There might be the odd sighting in the street, or a glimpse of her from her perch at an upper-story window. She might be walking with her mother-in-law, the woman's hand firmly on her elbow, going to the market and back again, stopping to talk to no one. It was like she was not there: the girl walked with her head down, her sari end pulled tightly over her face and arms.

Those who remembered the mother-in-law were not surprised. Likely, the woman had expectations that Menaka's mother never had—strict timetables for the preparation of all meals, rules about the clothes she might wear, endless lists of chores.

Nor were those who remembered the son surprised. He also had his expectations. She had her duties as a wife.

Soon enough, a child grew within her belly. For a time, Menaka reappeared. Her mother-in-law assumed some of the chores and paraded the girl in the streets, a proud hand on Menaka's belly as that old woman stopped to talk to friends. Menaka spent the last month of her pregnancy confined to her bed—not in her childhood home, as was tradition, but in her mother-in-law's room, as decreed by that woman and her son. Days passed, until the moment arrived—she gave birth to a girl who screamed so loud and long that the entire street could hear her arrival.

But the silence of the day's end told a new truth: the child was dead. Two months later, the mother followed, body sprawled in a tangled heap on the last steps of Mir ghat.

Must a ghost always be as extraordinary in life as it becomes in death? Many folk simply float through life unnoticed, until one day they are gone, and the hole they create with their absence is like a pinprick in fabric: hard to see, and easy to pull the fibers back into place. They live, they die, and one day they are forgotten.

Except. . . . When Menaka died, she didn't leave. She stayed, tied to the place she had last set foot while living. And because her spirit remained, albeit as a ghost, her story remained as well. Folk from the outskirts or from far-off neighborhoods had their own theories. But the people who had known Menaka—who remembered the life of the maiden girl and the married woman—had no doubts. They decided that they knew exactly what had happened, and who had done it. How easy, they said, to move from pushing a girl around in the home to pushing her down some steps at the river's edge? And how convenient, they said, that it took place in the middle of the night, when there was no one to see? They were so certain that, before long, what they believed became what they said. What they said became what they remembered. And what they remembered became the truth.

PART III

24

In every town there are people who, despite bad weather and ill omens, cannot sit still within the comfort of their own thoughts. Even when monsoon downpours force others into dry spaces, this other breed of folk moves about the deserted lanes and empty alleys, ears alert, happy just to be outside in the world, wanting only to be able to say later in proud tones, "I was there when it happened, Bhaiya! No one knows the story better than I!"

On the day that Mohan let loose the news of the weaver who had died only to return to life, more than a dozen such curious bystanders loitered outside the bhavan gates, eager for the chance to witness key pieces of what would doubtless become an oft-repeated story. They had seen the urgency with which the manager, his assistant, and Kishore hastened to the bhavan, and they followed after, drawn by the excitement in the air. Because business always trails a crowd, a paan-, a chai-, and a snack-wallah all set up temporary shop in the narrow lane. In between morning chews of tobacco and sips of chai, the onlookers updated each other on what had happened, and entertained theories about what would happen next, each man supporting his version with a story of a similar event, of which they all had at least one or two to tell.

"Dead, they say, and now back to life!"

"My father had a cow like that once. . . ."

"What if they were wrong? Probably the old fellow was alive all the time, and that Mohan made the mistake and started this whole drama."

"It's the rains, makes everyone a little crazy, nah?"

"But is he really alive after all? Do we know the facts?"

" . . . such a gentle animal, it used to eat grass straight from my hand. I cried when I heard it was gone. The second time it died, I mean."

True to his nickname, Bhut had stepped out of a side lane to observe the crowd and peer through the gates unseen. His house had been quiet when he'd left—for once, neither of his sisters had commenced the day by rehashing the quarrel from the previous night—and his mood had been light, his mind curious about the city folk's latest mania. The familiar street made something within him harden, like a clenching muscle he could not relax. He could feel eyes on him from above.

"Officer-sahib—chai? Pakora? Will you take some refreshment?"

"Keep the lane clear," Bhut barked in answer. He turned away from the bhavan, where more men clumped outside to peek through the bars of the gates, heedless of the order.

Though the bantering men outside the building did not know it yet, Mohan had spoken the truth: the weaver was indeed alive. With Kishore at his elbow, the manager hastened to the room of the man he had left for dead. He could read the truth in everyone's eyes. His wife, the priests, the other guests—their faces all held a mixture of bafflement and fear. The sight that met him in the weaver's room was no more comforting. The man's daughters appeared just as Pramesh had left them: two weeping girls, the older just on the cusp of womanhood, clutched at each other for support. The father, that skeletal man who had been a mere cold body just a half hour ago, flailed in weak motions on the concrete floor, his blankets tangling in his limbs and his eyes streaming with tears as he cried out, "Rama! Oh, Rama, Rama, Rama!"

So it was true. The man repeated the holy name over and over again, each cry setting a new weight on the manager's chest. It could mean only one thing. The man had reached the great God, had been at the point of assimilating his spirit into the divine Supreme Soul, only to be torn away and pulled back into life at the crucial moment.

Pramesh returned to the courtyard, where he could breathe easier. "How could this happen?" he murmured to Narinder. That old priest raised his eyebrows, but said nothing. The manager's question rippled out and echoed among the male guests who, like the curious men beyond the gates, clustered in the courtyard and outside their rooms, while the women formed their own group. A few ventured to the manager's family quarters, where they found Shobha waiting near the window, her hands absently picking over a thali of lentils for stones while Rani played nearby. She was anxious, but when the others asked her what was going on, the manager's wife only held her hands up, palms out, requesting patience. "Wait," she said. "I am sure we will all find out soon enough." To help the minutes go faster she tried to engage the women in light talk about their children and the homes they had left behind. Some responded, some remained silent, but in this way they passed the time. They were women, after all—their condition was not new. They had waited for other answers before, and they would find themselves waiting again many more times in their lives.

Of all the people in the bhavan, Kishore alone remained unruffled. "The man is certainly able to speak," he said. "Can you not ask him?"

"What would we ask?" Pramesh said, surprised. "What could he possibly tell us?"

"If he saw anything, heard anything. Words, a vision, something. One cannot go through such an experience with no memory of it." There was a hunger in his tone that Pramesh did not like, but the guests around him heard the ghaatiyaa and clearly expected an answer.

"Narinder-ji," he turned to the priest. "Would you?" The older man tilted his chin in assent. Pramesh followed him back into the weaver's room and was overwhelmed with terrible visions: the weaver confessing before all that he had actually died, that the merits of a good death in a good month in the holiest city had almost bestowed several lifetimes of exquisite karma on his future generations, and that he had been turned back not by a wronged ancestor or the ill merits of his own past actions, but something else. Someone else. In the pit of his stomach Pramesh felt the realization unfurl like a thundercloud.

The weaver had died.

The pots had shrieked.

The weaver had lived.

Of course Sagar was to blame for the dreadful change. How naive he had been to believe that the ghost's presence would impact the bhavan no more than a spider weaving its web in a high ceiling corner. All those weeks, with no death breathing activity into the bhavan, families arriving with hope and leaving with uncertainty. He knelt with a quaking heart as Narinder endeavored to communicate with the wailing weaver. After the intonation of the sacred syllable, the OM on whose breath Narinder began every religious rite, he began his interrogation. "Do you know who you are?" he asked.

"Rama," was the startling reply. Here was an explanation even Pramesh had not foreseen. The divine, come down to the bhavan through this vessel? For an instant, Narinder looked as if he had lost his famous composure, but the skeptical clicking of Kishore's tongue goaded the priest.

"Do you know *where* you are?"

"*Rama*," the weaver said.

"Do you know who these are?" Narinder persisted, pointing at the two daughters.

"Rama!" the weaver shrieked. He could not speak a word beyond that divine name, and any other syllable he attempted exited his mouth stillborn, his toothless gums smacking with the useless motions of a dog that can no longer chew. If he had seen or heard anything during his soul's flight and subsequent return, the secret remained locked within him, at least for now. And *now* was time enough for Pramesh to feel a temporary relief that the washroom and all its supernatural doings of the past months would not reach the ghaatiyaa's ears, and therefore the city's.

"Perhaps you need to bring a doctor," Kishore said once they were all again in the courtyard. "Someone to check this fellow out, nah?"

"Ji—this is a house of death," Pramesh said, careful to control his tone. "We've never had reason to call for a doctor."

Narinder touched the manager's shoulder with gentle fingers. "Perhaps we should discuss this elsewhere?" he suggested, his eyes indicating the guests who had attained a miraculous silence, ears straining to hear every word. Pramesh led the priest, the ghaatiyaa, and Mohan to the family quarters.

The gathered women covered their heads and filed out, and Shobha, happy to have a concrete task, served the men chai. As they talked and sipped, Shobha coaxed Rani to her side and slipped to the weaver's room to check on the weaver's daughters. She'd felt an affinity for them in those early morning hours, having understood their pain; hadn't she lost her own father in this very house? But now she tapped on the door with hesitation—she may have experienced a father's death, but she had certainly never experienced his rebirth. The sisters were crying, but were those tears of sorrow, joy, or both? Did they require sympathy or a show of happiness? She instead turned to the weaver. With the same gentle words used to soothe Rani before setting the child to bed, she persuaded the agitated man to lie still and tucked the blankets back around him. She met the eyes of his daughters, and their sobs subsided. "This is extraordinary," she said, sitting down, unsure how to continue. Rani stood next to her, leaning against her shoulder, pushing jasmine from the courtyard into the hair coiled at her neck. She decided to be frank. "What will you do?"

The older daughter swabbed her wet cheeks with the end of her dupatta and used the same soaked cloth on her sister's face. "They say this is a holy place," she said, her voice skipping with tears yet unshed. "We know that now."

"What do you mean?"

"All night we prayed," the older one continued. "We have been praying for days, and fasting too. Neither of us has taken anything but milk since arriving. When our father passed, we wanted to die too. Who else could look after us two in the whole world? When everyone went back to sleep, we decided to take all of Pa's sleeping pills between us." She showed the clear brown glass bottle to a bewildered Shobha. "We split them, one pile for each of us, and we decided to take them just as the sun came up, but we wanted to say one more prayer. We each made one more round on our prayer beads to the great God."

"And then?"

"He came back." The younger one choked on a sob, and her older sister smiled and squeezed her. The tears ran afresh down their faces, around the corners of their smiles.

"And your plans now," Shobha faltered. "Will you leave?"

The older one rocked her chin from side to side. "As soon as we can, with your and the manager's blessing. We'd thought this place would be our end. Instead, life is beginning." The girl's face broke out with such glowing radiance that anyone would have thought the monsoon had ended and the sun had returned. "Our father has such a gift, another life within this life, nah? Rama could not take him knowing that we were so unprotected. Now we will go home and Pa will settle everything."

Dismayed, Shobha could see that the girls foresaw a future no one else had considered: a father come back full strength who would regain the faculty of mind needed to manage his household and choose proper husbands for his two unmarried girls. The sheer implausibility of it! She wanted to tell these two innocent joyful daughters that yes, their father was alive, but that was as far as the great God's gift could go. Life, after all, did not automatically extend into *living*, being present and cognizant in the world. That was another gift entirely, and not one the weaver was likely to receive again. The girls rubbed their faces, sending a rush of vibrant pink to their cheeks and noses, happiness exuding from their pores.

A vision came to Shobha, an image of a pair of girls praying with the intensity of wizened sages; they held their prayer beads in their right hands, and in their left, a trove of white pills like some sort of toxic pearl. She shuddered. To go from one dead body to one living man was something, but how close they had come to going from one dead body to three! Pramesh would have been shattered by two suicides. *There is a blessing in everything*, Shobha's father used to say; she sat with living proof of the statement's truth. "Hai Rama," she murmured under her breath.

The younger daughter clasped Shobha's hand and smiled. "Yes," she said, not seeing the distress in Shobha's eyes. "Say the God's name—we will never hear it enough after this."

The four men sat in the airy corner room and fiddled with their empty chai glasses. They had reached an impasse. Though Kishore had been at his most persuasive, Pramesh would not agree to bring a doctor to Shankarbhavan. "Their skills only extend to the living," he said. "Once the body begins to deteriorate, there is nothing they can do. They cannot even predict the timing of the event. With death they are as helpless as any of us."

The ghaatiyaa sighed and rubbed his brow. The expensive embroidered shawl he wore had slipped from his shoulders, but he did not bother to adjust it. Irritation crept at the edge of his voice. "Tell me," he said. "Are we spinning thread from nothing? Are you absolutely sure that this weaver was dead to begin with? What if he has been alive all along, and this is an empty drama we are debating?"

Mohan, silent all this time, spoke. "The soul had flown," he said. "We were all witnesses. The spirit had flown! Why would it come back?" The assistant seemed to perspire sincerity, brow glistening with sweat, shirt damp in patches under his arms and on his back. The ghaatiyaa looked to Pramesh. The manager, after all, was in charge, and besides the weaver's daughters and Shobha—who, being women, no one thought to ask—only he and Mohan had seen that the man was dead. Only they knew the truth that, if known, would lead back to the washroom and Sagar's ghost. The answer Pramesh gave the ghaatiyaa this day would be the tale subsequently spread across the city, and in the years to come folk would look at him and his family and see not the faces of Pramesh and Shobha and Rani but *that story*. Bhut's warning rang out in his head, and he thought of the circle officer's two older sisters and the tale that had doomed them to spinsterdom. If he was not careful, he would ensure the same fate for his daughter.

"It is possible we were wrong," he began. Despite Narinder's sharp look and Mohan's audible gasp, he continued, his mind clearer with every word. "It was so early in the morning, perhaps we were all tricked by weariness."

Kishore's eyes hardened. "Then *who*," he pressed, "was the one to say the fellow was dead to begin with?" In that moment, if Pramesh had looked Mohan full in the eyes—he who had trailed by his side for so many years, who had shared his meals for so many nights, who had assumed the kindness of a blood uncle to Rani and a brother to Shobha—he might have lost his courage, for even a lie takes courage, though of a certain kind. But Pramesh did not look at his assistant. He thought only of Rani, and of getting the bhavan to the day of tripindi shraddha so that the ghost would leave and this entire thing could be forgotten.

"Mohan-bhai," he said. "It was dark in the room, nah? The weaver's daughters were wailing so loudly—you would not be the only one to make the mistake."

Mohan stood up, his agitation causing him to drop his steel tumbler to the concrete floor where it clattered and rolled to a stop at Narinder's feet. "It was no mistake, Pramesh-ji! The man was dead. I swear on the Mother!"

"No," Pramesh said. He had to make certain that none of the men would doubt what he was about to say. He looked straight at his assistant, feeling Kishore's eyes on him. He spoke so that even the guests loitering outside the room heard every word. "No, Mohan-bhai," Pramesh said. "You are wrong. It was a mistake. The weaver must have been alive the entire time. He was never dead."

25

The story that a disgusted Kishore left the bhavan with, that he shared in moody clipped sentences with the audience waiting outside, was based on a lie, but how could anyone know that? As the wandering gossips dispersed themselves and the tale across the city, they came to see it as something to be laughed at. "Imagine!" they said. "We all thought it was something extraordinary with a man who had died only to come back to life, and instead it is *this*!" And *this*, this joke, now made the rounds in and out of people's mouths. "I have many faults," the harangued husband, the underpaid office clerk, the child who'd come home with a rip in a brand-new frock all said, "but at least I know enough to see if a man is dead or not, ji."

Those bhavan folk had gone for so long without anything to do that they'd deluded themselves into believing that which could not be, the city said. What other excuse was there for such an idiot mistake? Even dogs could tell the difference between dead and alive. A man who couldn't was either drunk, aggrieved, or stupid, and while no one accused the bhavan manager of any of those three maladies, most people assumed Mohan to be afflicted with the last.

Mrs. Gupta knew better than to try the joke with Mrs. Mistry, but she repeated the lines loudly in the lane outside her house, within the bhavan's hearing, always on the watch for Shobha. Bhut, well known for his short temper, broke up several groups of laughing deputies with his mere presence, yet when he arrived home for lunch he tried the joke on his sisters, heart bloated with hope. Those two women sniffed in contempt and instead started on their latest grievance. They were not the only ones who refused to laugh. Mrs. Chalwah heard the joke from her daughter-in-law, who came in smiling with the chai tray and then had to retell the story to explain her mood. "I do not see the humor in it," the older woman said, her pace on her prayer beads stumbling.

Inside the bhavan, no one was laughing either, least of all Mohan. After Kishore left, the assistant had bolted out the bhavan gates into the solace of the city. Instead of the comfort he usually found, he encountered a group of his friends, all clustered in the marketplace, cackling so hard that some were bent, hands on knees, and a voice in the group saying, "At least he kept his head better than our Mohan at the bhavan, nah?"

All Mohan wanted was a confirmation that he had been right, that the weaver had died. But when he broached it with the manager, he was met with only a long stare, eyes that did not even seem to see him. "It will pass. It will end, Mohan-bhai. And anyway—"

The manager never finished his sentence. Something caught his eye outside his office, and he held a hand up to Mohan, hurrying to the courtyard, where the woodworker from No. 11 stood, surrounded by his family entourage of eight, their belongings packed and the women readying their dying mother for travel.

"Hemant-ji, surely you are not leaving?" the manager said. "Your mother hasn't been here the full two weeks. There is still time." A few days before, the weaver himself had departed, his daughters supporting his limp form on the rickshaw ride to the train station. The woodworker led Pramesh to a corner of the courtyard and faced him with folded palms.

"Ji," he said. "You have been good to us, and at any other time we would be happy to stay. But you must understand." He gestured to the blanket-wrapped bundle just inside No. 11's door. "That is *Ma*. She is the only one I have, nah? If I have promised her death in Kashi—and I have—I must see my word through to the end."

"But these things take time, nah? No one can predict when the soul will go."

"No, no one can tell when," the woodworker answered with eyes that avoided the manager's. "But I know where it *cannot* happen, and I tell you, Manager-ji, it will not happen here."

Pramesh could not have been more offended if the man had made an insulting comment to his wife. "What do you mean? This is among the best places to die! With the word of God going in the ears, and the family present, the atmosphere for a steady mind—what else is needed?"

"What of the weaver?" the woodworker asked, looking up to meet Pramesh's eyes. "The other guests have been saying he was dead, and that this place would not let him go, and pulled him back to life. What of that?" Pramesh could say nothing to this. Of course they would not stay in such a place. He'd supposed, with a presumptuous and wishful heart, that the guests would trust him, that they were all bound together to wait out the ordeal. But they owed him nothing, these families that merely wanted to see their loved ones die so that they could go home and resume their own lives. "I am not a man of much knowledge, but there are some things I know," the woodworker continued. He kept his voice low, mindful of the ears that strained to hear his words from the other rooms. "How can I stay in this place where my mother cannot die? Better to set her in some quiet spot near the river, as long as she can pass in Kashi."

"But surely," Pramesh persisted, "you don't mean to live with your family on the street? How will you manage?"

"There are other places in Kashi," the woodworker muttered. "Other hostels, other rooms. . . ." The manager was aghast. This man could not mean to let his mother die in one of *those* unholy rooms, some cheap and loose place where dancing girls brought their customers and men brought their mistresses. Even after Pramesh explained all of this to the woodworker, the man would not budge. Palms folded once again, he inclined his head toward Pramesh and then turned back to his family. Within the hour, they were gone.

Several other families left as well, each muttering in the direction of the washroom, explaining with downcast eyes that they would be taking their dying folk elsewhere, or back home. A week after the weaver's departure, for the first time since the bhavan's earliest days, the hostel was almost empty. Each room held nothing but the single rope bed, the single washing bucket, the single neatly folded blanket. Families still trickled into Shankarbhavan, but they siphoned out just as quickly, deaf to Pramesh's half-hearted pleading. Only one room remained consistently occupied: No. 5, in which a steadfast Sheetal continued to care for his steadfast father.

"It does not matter to us," he explained to Loknath, "whether we are here, or back in the village, we would be doing the same thing, nah? If I can keep him here in comfort for as long as you are happy to let me, I will do so." And so Loknath and Dev continued to chant their mantras during every waking and sleeping hour and provided Sheetal's father with tulsi water and daily blessings. Beyond that, there was not much for any of them to do.

That night, when the pots screeched anew, the manager met them downstairs as he always did. The sound was unbearable, long needles inserted into his ears, and he felt a quailing sickness in his stomach that weakened his knees and sent bile rushing to the back of his throat. Still, he strode to the doorway and called out the word that would silence the vessels. But the pots were louder than his voice, and they continued to clamor, ignoring him. Pramesh stood fast, mustache trembling, hands clenched, and summoned all his breath to shout out the word "Bhaiya!" The word bounced off the washroom walls and echoed out into the courtyard. The pots instantly stilled, cowed by the anger in Pramesh's voice. His hands were shaking, and his chest heaved with a burning heat that traveled up to his ears and encased his head. He stood there, daring the pots to move, half hoping they would so that he might fling them against the cement walls or out the gates. He had never struck anyone in his adult life, but he felt as if the fire would burn him from the inside out if he did not forcibly expel it. He'd only encountered such a feeling once before.

Folk said that the young Pramesh and Sagar were inseparable, without a single quarrel or moment of ill will between them, but that was untrue. They were boys like any others, as prone to fight as they were to defend one another. Their disagreements ended as quickly as they began, like a piece of straw that catches fire and sputters and smolders down to ash in seconds. Only once had one of their fights turned violent.

The rains were a month overdue, the air was dry and burned in their throats, the ground hard and unyielding beneath their feet. The Elders had raised their voices at them that morning for not rising earlier, and though Pramesh protested that he was at fault for sleeping in, the two men had showered Sagar with the brunt of the blame, until Bua stepped in.

"Leave them," she said. "I have an errand for them to run, and it cannot wait." The Elders relented, grumbling as they stalked off. She handed Pramesh a cloth-wrapped bundle. "I borrowed this from Champa-behan. She needs it back today—take it to her."

Glad for the excuse to be out of the house, Pramesh pulled Sagar behind him. They hadn't gone far when they ran into Jaya walking with her cousin. She saw the angry red mark on Sagar's cheek immediately. "What happened to you?" she asked, reaching out, but Sagar knocked her hand aside.

"You're always in everyone's business, and you don't even live here," he said sharply. Jaya colored, cheeks flushing in imitation of Sagar's. Her cousin put his arm around her shoulder and roughly shoved into Sagar as he walked past.

"Nothing but the son of a drunk," the youth said, spitting behind him at Pramesh's feet.

Sagar stood frozen, looking after them. "You shouldn't have said that to her," Pramesh said after Jaya and her cousin were out of sight.

"And you shouldn't have argued with the Elders," Sagar replied. "Why couldn't you just keep silent for once?"

Pramesh turned to soothe his cousin, but he saw the darkness in Sagar's eyes and they continued the journey in silence. Sagar glanced behind him several times as they walked. But Jaya was gone.

Champa-maasi would not allow them to go without a tall glass of aam paana each. "Too hot for both of you to be out," she said, eyes on Sagar's face. Sagar held the cool glass to his cheek for a moment, then downed the drink and stood. "We have to leave," he said amid Champa-maasi's protests, and Pramesh ran after him. Back out in the heat, Sagar trudged a long meandering route across a wheat field, Pramesh following word-lessly, until they saw the tree looming before them.

The colossal peepal growing at the far edge of the field had been there for hundreds of years, or so the stories went. The dense branches were so thick and far-reaching that the canopy seemed wholly unattached to the massive trunk. With its age came veneration: holy string in shades of red and orange and sun-bleached pink was knotted in and around the corded trunk and the low-hanging branches and tied around a thick root that had burst upward out of the soil and plunged back deep into the ground. The string symbolized hopes and wishes and pleas directed to a power that had existed long before them and would continue long after.

Pramesh made a pilgrimage to the tree as often as he could. His mother had told stories of men overcoming illness when they drank milk steeped with the leaves, long-barren women growing heavy with child when they rubbed the smooth bark, bandits fleeing in terror if they happened to pull a victim into the tree's purview. He remembered following her on some errand and having to wait while she tied red thread and muttered prayers beneath her breath, Sagar's mother at her side doing the same. *Sometimes, a tree like this houses the soul of a great sage, come down to Earth to perform some penance,* his mother had said. *It's important to venerate that being, to show it respect.*

Back then, Sagar had helped, holding whatever the Mothers had been carrying so their hands would be free, mouthing the great God's name in imitation of the women. Now, he waited in the shade as Pramesh bowed and stretched out on his stomach before the trunk, lying prostrate, fingers reaching to touch one of the thick roots straining out like veins beneath and on top of the earth. When Pramesh rose, he brushed the dust from the roots onto his own forehead.

"Do you really think it makes any sort of difference? Bowing to a tree?" Sagar asked, still in a foul mood.

"I do not ask you to believe." Pramesh was certain his devotion to the tree had sped his recovery from illness years ago. Even now, he was not sure he could have made the journey from home to the neighbor's and back again if not for that blessing, that fruit of his firm belief.

"But *you* believe. What do you think will happen? Will it bring our mothers back?"

"Of course not. But it works for other things. I am stronger now because of it."

"That is because I dragged you out with me to walk the fields each day, not because of some tree."

Pramesh sighed. He remembered Sagar pulling on his arms with a firm but gentle grip, insisting he walk from their room to the front door one week, then farther out to the tree outside the veranda the next week, then even farther to this prayer tree. Pramesh had been terrified that his wasted legs would collapse, but Sagar walked behind him, and Pramesh continued forward.

Sagar would have to let go of his temper before they returned to the Elders. "The stories are not untrue, Bhaiya," Pramesh said. "Otherwise why would so many speak of them? Think of the schoolmaster—lame so long, and suddenly he visits the tree and rubs the leaves over his leg and it is as straight as yours or mine. Can you explain that?"

"That is just one story, and we do not know that the man was lame to begin with. Probably the leg was ready the entire time and he never bothered to try it out. Like you, at first. And what about the Mothers? All those years of dragging us here—what difference did it make?"

"They weren't asking for anything specific," Pramesh said. "They were just paying their respects."

"But they were. They were asking for the tree to make the Elders come to their senses. They were asking for them to stop drinking, to stop . . . to stop with us. And with them."

Pramesh froze. "How do you know that?"

"I heard Ma one day. *Remove the nazar from them both*, she said." He laughed, an ugly sound without mirth. "As if the problem came from some bad spirit, some evil eye attached to them, and not their own hands reaching for the bottle."

"Even if they did . . . it isn't just a story," Pramesh repeated, uncertain.

"Isn't it? Stories are not true. And there is not a single seed of truth there in your sacred peepal."

"There's truth and there's belief. Ma taught us about both things."

"Fine, then. Become like them, like those other fools in the village—believe any story you hear. Just don't let the Elders find out. You needn't remind them again."

"Remind them of what?"

"You know. That you are *not like us.*"

Not like us—their pact, a bond that grouped them on the other side of a line that divided them from the Elders. But this time, as he hissed out the words, Sagar crossed that line, joining the Elders and leaving Pramesh on his own. The words struck Pramesh like a blow across the face, and he swung around and clouted Sagar on the same cheek his own father had struck just that morning. *Not like us*—Sagar returned the blow, and then all restraint fell away. There were no Sagar and Pramesh, but only balled fists, cocked elbows, fast-moving feet. They rained blows down upon each other, the anger of one fueling that of the other, until a hand reached out and grabbed Pramesh's arm.

Both he and Sagar lay flat on their backs, their arms held in a grip as fierce as their tempers, the blue sky so piercing that it hurt to look at. Nattu, the limping herder living at the crossroads, held them down, and released them only on a signal from someone beyond them. When they sat up, they saw their aunt looming before them, fear in her eyes. Their anger changed to dread. The mottled purple bruising on their skin would not dissuade the Elders from beating them again. The rest of the day passed in silent anguish. The Elders came and went, eyes sliding over the boys without seeing them. Their aunt laid out the midday meal, then the evening meal. When it was dark, they went to bed. She blew out the oil lamp, but remained in the room, her form an eerie black shadow. And then her voice sounded in the dark.

"Do you not even know when you are cutting your own hand?"

Standing at the edge of the courtyard, Pramesh rubbed his wrists and looked at his palms, flexed his fingers. He felt the heat within him dissipate. Moments before, he'd been so angered that, had Sagar been there before him, he might have done some violence to the man. But what harm could a living man do to a ghost?

The next morning, Pramesh was up early waiting on Narinder to rise. The head priest closed the office door without a word and sat in a chair opposite Pramesh, his hands looking frail and naked without the prayer beads he usually held. He listened as the manager made his case for performing tripindi shraddha early, starting that very day, if possible. He sat and stared out the window for some time after Pramesh had finished speaking, and the manager waited, trying to discern from Narinder's blank face what he might be thinking. "You remember our chat with Govind-bhai a few weeks ago?" Narinder asked at last.

"I do," Pramesh said, wary.

"He advised you to try and find what the man wanted so badly that caused him to linger as a ghost to begin with," Narinder said, eyes still on the window. "Well? Have you thought more about why he was here?"

The rains had begun again, and a heavy patter of drops sounded. Pramesh felt a rising desperation engulf him. "There is nothing to think about. He had a bottle with him."

"You believe he'd been drinking?"

Sagar raising that bottle to his lips, speech slurred, eyes rimmed with red—Pramesh shook the thought away. "He could have intended to use it as a vessel for river water. Perhaps it was late at night when he arrived here, and our gates were closed. Then . . . then he went to the river."

"But that cannot be it. What else did he do that day? What was he doing *on* the river?"

The boatman's tale returned to Pramesh. Was Sagar ill? Yet what ill man would travel all that way to see someone he hadn't spoken to for a decade? He tried to picture Sagar in a boat, discarding a lifetime of skepticism to chase after a city myth. The image would not come clear in his mind.

"The only person to know those answers is someone who is dead—and he isn't telling us, no matter how loudly the pots bang every night," he said instead, his voice rising against his will. "What good is asking?

Why should I continue to think about him when I must detach? *The body is burnt and so should the memory be*—we tell our guests this. Why should I be any different?"

"And yet you *are* different," Narinder said, turning his piercing gaze on Pramesh. "Those who come to Shankarbhavan are old; they have completed all the hurdles of life and are here for that one final step. They are not young, like your cousin, nor do they have any reason to linger. We can tell those grieving families to detach because we know that their dead have already done so, have released themselves. Not so with you."

As the priest spoke, the manager noticed how old Narinder had grown. For the past ten years, that head priest had seemed as steady and unchanging a fixture in the bhavan as the iron gate. His routines played out each day with the regularity of the sun's rise and fall. His presence in the courtyard, reading from sacred texts or circling the walkway with his prayer beads, was so fixed that one guest, who had been at the bhavan to see his father die and who returned with his mother years later, remarked that the priest seemed never to have moved in all that time. But time had passed, and Narinder had aged. "So it was just a visit, or so you say. No other thing on his mind when he decided to come here."

Pramesh hesitated. "I don't know for sure. But if his life was an unhappy one. . . . And there was his wife. Sagar-bhai knew I had hated the marriage, for his sake. If something happened . . . perhaps he changed his mind. Perhaps he meant to see me, but died before he could."

"Your cousin's wife, his marriage: why did you hate it?" Narinder sat immovable.

"It was a business transaction, not a marriage," Pramesh said. "My Elders, hers—they didn't think about whether their children would be happy, whether the families could blend and benefit from each other. She was meant for me at first—I had married by the time I learned this. Then Sagar-bhai married her in my place. They took advantage of her, of my cousin and me."

"Advantage?" Narinder leaned forward. "How so?"

Pramesh sucked his teeth in irritation. "She was young when she married my cousin, but even then she had a history. A story behind her name. Village gossip."

Seeing that Narinder demanded more, Pramesh brought out the long-buried story. "She was a repeat runaway. She used to do it as a child all the time. One minute she would be sitting by her mother, helping in the kitchen—the next she would be gone. When her family found her, she was always off by herself somewhere, near a pond or in a field. They said that each time, she greeted them with a blank face; she did not understand their worry, did not heed their warnings never to do it again.

"Perhaps all of this was tolerated when she was a child, but the stories became worse as she grew. Now they said she was no longer alone when she ran away. She met men, one in particular, a rich man's son, heir to a great fortune in orchards and acres of land. She followed him everywhere without shame and refused to leave his side.

"He bound himself to her. They said she bewitched him—foolishness, all of it," Pramesh spat out the words like a poison he'd long held inside. "Perhaps there was truth to her wandering off as a child, Rama knows, but as for the man: more likely he pursued her first. Her parents knew of that other family's wealth and encouraged it. Then the man's family found out and sent him away, paid the girl's family to leave them alone. They ended up leaving the village for another place. And right after they left, the man died suddenly—likely of any common illness, but everyone said it was because of her. When her people entangled themselves with my family, it was because they needed to be rid of her, having ruined her name. And the Elders needed the money."

He'd always felt pity for Kamna. She was lost in a family like that, with little control over her life. He had been able to leave—but she couldn't. She was like his mother and aunt, bound to the person and the place their parents chose, with little recourse even when that person put bruises on them, on their children.

But how could such a girl, with such a family—elders to rival his own—ever be right for his cousin? After the upbringing they suffered, Pramesh was certain Sagar required someone equally strong, equally intelligent. He needed the chance at a real family, one that loved and protected, and a proper partner who was loyal and reliable—not more grasping elders, more dark stains on a name that was already burdened with plenty of its own whispered stories.

"Did your cousin know?"

"He was the one to tell me. On the day I learned of the marriage agreement. Her family, her name—I knew nothing of them. The family had been wandering apparently, going from village to village. Living in each place for a year at a time, then moving. Because of the stories, he said."

Narinder listened in silence, betraying no emotion. "And yet he married her anyway. Did he knew how you felt about it?"

Why must you walk where you were never meant to go? Pramesh squeezed his eyes shut. "He did. I told him he was throwing his life away. He refused to listen. We never spoke after that."

"And your elders, your father and uncle—why would they have condoned such a match? And for you, the eldest son?"

Pramesh stared at his desk, rubbing a finger along the top edge, back and forth.

Narinder coughed, cleared his throat. "So it was an ill-matched marriage. Perhaps she was a runaway . . . perhaps not. Her family used her—they might have continued to do so after the marriage, and to use your cousin as well. Was that enough? Enough for him to leave the only home he had ever known? Enough to set off a desire to see you after ten years of silence, a desire so great that he became a ghost, rather than die a good death?"

You started your new life—why are you pulling me back from mine? He remembered the fury in Sagar's face, his voice, the memory so palpable that blood began to pound in his ears. "Why is it suddenly our duty to think of the dead?" Pramesh's words came out louder than intended, but he could not stop. "After the rites are done, must we still think of nothing but their wishes and the things they left behind? How then do we move forward? How do I continue on?" He heard footsteps outside the door that paused before turning back with tentative steps—Mohan, probably, wondering why Pramesh had raised his voice at their head priest. He swallowed his frustration and lowered his voice. "Narinder-ji, please. My cousin is gone; there is nothing I can do for him. My duty is to the living, to the ones who seek refuge here. The tripindi shraddha—will you do it now?"

Narinder's silence stretched until Pramesh felt he might burst from uncertainty. The priest sighed. "My duty is also to the bhavan. I too remember my failure."

"What failure?"

"I froze. You know this. Every time the spirit has asserted itself, you have walked right up to it, and Mohan-bhai has done his best to distract others from it; Loknath and Dev each continue reading the holy word— but I can do nothing."

"No one blames you—" Pramesh began to say, but the old priest held up his hand.

"I thought, after all these years, that I had conquered all emotion. That I was readying myself every day for the moment when I would follow the dying folk who come here and depart. But then the ghost came, and I was afraid. You saw this yourself. I am afraid because even living next to death, I realize I do not know everything about it. But I am learning, Pramesh-bhai. Each night, I am still afraid—but a bit less than I was before. To perform tripindi shraddha, one must have a perfectly focused mind. It is not easy; I have told you this. Even if you feel you are ready, I am not. I intend to use all the time I have, so that when the moment comes, I will not fail."

"But—"

Narinder was stern. "You know better than anyone that death does not come on our schedule," he said. "Why should it be any different with the timing of the rites?"

Pramesh was defeated. Narinder was right. He sat in silence, while Narinder continued to stare out the window. When the priest rose, the manager thought of something. "My question from before, Narinder-ji. I truly want an answer. After the rites. . . . Will I be free of Sagar-bhai, then? Will I be able to detach?"

Narinder, in the absence of his prayer beads, lifted the end of his shawl and gripped the fringe between his fingers, worrying at the threads. "All this time, you have detached, you have pushed your cousin and your past from your mind." There was no reproach in the priest's voice, but the manager blushed. "You ask the wrong question. Perhaps you should ask if the ghost has detached, Pramesh-bhai. You are so ready to leave that shade of your cousin behind, but are you sure that he, too, is ready to leave you?" Pramesh felt a sharp twinge through the center of his heart. He opened his mouth to speak, but his throat was dry. Narinder stepped to the door. "They are saying the rains will end in a week, Pramesh-bhai. We will take the first auspicious day after that. How you decide to spend that time is entirely up to you."

Pramesh sat in his office for some time after the priest left. The rain stopped, started again, stopped. Water trickled down from the roof to the ground. He fiddled with his pens, crumpled up some precious sheets of paper and then smoothed them back out again. Eventually, his hands wandered to his desk drawer, and as he picked through the scraps of notes and the odd rolling pencil, he came upon a dirtied card wedged beneath a letter opener.

Shankarbhavan, it read, *The premier luxe hostel of the great God's city.* He flipped the card back to front, front to back between his fingers. He flicked it back into the drawer.

He spent the day wandering among the rooms, sitting with Shobha and Rani, passing back and forth before the washroom. His mind felt like a sieve. That night, he was outside the washroom door before the pots began their evening protest, and he quickly silenced them, tone filled with the same iron as the previous night. Still, he felt as if the echoes of that ghostly sound coated his skin in a film he could not wash off even in the holy river. There were just a few hours left until dawn, and yet he had no desire to sleep.

Out of habit he walked one round of the courtyard, glancing into all the vacant rooms as he went. His heart grew heavier with each empty bed he passed, remembering when the guests and their dying folk had numbered so many that blankets and bundles spilled out of the rooms and into the walkway and courtyard. Even when quiet, there had been a kind of hum to the bhavan that was absent now. He glanced in Sheetal's room, saw the boy sliding a knife down a block of wood, whittling it into some form as yet known only to him.

Mohan's door was ajar and a small oil lamp was lit. The assistant was usually a heavy sleeper, quick to begin snoring even after the commotion with the pots was dispelled each night. He had never seemed to fully recover after his bout with the cold and had reached a constant state of glum stupor. Pramesh knew he owed the man an explanation. He stopped at the door and gave it a light tap before pushing it open. "Are you well, Mohan-bhai?" he asked, his eyes adjusting to the dim light. Then he took in the scene before him. Water lay in puddles on the floor near the window, and Mohan himself was completely soaked, with his wet hair plastered to his skin and his shirt clinging to his round body. Outside, the rain fell to the earth with such force that a fine mist rose up from the lane. "What happened? What reason was there for you to be out at this hour?"

"Nothing, Pramesh-ji," Mohan said, his teeth chattering. Pramesh's eyes wandered over to the steel cabinet, usually kept locked, but now the door was wide open and the contents were fully visible. He stared at the packets of biscuits and chocolates and fried mung that spilled onto the floor, and then he looked at his shivering assistant.

"Remember your place here, Mohan-bhai. Remember your duty." He pulled the door shut. Mohan had never broken the bhavan rules in all his years here. He must have done so now only because he knew, as everyone else seemed to, that the ghost had made his hostel into a hopeless place. Pramesh entered his office and pulled open a drawer in his desk. The smudged card was where he'd left it earlier, touting another Shankarbhavan in a very different part of the city. Here, in *his* Shankarbhavan, he was powerless. The ghost would not heed him. The head priest would not budge. The guests refused to stay with their dying within these walls, and his assistant had succumbed to temptation.

He flipped the card between his fingers and looked out the window. It was raining even harder now, the sound a low rumble, but morning would come soon enough. Perhaps he would try his luck.

26

Bhut had started his day early, setting off on foot patrol with a deputy to show the goondas and moneymen and dancing-house owners that he was, after all, responsible for his portion of the city. He'd just come from the cremation ghats, where he'd hovered at the topmost steps, watching the proceedings.

"So vigilant, Bhut-sahib!"

"A good fellow, that Bhut. Always keeping his eyes open, even here."

"The man who goes everywhere and sees everything, nah?"

These folk, who spoke so highly of the circle officer, never dreamed that Bhut envied the mourners. They had the luxury of circling the pyre, cracking the skull, and throwing the pot of river water over the shoulder as they turned away—concrete motions necessary for breaking ties to the person who existed no longer. Motions that others had denied his own family.

The priests of Kashi had relegated his sister, with her decidedly *not good* death, to the rites reserved for those whose ends were full of questions the living could not answer. Too obedient to urge his father to question the priests' decision, too young to speak to those holy men on his own, Bhut had stood by helpless and mute as strangers placed his sister's body on a wooden raft and set it afloat on the river. Having preceded her husband in that journey beyond life, she was dressed in her bridal sari, with the delicate ornaments of her wedding day sparkling from her ears and nose and throat and wrists, and the glinting gold was all the more painful to see for the pantomime of life it created in the body that lay on the raft.

But most devastating of all was that his sister's husband was the chief mourner. Bhut, who'd begged his father to intervene, to bully, to throw enough money at the priests so that they would turn a blind eye to the way things had been done for centuries and allow the woman's father—or even her only brother—to preside over the rites, had fixed his eyes not on a final glimpse of his sister, but on that man who everyone whispered about.

Shameful business. Such a light and happy thing, and such a change after she married.

His mother told him to do it.

It was only a matter of time. Doesn't he already have a new bride?

How long had that man known his sister? A scant year, pitiful when compared to the years, the lifetime that Bhut and his sisters and parents had known her for. And yet the husband had the privilege of wading into the river after the body with another priest, while Bhut, his father, and the city watched. The one who everyone said had pushed Bhut's sister to her death now pushed the raft further away from the ghat, while the priest muttered hollow chants. Once the water became too deep for them to safely walk further, he'd taken the rocks passed over to him by the priests remaining on the ghat and hoisted them onto the raft's edges, each weight sinking the wooden structure a little, until the border of heavy stones gave the body over to the river completely, the water embracing and pulling it into its depths with the silent indifference of a beggar who accepts a coin only to put his hand out for another.

No purity by fire, no freeing of the life essence. *The body is burned and so should the memory be.* His sister's body remained in Kashi, albeit at the bottom of the river; perhaps even now she walked its depths, pacing the sands deep below. And so too the memories remained, rotting in a hidden corner of Bhut's brain, growing putrid with time and festering no matter how hard he tried to forget.

He walked with his deputy through streets, the ground littered with refuse and drunks. As they approached Dal-Mandi Chowk, the infamous street of dancing houses and brothels, he was surprised to come upon the hostel manager, who seemed lost and relieved to see Bhut's face.

"What business do you have here?" the circle officer asked.

Pramesh held up the sullied card. "This other Shankarbhavan—do you know anything of it? I believe my cousin may have stopped there."

The circle officer stared at Pramesh and shook his head. "What point could there be in this journey? Go home, Manager-ji. Go home to your daughter. Live your life. Don't bother learning a story that can only bring you pain." He spat out those last words along with a wad of tobacco. A moment later, his deputy hailed him from a side street. "Mark my words, Manager-ji," he said before following the deputy. "Most times, it's better to know nothing."

Pramesh watched the man's back as he stalked off, but remained undeterred. Down an alley, then another, round a bend, and at last he found the place. In contrast to the wide expanse of street that his hostel occupied, this false Shankarbhavan seemed no larger than any other house in Kashi. The paint on the sign outside was worn and flaking, and the front desk, seen through the open door, was a rough, lopsided table where a boy not even in his teens sat scribbling away in an exercise book.

"Hello," he greeted the boy. "You have another man here, one who picks up guests from the train station, yes? Is he here?"

"Arrey, Sahib, who can tell?" The boy kept his head down, his pencil skittering across the page in a busy hand. "So many people in and out and in and out, all day long. All day I am here listening to orders: do this, do that, another towel, a lizard in the washroom, mosquitoes in the bed."

The manager looked around. Red paan spit stains spattered the walls, and an unpleasant acrid odor permeated the air. A staircase wound upward behind the desk, so narrow that Pramesh would have had to walk up sideways to traverse the passage, and loud yells and banging sounded from the upper floors. He noticed a rickety chair near the entranceway, and he sat down. "I will wait, then," he said.

The boy continued to mutter to himself as he finished writing and squinted at the page. Then, as if suddenly cognizant of Pramesh's presence, he looked up and stared at the manager, who tried to give a reassuring smile. But the boy bent his head and bit his lip, his hand now idle on the notebook before him, his complaint forgotten. "Another man, you said?"

"That's right." Pramesh could not remember any distinguishing characteristic about the tout. "He was passing out cards at the train station, cards for this place."

The boy looked down the short hall to his right and shuffled his feet. "Yes, yes. He's out all day today. Tomorrow, too."

"Where can I find him?"

"Who can tell?" the boy said again. The grip around his pencil was tight. "Honestly, Sahib, he is barely ever here. I'm sorry you wasted the trip."

A woman's laugh sounded from upstairs, and a man's voice, singing a song, answered. The boy's ears turned red. He closed his notebook and sat still, his hands folded in front of him. Pramesh could see that he was not wanted in this place, and he, too, wished to leave; every part of him felt repelled by the smell, the sounds, the sight of this false Shankarbhavan. He thought a moment. "Might I see a room?" he asked.

"Ji," the boy sighed. He beckoned Pramesh to follow him up the stairs. They stopped at the second floor, and the boy pushed open the door of the first room they came to. The manager felt his chest tighten as he entered the space. A single cracked window opened onto a view of the street, but the shutters were closed and no light entered the space. A narrow low bed with rumpled blankets sagged in one corner. The walls were water-stained and peeling, and insects marched from one corner of the room to a rupee-sized hole near the baseboards. The entire space had a sweet and acrid stench about it, like rotting garbage, an odor accumulated from beedi smoke and ganja and more, the years combining into a stink that lived within the walls. He heard feet running upstairs and the woman's laugh again.

"Well?" the boy said. His tone was defiant, as if he knew quite well that Pramesh was stalling. He should have been in school instead of scribbling away in this horrid place; he should have been playing cricket or joking with friends on the ghats instead of trying to squeeze a few coins from degenerates. A wave of pity for the boy overwhelmed the manager, and he felt cheap, wasting the child's time in an ill-advised quest.

"Arun!" a voice bellowed from below. The irritated look on the boy's face disappeared, and he turned to Pramesh, his finger on his lips, in a plea for the manager's silence. "Arun!" The second call came quickly after the first, louder and angrier, and the child left Pramesh to fly back down the stairs. The manager hesitated, then followed after just far enough so he could hear the conversation below. "Are you empty-headed?" the man asked. "How many times have I told you never to leave the desk?" The boy muttered apologies. "So, how many while I was out?"

"Just the ones from the night before," the boy replied. "And a couple."

"They asked for the hourly rate, I'm sure." The man laughed. A chair scraped. Pramesh crouched lower on the step. He could see the dark top of a man's head, the chair tilted back against the wall, beedi smoke blooming. The boy hovered near the desk but his face was out of view.

"You said you'd be back hours ago," the boy said. "You said I could have the afternoon to myself."

"Careful." The quiet in the man's voice had a lethal quality to it. Pramesh felt his stomach clench. More thuds sounded from the floor above.

"Well, are you staying here now? May I go?"

"*Careful*—didn't I say?" the man said. "I am here now. If I have something to entertain me, I may stay for a very long time." He grabbed the notebook that the boy had left behind and ruffled the pages.

"Manoj—Bhai, don't. . . ."

"Why not? My brother will be a famous writer, nah? Shouldn't I be able to read what he writes?" The rickety table sat between them, but the boy still made a grab for the notebook, which his brother held out of reach. "Which page?" the man said in a low singsong voice. "Which page shall we read today?"

"Bhai; please, Bhaiya, don't—"

Pramesh winced and looked away. His reluctant ears took in the mocking sounds of the man reciting his brother's poetry, pausing only to spout an exaggerated "Wah! Wah!" of appreciation after each verse. The boy had come around the desk, grabbing at his brother's arms to wrest the notebook away. "What's this, a longer poem? Is the famous brother writing a novel, now? *The man with the split eyebrow waited on the corner as we'd agreed upon earlier—*"

Pramesh's breath caught. He stayed absolutely still on the stairs.

"Manoj, please, please, Bhaiya," the boy tried again, his voice laden with panic.

"*He looks frail and thin, like a bird plucked of its feathers. His eyes are bright like a baby's and when he smiles I can see it go up and reflect in his eyes. This is how I know he is an honest man.* Honest man, wah! So, little Bhai is a writer and a philosopher now?"

The boy made a desperate grab at the book, knocking the beedi from his brother's mouth. At this, the man stood up and gave the child a swift slap and a shove to the ground. Pramesh stood, his heart bursting, and descended the remaining stairs before the man could strike another blow. He bent, trying to help the boy up, but the child wrenched away, tears streaking his face, and ran out into the street.

"The book is his," Pramesh said, facing the man. "Give it back to him. Enough fun for the day."

"Rooms are upstairs, Hero-sahib," the man said, putting a fresh beedi to his lips. He lit the end and flicked the match away. After the first puff, his eyes met Pramesh's, and he twitched. A flicker of fear passed over his face, or so the manager thought. Pramesh recognized him now, this tout, this man, who was really more a boy. He was like Sheetal in build, and he even carried the same weight in his face. But unlike Sheetal, there was a hardness in the young man's features, as if he were slowly turning to stone.

Pramesh pulled the card from his pocket. "You gave this to me in the train station. There was a man here, some weeks ago, a man who looks exactly like me. You tricked him into coming to this place instead of the death bhavan."

"No trick, Hero-sahib: if the names are the same, what can I do? I force no one to stay here. They may leave as they like. Anyway—do you really expect me to remember one man out of hundreds?"

"I know you remember him. The boy's book—you just read aloud a description of that very same man."

The tout took a long draw of his beedi. "If it's money you're after, if you've come to take back whatever you think I took from him, you are a bigger fool than you are a hero. I am no thief. He came, he looked at the place, and he left. If anyone is owed money, it is me—what of the time I wasted, bringing him here? What of the room I did not fill?"

The manager exhaled: Sagar had not stayed here. But a gap of time remained in between his coming to this place, his visiting Thakorlal's shop for an empty bottle, and his body ending up tangled in a boat's anchor rope in the middle of the river. The manager's eyes fell on the exercise book still in the tout's hands, but that man came upon the idea at the same moment as Pramesh. His eyes gleamed as he waved the notebook in front of the manager's face. "Perhaps we can both be satisfied, Sahib." His tone changed from mocking to businesslike. "I lost money on a room. You seem to want to know what my famous writer-Bhai had to say about your twin, nah?" He rubbed his fingers together in a gesture that Pramesh understood. Still, the manager hesitated. The man's brother was still a child, with a child's fancies. Who could know if what he'd written were actually true?

"Manoj? Manoj, are you back?" A woman's voice, the laughing voice Pramesh had heard from the upper floors, floated down to where they stood. She laughed again, and the sound extended to a metallic jingle, which landed in a tinkling shower at their feet: she'd thrown an anklet down. "Manoj, come up, nah? God, I'm so bored in this place! What are you doing down there—Manoj?"

"One last chance, Hero-sahib." The tout held his hand out. "You can see I already have a better offer."

The man with the split eyebrow. The child had written those words, and that, at least, was true. Pramesh reached into his pockets and placed money into the tout's eager palm. The tout looked to Pramesh, the fear gone from his hardened face. He ripped the notebook in half and tossed it at the manager's feet. At the same time he spit, and an orange-red paan stain bloomed on Pramesh's shirt. Then he was up the stairs, two at a time, and the woman was exclaiming and laughing and slamming a door shut.

The boy was nowhere to be found. Pramesh walked, searching, the notebook halves in his hands. The streets felt cramped, as if he were in a box with the lid fastened shut, and the air tasted tight and stale. A sour smell wafted up from his ruined shirt. He felt ill, and he gave up looking for the child and instead walked to the closest ghat. There, he stripped off his shirt and dunked it into the river, rubbing the fabric as best he could. The air was damp, and the shirt would never dry without the help of the sun, so he put it back on, sodden as it was, and shivered on the stone steps. Shobha would scold him later, but he did not want to walk back into his home, into the real Shankarbhavan, with the scent of that place still on him.

The notebook pieces sat next to him on the stone. All he had to do was hold the open halves together and begin to read. But as his eyes fell on the first few pages of verse written in the round scrawl of a child, he felt ashamed. These words were not his to read, even if they featured a story about a man he'd once known better than himself. He fixed his eyes on the black river and the bobbing boats, trying to lose himself in the ebb and flow of conversation and chatter from the folk walking up and down the steps, the women hauling laundry and a group of old men watching the crowd with milky eyes. He scanned the crowd, hoping to spot the boy, and return this thing that had never been his. When he felt he could stand the chill of his soaked shirt no longer, he stood, hesitating, then left the notebook halves where they were on the steps.

Halfway up the steps, he felt movement behind him and turned. His eyes locked with those of the skinny lad from the front desk, the exercise book gripped tight in his small hands. The child looked both terrified and defiant, his legs frozen. Pramesh managed a smile, and then he continued up the steps and into the lane beyond.

"Sahib? Sahib!"

Pramesh kept going, his steps swift and sure. He took a detour through a market lane crowded with people and stalls, folk out buying wares for the midday meal and for chai. Shobha would be looking for him soon. He thought of Rani, and his legs moved faster. He wanted to be away from the events of the morning, from that other life he'd come so close to touching. He wove in and out, nudging past housewives and packs of peons hurrying to fetch lunch tiffins for their bosses. He felt a tug on his wet sleeve.

"Sahib," the boy panted behind him. "You go too fast." The boy looked at him, the notebook pieces clutched to his chest. "You read none of it, Sahib. I was watching you."

"It was not mine to read," Pramesh said. Crowds pushed behind and in front of them, this odd pairing of man and boy. He moved to the side of the lane, close to a snack stall, and the child followed after.

"Manoj will not give you your money back," the boy, Arun, ventured.

"He should not have sold it to me in the first place. And I should not have presumed to buy it. I am only sorry about the damage. I can buy you another, if you wish."

"No, Sahib," the boy said. "This was not so bad. He's ripped the pages out before, ripped them into shreds." Then he hastened to add, "He is not all bad, my brother. . . ."

Pramesh watched the child. "Perhaps."

"He could have kicked me to the streets. But he took me along; he brought me to this place; he lets me stay here instead of chasing after people in the train station. He just loses his temper sometimes. Does things he doesn't mean."

He seemed desperate to convince Pramesh. "He is older than you," the manager conceded. "Older boys often act that way, at that age, and especially with their brothers. Men act that way, too."

"Did you ever do that to your brother?"

"No. Not exactly. That is, I can only hope I did not hurt him knowingly." His hand wandered up to rub his eyebrow.

"Twins." Arun nodded. "Perhaps it is different when your brother is a twin, and not the eldest." He spat, a gesture that looked too adult to belong to him. "Bhai is the one who brought your brother to the guesthouse. Your twin didn't stay long, though." He paused, a shadow crossing his brow. "Why didn't you meet him at the station?"

"I didn't know he was coming," Pramesh replied. "I wish I had."

The child contemplated the wad of spit bubbling on the ground before him. He smoothed the covers of the exercise book. "You truly did not read anything, Sahib." He presented the words as a statement.

"Yes. Truly."

Again, Arun drew his hand over the notebook. "Bhai brings me these notebooks. A new one every month," the child said. "He never forgets."

Pramesh thought back to the arrogant face at the false Shankarbhavan, the features that had turned to stone. Well, not quite stone—not yet. The child opened the halves, turning the pages of each. Halfway through, he grasped a number of pages and gave a gentle tug. The binding released the thin paper easily. "Here," he said. "It is my story, but it is your brother."

Pramesh felt a ball of dread in his stomach. "Is it a story only?"

The pages trembled in the child's hands. "No, Sahib. It is the truth." The boy shook his head and swallowed. In a year or two he would be a teenager, and then more years would pass and he would be a man like his brother. Time would determine how much his features would harden, would turn to stone or remain as they were now, so open, so clear. He would not meet Pramesh's eyes, and his upper lip trembled. "I am sorry, Sahib."

"I don't understand."

"Please, Sahib. Just take it." The boy tried to push the paper into Pramesh's hands, but the manager curled his fingers inward and folded his arms behind his back.

"I have no right to read your words," he said. He was surprised to see tears fill the boy's eyes, which shone luminous in the dull surroundings of the crowded lane. He seemed so lost, and Pramesh thought of the humiliation of his brother reading his words aloud with such mocking disdain, the fear he must have felt while watching to see if the manager would read the pages or discard them. The dread remained in his stomach, and yet he realized he *wanted* to know the story. He wanted something to fill the hole of the past ten years, and especially the hours of Sagar's last day. He wanted this knowledge in the same way a man waits to hear of his fate from a doctor or from a judge.

"Will you read it to me?" he asked the boy. The child seemed confused, but then his face cleared and he wagged his head. They walked to the steps of a nearby temple where it was less crowded and sat down, Pramesh one step lower than the boy. Arun smoothed the mangled paper, fitting the halves together, and began to read.

"The man with the split eyebrow waited on the corner as we'd agreed upon earlier. He looks frail and thin, like a bird plucked of its feathers. His eyes are bright like a baby's and when he smiles I can see it go up and reflect in his eyes. This is how I know he is an honest man." He looked up to determine Pramesh's expression. The boy reminded the manager of Rani, who often looked to him when she had done something either funny or praiseworthy, gauging his reaction, seeing if he approved. He mustered a smile and nodded at Arun to continue. *"He was a stranger to the city. Bhai brought him here to the hostel, but he left very soon after. He waited around the corner until Bhai again left for the train station, and then he came back and asked me if there was another Shankarbhavan around. A death hostel, he said. I had heard of the place, but I thought it was strange that he would want to go there. He asked me to be his guide, but I could not leave the desk just then, so he said he would return."*

"How long was he gone?" Pramesh asked. He regretted his question immediately; the look on Arun's face made clear his displeasure.

"I am telling you the story, Sahib. A moment, just a moment." He set the pile of read pages in a careful stack beside him on the steps, a round stone serving as a paperweight, and resumed reading: *"A half hour later he was back, now with an empty bottle in his hands. I was afraid because Bhai has always told me to stay clear of the drunks we see in our lane. But his eyes were honest, and different, and he told me he wanted to go to a temple first. And he'd brought me money—a real guide's fee! I had never had so much at one time. He was quick at the temple, and then we went to the death hostel."*

Pramesh frowned. Where had he been on that day? What had he been doing? It would have been the day before Bhut had visited him, the day before the story of Sagar's body being found in the boat whirled through the city. "You never brought him there." He did not mean to sound accusing, but the disappointment was heavy in his voice.

Arun looked up and held the pages out. "I did. And you would hear it yourself, if only you would let me read it. Or would you like to see?"

Folk hurried in and out of the temple; a flower seller sat on the topmost steps, an old half-clothed man dozing against the stone. When could Sagar possibly have come to the bhavan? Then he recalled a headache. His head bursting, shutting his eyes, sleeping away the pain. Mohan acting in his stead.

"Shall I keep reading?" Arun's voice was small. Pramesh rocked his head. "*I thought I would be too slow for him—he was tall, with long legs. But he seemed unable to keep up even with me. He must have been tired from the journey. Whenever I looked back to make sure he was following, he lagged, but he always kept me in sight. I took him to the place I knew about, and he asked me to wait outside. There was a dog sitting nearby, a white one with a brown spot on its side. Bhai doesn't like dogs around the place; he always makes me chase them away. So it was nice to just sit with this one, and I was even able to scratch its ears.*

"*The man was not gone long. He walked now as if his feet had weights on them. He said he'd come at a bad time, that the person he'd asked for was not there. 'Tomorrow,' he said. 'I will need to return tomorrow.'*"

Arun paused and looked up. "You see?"

A knot formed in Pramesh's stomach. "When you were at the bhavan—was there anything else you remember? Did you go to the gate?"

"I didn't see—I told you he asked me to wait, remember?"

"Yes. Of course." He could not concentrate. On the temple steps, all Pramesh could think of was another set of steps: the ones in the bhavan, the single floor that had separated him from Sagar on that day. And Mohan, where had Mohan been? A feeling of being trapped in a confined space, so like that terrible night when the earth had shaken with the ghost's rage at the bhavan, his limbs frozen, crept upon him. He felt the child waiting. "Please, continue."

"*He told me my duty was done. He said I could go back home. But the sun was about to go down, and I asked him where he planned on sleeping that night. And he said something strange. He said he wasn't planning on sleeping. He wanted to keep moving, that he might as well see the city while he was here. I* told him it was dangerous at night; he couldn't wander where he wanted to. He wouldn't listen; just kept walking. So I followed him."

"Why?" Pramesh asked. Any child would be quick to run, to spend the coins as quickly as they'd come.

"A moment, Sahib; you'll see," Arun said. "He tried to go faster than me, at first. But he was so tired, and I would not leave him alone. A few times, I asked him where he wanted to go. He ignored me at first, but I noticed he would look at me from the side, watching where I would turn. At last he said he wanted to see the river. So I led him, and slowly he started to talk to me.

"This time, as we walked, he talked the whole way of this other man, this twin of his. He said this twin had lived here many years, and that he'd sent letters a very long time ago of how life in this city was, how things looked. He said that he'd neglected his twin for a very long time, but that everything was about to change. He said that people make mistakes, but that there is always time to fix things, if we truly desire it. I asked him what he was fixing. He stared at me and did not give me an answer. Instead, he began to ask about me—how old I was, how long Bhai and I had been alone, what I liked doing best."

The knot in Pramesh's stomach pulled tighter. His head began to ache.

"I don't know why I did it, but I told him I wanted to be a writer. I have never told anyone this. Bhai knows, but only because he sees me doing it every day, and he laughs at me, most of the time. But this man didn't laugh. He listened to me. And because he listened to me, I decided to tell him something. I'd figured his secret out by then. I knew why he was here."

The temple bells rang out, drowning out Arun's voice, signaling the last call before the doors closed for the afternoon. He paused as folk streamed down the stairs, dusty sandals passing on either side of them. Others pushed upward through the crowd, struggling to get through for one final prayer, one final blessing. Even when the bells ceased, the boy sat there, smoothing the pages over and over. He no longer seemed as eager to read aloud as when he'd started. "I'm sorry, Sahib. I only meant to help him."

"What is it?" The child shook his head, unable to speak. His hands shook as he struggled to keep the crinkling pages from curling upward.

He was frightened, Pramesh realized. "Whatever you tell me. . . . The man I am looking for is already dead. Nothing you say will change that."

Arun struggled with the words. His voice broke. "I told him something. It was meant to help—nothing more."

A chill washed over Pramesh's heart. "Tell me."

"He was ill. The river, the death hostel. Why would someone travel all that way and only go to those two places? Before, he at least kept up as best he could. Now, he didn't try to hide his weakness. He stopped to rest often. And his eyes were bright not so much with happiness, but with fever. It was a hot day, but he looked chilled in his shirt. And when he talked, he no longer seemed as calm as he had been earlier. He talked quickly, with no logic, and his sentences had no end and no beginning. He had kept up the play of a normal, healthy man, but I saw what he was hiding. He was doing what all the pilgrims did—he wanted to visit the holy river, and then he wanted to gain admittance to the death bhavan so he could die.

"But I had my own secret, one that not even Bhai knew. And I had never told it to anyone, because the man who told me made me promise to keep the knowledge close. Here was a good man. I felt sorry for him. I wanted him to have this chance, while he was in Kashi."

"Magadha," Pramesh said aloud. He felt the finality alight upon his chest like a fifty-kilo weight. The boy had told Sagar to go to that cursed land, to plead with the Bearer of Death.

"What?"

"You told him to go to Magadha. To ask Yamraj for a reprieve . . . didn't you?" The boy shook his head, eyes bright, and resumed reading. Gone was his confidence from before. Now he assumed a monotone, his voice at times so faint that Pramesh had to strain to hear.

"A year ago, a holy man came to our hostel. He was not a fake, like the others. I was ill the year he came—a strange illness that made me fall asleep whenever I was sitting. I could not keep my eyes open; none of the doctors understood what was wrong. Even Bhai was worried, and he asked this holy man to do something. The man did a small puja for me, and the next day I was completely better. When I was bending to touch his feet and thank him, he grabbed me by the ear

and pulled me up. And then he whispered the secret so that only I could hear. He said to save it for a moment when I would truly need it.

"The middle of the river was the answer. Any sick person could make himself well again if he drank from the river at the exact point the waters of Kashi met the waters of Magadha. He only had to guide the boat and fetch the water himself. I repeated this to the man. I was excited to tell him. But he didn't seem to care. He didn't ask me questions like he had before. So I didn't speak of it again.

"When we reached the ghat, he sat down on an open space of stone. He was very tired; I could see his eyes closing more and more. I told him to lie down and I would watch over him while he rested. So he did."

Arun paused, as if knowing Pramesh doubted him. "I didn't leave him, Sahib. I got up to get a snack, but I could see him the entire time, and I came right back. I sat next to him and worked in my book, but I never left him."

Pramesh could only look at the boy, the knot in his stomach pulling tighter.

"When he woke, it was dark. He was very worried when he saw I was there. He said I needed to go home. But Bhai wasn't going to be home that night—he wouldn't know if I returned or not. I said I would rather sit with him.

"He seemed a bit better, after he woke. I shared my chaat with him, and he went down to the last step and scooped the river into his mouth. I asked him what he planned to do then, but he just sat there, on the last step. We watched the last boats come in. We must have been there a long time because then the ghats were clear. We were the only ones left. Bhai had always told me I was never to walk the city at night by myself, but I wasn't alone. I liked sitting there with him, no one else, at night.

"I thought he'd forgotten all about the story, but then he asked me to repeat it. Even then I thought he listened with half an ear. But when I finished, he stood up. He walked down to the boats tied at the bottom. He touched the ropes. Then he sat back down again."

Dread enclosed Pramesh's heart. He knew how the story ended. Yet he listened for the words, hungered for the details even as they caused him pain. The boy gave him a worried glance and continued.

"He did that maybe twice more. 'How far to the other side?' he asked me, and I said it wasn't far; perhaps twenty, twenty-five strokes to go halfway. He kept looking at the boats, then up again at the darkness, then back at the boats. And then I told him I thought he could do it. Because I could see he could not decide.

"He still did not move. And then he took out the glass bottle he'd been carrying and he put it in the end of the boat. He didn't say anything, but I understood what he was trying to do. I asked him if he was sure, but he was already turning to get into the boat. I helped him get his footing, and I pushed him off. He wobbled a bit, at first, but then he seemed to get used to the oars. The path was not straight, but that didn't matter. His strokes were strong. It was as if the river was already working its magic on him, giving him life. I knew it would work; I knew he would live. He only needed to go halfway; then the river would give him strength and the return would be easy. He waved to me just before I lost sight of him in the dark."

Arun stopped here, a sob nestled in the bottom of his throat. "I waited for him. By the Mother, I swear to you that I waited as long as I could. I even ran to the ghats downstream to see if he had come totally off-course on the return journey." The pages fluttered at Arun's side, and Pramesh marveled that such flimsy material, thin as onion skin, could hold so much pain.

"Go on," he said, his voice hoarse. "Tell me what happened next."

Whether the rest of the tale lived in those pages or not, the boy refused to read them. He stared straight ahead and tried to control his voice as he finished the story. "I stayed awake that entire night, my eyes never closed. At dawn, I thought perhaps I might see something, but the fog was too thick. I heard some boatmen coming down and pushing off. I did not know what to do. The sun rose higher and people began to come to bathe and pray. No one noticed me. And then I saw two boatmen from earlier come back, but this time they dragged another boat behind them." Arun turned to Pramesh, his eyes bright with anguish. "How was I to know, Sahib? How was I to know that your brother would not come back?"

Pramesh was frozen. He marveled at his cousin's foolishness even as a wave of despair descended upon him. He must have been more than ill to believe the child who had guided him. He must have been certain that death was near. He must have been desperate for life.

"Sahib?"

"Go home," Pramesh said, his voice faint. He felt as if he were speaking from the bottom of a deep hole. He pushed some coins into the child's hands. "Go home to your brother. He will be worried for you." He stayed on the steps as people streamed around him. When he looked up, the child was gone, but the money and the pages remained, fluttering in the light breeze.

He didn't see the street before him as he walked home, didn't notice if any faces recognized him and called out hello, didn't register how low the sun was in the sky. But coming upon the bhavan, he saw Mohan waiting outside the open gate. The assistant's face flooded with relief, and he yelled something into the bhavan, then walked with swift steps to meet Pramesh. A sudden engulfing anger burned through him, followed by a wave of despair at the chance he'd so narrowly missed at seeing Sagar.

"Pramesh-ji! You had everyone so worried—it's late; didn't you notice the time?"

"Is it true?" Pramesh spoke calmly, but his jaw trembled.

"Ji?"

"He was here? And you never told me?"

The color drained from Mohan's face. Pramesh could feel Mrs. Chalwah looking at the pair of them from above. He didn't bother to modulate his voice. He picked out each of his words carefully. "So it is true. You cannot even tell a dead man from a live one, can you?"

"Pramesh-ji, it isn't—"

But the manager brushed past his assistant and went through the gate, leaving Mohan in the empty lane.

That night, when the ghost in the washroom began to clatter and wail two hours after midnight as always, Pramesh went downstairs and, as he had never done before, he entered the washroom and pulled the door closed, shutting himself in with the ghost. The sound was excruciating to hear from the outside, but with the door closed, the pots suddenly ceased. The ghost was still there—the vessels quivered on the stone floor—but the shrieks wore down to a metallic murmur. His presence calmed the ghost. Was that what it wanted? For Pramesh always to hover around the washroom?

The manager leaned his head back against the door. His mind was screaming with questions. *Why didn't you tell me you were ill? Why didn't you insist on waiting here instead of turning away? Why did you believe a child—a fairy tale?* The words remained dead on his tongue. The past was past. He had to move on. "Bhaiya," he whispered. "Enough. There is nothing more I can do for you."

In answer, the pots resumed, calling out with desperate urgency into the night, speaking in a language that Pramesh could not recognize.

27

Shobha was worried. Since yesterday, her husband had seemed even further lost within himself. He did not answer when she asked him a question. He paid no mind to Mohan, who lingered outside the office or in the courtyard, his face twisted in concern. He did not even notice Rani pulling at his fingers, her playful face becoming frustrated when her father ignored her, as he'd never done before. In the middle of the night she'd woken to find his eyes still open, his face toward the ceiling. When the pots wailed, he was gone for much longer than usual. Now he stayed in his office with the door shut. But a look from Narinder told her to be patient.

With the housework done and her husband isolating himself, Shobha took Rani's hand and set off for the market and the post office. She checked almost every day, but still she hadn't received a reply from Kamna. Shobha was prepared to be patient. Kamna probably knew as little about the bhavan mistress as Shobha knew about her, perhaps even less. So that morning she'd written one more letter, one that sought to tell Kamna more about herself, and perhaps open that woman up to her. She was careful in what she said, and she wrote several versions before she was happy with it. She wrote about herself—*Kashi is my home; I have lived here all my life*—and included just one line about Rani—*She grows bigger every day, and her smile by far grows the biggest.*

Still, she hesitated outside the post office. Rani pulled on her sari, and she placed one palm on the child's head, looking at the letter, then looking up, thinking. She spotted a familiar form coming toward her, and her heart sank; it was Mrs. Gupta. She quickly walked the letter over to the postman waiting behind the metal grate. Then Shobha picked up Rani and turned to the woman. "How is your health?" Shobha asked. She could think of nothing else to say.

Mrs. Gupta frowned at the sight of Rani's round face and Shobha's empty market bag. "You are too late today," she said, pointing to the limp jute bag. "All the best bits will have been taken. You should have been here hours ago, as I was." She held up her own bag, which overflowed with greens. She looked at Rani again and pointed a finger in the child's face. "She looks peaked. What have you been feeding her? Sweets, probably, no proper nutrition?"

Shobha shifted the girl to the other hip. "How is your family?" she asked.

"Mailing something?" Mrs. Gupta said, ignoring Shobha's question. "The postman's wife is my fast friend; we've known each other since grade school. Did you know that?" She did not wait for Shobha to answer. "Who were you writing to?"

"Just a relative." Against her will, a deep flush erupted on Shobha's cheeks. She tightened her grip on Rani.

"But I thought you had no other relatives?"

"A cousin."

"Hmm. How is your husband? Have you quarreled?"

"Of course not." Shobha did not hide the shock in her voice, but Mrs. Gupta only smiled.

"Couples quarrel all the time. Ill-matched couples especially." She slid the coins in her palm back into her money bag. "But my nephew— oh, he is different. You never met a more even-tempered man. And he treats his wife like a goddess. She thanks the great God every day for such a husband."

"As you say, it is late, and the markets will be closing soon—"

"And what's this I hear about your husband?"

Shobha exhaled. "I couldn't tell you. I never listen to gossips." At this, Mrs. Gupta smiled even wider.

"Well then, I'm sure you already know. It just seemed so strange for him to be walking near. . . . Well, you know." The woman lowered her voice to a whisper that was yet still loud enough for any passerby to hear. "Where the *bad* women are. On the other side of the city." The flush returned to Shobha's cheeks. "Men will do that, you know," Mrs. Gupta murmured. "If there is nothing keeping them at home." She leaned forward, as if she wanted to say more, but she stopped when she saw the bhavan mistress's face. Her own eyes narrowed.

Shobha's mouth twitched and her eyes sparkled, until she could contain herself no longer. The peal of laughter that escaped her lips was so loud that the folk passing in the lane stared openly at her, some smiling at what they assumed was a good joke. "So kind of you," she managed to gasp out. "So kind of you to tell me." The outrage on Mrs. Gupta's face was enough to set Shobha off again, and she pulled the edge of her sari up to her mouth and bit down on the cloth, trying to stifle the sound. When she mastered herself, she bounced Rani on her hip, one hand reaching up to brush away the tears springing to her eyes above her aching cheeks. Mrs. Gupta was fumbling with her bags, her face awash in heat, her eyes furious. "I should be going," Shobha said with a gentle hand on Mrs. Gupta's shoulder. That woman turned her back without a word, and Shobha could only shake her head and try to catch her breath. She felt a brief prick of regret for her behavior—the woman was her elder, and Shobha should have had more control over her emotions. But really! Her husband, wandering in the red-light district? The idea was so ridiculous that Shobha could not even picture it.

And yet, despite Shobha's good mood, nothing else went well for her that day. True to Mrs. Gupta's prediction, the market stalls held only the last leavings, and after much back and forth with the vendors she was successful in buying only half of what she really needed for the evening meal. She arrived home late, a cranky Rani pulling at her hair. She was late with the chai, and in her haste she added so much ginger that even Narinder, who sometimes partook but who never offered an opinion, opened his eyes wide at the first swallow. Pramesh merely blew at the

THE CITY OF GOOD DEATH

liquid, his eyes distant, before putting down his still-full cup and ignoring it. Shobha thought to cheer him by telling him about what had happened to her that morning, but before she could start the story a crash sounded behind her. Rani had pried open the lid of the rice tin and upended the contents onto the floor, leaving nothing for the evening meal.

"Rascal child!" Shobha gasped. Rani grabbed fistfuls of rice, smiling at the stream of grains falling between her fingers. Shobha stepped over the mess and grabbed the girl, hoping to salvage some of the rice, but when she brushed Rani's arm, the child shrieked and burst into tears. Before she could comfort the girl, Rani ran to Pramesh, who came up behind her and scooped the girl up.

"Careful," he said, his tone sharp. "It was an accident. Leave her." He walked out of the kitchen with Rani, leaving Shobha amid the mess.

She cleaned up the rice grains, her heart pumping, shame sending a rush of blood to her ears. The feeling remained all afternoon and evening as she cleaned the vegetables and sweated over the fire, and especially when Rani ran into her arms, the earlier incident already forgotten. But after everyone had eaten, after the priests, Mohan, and Sheetal had thanked her for the meal, after she had cleaned the dishes and the kitchen and after she'd had a moment to think, her shame turned into something else. Anger rose at the back of her throat and radiated down to her stomach. Ever since the day Rani was cut at the Mistry house, Shobha had felt that the mantle of guilt was hers to wear. Pramesh certainly had not tried to make her feel otherwise. For days, his every action and look seemed to imply that she was a neglectful mother. She, who had to be everything to everyone, who reserved every worry, every prayer, every thought for her daughter and husband. Who dealt with her husband's moods and infuriating silences, his secrets that drove her to go seeking for answers herself.

That night, after she'd tucked the blankets around Rani and drawn the privacy curtain around her daughter, she lay in bed, careful not to let any part of her touch her husband. She was conscious of his every movement, his every breath. Anger kept her awake, and so when Rani woke a few hours into the night, throwing her blankets aside and kicking at the privacy curtain, Shobha was quick to get up, quick to rest a cool palm on the child's hot forehead and fetch her a glass of water, to hold her daughter's hand until she fell back asleep. Only when she turned back to the bed did she see that Pramesh was also awake, observing her.

"Is she well?"

These words after his long silence sparked the anger that had smoldered hot inside of Shobha for hours, and she struggled to control her tone. "She is asleep, finally."

"I noticed a bruise."

"She was with *you* all afternoon."

Pramesh blinked. He peered at her in the dark. "I am only worried."

"I am the one who is with her, always," Shobha said, her voice rising. "But you—you were gone for hours yesterday. Wandering in such places. . . ."

Pramesh sat up. "What places?"

The words escaped Shobha before she could stop them. "Everyone is talking about it. Places where family men do not go. . . ." She clapped her hand over her mouth, instantly contrite. There was only malice in everything that Mrs. Gupta ever said; why would Shobha think to accuse her husband now, with *that*, with the thing that she herself did not even believe?

He was silent, but she recognized the look on his face from the many times he'd been confronted with an especially hysterical family. "They do not speak an untruth," he said. He looked down at the thin blanket and picked at the threads. "I was there, or close to it." Shock sealed her mouth. "I was looking for Sagar-bhai. I was searching for the last hours of his life."

"In that place?"

"Not there exactly." His eyes flicked to her, hesitating. Then his mouth opened, and the words spilled out. The false bhavan, the boy, the notebook; the near miss when Mohan turned Sagar away.

Shobha felt a tight knot loosen within her as she listened. When Pramesh was finished, they sat quietly for some time, side by side on the bed. She felt him reach out, his fingers searching for hers. She could picture everything as he spoke, his walk to the other Shankarbhavan, the scene inside, the boy with his carefully written words, the story within the story that her husband told. But all she could think of was someone else entirely. Who would tell Kamna the story? If she were that other woman, if Pramesh had been the one who was sick, who had died and left her a widow, she would want to know everything. Every detail of every minute of his final day.

She chanced a look at him in the dark. *When will he be here? We are waiting.* The letter was in her almirah; it was a moment's effort to get out of bed and fetch it for him to read. But she wasn't sure what his reaction would be. "Should we write to them? His wife, his in-laws?"

"What for?"

"To tell them what happened, what you found out today."

His hand lifted from hers. "I already wrote that family twice before."

And I've written twice as well, Shobha wanted to say. "What about just her?" she asked. "If we write specifically to her—"

"How do we even know she is there?" Pramesh cut her off. "They may have all moved on by now; her elders probably sold the land and pocketed the money, all to escape those stories."

Shobha's breath caught, heart pounding. "What stories?" She spoke slowly and carefully, as if she were trying to convince Rani to do something she very much did not want to do. She had waited so long for the story.

"That she knew how to bewitch men," he said. "Make them follow her, fall in love with her. Foolishness." He exhaled deeply. And then he repeated to her what he'd told Narinder.

Shobha struggled to keep her breath even, her hands from trembling. A new feeling tingled within her. A woman like that might be capable of anything. Black magic. The ability to cast the evil eye. Silly things, silly accusations. . . . Gossip at the well, at the market, in the kitchen of a neighbor. But a small voice in her head persisted. Sometimes, such stories carried a thread of truth. A slow wash of unease ran through her veins, and she thought of the letter she'd mailed just that morning. Her fingers curled inward, the nails cutting into her palms. She should have waited. She knew no more about Kamna than she had ten years ago. Why hadn't she waited to mail it?

"He was ill," Pramesh interrupted her thoughts. Something in his voice made her look closer at him, trying to make out his features in the dark.

"But they let him go," she said. Again, she put Pramesh in that place, herself in Kamna's. What could be so important that he would need to leave the city, take a long and tiring journey, when his body was deteriorating? She would have blocked the door, would have held onto his feet and pulled him back into the bhavan before allowing him such a thing. "If he was as sick as you say—dying—why would they have let him leave?"

He held his hands up in a helpless gesture, then let them drop. "He needed someone, he needed a family, an equal partner. But he had no one at the end."

There was a quality of sadness and hopelessness in his voice that penetrated her bones. She picked up his hand and squeezed it between her warm palms.

Pramesh stayed awake for a long while. He remembered the old holy tree he'd visited as a child, the fight he'd had with Sagar, who scoffed at superstitions; Sagar, who preferred the logic of self-determination and will over the dubious boons of a village-designated idol. To abandon that so suddenly, to alter that essential part of himself and place his hopes in a dream, a fairy tale told by a strange child in a strange city. . . .

He saw Sagar getting into the boat, pushing off with such desperate purpose. He saw the weak arms pulling the oars, the legs bending and straightening in an unfamiliar motion, propelled by the darkness of Magadha, so tantalizingly close. He felt the same fear Sagar must have felt as the river took control of the boat, shuttled it wherever the strong currents willed, pushed it further into darkness. Had his resolve wavered then? In that moment, had he wished for dry ground, for a return to the city and the chance to see Pramesh? No matter—in the end, the temptation of surmounting death, of eluding the Bearer for just a little longer, had sealed Sagar's fate. He must have held such hope as he bent his body to the water, scooping the holy river into trembling palms, lips burning to taste that miracle that would give him the thing he wanted most, and then, then, *then*. . . .

28

The rains poured and poured and poured until finally they stopped, and the monsoon season ended. What was wet became dry, what was submerged became visible, the ghats seeming to rise out of the river, the buildings growing out of the ground, the city stretching upward and unfurling from its submissive curled state like the many-hooded serpent king Kaliya rising up from the river. Folk emerged from their homes, blinking and anticipating the festival season that would arrive in two months. Inside Shankarbhavan, the mood was one of purposeful determination.

Narinder sat cross-legged on a low stool in the priests' quarters, scrutinizing a star chart and counting out mysterious figures on the knuckles of his right hand.

"Today?" Pramesh asked.

"Tomorrow," Narinder said. "We will leave early."

Pramesh busied himself, taking inventory of the rooms, checking the state of the rope beds and blankets, making note of which rooms needed replacements. He strode from room to room inspecting the windows and doors for squeaky hinges and faulty locks, looking over the water tank, assessing the fastness of the main gate, tackling the paperwork and old files in his office and fiddling with the budget so that he might buy newer linens. When his thoughts began to wander, he forced himself to think only of the next hour, the next day, and everything that needed to be done.

Shobha watched him from the kitchen. She knew what the end of the rains meant for Pramesh, but her mind still went to Kamna, as naturally as a bird alighting on a favorite perch. Something about what her husband had revealed kept asserting itself in her mind. She pushed it away. Perhaps, she thought, with the exorcism of her husband's cousin's spirit, she could also exorcize that man's wife from her thoughts.

The thick sound of a clearing throat alerted her to Mohan standing at the door. Rani was sick with yet another cold, and the assistant offered to do the marketing for Shobha. "Just one second, Mohan-bhai," she said with a smile of apology. "I have nothing ready. Ah, and I have all my writing things upstairs. . . . Maybe you don't need a list? Just some ginger, potatoes, coriander? And I have run out of black sesame seeds as well." She would have continued with the few more trivial things she needed, but Mohan held his hand up in a limp motion.

"I think," he said, "it is better if you write them for me, ji. I do not want to forget and come back and disappoint everyone. I don't want to forget my duty."

She looked up, assessing his face. "Mohan-bhai, you always do your duty." She thought of what Pramesh had said about Mohan turning Sagar away from the bhavan. She never interfered between her husband and the assistant, but something in his tone—or in how he couldn't look at her and instead looked at Rani, who sat curled on the rope bed—alerted Shobha to the sadness emanating from the assistant's figure like a haze. He was tired, dark circles stamped his eyes with a haunted look, and his usual cheerful greeting came unaccompanied with the joke or bit of gossip that he always had at the ready. "Are you well?" She received no answer but a drooping smile. "Just one more day, and then it will be over. Narinder-ji will begin the rites tomorrow. We all just need some patience and strength."

Mohan's eyes flickered up to meet hers. "I didn't do it on purpose, Bhabhi. I wanted to tell him. But it was my fault. I accept it."

Shobha wagged her head slowly, unsure yet wanting to provide comfort.

"But one thing. If you could only tell me—he was angry, and he was right to be angry. But before then, on the day that Kishore came—does Pramesh-ji know that I was right?"

"What do you mean?"

"Ah, Bhabhi, tell me that Pramesh-ji knew the weaver *was* dead, that I did not make a mistake!"

"Well, I—" Shobha faltered. She'd seen the lie her husband had told about the weaver as a sacrifice Pramesh had made for the bhavan and the family. She hadn't thought of Mohan then at all, and now realized what a blow it must have been for him. "What I mean to say," she began, trusting her tongue to find its way, "is that he did what he thought was best. And we must follow him in that."

He did not look well. He sighed and seemed to shrink within himself. Shobha dipped a clean metal tumbler into the clay water pot nearby and carried the full cup to the assistant. As he drank, Shobha spoke. "He *was* dead," she said. "You were right. And my husband was wrong to say otherwise." Mohan ceased drinking, but this time she would not meet his eyes. She excused herself to fetch a pen and paper. "The list," she said as she hastened up the stairs. "I will get you the list so you may be on your way."

Once in her room, she leaned against the old wooden almirah, trying to remember the market items that had seemed so necessary minutes ago. Her face felt heavy and hot, as if all the exertions of her heart were working to pump blood to her head only. The very ends of her hair burned. But she gathered herself, reaching her wrists up so that the metal bangles she wore might cool her face. She uncapped a green glass bottle and rubbed a small amount of oil into her temples. The pungent medicinal smell cleared her mind, and she remembered her errand. She slipped out a torn scrap of paper from the small pile she kept for such things and then rummaged for a pen. And then she spotted something in the pile.

Your Sister, Shobha.

It was one of the versions of her most recent letter to Kamna, every word labored over, only for her to tear the paper into four equal squares for later use and to try again on a fresh sheet. Only now it delivered a truth that was achingly stark in its simplicity. She had just betrayed her husband. She had not told a lie, and her intentions were for the best, but still—she had spoken words against her husband, who had given her comfort after her father died, who had never breathed a word of reproach as her womb refused to hold fast to the soul that had entered and fled before Rani, who'd ignored his family's wishes and put her before all. She could not have done worse if she'd announced to a bhavan full of priests and guests and dying folk, and to stragglers in the lane, within Pramesh's hearing, that he was guilty of wrongdoing.

This letter was another betrayal. Pramesh's pain was equally hers, and she had forgotten this in her passion to understand this woman she'd wondered about her entire married life. How certain that handwriting looked as it marched across those four scraps, how assured! She grasped the square and tore it into tinier pieces, and then she dug the other scraps from the pile and did the same. She flung all the bits save one out the arched bedroom window. As they floated in a confused haze before drifting to the ground, she printed the day's market list for Mohan on the remaining scrap and then went downstairs.

29

At sunrise, Narinder led the way to the ghat, Loknath and Dev at his side. Pramesh in a dhoti and Shobha in a new sari delivered a sleeping Rani to Mrs. Mistry's care for the day and followed after. Mohan stayed behind to look after the bhavan. Narinder chose a high platform overlooking the bloated river away from the busy traffic of the steps, and he directed Pramesh to sit across from him, Shobha sitting just slightly behind her husband. Loknath and Dev lined up an array of offerings between them, bananas on green leaves, a row of rice balls, copper vessels filled with holy water, copper lamps with ghee-soaked cotton wicks, small piles of flowers, and then they sat on either side of Narinder. As the sun rose higher and the ghats filled with people coming and going to bathe and pray, Narinder began.

He recited mantras for hours, his breaths so seamless between the natural breaks in the line that he seemed to Pramesh not to pause at all. The manager listened closely, watching as the head priest's hands indicated he pour water with a copper spoon into his hand, that he light one of the lamps, that he place one of the rice balls in front of him. Shobha sat with her hands folded in prayer; now and again Dev or Loknath leaned forward to push an item closer to Pramesh's reach so he might be able to access it at exactly the point when Narinder indicated it was time. A vein stood out on Narinder's forehead as he unfurled word after sacred word. Pramesh's hands did not tremble, and his voice was strong in repeating back the mantras the priest nodded at him to say.

All the while he concentrated, his mind fixed not on Sagar or pots or the washroom but on the great God, and soon the crowds of people who drifted their way and watched, curious, or the ones who walked by indifferent, the chatter and laughter and distraction of the ghats all melted away, and he felt himself so fully immersed that he did not notice the sun's passage across the sky, forgot even that Shobha was just behind him, saw nothing but the task at hand, focused on performing this ceremony of appeasement for Sagar perfectly, so that everything he had done wrong the first time, and every element of his cousin's bad death, might be wiped away completely.

Walking back to the bhavan, Pramesh was exhausted, but at Mrs. Mistry's, Rani ran straight into his arms and he swung her up and to his shoulders, grasping her chubby legs to steady her. Her short fingers gripped his hair, grown back to what it was before Sagar burned on the pyre. He breathed deeply. At home, he ate the simple meal that Shobha prepared, and before putting Rani to bed, he carried her out to the courtyard to show her the sky stippled with stars.

"I will stay up," he said to Shobha once he'd tucked a blanket over Rani.

In his office, Pramesh waited out the time. He'd made many mistakes in his lifetime, perhaps more than any man had a right to. Yet to regret what had gone wrong, he would also have to regret what had gone right. His wife. His daughter. His livelihood. His city. All this had come out of a single act of selfishness, an act that doomed Sagar to one kind of life even as it raised Pramesh to the happiness he'd come to know in Kashi. The new life, the one that remained with Shobha and Rani, would not have been possible without Sagar. He could trace it all back to a single moment, a single word.

They were men, twenty-one years old and tall, Sagar more muscular than Pramesh, with identical neat mustaches.

"Kashi?" Sagar had said. "Why would you want to go to Kashi?" They sat on the kitchen floor, eating the rice and dal that Bua spooned onto dried banana leaf plates, talking of where they might go if they had the choice and the means.

"Well, what is wrong with Kashi?" Pramesh said between bites. "The holiest place in the world. Doesn't that interest you?"

"Holy, unholy, it's all simply *land* to me."

"Always the farmer." Pramesh shook his head.

"I know what it is with you and Kashi," Sagar said, taking more dal and shoving a great fingerful into his mouth. "It's the Mothers. You listened to the stories too much, Bhai. You always took them as truth."

Pramesh flushed. "It's not a serious thing for you," he said.

"I'm not laughing at you, Bhai. You should go! See all the places Ma and Tayi talked about—why not? All those thousands of pilgrims going to Kashi every year—you're not the only one following a story."

Pramesh couldn't tell if Sagar was being serious or jesting. "Forget, then, that it is holy," he said. "It is still a city, nah? Neither of us has been to one; Kashi is closest."

"But *Kashi*?" Sagar wrinkled his nose. He had not shed certain facial expressions from childhood. *Sagar smells something bad!* Pramesh would shout when they were younger and his cousin made that same face. Now he laughed as he ate.

"Bhaiya," Pramesh said, smiling as he scooped more rice and dal into his mouth. "I am talking of where it is *possible* for us to go." He glanced down the short hall to the front veranda where the Elders lounged in the evenings. Usually, they were obliged to take the evening meal with them, eating in silence and communicating via small motions of the hand or a smirk.

"They are out late tonight," Sagar said.

"Doing the usual?"

"No, something different. They wore their best sandals. They were walking somewhere, it seems."

The cousins fell into a different line of talk as they ate. After, they lay outside on the veranda on low rope beds, a kerosene lamp flickering between them.

"Well, where would you go?" Pramesh asked, yawning. He lay on his stomach, the dinner a satisfying weight within.

Sagar reclined on his side with his head propped on one hand. "Oh, I don't know," he said. "Perhaps I would visit you in your Kashi, or wherever you might go. But I suppose I would simply come right back here."

Pramesh smiled. For three years, Sagar had carefully won the favor of the surrounding farmers. He'd looked over the messy account books, created schemes to increase their meager production and bring in money for more land. He was so young, yet he had a head for such a life, the neighbors often said in admiration. The Elders, meanwhile, spent their days on these same rope beds and drank and smoked beedis and remained mostly silent. The land had shrunk since the family's prime years, when fields fanned out around them in all directions. But it was enough to make a life.

A life—just one. Pramesh had never felt at home with farming, preferred listening to their neighbors tell stories rather than their advice on how to approach the coming planting season. When Sagar was outside, Pramesh remained in, reading from his mother's collection of religious texts, the Bhagavad Gita and Puranas long since falling to pieces.

"And the land is the only reason you'd come back?" Pramesh raised his eyebrows at Sagar, who now lay with his arms folded beneath his head, eyes closed. A small smile curled his mouth, and Pramesh laughed. His cousin couldn't keep the secret, no matter how he pretended to. The previous summer he'd begun to make excuses to go to Jaya's grandparents' house while she was visiting—to borrow this or that, to drop off something ostensibly at Bua's request.

"As if she would have you," Pramesh teased. "You were so mean to her when we were children!"

"Me? I was a prince of a boy," Sagar retorted. "No finer manners anywhere." He listed his best qualities as Pramesh snickered. They stayed up late, talking, and eventually fell asleep. They did not hear the Elders come home.

In the morning, the cousins rose and washed and went into the kitchen for their chai. Bua handed them steel cups and continued thumbing her prayer beads while they drank. When they were finished, Sagar headed outside as usual and Pramesh went to continue his reading, but their aunt stopped them. "Your fathers are waiting to speak to you," she said. Something in her tone was off, and Pramesh caught Sagar's eye. "Outside," she said. "They are waiting on the veranda."

The men were seated together on one of the rope beds and indicated that the cousins should share the other. When they were children, the cousins had felt the Elders to be giants; they had dictated Pramesh and Sagar's every motion. At some point the beatings had stopped, though the drunken diatribes and evenings of shouted vitriol continued. As the cousins aged, the Elders shrunk to average size, or perhaps it was only their own arrival into adulthood that balanced their perspective.

"There is a man in town," Pramesh's father said without preamble. "A man whose nephew is very important at the university in Kashi."

"The head of sciences," Sagar's father added. They went on, one speaking and the other elaborating: Though the admissions period had passed, though both cousins were older than the usual incoming students, though they still required a personal interview and much convincing, this uncle of the head of sciences had agreed to have his nephew make an exception for somebody from the Prasad family.

"For one of you," Sagar's father said. "Just one."

Pramesh's father cleared his throat. "You will go," he said.

And he looked at Sagar.

Pramesh had listened with increasing excitement, and though his heart dropped when the Elders indicated Sagar, he did not feel jealousy. Sagar had proved himself the ambitious one in the Elders' eyes. Sagar in the fields, Sagar conversing with workmen, Sagar thinking up new ways to do things. Of course Sagar must go.

Except—Sagar did not want to. "He is older," he said, pointing to Pramesh, who felt shocked by this fact, as if his cousin had just accused him of something terrible. "He should be the one to go."

"That is not your decision," Pramesh's father said, refusing to look at his son. After all these years, that man still felt the sting of coming in second, of having a child whom he saw as inferior to his brother's. "We have evaluated your character, your prospects, the way you have lived thus far. We have agreed."

"You have proved yourself more capable, physically and mentally," Sagar's father said, not without a ring of triumph in his voice as he looked at his son. To these older men, the cousins were merely players in another contest, one that had taken many years to come to a climax. Sagar was the victor, the one who could do what Pramesh could not.

Sagar was disgusted. "This is nonsense. Why gift us this thing if you are giving the gift to the wrong person?"

"Careful," Sagar's father said, the warning in his voice that once terrified the cousins as children.

Sagar grabbed Pramesh's hand and raised it in the air. "This is the one who should go. When will you wake up and see that?"

"Sagar!" Pramesh's father roared, a man who had once beaten them equally for the most insignificant of faults. But the cousins were no longer children, and they were no longer afraid. Sagar stalked off the veranda and disappeared behind the house and into the fields. Pramesh followed.

Sagar had devoted one field to wheat, one to mustard, one to rows of different vegetables. A fourth plot, the smallest, was overrun with sugar cane. "Something different for each one," Sagar had explained to Pramesh. "In a year, we will see what does best and go from there, expand, increase production." The Elders disapproved of this tactic, waiting for the experiment to fail, but so far the fields seemed to support everything, each crop flourishing in its own plot. Pramesh found his cousin at the edge of the wheat field. The green plants reached his knees. The air smelled sweeter here than by the house, where beedi smoke and cooking fires colored everything with a dark smoky taint. He stood beside Sagar and surveyed the field, trying to see the land with the same eyes as his cousin.

"You are angry," he said after a time.

"And you are not," Sagar replied. There was both irritation and weariness in his voice.

"What they say is true. You will get more benefit from it. Go, learn something, and bring back what you know when you are finished. It is only four years."

"A wasted four years," Sagar muttered. He reached out to grab a thin wheat stalk and tore the top away from its root. A green smell rose from the exposed broken ends. "And what will *you* do while I am gone? Will you take care of all of this?"

"I won't be totally helpless," Pramesh said with a rueful look. "The neighbors will be there to advise me. We will write; you will tell me what to do. And when you return, you will have your fields again."

"And then? What will *your* life be then?"

"My life?" They had never talked of lives as separate things: *your* life, *my* life. *Our* life was the way they'd always thought of it. A journey they embarked upon together. They had their differences—Sagar with his land, Pramesh with his books—but those were just likes and dislikes. Fundamentally, they had grown together, like two tree trunks growing so closely that the trunks entwine and mesh. No difference between where one tree began and the other ended.

Even when they each married, they would still be together to raise their children in the same home. And then Pramesh understood. "We can go talk to her parents, her grandparents, together," he said. "We can ask them to wait. To have their daughter married to a university-educated man—what family would refuse that chance? Perhaps they might even consent to an engagement. We can tell the Elders, say you won't go unless they speak on your behalf as part of the bargain."

"The Elders?" Sagar laughed. "I wouldn't dare send them. It would be a disaster, Bhai—they know us only as the sons of two drunks. As does the whole village."

"No," Pramesh said. "They know us for us now. Separate from the Elders. And you know they respect you." He couldn't tell if Sagar was listening to him. "Four years," he said again. "It isn't such a long time. Then life will be as it was."

Sagar threw the torn wheat stalk away from him, where it floated to rest near its root end, still firmly planted in the ground. "Don't you see? Nothing will be as it was, Bhaiya. They've made sure of that." He turned abruptly and stalked off. His gait, the stiff way he held his shoulders, told Pramesh that he wanted to be alone.

That night, Sagar arrived late for dinner. They ate in silence. Before he rose, his father spoke. "You will leave in a week," he said. And that was all. Discussion over.

Because Sagar refused to prepare, Pramesh did so for him. He laid out his cousin's new shirts and pants that Bua had quickly made, and packed a small bag with all the things he thought were needed. Sagar neither helped nor advised, except to take his handkerchiefs—embroidered by his mother and Pramesh's—and hand them to Pramesh to be packed away with the rest of it.

On their last night, Pramesh lay on his reed mat. He tried to imagine what the farm would be like for four years, all that time without his cousin, and could not. He hadn't really believed in this imminent parting; he wouldn't until the event actually happened and he was left alone as the train pulled away, watching Sagar go farther and farther until his cousin was gone.

Sagar came in and closed the door. "Listen," he said. "You know you must go in my stead."

Pramesh kept his eyes closed. "The bags are packed. Your letter of introduction is waiting. Why start this again?" A kick in the legs opened his eyes. Sagar stood over him.

"This is not a joke."

Pramesh sat up. "No, it isn't. Everything has been prepared. We can't simply decide differently. The Elders decided; the letter of introduction is for *you*."

"Forget the letter, forget everything. This is the chance for you, don't you see?"

But Pramesh didn't see. "I am not jealous, Sagar-bhai," he said. "I want you to go. The Elders are right, you will get more benefit from it."

"No, you are wrong, completely wrong." Sagar was whispering fiercely to avoid waking the others in the house. "They care nothing about the benefit to you or me. They care only about their game, about the winner. We are pawns, Bhaiya—we always have been. No more. I will not go in your place; I will not take the path you have the most right to. I refuse."

He was serious; Pramesh could see it in his face. His heart sped. He had not allowed himself to yearn to go because he had truly felt that his cousin should have the chance. "You are sure?" he asked.

"I am, Bhaiya," Sagar said.

"The Elders. . . ." Neither had so blatantly disobeyed them before.

"They made their choice. We made ours. What can they do? We are not children anymore, Bhaiya. All our lives, it has always been the two of us, taking care of each other. Why should it be different now?"

"One word," Pramesh said. "One word from you, Bhaiya, and I will go. But you must think carefully before you speak. Think it over first."

Sagar stared at his cousin. They both knew what the answer would be. "Go."

That was how Pramesh allowed himself to be convinced. "I will visit, every year. And after the four years, I will be back for good."

Sagar flopped down on his reed mat, assuming Pramesh's position from moments before. "Look at you, Bhaiya," he said, eyes closed. "Going to Kashi after all."

Early that morning, before leaving, both Sagar and Pramesh knelt to touch their aunt's feet. She hugged Sagar, lightly running her hands over his hair, and she held Pramesh tightly. She handed Sagar a packet and then turned away. The Elders said nothing as the cousins set out for the train station. As soon as they were far enough away from the house, Sagar pressed the packet into Pramesh's hands. "She knows," he said. Pramesh opened the cloth covering and found a stack of warm rotis slick with ghee. "I tried to tell her this morning, but she already knew, somehow."

Pramesh peeled one from the stack for Sagar and took one for himself. It was just roti, just water and flour, but he savored this one, knowing he might not taste another like it for some time. How many had Bua made for the boys over the years, rolling out round after round, hunched before the hearth? "She is a good woman," he said, putting the packet into the bag that had been Sagar's, packed so hastily the night before with his own things replacing his cousin's.

They walked in unaccustomed, awkward silence. "I will be back soon enough," Pramesh said to dispel the quiet. "Even if the school takes me in. . . . Anyway, it will be as it was before."

"Will it?" Sagar said absently. Pramesh looked closely at his cousin. More often lately, a blankness swept his cousin's face that he couldn't read. Pramesh was becoming used to the idea of being two different people, rather than the one fused together that they had been for so long.

"You should ask Jaya now," he said.

Sagar laughed. "And offer her what? I barely know what I'm doing, Bhai—how am I supposed to give her any kind of guarantee of what our future will be like? Besides—they've probably already picked out their future son-in-law. Her parents won't want her marrying a failure."

"Don't ask them to promise anything, but at least let them know your interest, your intention. Don't work in silence, waiting, assuming."

Sagar walked on, thinking. "Well," he said at last, "you might be right. Anyway, even if I was settled, it isn't as if I could marry her straight away." He glanced at Pramesh. "The elder is supposed to marry first, after all. How would it look? What would they say about the Prasad boys otherwise?" he asked in mock horror.

"Idiot." Pramesh flicked Sagar's ear lightly. But he was glad that Sagar's tongue had loosened, and they talked freely as they walked the five miles to the platform at the station.

Theirs wasn't a popular stop, and only a few people milled about. Pramesh paid for his ticket, taking it from the agent. His heartbeat quickened. The ticket made the journey real.

Sagar was standing at the edge of the platform, looking down the tracks in the direction the train would arrive from. He pointed, and Pramesh saw it, a black dot topped with white steam. "Listen," he said. "You must promise me something."

"Anything!" Pramesh felt suddenly excited. Adrenaline powered through his limbs. He was not sure he would be able to sit still for the duration of the journey. "Whatever you wish."

"Forget this place. Do not come back."

Pramesh looked at Sagar, but his cousin kept his eyes on the train. Pramesh laughed. "You are joking."

"Am I?" Sagar said, his lips tight.

"I cannot do that."

Sagar turned to look at him. "No," he said thoughtfully. "I don't suppose you can." The faintest of vibrations began to roll beneath their feet. Pramesh reached out and squeezed his cousin's shoulder.

"Listen," Sagar said again. "Just listen once, before you protest. What is there for you here? They will not allow you the life you want, not while they continue to live. They think I am the winner and you are the loser in one of their contests; they will continue to think so for the rest of their days. This is *life*, Bhaiya, yours and mine—not a contest. Until today we shared everything, but this is where we must part. You are defying them once; do you think they will allow it to happen again?"

A sick feeling burned in Pramesh's stomach. "But to leave you here, with them. . . ."

"That is different. I have chosen my life here. I want the fields, I want to recreate what they lost. You do not."

"And because of that we should never see each other?" The idea was ridiculous, and Pramesh laughed. Sagar did not return his cousin's smile. Pramesh gripped Sagar's shoulders again and squeezed hard. He was yelling now to make himself heard over the loud jangle of the locomotive on the tracks. "You cannot ask me for such a thing."

"I know I cannot," Sagar said, turning to Pramesh. "But I am asking you regardless. How else can you build a life for yourself if you are always tied to the past?"

The train slowed as it approached, steam billowing behind it. They were too far to the front, and they began walking quickly to the back, where the third-class cars were. People streamed off, some of them jumping from the top of the car or alighting as the train moved.

Sagar pushed Pramesh toward the open door of the third-class carriage. The wails of a screaming child poured from the car; a man blocked the stairway as he glanced backward and chatted with his companion. "Bhai, just a moment, can you move just a bit?" Sagar yelled at him, and then he gave Pramesh a hard piercing look and pushed him up the stairs. There was no available seat, but Pramesh shoved his way to an open window and leaned over the annoyed man seated there so he could look down at Sagar waiting below. The train jerked forward, and Sagar lifted his hand in farewell.

"I won't make you that promise," Pramesh said, his voice rising above the talk and rickety wheezes from the engine.

"I know. I knew you wouldn't," Sagar said. "You will always do the thing that I cannot."

"Really, Bhai," the man at Pramesh's elbow said, glaring. "Must you?"

"A moment," Pramesh said. "I'm sorry, but just until the train leaves." He felt his heart in his chest. This was not how he envisioned his departure. He was not supposed to give up one happiness in exchange for another.

A low grasping rumble vibrated beneath him. "Just one thing," Sagar yelled up at him in a rush. "Make me another promise if you cannot hold to the first one."

"Anything sensible," Pramesh said, hoping for a return smile.

"When the train leaves, don't look back at me, at anything."

"But—"

"You've already committed. You are starting a new path in your life, so start it correctly. Look to the future, not to the past. Keep this promise for me, at least." The engine rumbled louder, the wheels groaned and began to move forward. Sagar looked so sincere. Desperate, even.

"All right then. I promise."

One last look at Sagar: the split in his eyebrow, the identical mustache, the sweat on his forehead. And the eyes, the eyes in which he longed to see a spark of laughter but which instead met him with a determined and steady look. The train continued to creak forward, getting faster. Pramesh leaned forward, craning his neck, but he remembered his promise just as Sagar shouted, "Never look back, Bhaiya! You promised!"

Pramesh straightened from the window and turned his eyes to the front. He imagined Sagar standing on the platform, watching the train pick up speed. He pictured Sagar's dusty sandals, his worn cotton trousers. He'd had his whole life to memorize Sagar's features, and yet now Pramesh was burning, even frantic, for one last look at his cousin. The other request, the one Pramesh refused, throbbed in his mind.

Forget this place. Do not come back.

That promise was unthinkable, but he kept the other. He did not look back.

The clock hands reached two hours past midnight. Pramesh walked out to the courtyard, pausing in front of the quiet washroom. Narinder and Loknath came to the door of their quarters, Dev lingered with the book he'd been reading from near No. 5, Sheetal sitting in the open doorway. They all waited.

The washroom was silent. The pots were stacked in neat rows, static. He walked around the room, stood in spots where he'd felt the pain of that sound, the horrible thoughts slithering through his mind, under his skin. He felt nothing but the emptiness of the room. He wished for Govind, wished he knew what to look for. Yet here was proof: in a place and at a time of night when his thoughts had only been in chaos, he now had a clear mind.

Sagar, the last vestige of that old life of Pramesh's, of that first family whose blood was his own—was he truly gone? Was he now making his way to the Vaitarani river? Pramesh hoped for it, hoped that the calm that descended on him in this place that had held so much pain meant that Sagar, too, was appeased.

Narinder hovered near the doorway, then crossed the threshold. He took a turn about the room as well, completing the round with sure steps. When he was finished, he looked at Pramesh, a grim satisfaction in his eyes, and he walked out the door, murmuring the great God's name beneath his breath.

Shobha was awake and waiting for him, her eyes bright with the question he could see even in the dark.

"Nothing. Not a sound." He lay down next to her, wrapping his arms around her and resting his head atop hers, feeling her nestle closer. He searched himself to see what he felt, where Sagar was in his mind. There was sadness—but more than that, a desire to move forward and leave the past behind. *Gone.* Soon he fell into dreamless sleep.

30

Mohan held vigil in his small room. When the others had returned from the tripindi shraddha, he excused himself, fixing his face into a pained look while holding his stomach, but the manager hardly acknowledged him, his focus elsewhere. Late that night, he heard the priests gather in the courtyard, waiting to see if the pots would ring out, and the assistant took his chance, slipping through his window with his small bundle of clothes. He stood outside the locked gates, a thickness rising in his throat like dough. For so long he'd guided pilgrims through the city, but he'd never imagined that he'd one day have to guide himself.

Into the night's embrace he went, feeling no weariness despite the hour. His loyalty, his unswerving good faith, his true fellow feeling for that family that had replaced the one he'd never known—what had been the use of any of it? Tonight, he was determined to leave the past behind him. Yet uncertainty dogged his steps. Guilt that had been his companion since the arrival of the ghost in the washroom continued to walk with him. And one other thing refused to leave Mohan—his frantic bowels, which forced him to make a detour.

The swollen river lapped at the first few stone steps of Mir ghat as if to touch the feet of the city. Boats bobbed and swayed on the water as far as their tethers allowed. Mohan kept to the topmost steps and walked to the middle of the ghat, to the place that street-sweeper child and holy man alike often used as their toilet according to urgency and the audience. Often he had cringed at the thought of such filth near such holiness, of man indulging in that essential earthly act when the divine Ganges and several temples were so near. Why couldn't they walk the short distance to the line of public toilets just two lanes behind? How could control elude them *here*? Now he longed for restraint even as he tore open his pants and squatted in the dark, his brass lota beside him at the ready with water he'd dipped from the distended river.

"Hai Rama," Mohan groaned. "Hai hai Rama." He leaned his forehead against the concrete wall that rose in front of him with its scabbed-over layers of paint and grime. As he felt the more tangible of his troubles slip from his body, he relaxed, and, for just a few seconds, he forgot all the awkwardness of his situation, forgot all that lay before and behind and beneath, forgot himself completely and experienced the bliss of a blank mind.

And he forgot one more thing. In all of his nighttime excursions, he had always locked onto one face and one memory: the warning of old farmer Ramu, squeezing chunks of sugar cane between his ancient teeth. *Never go at night! Never!* Always Mohan had been on his guard against those spirits preying in the dark—but if Ramu could have seen his erstwhile disciple now! Mohan, back exposed to the wide expanse of steps fanning behind him, to the river, and to the gaping maw of Magadha, a country of spirits unto itself. His sealed eyes, shut not in prayer but in contentment. A wisp of warm air emerging from his parted lips as he exhaled, a stench rising from below him as he lingered, and the false belief that all was right and well. In those few ruinous seconds, Mohan did not exist in the world. But the world came to pull him back.

Someone, somewhere, sneezed with such violence that Mohan almost lost his balance. Now alert, he flung hurried splashes of water onto himself from his lota and sprung to his feet, pulling his pants up and stepping down from the top ledge to assess the ghat. Ramu's warning rang anew in his mind and echoed his fear. "Who is it?" he called out into the night, his voice quivering like a flame in the breeze. "Who is there?"

He didn't know what he expected. Ghosts, after all, never arrived with a specific physical form. They revealed their presence in the things they did and the sounds they made, like the raucous spirit he had just left behind in the bhavan washroom. He heard sand scraping stone, and footsteps first hesitant and then certain. From the dark, a figure emerged. At a different time, Mohan might have thought the shape coming toward him was a walking corpse, a half-burnt body emerging from the sticky slurry of river and mud and trash at the base of the ghats. But lately he'd had enough of dead men come to life. Impatience settled into his limbs as his eyes traced the figure of a living man, one Mohan recognized. Maharaj walked toward him, hugging his clay pot in the darkness.

"Ah, Rama," Mohan groaned beneath his breath. If only emotion could be like a muscle, something he could exercise at will, but he could no more control his feelings than he could rein in his bowels. Still some paces away, Maharaj slipped on the wet stone and only just caught himself with one hand on the step behind him, the other holding tight to his precious pot.

Pity and obligation, and some resentment as well, welled in Mohan's chest. How could he leave now? How could he abandon Maharaj on the ghat, where he might slip again on the wet stone or be easy prey for thugs? No, Mohan had seen the man and now it was his duty to protect him, the task as good as assigned to him by the great God.

"Don't you know this isn't a safe place for you, walking alone in the middle of the night?" he asked, coming to meet the man on the same level.

"Some nights it is difficult to sleep," Maharaj said. "Some nights a man must walk." He seemed unsurprised at meeting another wandering the ghat; his tone was companionable, as if he had only been waiting for someone to come and chat with him.

"Where do you usually sleep? I will take you there; it is no trouble."

The drunk instead lowered himself to sit on the cold stone, hugging his clay pot. After a moment, he set the pot down by his side and then looked up at Mohan, his eyes hopeful. The assistant sighed, looked toward the sky. "From Shankarbhavan, yes?" Maharaj asked.

Mohan winced. Was he still from the bhavan? Was he still from anywhere? "Yes," he said, and left it at that.

"What were you doing up there?" the drunk countered. "All alone, in the middle of the night—such a thing is to be saved for the morning; don't you know this?"

"Yes, yes," Mohan sighed. "But sometimes it cannot be helped."

"It's simply a question of proper diet," Maharaj said with airy comfort. "Eating the right things at the right time, nah?"

Mohan suppressed another sigh. "Come," he coaxed. "No need to continue to speak of it. Shall we go?"

"But this is a dangerous place!" the drunk said, evidently excluding himself from his own warning. "To do such things here. . . . You were lucky this time. Find some other ghat if you must—Lalita ghat is right there," Maharaj continued. He smacked his lips and shook his head. "But to stop *here*, of all places. . . . Such is the action of a man who does not fear a cursed fate." He peered at Mohan. "Don't you know the story I speak of?"

Mohan tried not to let his interest catch. "This city has many stories."

"Yes, but what of *this* story? The story of the ghost that wanders here."

"Ah," Mohan said, disappointed. Everyone knew the story Maharaj spoke of, the story of the Green Parrot Girl. The drunk was like someone's grandfather left out on the porch, calling out to all who passed by, declaiming the same story that had already been told so many times it was falling apart at the seams.

Maharaj chuckled. "You think it is nothing, that it is *just* a story, nothing real in it. But all stories were alive for someone, once."

"As many as die here still linger afterward," the assistant murmured, and then, louder: "Well, they say the spirits are everywhere, not just this ghat."

"All the more reason to be careful, nah?"

"Yes," Mohan said, changing tack. "Yes, you are right. I have been a fool." He held his hand out to Maharaj. "And because this is such a dangerous place, we should go now. Come, where do I take you?"

The drunk looked down at the assistant's hand as if he had never seen one before. Then, he faced the river and blew a long stream of air from his mouth. "It is a woman's, they say."

"Yes, yes, I know."

"Do you? And what else do you know?"

"From a Kashi family. Married, I believe. A sad story—she birthed a child and lost it, all in the same day. And then the lady herself, just some time later, dead. Grief, they say."

"But it was more than grief." There was a tone in the drunk's voice that made Mohan's heart sink: the man was enjoying himself, and once he began speaking he was likely to continue for hours into the night. Mohan sighed, accepted his fate, and took a seat on the ghat.

"She talked in her sleep," the drunk said. "From the wedding night until her final evening on this earth, she said things, whole conversations, her eyes closed. And always, always she said the same words in her dreams. Over and over. *Hari, don't leave me.*"

This part was new. "Hari—her husband?" Mohan said.

"No," the man said. "Nobody knew who this Hari was, but, of course, when a woman begins to say another man's name in her sleep, there is always trouble. And then she began leaving her bed at night as well. She would find some way out of the house and go walking: down her street, to her neighbor's, in the alleys. Sleepwalking. Traveling in her dreams. She never remembered any of it when she woke. They found her on the ghat near her home once, sitting with her eyes blank and open. It was all very puzzling, because she was fine during the day, you see. And soon, the city began to talk."

"The girl who danced with ghosts, the girl turned into a parrot, the girl who caught the glance of the evil eye. . . ." Mohan listed off all the different iterations of the tale he knew.

"See, you *do* know! Those stories, others, all flying through the air in Kashi like a swarm of gnats, until the gossip shifted direction. She stopped with the nighttime walking, she stopped asking for Hari. That was when she carried a child within her."

"Yes," Mohan said. He knew the rest: a girl was born, cries of happiness exploded in the streets only to turn into cries of despair. The babe passed even before the girl could first put it to her breast. A quick summer fever, they said.

"Very soon after her child died, she again began asking for Hari again. *Hari—why have you left me? Hari, I am coming.* At night, the sound of her anklets made the rounds down the lane and back. Each footstep like a shower of tears." Maharaj paused, his breath halting in his throat like a scarf caught on a thorn. "She must have walked so far during those nights! Her feet must have touched every part of Kashi, eyes open, but dreaming all the while. And then, the day arrived that all of us knew was coming. Or rather, the *night* arrived. She left the family home, fast asleep as always. The hours slipped by. And the sun rose, the city awakened, but she did not return." Maharaj's voice faded away. He rubbed his bearded chin with the back of his hand.

"Yes?" Mohan prompted. The drunk said nothing, but his jaw worked silently. He gestured behind him.

"They found her on the ghats," he said. "On *this* ghat. She had slipped, they said, slipped on the wet stone, for she walked even in the rains. Her neck broke while she slept."

"Her family," Mohan said, "her husband's people—why did they not watch over her in the night? Why did no one follow her, protect her?"

Maharaj's shoulders slumped. "Who can tell?" he said. "But they say that the woman did not have another child because she refused her husband, that whenever he attempted to come near her she cried all the louder for her Hari. And they say that the mother-in-law had begun to make inquiries about a *new* daughter-in-law, one who might fill the current one's space."

"Hai Rama," Mohan murmured. "How do you know all this?"

"They say—" the drunk continued, his voice low so that the assistant had to strain to hear him, "they say other things. That the ghat steps had been dry that night, and that the water appeared afterward. And that the woman had been awake for her death."

"What?"

"They say that she screamed, or tried to scream, but someone covered her mouth as they—he—dragged her across the steps."

"Rama."

"And that you could hear the anklets chime, those tiny bells ringing as her body fell to the stone."

"*Rama.*" Mohan covered his mouth. He looked at the drunk and saw a small bead of wetness trace its way from the man's eye down the side of his nose to the corner of his mouth. "You were there," the assistant realized. "You saw it happen."

"She would take my hand, sometimes, in the days before she married," Maharaj murmured. "When I heard her going too far down, I would wait for her at the bottommost step, and when she reached me I would lead her back up to the top."

"But after she married? What about that night?"

"That night. . . ." The drunk's voice quavered. He shook his head and tapped his skull, and Mohan understood. Maharaj may have been there on that night in body, but his mind had been absent, arrested in a state of blackout that prevented any new memories from forming. He seemed to remember himself, and he brushed a rough hand over his eyes and straightened his back. "The point is that her ghost still lingers."

"Of course."

"You don't believe me. You don't believe that she is still here, in this world."

"I do, by the great God I do," Mohan said, suddenly aware of the time. Soon he would lose the advantage of darkness.

"How could you know?" Maharaj choked. "Everyone says they *know* of these things, but does that mean anything?"

"I am not simply saying it," Mohan replied. "I believe you because I have seen it."

"What? When did you see her?"

"Not *her*," Mohan replied. "Another ghost. In another place."

"Where?"

"At the bhavan," Mohan said.

"The bhavan!" the drunk said. "At Shankarbhavan? No, you are mistaken. Anyway, how could you know that was what you were seeing?"

Mohan hesitated. His answers heretofore had been firm and confident, but the next answer was not his to give, because the secret belonged to another. Yet what could it matter if he told just one person, and a drunk man at that? If he was leaving the bhavan, he needed to leave *all* of it. Not just the place, the people, but also the pain that had forced him out. "Most certainly a spirit," he said. "Every sign was there. Pots rattling in the early morning hours and other events."

"That is nothing," Maharaj scoffed. "Pots! What can pots prove about a ghost?"

"Well," Mohan began. Again, he hesitated. *He was not dead*, Pramesh had said—had lied—in a declaration before everyone who mattered. And worse: *You cannot even tell a dead man from a live one, can you?* Mohan, at least, would be telling the truth if he continued, and he could leave this place with the satisfaction that someone outside the bhavan knew his side of things. He could unburden himself, here, with the holy river as his witness. "We had a dead man come to life."

"Oh?" The drunk's eyes opened wide. "Is it so?"

"Yes," Mohan said, at once relieved and unsure about what he'd just revealed. "No deaths, ever since the ghost appeared. But this man was dead."

"Are you sure? Aren't you the one they say cannot tell—"

"A lie," Mohan said firmly. "I swear it on the Mother. He was certainly dead, and for some hours. And then, back to life."

"Back to life," Maharaj murmured to himself.

The night was still but not silent: water lapped in wet thuds, insects murmured in rhythmic lullabies. Yet no sound came from the two figures sitting midway up the ghat, their elbows resting on bent knees, their features arranged in identical stoic masks. Facing the river, with the infinite blackness of the night sky reflected in its quiet depths and Magadha beyond, perhaps the two men thought that only they existed in this moment, this city, this world. Then something insinuated itself into their silence.

"What was that?" The drunk cocked his ears toward the sound.

"I heard nothing," Mohan said, his attention only half present. Then he too heard it. A strange scraping sound, like a piece of wood being dragged down the ghat. Low and gravelly, this stretched growl soon turned into a rhythmic knock, a repeated *thuk thuk thuk* that echoed. Something beyond them was moving. "Is that—" Mohan began, his tongue losing its way in the middle of the thought. Louder and faster came the *thuk, thuk, thuk,* and now there was something else besides. A lighter, silvery sound floated above the heavy plodding. Perspiration bloomed on Mohan's forehead. "A bell?" he whispered. "Hai Rama, are those *bells*?"

"This is the hour," the drunk murmured. "Oh, Rama; this is the hour."

"The hour for *what*?" Mohan croaked.

"The hour for these things to roam. The hour for worlds to cross." Maharaj stretched his arms out toward the river, as if he were presenting that holy water to the assistant, embracing it. "One land cursed," he said, pointing in the direction of Magadha. "And the other blessed, and the water a thin bridge between. Did I not tell you? This is a dangerous place." He continued his muttered mantra: "This is the hour, this is the place, this is the hour. . . ."

"Come, whatever it is, we should leave," Mohan said. Brass water pots in the bhavan were one thing, but an unknown spirit on the ghat was another. He stood, knees shaky, and attempted to take Maharaj's elbow, brushing against the pot sitting at the man's side. As if prodded with a glowing hot iron rod, the drunk jerked himself away with a snarl. "I meant nothing," a worried Mohan said. "If you'd only give me your hand—"

"Yes, and give you everything else of mine as well, I suppose," Maharaj said as he backed away with his pot in his arms, his movements devoid of the earlier stumbling and caution that had worried the assistant so.

The *thuk thuk thuk* behind them quickened.

Bewildered, Mohan walked toward the drunk. "Come now," he said as he took slow steps on the ghat. "It is late and you are tired."

In answer, a hollow thud sounded some meters away. An abandoned wooden crate had bounced down the steps, as if by an invisible hand, landing some paces away. The sounds of *thuk* and bells ceased, and several things happened at once:

Mohan leapt forward, hoping to catch Maharaj before he stumbled and injured himself.

The drunk fell back, releasing his hold on the pot and sending it tumbling down. On the last step, it cracked open, and half the shards fell into the waiting river. With a yelp, the drunk slid down after it, spitting the great God's name. Mohan cried out, stumbled and grabbed Maharaj's shoulders, trying to drag him further up into the safer and higher regions of the ghat.

"You cannot have it," the man snarled as he reached his hands into the water and grasped about the wet darkness. His fingers felt something, his hands curled and lifted, and he flung his prize—a hardened bit of stone and earth—in a wild arc that ended at Mohan's head.

Mohan landed on his back with a shocked gasp and spoke no more.

⚬

Staggering about in the dark, Maharaj made his way up the stairs. He reached Mohan and touched that man's hands and stomach and legs and face, searching for clues of movement, of warmth, of life, and instead finding stillness and damp. His hand rested on Mohan's head and came upon a wetness whose odor he recognized. "Ah Rama, Rama, Rama!" the drunk cried.

He knew enough not to remain in this place. He carefully made his way back to the last step and felt about the stone. So dark, impossible to see, yet he knew he'd heard that bag pop out of the shattered pot. Maharaj's eyes strained, and his hands came upon a limp piece of cloth, the ties undone. He upturned it and emptied the remaining contents into one trembling palm. For years, he'd safeguarded that pouch of treasures, the last remnants of that other life, in his clay pot. No one had thought to look there, not even Thakorlal. Over and over his fingers searched through the small trinkets therein, but he could not find the one thing he was looking for. "Where is it?" he whispered. "Oh, my love—where are they?" Desperate eyes turned back to the river, and he knelt and ran his quivering hands over the stone. Nothing.

He dared not tarry any longer. Maharaj flew up the stone stairs, bound for the house of the only man he trusted and the only substance guaranteed to clear his mind: the metal-man Thakorlal and his home brew. As he ran from the ghats his thoughts lingered on the man he'd abandoned. "Dead!" he said to himself as he ran into the night. "Dead!"

The ghat was still. Even the river paused in lapping against the unyielding stone. No movement came from the man sprawled on the steps. The blood that had spread in a steady trickle from his head ceased its flow. His chest lay as flat as unleavened dough. All was quiet.

Thuk thuk thuk.

The wooden crate, on its side on the hard stone, began to move again. It inched slowly across one level of steps. At an uneven joining of the stone, the crate came to a struggling halt. The crate pushed and pushed, trying to get over that lip in the steps, until it turned over and tumbled down the stone again, this time landing in the water with a melancholy gulp.

Something stirred from where the crate once lay, stretched, and moved. A glint of silver flashed in the dark, accompanied by a tinkling chime. And out stepped a cat.

Gray, placid, the cat glanced around, green eyes taking in with lazy interest the scattered tableau before it. The bobbing crate under which it had been napping. The black water. The man on the steps. And the silver anklets curled under the man's foot, wrapped in a dirty bit of green silk. The cat opened its mouth and yawned. A pair of silver bells, affixed on a ragged length of string tied around its neck, sang out in soft notes. It licked its paws and then stalked up the stairs, disappearing into the dark.

Sometimes, only questions remain.

How could a docile girl, an ordinary woman, become a malevolent spirit that even the strongest and most practical of men feared? How to reconcile the girl who sat by the window, waiting for her husband and waving to little children who yelled at her from below, with the ghost whose reputation controlled the movements of an entire city when they traveled to one tiny ghat? How to create a logical path between the living and the dead?

Where did she go when she walked at night? Did she take the same path each time, or did her steps deviate? Did she stay in one part of the city? Did she really walk the entire time, until the sun rose and found her in bed, or did she stop and rest? Did her eyes remain open or closed? Did she sleepwalk before her marriage? Did she know what had happened when she woke? Was she like a body housing two souls, one dominant during the day and the other presiding at night?

And Hari: a lover, of course, but who was he? Perhaps a man she had met while traveling? Was he a guest whom her family had hosted, the son of one of her father's school friends? An old love, no doubt, but what were the circumstances of their first meeting? What of the love letters they might have exchanged, the tokens of affection passed between their hands? Did her parents know and disapprove? Or did Hari jilt her? Did she enter her marriage in a pure and true state? Or was she willfully deceitful? And did the deceit eat away at her soul, her sense, did it goad her feet to walk until the streets were marked with her footprints?

How did her parents arrange her marriage? Did they know? Did they suspect that a demon sat on her shoulder, nudging her along at night, or did they worry that her mind was fragile? Did they think the evil eye rested its gaze solely on her, or did they seek out doctors, holy men? Did they attempt to exorcize her, or did they leave her be and hope everyone else would as well? Did the sickness exist elsewhere in her family?

Did she goad her mother-in-law or did she wear the mantle of duty, no matter how difficult? Was her husband good or bad? Did he force himself upon her when she pushed him away, or did he keep his distance and nurse a wounded heart? Did marriage turn her into a different person, or had she been the same all along? Did she kill her own child?

Who did she blame for her death? What did she want, what made her linger? When would her ghost be satisfied and leave? And when she finally departed, would she still receive the boon of an end to her incarnations, or would she suffer rebirth? Are the actions of a ghost the same as the actions of a living person? Are they weighed on the same scale of good and bad, duty and sin?

Did she cling to life until the end?

Was she relieved to die?

Was the yearning mapped in her human heart something she was permitted to keep as a wandering ghost?

PART IV

31

Shobha had always been an early riser, but the day after the tripindi shraddha she allowed herself a few extra minutes in bed, stretching out her limbs, listening to Pramesh's deep slumbering breaths. She rose, pressing her husband's feet and pulling the blanket back up over Rani, who'd kicked it off in her sleep, before heading downstairs. She tended to the bhavan's home shrine, lighting incense, circling each picture and silver figurine with the flame ensconced in the small copper lamp she held, applying red sindoor and rice to the holy foreheads. She finished her puja with two quick rounds of her prayer beads, reciting the great God's name.

She picked through the rice and set it to soak, then checked to see if there was enough roti left from the night before for the morning meal. She dusted off her hands and opened the kitchen shutter a crack. And she allowed herself to think about Kamna.

The ghost might have been gone, the washroom quiet, but her mind still rattled with questions, wondering which version of Kamna's story to believe. But did it matter? On the train platform after that disastrous village visit Pramesh had asked her whether she believed in not looking back. She'd said yes—but then what had she been doing this whole time? How easily Pramesh was able to shut the door on any portion of his past life. She needed to learn that trick. She thought of the last letter she'd sent, regretting her haste.

The air was crisp and thick and laden with the scent of the city, of earth and river water and smog and incense. Today was, after all, just a day, a single bead in the necklace of her life. The day would pass, tomorrow would come, and the next day and the next. It would not matter to her fifty beads later on the necklace. She would forget in a hundred. A splinter from the shutter caught on her skin, and she looked down to brush it away. A step sounded; not the milkman's clank and squeak, but someone coming on foot. She turned back to the window and pulled the shutter a hair wider.

The alleyway was empty. *A ghost*, she thought, and a laugh escaped her lips before she clapped her hand over her mouth in dismay. *Shame*, she chided herself. One more glance down the deserted lane, a regretful shake of the head, and then she was back inside the bhavan, readying for the start of the day.

In a way, Shobha had been right. A ghost *was* walking the lane, unseen, one who caught sight of the bhavan mistress and halted in the gully beyond until she slipped back inside. Unlike the other spirits purported to wander Kashi, this was a ghost in name only, dressed in a khaki uniform, making noiseless footsteps even in the most debris-strewn lanes, a ghost who smoothed his hands over oiled hair as he walked.

Bhut was in a foul mood. He was not an early riser, but on this day a fit of insomnia forced him to his feet at an hour that caught his wife, a lover of mornings herself, by surprise. While taking his chai, he thought he'd take a stroll around the lanes, as he'd once done back in the days when necessity and his lower position forced such patrols. "Not a bad thing, being up now," he had said more to himself than to his wife or his two older sisters, who yawned and picked through trays of uncooked rice and lentils. "Not a bad thing," he said again, "to see my city at all times, in every light," and he laughed at his own unintentional joke, for anyone could see that no light had cracked through the darkness just yet. Bhut caught a signal passing between his sisters in the way that only siblings can detect. "What is it?" he asked, wary.

"You never wake up early," his eldest sister said.

"Except for this day last year, yes?" the second eldest said, as if the thought had only just occurred to her.

"And the year before last," the eldest said. She picked out a small stone and tossed it over her shoulder with relish, or perhaps bitterness; Bhut could find no difference between those two emotions when it came to his siblings.

"Is there some point to all of this?" He drained his cup, preparing to leave the room, his new tactic for resolving their arguments. But his sisters' words moved more quickly than he could.

"Since he was thirteen," the eldest said, never looking up from her dish of lentils even when her sister contradicted her, saying that no, it was not thirteen, Bhut had been twelve, or didn't she remember? They had only been in their teens themselves when it happened.

That was all it took. The irritation Bhut had felt as a mere itching flared into something far fiercer. He stood with such violence that his stool shot backward into a wall. His emotion fairly propelled him out the door and into the lane and onward, until soon he was passing the bhavan and avoiding the hostel manager's wife, blinded with temper. Passing beneath Mrs. Chalwah's window, he felt her eyes on him, and though his knee ached, he quickened his pace, refusing to look at her.

Today marked the day of Menaka's death, as Bhut's sisters had so helpfully reminded him. More than fifty years had passed. So many memories, so many things he wanted to forget. He walked to escape all thought, to give movement to his anger. In earlier years, he had imagined that he traced the steps *she* had taken on her last night all those years ago. Now, he scoffed at his own naivete, his hopeful idiocy. Age had taught him which things mattered and which did not. All he wanted now was peace, but the memories kept coming unbidden.

Before she died, there was that awful day when her eyes had brightened as she'd taken her newborn into her arms. His sisters had been at school; he'd feigned illness to witness the excitement. He was the only one left alive who remembered her pained cry, her confusion and despair at holding a baby that abandoned its life as quickly as it had come into it. . . . He would hear that cry for as long as he lived.

Shobha opened the tall kitchen shutter to throw out a bucket of dirty water, and something caught her eye. It was Mrs. Mistry, beckoning wildly. Shobha waved back and stepped through the window to cross the lane.

Mrs. Mistry poured a cup of chai and pushed two low stools together in her kitchen. "Only a moment," she said when she saw Shobha's face.

"There is so much to do," she murmured as she attempted a smile.

"It can all wait," she said as she patted the stool next to her and handed the cup to Shobha. "You must not fatigue yourself. Rest a little, nah?" Shobha nodded and sipped the chai.

"Everything is okay?" Mrs. Mistry asked.

"Yes," Shobha said. "And with you?"

"Yes, yes. And your husband?"

"We are all doing well, praise Rama." Shobha smiled. She did not mind these questions. Unlike Mrs. Gupta, Mrs. Mistry had no ulterior motives, nothing but goodness in her heart. She had as much right to ask about her family's welfare as anyone of Shobha's blood.

Mrs. Mistry swiveled her chin briefly and squeezed her palms in her lap. "There is something I wanted to ask you about," she began. Shobha put her cup down and focused her full attention on her neighbor. "There are times . . ." Mrs. Mistry stopped, then started again. "What I mean is, I learned myself, quite early on after I married, something about my husband. All husbands." Shobha wondered what was to follow. She'd been married nine years; any nuptial advice would have been quite late in coming. "Sometimes you needn't tell them *everything*. Sometimes there are things that they do not need to know. Like that picture over there," she said, pointing to a painted watercolor of a flower one of her daughters had made years earlier. "See that? Now, when your Mistry-maasad sees that picture, he only thinks *Oh! Such a beautiful flower!* He doesn't know as I do that it is there to hide a water stain. See it there?" She stood and walked over and removed the watercolor. A brown stain rippled through the paint on the wall. She rehung the picture and returned to Shobha.

"It's a lovely picture," the bhavan mistress said, "but I don't understand."

"He sees only the good thing, not the bad, because I hide it from him. But does he *need* to see the bad thing? What would it give him if he knew? It would only upset him, so better not to say anything at all."

"Of course," Shobha said. Why had this been so urgent for Mrs. Mistry to relay to her? And then she understood. "If there is something concerning you, something you cannot say to him—"

Her older neighbor waved her hands in the air, as if to dispel the evil eye. "No, no, you must let me finish. *Some* things must be kept from the husband. Only some. And it is our job to determine what those things are. But we must not be too proud to continue hiding the things that get beyond us."

Shobha looked upon her neighbor, this woman whose face was as familiar as her mother's, who had seen her grow up, who had dressed her in her wedding sari, and felt an overwhelming tenderness. She took Mrs. Mistry's hand in her own, the skin as soft as a bird's wing, and looked that woman in the eye. "Tell me what is wrong."

Mrs. Mistry seemed to have run out of words. She squeezed Shobha's hand and pulled something from her blouse. "This isn't a water spot to be keeping from your husband."

Shobha took it. It was a letter, addressed in her own hand, to Kamna. It was the one she'd given to the postmaster in haste on the day Mrs. Gupta stopped her. "Why do you have this?"

"You forgot the stamp," Mrs. Mistry said. "By the time the postmaster noticed, you were gone. But his wife was there, and she saw Mrs. Gupta—they are old friends. And she gave it to her, for you."

The stamp was indeed missing. Shobha turned the envelope over, wondering how she could have forgotten, feeling relief lift her shoulders. Kamna would never receive this letter, at least. Her fingers ran along the top edge and hit a snag. The envelope was open. "Someone has read this," she said, slowly. Her heartbeat quickened, and she looked up, searching the woman's face.

"Not Mrs. Gupta," the old woman said quickly. "She has her faults, but she brought me the letter, whole. She thought it would be better if I gave it to you."

"You opened it?"

"I was worried about you. I knew something was wrong, and you weren't telling me. You never ask for help when you need it; you try to do everything on your own."

"But you read it?"

Mrs. Mistry looked down. "Before your mother died, I promised her I would always help you, even if you did not ask. We both knew how stubborn you can be. I read it because I remember who she is—that Kamna. I remember everything you told me after that village trip when you were first married."

Heat rose into Shobha's face, and all the relief she'd felt at the letter being in her hands instead of on its way to the village disappeared, replaced with mortification.

"Why are you writing to her?" Mrs. Mistry pressed. "Why are you telling her things about yourself, about Rani?"

"It isn't—" Shobha stopped, shaking her head. "How could you do that? How could you simply read it without asking me?" She felt as if she could not breathe.

"That day on the terrace—you asked me if something bad can happen simply if someone wills it. I wasn't paying attention to you. Were you talking about her? What do you expect to gain by writing her?"

"What do you mean?"

"Her nazar—were you saying she'd cast the evil eye on your house?" Shobha felt nauseous. "No," she managed to whisper. "That's not—"

"Does your husband know?" Mrs. Mistry continued. She reached out to cup Shobha's face between her palsied palms. "You cannot keep communicating with this woman without telling him. It will destroy you both."

Shobha jerked away and crushed the letter in her hands. All that she'd left unsaid, all the despair and frustration that she had pushed down, bubbled forth like an overburdened boiling pot. "You are stepping where even my own mother would never dare," she managed to say. Mrs. Mistry's face blurred in the thick haze of her anger. "None of this was your business to fix, none of this—nothing of what happens in *my house* is yours to comment on. It isn't something to laugh about later with Mrs.

Gupta. It isn't—" Tears choked her, and she swallowed a sob, unable to finish. The letter was still balled in her hand, the paper softening from the sweat seeping from her palms.

She rose and left the house. Once in the bhavan she threw the paper into a clay pot and sent a burning match down after it, transforming it into a pile of ashes that would not even fill a teaspoon. Shobha watched the flame and felt her anger recede along with the heat in the pot. She could not understand how the emotion had engulfed her so quickly. Seeing the letter in her neighbor's hands, Shobha had felt like a woman caught without a clean sari on the riverbank. She was humiliated that someone else could know her deepest insecurity, no matter how close, how beloved.

But something else upset her even more. She set to work, threading her thickest needle with a length of strong white thread. She gathered a lime and several fresh chilies, and after spearing a steel skewer through them, she strung them together with the thread, the lime sandwiched in the middle, with the chilies crisscrossing above and below that green orb. Then she gathered dried red chilies and black salt in her fist and went upstairs.

Rani was sleeping quietly, the blanket rumpled at her side, her dark curls haloing her face. She did not stir as Shobha reached up and hung the fresh lime and chili garland from a nail near the window, in a spot directly above the child. Then she knelt, pushing aside a strand of the girl's hair, feeling her temperature with the back of her hand. Rani was cool, and she stirred at Shobha's touch. Shobha held her spice-filled fist up over her daughter's head and circled it over the child seven times, counterclockwise, concentrating on the great God. Then she ran downstairs and emptied her fist into the pot of ash, dropped in another lit match after it, and watched as the spices burned, and with them the evil eye attached to Rani.

She'd never done such a thing in her life. Other mothers were vigilant with lining their children's eyes with black kohl, with dressing them in torn or dirty clothes, all to deflect the evil eye. Had Kamna really set her nazar on the bhavan, on her child? *A woman like that does not forget.* All those years, her imagination had sought to fill in the blanks in that sentence—what kind of woman? Now she did so easily. A vindictive woman. A revengeful woman. A woman who was the reason for Rani being so endlessly sick the last few months, so susceptible to injury. Her hands rose up to her face where Mrs. Mistry had held her, up over her eyes, and she breathed in and out deeply in the way her father had taught her to do when she felt overwhelmed and unable to think for all the thoughts running in her head.

She sighed and turned to the window. Shame over the letters now turned into shame over something else: Mrs. Mistry's house, usually one of the first to open itself to the world, was still shut up; doors barring the day, walls stretching up to the sky. What had she said? Those words had flown with such speed from her mouth that she could not recall them even minutes later.

She took up the clay pot of ash. As she blew the black dust out the window, she took little satisfaction in knowing that, this time, those words would not float back to her.

3 2

Despite his aching knee, Bhut's legs moved to an angry beat until the heat within him cooled, and his pace slowed as his mind cleared; he looked up and took note of where he was. Dal-Mandi Chowk. He had to laugh; his body had known him better than he'd known himself. What better remedy to forget something awful than to come to the place where men came to forget themselves? People paced or loitered outside the dancing houses, but most turned away at the sight of the circle officer. Sickly sweet smells of perfume and moldering refuse surrounded him. A curtain shifted in one upper window, scratchy music emerged from another. He bent to rub his knee, and straightening, he heard a surprised intake of breath just behind him.

A sniffling man stood there, his face stained with tears, his eyes wandering over the smart starched pleats in Bhut's pants and shirt sleeves.

"Ah, here comes the sun," Bhut said dryly as he looked over that man's stricken face. "Shouldn't you be with your moon right about now?"

Raman, that lovesick boatman whose boat had cradled the dead man, was entering Dal-Mandi. The boatman's obsession with the dancer Chandra was well-known. Money was a prerequisite to wooing his paramour, and for so long his mother's savings had been the never-ending pool that he'd dipped into again and again. That woman had long maintained a blind eye to her son's doings, but when he came to her pleading for funds to pay priests to exorcize his boat, the superstitious woman's eyes opened and her pockets closed. One thing for her son to go about with a dancing girl, but to leave his boat—his livelihood!—unsecured as open prey for drifters and malevolent spirits? That was inexcusable. Now she demanded accounting for every coin she put into her son's hands. When Raman found himself without money to finance even his ever-worsening beedi habit, let alone the expensive tastes of his Chandra, the dancer had closed her door against him. He continued to visit her famed house every evening, and though continually rebuffed, he believed each night that this time might be different.

"Ji, I was just with her," he said, which was true in a way.

"What presents for the lucky lady this time?" Bhut pressed. Raman's frivolous largesse with his dancer was just as storied as his ill-placed affection.

Raman breathed in and made a valiant effort at articulation. "Some ornaments, a strand of flowers. . . ."

Somehow Bhut found the presence of this silly fellow to be calming. He reached into his pocket and pulled out a few cloves, which he chewed on as he looked at the boatman. He was old enough to be Raman's father. "You are young still," he said. "It's best not to set your heart in only one direction, you understand?"

"Ji." Raman wagged his head. "Even my Ma has told me this."

"The wisest man always follows his mother," Bhut agreed.

"But it is no use. No, ji, only Chandra, only she."

"You haven't seen the world though, nah?"

"Mother has mentioned other girls, yes," Raman said. His face crumpled. "But who could compare to my Moon?" he moaned.

Bhut was disgusted. Such a man as this, if one could call this weeping sniveling specimen a *man* to begin with, still had families clamoring to have him as a bridegroom for their daughters. And at his own home, two sisters had sat adrift in their own bitterness for years because no man would deign even to take chai from their hands given their family's story. He swallowed his bile. He would not think of that, not today. Raman was not to blame. He was a simpleton, yes, but not at fault. The boatman lifted his shirttail to rub his eyes dry. A faint jingle sounded from his pockets. "What's this?" Bhut asked. He forced a lighter tone. "Some last trinket that couldn't wait until this evening? Is that why you've been straggling back this way?" Raman managed a smile and wagged his head. "Come, come," Bhut said. "Show me the offering you've brought for your goddess."

Raman could not resist. He pulled the bundle from his pocket and held it for the circle officer to see. "Perfect, ji," he said with giddy anticipation as he unwrapped the bundle. "See how slender the chains are? Only an equally slender foot could fit these, only feet like hers, ji!" A pair of silver anklets lay coiled on a wrinkled bit of dirty green silk, like a snake gleaming and reborn from its old papery shed skin. "The shine, see the shine!" Raman babbled on. "A piece of the moon for *my* Moon, nah?"

Bhut stared at the anklets intently. "Where did you get those?" he asked. His voice was just friendly enough for Raman to look up, terrified.

"They were my mother's," Raman said.

Bhut looked at him.

"My sister's!" Raman said.

Bhut looked at him.

"I bought them," Raman said.

Bhut took a step forward.

"Found—I found them," Raman at last said, and when it was clear that still the circle officer did not believe him, Raman became breathless in his haste to push out the truth. "Now! This very morning, only some minutes ago, I swear it, ji! They did not appear to be his—anyway, I did not think he would miss them. How could *he* have a use for them?"

Bhut spoke softly. "Who?"

"The man."

"*What man?*"

"The dead man. The dead man on the ghat."

＊＊＊

With the ample patience of a flower unfurling its first petal, the sun began to rise, illuminating two men walking together in the first light of morning. When early risers noticed the district circle officer together with the boatman in whose vessel a dead man had been found only some months before, wives sent menfolk as emissaries to find out what was going on. Soon Bhut acquired a trail of citizens who bickered and chatted and called after him with all the conviction that men without their morning chai could muster.

"Officer-sahib! Just one minute; some seconds to talk?"

"Someone give that Raman a handkerchief, nah? Crying so many tears that his eyes will swell shut."

Bhut was aware only of the path before him and the weeping boatman behind him, his ears wincing at the soft chimes whispering from the chains wrapped around his fist. The pair of delicate silver anklets felt as weighty as a small mountain. He marched on, his eyes fixed on a single point, his features stiff and unmoving.

"That Bhut," a man whispered to his neighbor. "Arrey, look at his face. He must have the cramping stoppage issues, nah? My missus gave me this remedy: three dried plums. . . ."

One man observed the crowd, Bhut pulling Raman along by the elbow, men tittering over the silver anklets the circle officer did not bother to hide. He watched and waited until all had passed through his lane. Then he called for his wife, who draped his woolen shawl over his shoulders and placed his walking stick in his hand. He headed out the door and down the street in a direction opposite the ghats and the crowd. He'd been thinking about his destination since the black hours of the morning, when an urgent knock on his door had wakened his household. Thakorlal had stood waiting, shivering with nerves and anticipation, and before he could be denied admission, an astounding story had emerged from that metal-man's lips, a story of a well-known hostel assistant, a ghost, and a lie fabricated to cover a death that was actually life. "From Maharaj," Thakorlal had gasped, "a *sober* Maharaj—I know the difference, after so many years. And I also know if he is telling a falsehood."

"And?"

"He was not."

The gates were still closed by the time he reached Shankarbhavan. He peered through the bars: no movement within, and the only sound was of those chanted mantras so familiar to him that he barely registered the pious drone. He laid a hand on the gate and snatched it back as if he had been burnt. The metal was chilled. But he would not be so easily deterred, not after the story he'd heard. He rubbed his fingers and wrapped his palm with the end of his shawl. He grasped the iron bars again and gave them a quick shake. Closed gate or no, they would not be able to avoid him. Kishore would speak to Pramesh.

They arrived at the ghat, a small gathering squeezing through a narrow alleyway that opened up to the stairs, the crowd like water eking out drop by drop from a narrow crack in a bowl. They jostled from behind, pushing the men before them who in turn pushed those in front of them, the slow ripple reaching Bhut and sending a sharp elbow into his back. He turned and glared at the crowd.

"Bhut!" someone called out.

"Where?" the circle officer said, swiveling around, forgetting for a moment that he was the ghost in question. The men surged forward, each eager to lay his claim on the circle officer's attention. Bhut ignored them, heeding only Raman who pulled on his sleeve. "Where did you see this man?" Bhut asked. He shaded his eyes against the sun and squinted.

"Down there," Raman sniffled.

The river sparkled with the sun's radiance, and Bhut's gaze was briefly caught like a bee hooked midair by a particularly fragrant blossom. But then a wet and heavy clap sounded and Raman gasped. Bhut turned. A large sail of green fabric billowed, and he blinked.

He was no longer the circle officer. No longer surrounded by a simpleton busybody mob.

He was transformed back into his twelve-year-old self. A boy surrounded by inept adults, a boy who dreamed for months afterward of what he had seen only in his imagination.

His sister's body, Mini's body, swathed in parrot-green silk, limbs twisted in the fabric, slim feet with naked skin shining where silver anklets usually rested. Blood streaming in the part of her hair where the red sindoor mark of a married woman should have been. Black, kohl-rimmed eyes frozen open. Mouth parted for words never again spoken.

Bhut squeezed his eyes shut. He did not want to see. The anklets coiled around his hand wept in response.

"Well, there is nothing," a voice behind said.

The fabric snapped with a withering crack and Bhut remembered himself. On the lowest step of the ghat, where the stone met the water, a small girl crouched. She squeezed the fabric that seconds ago had been spread out to the wind for her inspection. An arc of droplets flew upward as she rubbed and beat at the length of bright green cloth.

"All this way, for what?" someone tsked.

"A good lesson: follow Raman and you follow a fool." There was more yawning than murmuring amid the small gathering, more impatience than curiosity at whatever Bhut's errand had been.

Bhut focused his fury upon the man who had brought him this far. "So?" he said, each word bitten off with disgust, "This? This is the spot?"

"He was here, he was," Raman gasped. "Where would a dead man go? Where would a dead man *want* to go?"

Bhut's anger emanated from him like an aura: hot, fevered, irrepressible. Hushed at the whiff of violence in the air, like the mynahs that go mute when a tiger passes in their midst, the crowd of remaining men leaned in.

A crack sounded, skin on skin, Bhut's hardened palm hitting Raman's soft dampened face. Red bloomed from the boatman's nose. As if they, too, had been struck, the crowd surged back but pulled forward again, intoxicated by curiosity.

The paternal feelings Bhut had held for this boatman—who cupped his bloodied face in his hands—had vanished. Bhut stared at the air above that crowd of men and chose his words with care. "You were not old enough to have been there when it happened," he began, and the men surrounding him leaned in to better decipher his words. "But you took them." Here he raised his hand, unleashing a melancholy jingle. Raman stared as Bhut turned and faced him. "You took them from someone who *was* there," he said in a hiss audible to everyone. "Who?" Raman swallowed a sob. He opened his mouth. Bhut leaned forward, and he felt the other men in the crowd do the same.

"Ji," was all the boatman said, sobs choking his throat. "Ji."

33

Pramesh had been unable to sleep. His eyes fluttered open at the slight-est creak of the shutters; the bed groaning as Shobha turned jolted him awake. Each sound made him wonder if he was mistaken, if the peace he'd felt earlier was false. But nothing happened; the washroom stayed silent. In the still-dark morning, the first of the birds began to chirp softly, and only then did his eyes droop. Yet it was enough to refresh him, to send a new energy pulsing through his limbs. The ghost had exited; he wondered if death would come back to the bhavan just as suddenly.

He was organizing papers in his office when the front gate rattled; prob-ably some child making mischief on his way to an errand. Mohan would see who it was. On his way out of his office he heard the rattle again. Mohan's door was open a crack; perhaps he was in the washroom. He went to check the bhavan entrance.

"Pramesh-ji. Does the bhavan no longer open itself to sons of the city?" Kishore stood outside the bhavan, walking stick in hand.

"Of course, ji," Pramesh pushed open the gate and beckoned the man in. "I am sorry; I suppose Mohan is not up yet."

"No matter, Manager-ji, although I wonder sometimes if your bhavan is more welcoming to strangers than to locals," Kishore said pointedly.

"How could that be, Kishore-ji? You are always welcome. Will you stay for chai? Come into the office."

"Not today, though I am sorry for it," Kishore said. "I still have my daughter-in-law's chai in my belly, Manager-ji."

"Is there something I can help you with?"

"We have known each other many years now, nah?" Kishore eased himself into the chair opposite Pramesh's desk and settled his walking stick in front of him, his hands resting on the ornate wooden handle. "Manager-ji, tell me: have I ever offended you?"

Pramesh focused his eyes on the man sitting across from him. "Kishore-ji—such a respected man as yourself—how could you have offended me? Ji, we have barely even seen each other since. . . ."

"Since the day of the weaver." The ghaatiyaa gripped his walking stick and leaned forward. "Understand me, Manager-ji. I would never have believed you capable of giving offense. You, the man I led to the bhavan! Do you remember that day ten years ago when you stumbled upon my ghat? Do you remember how I calmed you, how I guided you through this city like a most honored guest?"

"I will always remember. I was a stranger, and yet you treated me with such patience," Pramesh replied simply, truthfully. There was an odd sheen in the ghaatiyaa's eyes.

"Yes. And I have never regretted it, Manager-ji. Even when you avoided me for all these years—you cannot deny that you did. And when such stories started to come my way—stories about that dead man, your cousin. A bad death, they said. And then the bottle they found with him . . . a shameful thing, to have something like that in the family. But even when they were all talking of it, I told them to separate that judgment from you. *A different man, an honest man*, I told them. That is what I believed. And yet, one hears other stories, Pramesh."

"Stories?"

"Oh yes. This man says something, that man says something. Different tales coming from all directions. That Govind—an exorcist, once, he was here, at your bhavan. Then weeks later, you and your priests and wife on the ghat. Many people saw you. Doing tripindi shraddha, they said. One becomes confused, hearing so many stories, and doesn't know what to think. One decides to go to the source and ask the man himself, because is there any other way to ascertain the truth in this world?"

"No, ji," the manager said, carefully. "There is no other way."

"Yes." Kishore wagged his head in agreement. "That is what I thought as well. But a curious thing happened, Manager-ji. I went to the man to ask him the truth, and instead, he told me a falsehood." Pramesh thought he heard Narinder's familiar step outside the door. He glanced out to the courtyard and saw the head priest's straight-backed form. Kishore cleared his throat and spoke louder. "Many wanted the job at this death hostel, yet here you are sitting in that chair. I simply had to say one word, and you got the thing so many others wanted."

Pramesh folded his hands upon the desk and leaned forward. "Much of my life in this city is because of you, Kishore-ji. I have never said otherwise."

"There is only one way for me to believe you," Kishore said with quiet authority. "You had a chance before and did not take it. Do not lose your chance now, not when it is your final opportunity."

"I'm not sure I understand what you are asking of me." Pramesh sat up straighter, and his eyes never left Kishore's face.

"You must tell me what I already know, what I had to hear from someone else, someone far beneath you. Tell me that you lied. Tell me that you made a fool of me. *Tell me that the weaver was dead.*"

Pramesh kept his gaze steady on the ghaatiyaa. Kishore waited. Pramesh's face betrayed no fear, his gaze did not flicker, and his hands remained folded on the desk. "I believe you are mistaken," the manager said. "The weaver was *never* dead, Kishore-ji. You were there when we had this discussion. You were not the only man in that circle. Shall I fetch Narinder-ji, to verify what I have said?"

Kishore tapped his walking stick against the concrete floor. "What is the point to these games, Pramesh-ji? Your head priest wasn't there in the room, I remember this. No, only two of you saw what really happened. You and that assistant of yours. The truth could only come from one of you, and I have received it from that other man's mouth. I should have listened more closely to him the first time. I trusted your word over his. An error I won't make again."

The manager's heart skipped, but his face was as resolute as stone. "You are mistaken," he said again.

"I do not think so. I do not think your Mohan was mistaken either." Kishore stared at him intently. "Wasn't that bad of you, Manager-ji?" Kishore continued. "To blame that poor man when he was right all along? To do such a thing! What kind of a man tarnishes another's reputation just to uphold a lie?"

Still Pramesh said nothing, but his heart beat with a sole truth—Kishore was right. He could not assign any blame to Mohan. Mohan was many things, but he was loyal above all. He would not have wantonly revealed the bhavan's doings unless something had pushed him to do so, and Pramesh had. He'd crossed a boundary. *You cannot even tell a dead man from a live one.* He cringed at his words, spit out in the lane with no forethought, no control over his emotions.

"*I* would not want to know such a man." Kishore rose. "It happens rarely, but it happens, Pramesh-ji. I misjudged you. I thought you were honest, pious. I thought it was a good thing, to give you—a nobody, remember that—to give you a chance that so many others wanted. But how can anyone trust a stranger, not even born in the city? Your bones aren't clean; neither are your family's. One a liar. The other a drunk." He planted his walking stick into the ground and levered himself out of his chair. "And I would not want the pilgrims coming to this city, coming with their dead, staying in the house of such a man. Although it seems you may soon have the opposite problem, Pramesh-ji."

Pramesh had heard enough. "Kishore-ji," he said with as much calm as he could muster as the blood pounded in his ears, "I think you have said what you needed to." He pressed his palms together and tilted his head. "No matter what you think of me, the bhavan is my jurisdiction. The mission of this place is my duty, and I must now get on with it." He stood. A low murmur, heretofore unnoticed, wafted into the room. The sound rose outside the bhavan.

The ghaatiyaa turned slightly. A slow smile caught one corner of his mouth as the murmur became louder, a thick buzzing. Kishore leaned close to the manager and spoke in a loud hiss. "Shall I tell them? Shall I tell them that *you had a dead man come to life?*"

Now Pramesh recognized the sound. It was like the din in the bazaar, but condensed, and it was coming closer, getting louder. "You have it wrong, Kishore-ji. That is not what happened." And then the wave of sound, which had slowly been churning toward the bhavan, crashed against the gates. The priests gathered in the courtyard turned and stared.

The ghaatiyaa walked past Pramesh, through the office door, and into the courtyard. He looked out the gates, stopped and smiled. "You say I have it wrong, Manager-ji. Perhaps. But you've already seen that what matters most is the story that people hear. And *these* people"—he gestured to the gates, which now shook and rattled with the mad energy of idle hands—"seem eager to know the story from you."

Pramesh walked forward, oblivious to the priests behind him. Even Shobha had come out, her sari end draped over her head, Rani clutching at her skirts. "Who is there?" she asked.

In the lane, with the closed gates barring their way into the bhavan, stood a crowd composed of every strata of Kashi's menfolk. Some were still in their bathing dhotis, the soaked cloth dripping into the dirt lane. There were young boys who shoved their way to the front and pushed their faces into the space between the gate bars. Youths passed early morning beedis back and forth. Men with white hair tucked into lumpy caps peered from behind thick-lensed glasses. Others waited with irritated expressions, hands supporting chins, eyes glancing between the sun and the manager and back at the sun again as if Pramesh was at fault for the passing time. A young mendicant thumbed his prayer beads and held up his begging gourd with a hopeful look. A boatman stood at the front, his face streaming tears. Beside him was Bhut, arms crossed, grim and furious.

"Won't you tell them?" Kishore asked. "Won't you give them the story you refuse to give to me?" He bowed, a hint of a smile playing on his face. "Excuse me, Manager-ji. My grandson is waiting. I promised him a game before I left, and I keep my promises. I leave you to them."

The ghaatiyaa yanked open the gates and blended into the crowd, pushing into Bhut as he passed. The circle officer ignored him and stared through the bhavan gates at Pramesh.

"You! You are alive!" he exclaimed.

Shobha breathed out the great God's name in horror. Pramesh was struck dumb, but then he managed to stutter, "Well, why wouldn't I be?"

"*He*—" Bhut gestured at the boatman in disgust, "said you had died."

"Not that one, not him!" came Raman's desperate whisper.

"What other one is there?" a voice called from the back of the crowd as laughter rippled among the men.

"Yes," Bhut said as he focused his gaze on the hostel manager. "Who else could he mean?"

Pramesh's eyes opened wide. "Where is Mohan?"

34

All he saw was blood: pooled in a dark stain on the steps, flaking from his hair and into his eyes, splotches on his pants. There was so much blood that Mohan wondered if he'd fallen under a ghost's curse; perhaps he'd been turned into metal overnight, and the brown bits that freckled his skin were spots of rust, corrosion from the river lapping his body in the hours after he ended up on these stone steps.

A ghost? A memory tripped at the edge of his brain, came closer in a tantalizing dance and then whipped away just as he thought he remembered. He moaned as he sat up. "Rama." He grimaced as he bent his knees and raised himself to standing. The sun was not yet up. He had a dim idea that the ghat was not a good place to be, and although he could not remember why, he obeyed this internal warning. He stumbled down the street, one hand against the walls, and he got as far as a dozen houses and half as many home temples before he could go no further.

He collapsed on the closest stoop and tried to decipher where he was, but his head felt like a cotton boll, his senses all stopped up. He, who knew every crevice and gully of this city, found no familiarity in his surroundings. There was no one to ask, either; those few who passed him on the way to the ghats opened their eyes wide and murmured the great God's name when they saw him but hurried onward, distancing themselves from this man who had no doubt run afoul of some crime lord's goondas in the middle of the night.

The stillness embraced him with a kind of comfort he sensed he had not felt for a long time. Then, music slowly drifted down in a morning song: the plucked notes of a sarod shimmered out of an upstairs window. He heard stirrings behind him, a door opened, and a woman came out.

"It's that what's-his-name again—haven't we told him so many-many times to not play so early?" She caught sight of Mohan and gasped. "Rama!" she shrieked. "Rama!" She slammed the door shut. Mohan blinked. He strained his ears toward the music, the sound covering him like a blanket. The door opened again, and this time the woman stood behind a man who stared with bleary eyes at Mohan and yawned.

The assistant opened his mouth, intending to ask where he was. "Is it—where—" he said, his tongue bumbling over the words.

"*Drunk!*" the woman hissed over her husband's shoulder. "Hai Rama, look at the mess of him! It's the fault of that metal-man, haven't I told you?" Her husband grunted in response. "And will anyone *listen*? Must every man be stumbling down the streets, smelling of home brew, before someone *acts*? Well? Will you just stand there?"

"Yes, yes." Her husband waved his hands back at his wife, as if that gesture would somehow quiet her, or better, make her disappear. "I suppose we should take you to the police station," he said, facing Mohan with glum authority. "Listen," he said. "Ey! Are you listening?" He kicked Mohan, then leaned down and stared. Head tilted back, cheek against the dirt-smeared wall, hands limp at his sides, the would-be drunk did not respond. "Huh." He pushed at the fat man's shoulders. "Hai Rama," he said, more in surprise than shock.

"Don't bother with Rama right now," his wife hissed. "Get him up and drag him to the station. Come, I will call the neighbor to bring her husband."

"Yes, I suppose you should, although no need to rush about it," her husband said. "The fellow is dead."

Pramesh's heart assumed a furious beat. He strode away from the gate and into Mohan's room. His assistant was gone—of course. It had been clear for hours, though he'd been too preoccupied to recognize the signs.

When had Mohan ever let folk wait at the gate? When had he ever slept in, ever left without informing either the manager or the bhavan mistress; when had he ever shirked his duty in anything? The bed with its neat folded blanket and Mohan's empty steel cabinet were the only objects in the room.

"He must have left last night," Pramesh said to Bhut as he opened the gates and joined the men in the street, taking care to close the iron bars behind him. "He had no family, no one but us." *Only us.* A sick feeling churned in his stomach. Pramesh looked from sniveling boatman to the circle officer, Bhut's face a mask of fury. "Where is he now? Who saw that he was dead?"

Bhut gave Raman a rough shove. "This one seems to think so. But no one has seen this dead man, and the body is no longer there."

"He *was* dead," Raman whimpered. "So much blood everywhere. And a gash, right here, on the side of his head. Ah, Rama, Rama. . . ."

"Where?" Pramesh said again. He would not believe the thing until he saw for himself. "Which ghat?"

A shout went up from the back of the crowd. "Does it matter? Does a dead man *walk*, Bhaiya?" The crowd laughed. When the last wheezing giggle died out, they heard it: a familiar chant further down the lanes. *Rama Nam Satya Hai. Rama Nam Satya Hai.* Some turned toward the crossroads, curious about who was coming with a body here, in a direction opposite the ghats; others shifted from one foot to another or stared at Raman and Bhut, willing the drama to continue.

Pramesh focused on the bier, which was supported by four men, their arms quivering beneath the weight of the body. Slowly, they made their way into the crowd. Several of the men clicked their tongues or raised their eyebrows. The body had not been dressed properly or wrapped in cloth. In fact, the round person on the bier still wore his leather chappals, his torn pants, his woeful shirt. The carriers cut their way through the mob until they reached the manager and the circle officer. Then, none too gently, they set the bier down on the ground before those two men. "He is yours?" one of the men asked. All four panted with exertion.

Pramesh's heart dropped when he saw Mohan's battered face. Blood matted the black hair, only recently grown back to its former lushness, streaked the forehead, tinted the ears. There were scrapes and bruises on the man's hands and feet.

"See?" another of the bier carriers said. "I told you he was a bhavan man."

"Where did you find him?" came Bhut's sharp query.

"In our lane," the first man said. "My wife saw him. Frightened her most dreadfully, Officer-ji. She is still hysterical; not a nice thing for people to just die in the lanes, nah? Isn't there some other better place to do it?"

Pramesh knelt at Mohan's side and touched the man's shoulder. Another body stretched on another bier came to mind; slimmer, with a face to mirror the manager's but for a split right eyebrow. Pramesh had failed that man in life. He had never imagined the same could happen with Mohan.

"Him? Is this him?" Bhut asked Raman with gritted teeth. The boatman wagged his head quickly and swayed from one foot to another, while the men behind them, cloaked in the anonymity of the crowd, grew bolder.

"Sahib, what will you do with him? I thought the police only arrested living men!"

"Ah, Manager-ji; you will be needing a new assistant, nah? My brother-in-law is most suitable."

"So much wood it will take to burn that one, nah?"

"Something is wrong," Pramesh said. He moved his hand to the assistant's chest, then raised his palm just beneath Mohan's nose. "Hai Rama," he breathed in relief. He gave the assistant a shake. "Hai Rama!"

"Hai Rama," came an answering groan. Mohan's eyes popped open. He blinked and looked at the faces staring down at him.

"You!" Raman blustered. "You were dead!"

"Was I?" Mohan said. He rubbed his eyes and sat up. When he saw Pramesh, he was unable to meet the manager's eyes. "Dead?" he asked, looking at Bhut, at Raman, at the other faces hovering above him.

Bhut frowned. He squatted down and looked Mohan in the face. "Where were you last night? What happened?"

Mohan's ears and neck flushed. "I was at Mir ghat," he mumbled.

"Doing what?"

"Ji, does it matter?"

Bhut's face darkened. "*I* say it matters. What were you doing?"

A light clatter of bangles sounded behind Pramesh. He turned to see Shobha giving a cup of water to Sheetal, who then brought it with swift steps over to the crowd and handed it through the gate bars to Mohan. The hostel mistress kept her distance, about halfway between the gate and the kitchen so that she was shielded from the mob's gaze. Mohan managed a wan smile in her direction, but he still refused to look at the manager.

Pramesh could see that Bhut would not stop his questioning. "Bhut-sahib, Mohan will remain here. I give you my word. But he needs a doctor, he needs rest."

"And I need an answer," Bhut said, his gaze never moving from Mohan's face. "Now, again: what were you doing on the ghat?"

Mohan groaned. "I cannot remember it all." But he gathered himself and told Bhut and all who listened of his nighttime toilet habits, his sudden trip to the ghat, and his meeting with someone whose name he could not recall. Beyond that, he could remember nothing.

Bhut was silent for a long time after Mohan finished. He stared at the assistant, as if the pressure of his gaze could pull something else out from that man's mouth. Then he held out his hand, unfurling the set of silver chains. "And these?" he asked. "How did you come by these?"

"Oh!" a voice from the crowd shouted out. "Does Mohan-sahib have a secret lady friend? I thought that was Raman's game, nah?"

"Silence!" Bhut roared. "Or I will throw each of you do-nothings in jail, understand?" Everyone knew Bhut had no authority to throw *all* of them in jail, but the men obeyed, more because they feared missing the rest of the story than Bhut's threat. The circle officer shook the chains. Mohan's eyes crossed and he clutched his head. "Sahib, ji, what are those?"

"You have never seen these before?"

"Never, ji."

"This man"—Bhut glared at Raman—"says he found them at your feet. Strange, isn't it?"

"Ji," Mohan said again.

"What of this person on the ghat you spoke to? Who was he?"

"Bhut-sahib, please, you have talked to him enough," Pramesh said.

The crowd jostled, and a man pushed his way to the front. The manager recognized him as a doctor who made monthly house calls to Mrs. Chalwah across the street. "Let me examine him, Bhut-sahib," this doctor now said. "Surely you can see the man can barely remember his name, much less anyone else's."

Bhut ignored them both. "What did he look like? Where did he come from? Where did he go?" His voice rose with each new question, spittle flying from his mouth.

Pramesh stood. "Ji, I must insist you stop. You may speak to him later, but he is injured and exhausted and cannot answer you now."

"Our hostel manager is absolutely correct," a voice rang out in the crowd. "Coming back to life after being dead is certainly tiring, nah?"

Pramesh gritted his teeth as laughter again suffused the crowd. He focused on helping Mohan sit up and stand.

"Mohan-bhai, put your arm over my shoulder," Pramesh said. Mohan shrunk away; he averted his eyes from the manager's and instead attempted to rise on his own.

"Manager-ji, I can help." Sheetal had appeared from the other side of the gate. He meant well, but he was not very successful in raising the assistant's heavy form from the bier.

"Yes, ignore us, Manager-ji," the earlier taunting man called out. "But you cannot hide the truth, all the men have seen it."

"Seen *what*, Bhaiya?" a man in the crowd asked with genuine confusion.

"Isn't it obvious?" the first voice bellowed. "A dead man came to life right here, so close to these bhavan walls." The crowd turned to the speaker. Many of them were satisfied with the morning's events: such a story to tell their families and neighbors when they returned! But they all stayed where they were, the promise of more fun glittering in their eyes.

"But he was not so close to the bhavan, Bhaiya," someone said in a helpful tone. "He is outside the walls, nah?"

"And doesn't that show you how powerful the thing is?" a second voice from the opposite end of the crowd asked. "Such wonders it can do outside the bhavan; imagine what it does *inside*."

Between the two of them, Pramesh and Sheetal lifted Mohan into a standing position, though they wobbled with the assistant's weight. The manager glanced around for Bhut, but he had disappeared with the characteristic quiet of his nickname. With the circle officer gone, the surrounding mob swelled. No one offered to help, but then Raman stepped forward. Out of Bhut's grasp, the boatman had gathered together the remains of his composure. He motioned Sheetal aside and took up Mohan's other arm and draped it across his shoulder. "Come, Manager-ji, come," he said, already panting beneath his share of Mohan's weight.

The mob, however, would not let them go. "Does no one care to know what this *thing* is?" the two men from earlier cried out. "They were all out there just yesterday, doing tripindi shraddha—isn't it obvious? Does no one in Kashi care to know what happens in their city?"

"Well, speak up then, don't go on and on about it," someone answered.

Pramesh had his hands on the gate door, and as he struggled to pull it open while balancing Mohan, the two voices spoke up from either side of the mob, rapid and loud.

"You all think Shankarbhavan is so holy, nah?"

"Bring your dying here, bring them to end their lives in Kashi."

"But Manager-ji! Are you listening? Why have you kept *it* hidden so long?"

"Why haven't you told us about the ghost there? The ghost who brings folk *back to life*?"

The effect was immediate. Raman stopped to turn and look at the speakers; Mohan felt the sick queasiness of shame as the words he'd revealed the previous night came back to him in this twisted reincarnation. And Pramesh, though desperate to get back inside the bhavan, knew that such a statement required an answer. The men would never believe his side otherwise. He turned, still supporting Mohan's weight on his shoulders.

"Listen to me," he said. "There is nothing here that shouldn't be. We are a house of death; what is this nonsense about life?"

"There *is* a ghost, don't deny it!"

A man pushed himself to the center of the crowd. "For how long? For months! Months, to keep such a thing hidden?"

"Such a ghost, Bhaiya, and we saw it with our own eyes, didn't we? That assistant was certainly dead, even as those fellows were carrying him through the streets. And back to life, before our eyes!"

"And yes, we *did* hear of some ceremony these bhavan people did yesterday, didn't we? And this was the reason? Such a thing, hai Rama—"

"All of you, listen," the doctor called out. The fractious chattering ceased for a moment. "I have treated so many of you. I have been there to check on your children and see your wives through difficult births. You know that what I speak is true: there is no such thing as a dead man coming to life. It is simply impossible."

"But you are a man of science," came an answering cry. "What could *you* know about such things? When was the last time you were even in the Mother's temple? When have you last bathed in the river, offered prayers to the sun? How can we listen to a man who does not even count on his prayer beads each morning?" The men pushed closer and closer, their movements as restless as their words.

Pramesh moved in front of the doctor as if to shield him. "If you would let me explain," he said over the voices. "If you would listen—"

But the time for listening was past. No one but the boatman and the assistant heard him; every other man in the crowd was occupied with stating his own opinion and feeding off the conclusions from his brothers in the mob. And as their tongues moved, so did the men themselves, jostling, pushing closer and closer to the bhavan gates until manager, assistant, boy, doctor, and boatman were all pressed against the iron bars. The door was forced closed, with Shobha and the priests helpless on the other side.

"Wait, wait! Hold your tongues!" Mohan shouted. "Come now! Be reasonable! I was never dead—how could you think such a thing? And this lie you have decided to believe—no one has ever suffered such a thing in our place. Do you hear me? *Never.*" Pramesh watched the assistant valiantly repeat his own lie, but Mohan's words had no effect.

"How can we believe *you*?"

"You cannot even tell a dead man from a live one, remember?"

"Bhaiya, remember the weaver? *Remember*? I bet you a hundred rupees that man *was* dead!"

Into this fray Sheetal ventured. "I have no ties to the bhavan. I have been here with my father for almost two months now. None of the things you accuse the manager of hiding have happened in the bhavan." He did not back down from the mob's gaze. The youth's words, however well-intentioned, became more fodder for the mob.

"*Two months*, he says! Two months with who, his father?"

"And still he lingers here. Child, don't you see? He should have died long ago but for that ghost!"

"He is proof, even more proof! What dying man lingers for another two months when in Kashi?"

"My sister has been ill—"

"Father cannot miss the birth of his first grandson. . . ."

"The ailment has been there for so many years; no cure, they say, but now—"

The crowd surged, each pushing forward until this human mass threatened to crush the five standing before the iron gates. The iron, weak and rusted at the hinges, only symbolically imposing, creaked and groaned as the mob surged again and again.

"Wait!" Pramesh cried out as the many bodies threatened either to smother him or to pull him apart. "I will open the gates for you! Move back and I will let you through!" But the mob refused to move back, each man now a cell in a gigantic and ravenous organism. They continued to push forward, spurred on by the secret wish that each of them carried in their hearts for someone they loved best and did not want to lose just yet.

"There is a ghost in there!"

"Don't deny it!"

"Show us the ghost!"

"You have lied to us!"

The iron bars swayed, the hinges rocked, the ancient metal pulled apart from concrete walls, and the gates that had stood for centuries fell with a crash that would have been thunderous if not for the mob's roar. The crowd rushed in, pushing aside the manager and assistant and boatman, Sheetal and the doctor, in their hurry to see or hear the miracle. But as they fanned out into Pramesh's office and Mohan's room and the priests' quarters and the kitchen area—which a terrified Shobha vacated to wait with Rani behind the locked bedroom door—they found nothing and funneled to the washroom. Here they encountered one more barrier, which, unlike the gates, was far stronger and would not yield as easily.

Narinder waited at the door.

35

Bhut detached himself from the mob with the quiet ease of a leaf separating from a tree branch. He wasn't interested in a dead man; he wasn't even interested in a live one. He was interested only in a woman—the woman living just across the street. The woman whose gaze he could feel on his neck as he took slow deliberate steps to a door he knew quite well. He looked to the upper-story window, where he knew she would be, where she always was. Their eyes met; she was the first to turn away. He heard her give a sharp order, and in response he moved to the door, waiting.

Mrs. Chalwah saw him standing outside her house as he had all those years ago, the boy turned man, fast becoming an old man. She had waited so long, had lived in both fear and expectation of this meeting, but now she felt nothing. She called again down the stairs, and her daughter-in-law, unaccustomed to such a sharp summons from this older woman whom she'd only known to pray and speak in submissive tones, raced up the stairs to see what the matter was. "Open the door," Mrs. Chalwah said.

"Ma?" The younger woman looked at the old one with questioning eyes.

"The door, the door," Mrs. Chalwah said again with impatience. "Open it. The Officer-sahib is here."

Inside the bhavan, the head priest stopped the crowd from moving forward, but the men did not spare Narinder their words. "We know there is a ghost in here. You cannot deny it."

"I deny nothing," Narinder said. Pramesh pushed his way to the front and stood with his head priest. "But you are wrong," Narinder continued.

"So you *do* deny it!"

"Hai Rama! The manager has even a holy man lying for him."

"How can this be a holy place, Bhaiya? I would not let my daughter even cross into the lane where this house stands. How could someone bring their blood to die here?" Individually, these men would never be so bold as to contradict a priest, but their collective power imbued them with daring. "Narinder-ji, will you lie to our faces? Even as you speak the great God's name on your prayer beads? Will you tell us there was never a ghost?"

"Did I say that?" Narinder put his hands out in a helpless gesture. "You are perfectly correct. There *was* a ghost. But no longer."

"No longer? Did it simply walk away? What nonsense is this?"

Narinder smiled, his expression so strange in that atmosphere of accusation and anger and primal desperation that Pramesh blinked, wondering if it was a trick of the light. "No, Bhaiya. It cannot walk away. But it can be convinced to move along via the proper rites."

The crowd, quick to believe the presence of such a miraculous spirit, was less eager to take in the truth about its disappearance.

"It is clearly a lie. How convenient that the ghost should be gone just when we all know."

"Perhaps it is still here. How do we know it was truly banished?"

"But they were seen doing tripindi shraddha yesterday—what if it really *did* leave?"

"Where did you send it? Where would such a ghost go?"

Narinder looked away and loosed his prayer beads from his clenched hand. "Who can tell where any of us will go in death, Bhaiya? You can hope for a good death in Kashi, but no one knows. Neither can I tell you where the spirit will go. But the thing you want is no longer here. That is all I can say."

He folded one free arm behind his back, and with the other he commenced thumbing his prayer beads and making a round of the walkway, pushing through clusters of men. He walked on, maintaining his usual steady pace, as if this was a day like any other.

Bhut had not expected to be invited in with such ease. As a boy he'd dreamed of gaining entrance and concocted wild fantasies of what he would say and do, though he could remember none of these schemes as the younger Mrs. Chalwah led him into the small sitting area and gestured for him to sit. She did not seem to know what to do next, but a sharp cry from above sent her upstairs. When she came back down again, her face held an air of nervous apology. "Ma asks you to see her upstairs," she said. "She can no longer come down on her own, you understand."

Bhut followed as the younger Mrs. Chalwah pulled the end of her sari closer over her head and led the way to the staircase. The steps were high and narrow, set in concrete, and Bhut could understand what a formidable obstacle an older woman might find them to be. Then he remembered another set of stone steps and the girl who had not fared as well as Mrs. Chalwah had all these years, and his mouth set into a flat line.

She sat in a cane chair with many pillows and cushions surrounding her, as if their support kept her body from crumpling into a heap. Patches of skin peeked through the sparse strands of stringy white hair pulled back and rolled into a bun the size of a small ladoo. A pair of spectacles sat propped on her nose. A tray with chai and two digestive biscuits sat untouched on a nearby table, and her prayer beads lay curled in her lap like a tame snake that she stroked habitually with her fingers. The bed was the only other piece of furniture. No books, no pictures on the walls, not even a colorful blanket. The room was as devoid of life as Mrs. Chalwah seemed to be. *So*, he thought. *She has suffered, too.* He imagined he might feel satisfaction at knowing this, but he felt nothing.

She looked at Bhut as he stood next to the chair that her daughter-in-law dragged in from another room. He waved away the water that she brought; declined her offer of chai. "You have come," she said. Bhut only granted her a stiff nod. His eyes avoided hers and instead studied every crack in the floor and chip in the paint, as if the dilapidated furnishings might give him some pleasure, some power over her. "And what is it that an old woman can do for you?"

Bhut had also been turning this question over in his mind. All the rage he had felt earlier—toward Raman, then the crowd, then at himself for believing that the answer he wished for could be so easily found all these years later—all that anger was churning and turning inward. He was infuriated with his own inadequacy. What did he expect? What could he take from an old woman? He stood, saying, "It was a mistake to come here."

"I know why you are here, even if you do not."

She gazed at him, as she had gazed at him whenever he passed by these many decades since he'd lingered for hours outside her home as a boy, full of fire and despair. She closed her eyes. "Strange, yes? That you and I should be so linked." The circle officer's eyes widened in anger, but she shook her head. "You know we are. We are among the last who remember."

"*You* remember," Bhut snarled. "Only you could truly remember. You and your son, the only two who were there—you told him to do it, didn't you? You could have been a friend to her, but you protected him instead, all these years."

"Did I?" Mrs. Chalwah's smile was sad. "You've given me a far bigger part in this than I deserve, Officer-sahib."

"Yes? Then what was your part? Tell me, set me straight after all these years."

"The whole story?" she said, offering him one last chance to turn away, to remain in ignorance.

"Everything." The anklets shifted in his shirt pocket, and he put his hand to his chest, feeling his heart beat. "Tell me. Tell me what really happened to her."

She gestured to his chair with one papery hand. "Sit, please," she said. "Sit, so that I may tell you a story."

36

Though the sun would not dip below the horizon for several hours, and though no one man made the suggestion, the mob decided: the men would stay through the day and into the night's prime spirit hours and wait for the ghost to announce itself.

Pramesh did not care whether they waited or stayed. When the gates fell, so too did all the concerns tugging at his mind except for one. He turned his back on the courtyard and headed up the stairs to the bedroom. The door with Thakorlal's new key plate was locked; Shobha would not open it until Pramesh assured her many times that it was only him. When she turned the key and eased back the door with Rani held tight in her arms, her face relaxed, but she did not loosen her grip on the child. "Are they still here?"

"They think they will get the proof they want." He stretched his arms out, and his wife passed their daughter over to him. Rani's weight made him feel lighter. In spite of the commotion her eyes were half-closed, lashes trembling with the effort of staying awake. "She seems a touch warm," he said as he laid her down on the bed. Shobha followed, but not before first shutting the door and locking it. She placed her cool palms on the child's forehead and frowned, looking toward the window where the lime and chilies hung. "Probably just a cold," the manager said, following her gaze. "Did you just put that up today?"

"She just got rid of a cold last week," Shobha said, ignoring his question, her brow wrinkled. "She shouldn't be ill again, not so soon."

Pramesh lifted the child's chin with his finger, but Rani turned away and burrowed deeper into the pillows. The manager looked about the room, found the girl's favorite wooden horse, and nestled it on the bed near the child's hands. "It's been a shocking day, and it is still only morning. Let her rest."

"The men—what proof do you mean?"

"The ghost. They're intending to stay, thinking they'll hear the pots. It's not worth thinking about—they do not matter," Pramesh said. It was true; he did not care what the men would do. "They will be gone soon enough. They will wait all day and all night, and nothing will happen, and eventually they will leave," he continued, as much to himself as to his wife. He looked out the window to the Mistrys' terrace, which was free of its usual pack of screaming grandchildren. "Mrs. Mistry will not mind if you both stay with her for a few nights. You cannot stay here; not when it is like this."

But Shobha would not meet his eyes or accept. "She has many people in her house to care for. We will be fine here," she murmured as she moved a curl of Rani's hair.

"Is that wise?"

"As you said, the men will stay the night, and they will leave in the morning when they see the ghost is gone." Shobha attempted a smile and placed her hand on Rani's leg. "Better for her to sleep it off here. It is only for a day and night."

Pramesh did not have the energy to press the point. He laid his palm on Rani's forehead again, then left the room and shut the door, hearing the lock click back into place behind him.

The vantage from the kitchen showed the full range of the mob's assault. He had left behind a pack of about thirty men. Now, with the fallen gates leaving the bhavan open to the street and the city, that number almost doubled, with folk observing the crowd from the street and then plunging in to investigate.

"How will we know the ghost's presence? What will it do?"

"It differs, doesn't it? There was one in the woodworker's lane that used to do nothing, showed no outward sign of its presence, but if you entered the space it occupied, every bad memory in your life would come back to you, and you would not sleep for days after."

"Or that one that sang at night, remember? If you were walking that late—not that *I* ever did, Bhai—you might hear it singing at a certain hour in a certain lane. If you returned the tune with your own, they say it would leave you alone. But if you stayed silent. . . ."

"My cousin told me of one that rendered every man impotent if he were to walk near. Of course, none of them would really admit to it, but it must be true."

"We could simply ask the manager."

"And hear more of his lies? Better to wait. We will know when we see or hear it."

Pramesh paused in front of the gaping space where the gates had once stood. The men, more out of practicality than conciliation, had propped the halves up against the walls. The air rushed into this newly made wound in the bhavan, and Pramesh stood in this space and wondered how men could be capable of so much in mere minutes. He felt drained. His office and Mohan's room were in disarray, his assistant was badly injured, and his wife was terrified to venture into her own kitchen.

Narinder continued his rounds on the prayer beads. Pramesh watched the priest pick his way through the men as he traversed the walkway. His reassuring way of moving, neither too fast nor too slow, with an unbroken rhythm, had a calming effect: the men ceased chattering, and some moved into patches of sun coming into the courtyard and began to drowse. Narinder was an unswerving pillar of duty who never shirked his responsibility, just like that other, battered man now back in his room. He owed Mohan an explanation.

Bhut's face was pale. Mrs. Chalwah looked out of the window. She felt a strange calm envelop her.

"That was the truth?" Bhut asked.

"It was. It is."

"Why did you never say anything? Why didn't you tell anyone?"

Mrs. Chalwah looked at him with piercing eyes. "And do you really think, do you *really* imagine that anyone would have believed me?" He stared at her. "After all," Mrs. Chalwah continued, turning from Bhut to look out the window again, at the last mob stragglers, "an accident is far less entertaining a story than a murder. If they do not get what they need, they have the means to turn it into the thing they want."

"Who?"

She gestured out the window to where the mob had been. "*Them.* You must understand, in your line of work. You know them so well."

"But our family, and me—why did you never explain to *me*?"

"Would you have let me?"

"I don't understand."

"You were eleven, twelve, yes? You stood in front of my house every day for six months, in the rain, when you should have been in school, probably even at night. You were not a boy who would have accepted any explanation I might offer." Bhut did not contradict her. "In any case," Mrs. Chalwah continued, "what of the things your family never explained to me? They must have known. A girl does not begin to sleepwalk, to call after someone else, simply because she becomes a wife."

Bhut opened his mouth to speak, but no words came. Then a new understanding dawned on Mrs. Chalwah.

"You didn't know," she said. "Of course. You were too young, and they kept it from you."

Bhut rose, cap in hand. "You could be saying anything—any lie to save your face," he said, stepping to the door.

"I could. But there are two in your house you could always speak to." Bhut turned back to her, and she fixed him with a curious look. "You've asked them about this before, haven't you? The whole story?" He only stared at her, and she allowed herself a sad smile. "All these years, I dreaded you coming," she said. The circle officer did not linger. He turned his back on her, and she listened to his footsteps on the stairs.

For so long, Mrs. Chalwah had longed for death. Each Shraavana month, cycling through year after year, she prepared her soul and willed her body to perform the exit that simply did not come. A part of her knew why she refused to die. She had been waiting for Bhut. She heard her daughter-in-law bid the circle officer her usual goodbye—*Do not be a stranger, Sahib*. The sound of his footsteps crunching outside drifted up to her window, and she whispered to herself: "I wish you had come sooner."

37

Shobha felt Rani's forehead again. The child had fallen asleep and made no protest as Shobha pulled off her dress and put her into a different, softer garment, one with buttons that could be easily undone if the girl felt hot later on. Shobha felt warm herself; the bedroom was stuffy. She opened the window, frowning at the lime hanging just overhead, and she saw a boy down below, staring up at the bhavan.

She pulled back. He didn't look like one of the Mistry grandchildren; they usually came to the door. She felt a pang. She did not have those children in her home often, given the guests and the dying folk, but she loved the way they all clustered around Rani and made that girl seem like the brightest flower in the bunch. If only she'd done something else with the letter, if only Mrs. Mistry had never seen it. . . . Time, she hoped, would soften the quarrel between herself and her neighbor.

After a moment, she heard the *ping* of small stones being thrown. They did not quite reach the window. She could hear them patter on the wall just beneath before falling back to the ground between her house and Mrs. Mistry's. She looked down again. "What is it? If you want your father, you'd better go through the front and find him yourself."

The boy was undeterred. "A message for you, Madam."

Shobha pulled her sari over her head. He was just a boy, and she had to lean out of the window to hear him. "What is it then?"

The boy held up a paper packet. "I tried to go through the front, but I didn't see you, Madam. He expressly asked that I put this in your hand only."

"Who said? Who sent you?"

"The postmaster, Madam!" The boy held up the parcel, as if Shobha might fly down and take it herself. The sun was beginning to go down, but there was still light enough for anyone passing by to see the awkward tableau.

"Fine, yes, a moment." She went to her almirah and opened the drawer that held spare petticoat drawstrings, which she knotted together into one long rope, and then she dropped one end down to the boy. He secured the packet and waved up at her. As soon as she began to pull it up the child bolted, running out of the gully and into the lane.

The packet was heavy, but its weight was misleading: a sealed envelope had been rolled and wrapped around a stone. The envelope was shriveled and stiff, like a soaked book left out to dry in the sun. A note was attached, and she recognized the old postmaster's hand, explaining that the letter had dropped from the mailbag into a crevice behind a desk. It stayed there for many weeks, soaking up all the water from a leaking window. Only when the postmaster's wife was cleaning did they discover the misplaced piece of mail.

She could not open the envelope seal without taking some of the paper as well. She slit open one side along its seam with a penknife but discovered that the letter inside had meshed into a thin slab of paper fibers. Still, she worked the knife as best she could along the folds and creases. The ink had faded in spots and ran down in weepy lines beneath the letters. It was good that Pramesh was occupied downstairs, because Shobha spent the next hour salvaging the scraps, and then arranging and rearranging the ones she was able to read. In the end, what she had was this:

> . . . *who understood* . . .
> . . . *a beautiful* . . .
> . . . *strong but c* . . .
> . . . *of my own.*
> . . . *promised before* . . .
> . . . *so long since* . . .

. . . rainy and wh . . .
. . . told him he . . .
. . . kindness?

Nine pieces, nine fragments of stories that Shobha had no hope of deciphering. But her fingers held fast to the one piece that she valued above all.

. . . ister, your Friend,
Kamna

After Bhut left, Mrs. Chalwah took to her bed. Without the ever-present prayer beads, her fingers had nothing to do. Even now, as if they were separately cognizant of that loss, her palsied hands trembled on the blanket that her daughter-in-law had spread over her. The younger woman had offered to sit and read from the worn Gita that always sat on the bedside table—a marked change from her earlier attitude toward her mother-in-law's devotion, which bordered on derision. "Ma prays as if she is the biggest of sinners," the older Mrs. Chalwah had often heard the younger say. "As if being in Kashi is not enough; living here, why does she have the need to pray at all?"

Mrs. Chalwah had not always been so pious, but she'd never bothered to contradict the younger woman. She simply continued to pray because that was the only solace she had. Even then, she wondered if such prayer would be enough when her soul begged passage across the Vaitarani river. One could reach moksha only if they were able to cross that divine waterway, and one could cross only if they'd been given the right words, the words a death in Kashi were guaranteed to provide. Mrs. Chalwah's fear, the dark knot she refused to acknowledge even to herself, was that at her turn, the great God would have nothing to say to her, no words of passage would be whispered into her ear so that she might cross. Kashi or no, some souls were unfit for the final freedom of moksha.

"Ma." Her son stood at her door. "I am going over to the bhavan to see what has happened. I may stop at the market as well. Shall I get you anything?"

She shook her head. She needed nothing, but she knew her son would bring back fruits and fresh coconut water and powders from the pharmacist, as if a simple herbal concoction was all she needed to be herself. She had not been herself for a very long time, and no amount of turmeric or triphala powder would fix that. She wanted a drink of water quite badly, but she bit her dry tongue and returned to the habit of praying. She'd had two sons, but only one remained. This one had chosen his wife himself, and since the day that new daughter-in-law had crossed the threshold of her house, Mrs. Chalwah had said not a single word of reproach to her, never an order or demand, certainly no harsh words of criticism. Her reward was that her younger son's wife paid her no respect, the exasperation heavy in her voice when she spoke of Mrs. Chalwah to others.

"She must know nothing of *anything*," the younger Mrs. Chalwah had often mused to her friends, unaware, or not caring, that her clear voice carried to the older woman's upstairs sanctuary. "If you ask her for help or advice—nothing. As if she was never responsible for a household in her life. As if she doesn't know what to do with a daughter-in-law." How wrong, how utterly and completely mistaken that younger woman was, but who was there to tell her so? Who was left to tell the story of Mrs. Chalwah's year with her first daughter-in-law? The year she never spoke of, the year with Menaka, wife to her other, now dead, son.

With what happiness they had brought that girl into their home! After her own husband's death, Mrs. Chalwah had assumed full responsibility for fixing the marriage. She had never doubted her choice; even as her older son and Menaka made the seven rounds around the wedding fire and garlanded each other with fat joyful marigolds, she'd felt not a single prick of hesitation.

Mrs. Chalwah did not think she had been a bad mother-in-law—at least, she had not set out to be one. In the beginning, she had resolved to bite her tongue. Hadn't she kept quiet when Menaka insisted on sitting by the window, her hands idle, while Mrs. Chalwah was busy at work with the evening meal? Hadn't she turned a blind eye when the girl again failed to count the pieces of laundry that the dhobi's boy brought back, when she didn't see that Mrs. Chalwah's best-fitting blouse and an embroidered handkerchief gifted by the late Mr. Chalwah were missing? Eventually, she began to complain to her son, but what mother-in-law didn't do this? She was not unusual in her treatment of Menaka. She was not like the Singhs, who everyone knew were shameless in beating their son's wife, and who had shut the girl up in the house for a week so that the black eye clouding her face would not be on display for the entire street to see, never mind that the man selling shawls door-to-door had glimpsed that bruised visage and reported it to everyone immediately.

Bad fortune had a way of moving like a stone tumbling down a hill: its descent only quickened. When Menaka began slipping out night after night; when she lost the baby, the grandchild that Mrs. Chalwah had not been able to hold; when she screamed all the nights thereafter; when the neighbors began to avoid Mrs. Chalwah or to talk to her solely for the pleasure of prying—she had accepted all of it as her lot. Barring leaving the city altogether, there was not much she could do. Her mistake was assuming that the stone had finally halted, had reached the true bottom. Life could not get worse.

On That Night, however, it did.

She had followed Menaka out as she left the house. She knew the girl's sleepwalking footsteps; Mrs. Chalwah herself felt as if she had not slept in months, in years. She knew the routine by now: follow, follow, follow through the streets, don't lose sight or sound of the girl! Down lanes and past houses, she prayed that no one would look through the windows and see, that no one would step out the door and inquire, even though she knew that they *all* knew. Of course they did, when that girl insisted on wearing those horrid silver anklets that were a clear warning to all that she was walking in her dreams.

Down to the ghats, and Menaka took those steps down two at a time as if she were leaping into the arms of a lover rather than hedging close to the black glistening river. If only she *were* going to a lover, Mrs.

Chalwah had thought so many times—such a thing would have been so much easier to manage, so much more ordinary than this bizarre and awful truth. And why did she always have to go so close to the edge, feet dancing about the lapping water, coming closer each time and yet never getting wet?

That was how it had been before, night after night. But on That Night, that last time—even now she remembered every detail, for she had dissected the scene endlessly, trying to understand what had happened, how that night could have ended so differently. She clearly remembered Menaka lingering on that last step. This had always angered her, this blatant disregard for her own life, as if the girl were forcibly pushing it into Mrs. Chalwah's hands for safekeeping. Yet she *was* asleep, the older woman had seen it for herself during those first shocking nights when she'd held an oil lamp close to the sleepwalking Menaka's face, when she'd pricked her hand with a pin, when she'd snapped her fingers next to the girl's ears and yet still failed to bring her back into this world.

Why did That Night end so differently? Menaka had done the same dance by the water's edge before, had come back up the stairs and safely into the lanes hundreds of times with no mishaps. Sometimes, in her memory, Mrs. Chalwah imagined that someone else had been there, because there had been movement, a cough, a step.

Menaka had been swaying back and forth, back and forth, singing as she sometimes did at the water's edge. *Hari, Hari, I am here. I have come. I am here for you.* Her parrot-green sari glowed even in that ink-black night. The awful chiming sound that came from her feet! Even from the safe distance of years, Mrs. Chalwah shuddered to recall it.

She had only been a few steps away, watching from a higher level on the stairs. When Menaka *did* slip, as Mrs. Chalwah had always feared the girl would, the older woman had the time to be quick, to grab one of the slim wrists and pull her back. If only Menaka had not screamed—if only she'd kept quiet! If she'd been silent, Mrs. Chalwah would have had both hands free to drag her son's wife away from the river, closer to the dry safety of the top steps. Instead, Menaka had screamed at the touch of her mother-in-law's hand on hers, just as she'd screamed all those times

Mrs. Chalwah's son had tried to come near her after the baby died. Mrs. Chalwah had clamped her hand over Menaka's mouth while praying hard that no one would hear. The remaining hand had not been strong enough to hold the girl, and Menaka, still screaming, wrenched herself away.

And so Mrs. Chalwah lost her grip.

And so her daughter-in-law slipped.

And so Menaka fell, head meeting the unforgiving stone, soul soon in flight.

She died with her eyes open, and Mrs. Chalwah had hated her for it. When she was awake, Menaka's eyes had been as commonplace as any schoolgirl's: downcast and plain, with little mystery or depth. They had tricked Mrs. Chalwah into thinking the girl was simple and ordinary—wasn't that what every mother wanted for her son, for her family? *Special* was simply another way of labeling a girl who was trailed by talk and therefore by scandal. Yet when Menaka was in the thick of her sleepwalking, the look in her eyes spoke of some place that Mrs. Chalwah could not get to, a place she couldn't comprehend. Now dulled by death, Menaka's eyes contained a shadow of that place, as if to taunt Mrs. Chalwah that *she was there*.

Mrs. Chalwah could do nothing else but flee.

She'd never told anyone, even as she observed the young Bhut standing and staring outside her house, his hate and despair as tangible as glass shards thrown in her face. She allowed herself tears only once, and that was for her older son. He had loved her, his mother, but he had loved Menaka more. Mrs. Chalwah knew what things the city had whispered about him, about her, she knew how those lies had seeped into her son's skin, poisoning him from the inside, his hair falling out, his teeth rocking in softened gums, eyes bulging from his hollowed face. The doctors had no advice, so she'd paid to send him away, hoping he could forget Menaka and start a new life, and the city talked about that as well. But when he died, when she received word and, with no body to wash, no ashes to cry over, she performed rites of her own kind at the ghats, the city was indifferent, their mourning akin to what they might feel for a beggar crumpled in an alley corner. She cried then, in her room, but after that, Mrs. Chalwah's eyes remained dry, her mouth stopped. She remained silent as she heard the false tales that made the rounds. She did not even tell her remaining son what had really happened, and as the years went by she sometimes wondered if she despised him, her own flesh and blood, for his ignorance about the thing she lived with.

The city didn't forget about the scandal, but they chose to remember only certain parts, twisted to suit the way they wanted to tell—or hear—the story. The girl, the ghost, green parrots and silver anklets, something strange and abnormal hovering over the things they left out or forgot. But Mrs. Chalwah remembered. Bhut remembered, and his sisters remembered. They were all linked to one person and her passing, and yet none of them could discuss it with the other for fear of the pain of bringing that truth into the open.

38

Children, emissaries of mothers who'd learned their husbands' where-abouts and had sent over hot lunches and dinners in tiffins for their men, streamed into the bhavan and handed their cargo to their fathers, who either took the packages and sent them away with a grunt or bade the little folk to sit and share their meals. Shobha began to serve the priests behind the privacy of the kitchen curtain, which someone had tacked back up into place. Some of the children had brought rolled blankets and pillows, and after eating and washing, the men laid out this bedding in whatever free corner they could find and reclined or dozed, waiting for the promised moment. Amid the mood of eating and drinking, of bed-ding down and idle talk, Pramesh could almost fool himself that things were no different from the bhavan in busy times, when families occupied every room and claimed any other available space.

Shobha prepared a thali for Mohan, which Pramesh carried over. He found his assistant sitting up in bed, a compress placed over the large bump on his head, his face cleaned of blood. The manager wondered who had cleaned it off, wishing he'd been able to do it himself. He handed over the thali of food and sat, not knowing how to begin. The assistant chewed in silence, and when he was done Pramesh fetched a brass lota of water and a basin so that Mohan could wash and rinse his mouth.

"Too much, Pramesh-ji," Mohan said. "You are doing too much."

The manager shook his head, mouth dry. He took the empty thali from Mohan and stacked the lota and basin in a corner to take away later. But he didn't leave. He traced the outside edge of the thali with one finger. "How did he look?"

"Ji?"

"When you saw him. How did he look?"

Mohan flushed. "I didn't see him, Pramesh-ji. We had so many deaths that day—I tried to make it to the gate in time. He was gone. I saw him walking away, when he was already at the end of the lane."

"So you never spoke to him?"

"No. If I had seen him—I think I would have known, ji, if he looked like a dying man."

Pramesh swallowed. "It was my mistake, Mohan-bhai." Mohan held up his hand, but Pramesh forged ahead. "You have always done your duty. Even when I have not."

"I should have run after him," Mohan said. "I thought it was you at first, walking away from the bhavan. He was so like you. I thought it was a dream, some trick of the light."

Pramesh could see it, the straight-backed walk, the long strides. He allowed his heart to ache for a moment, to feel the loss of that meeting. Then he put the feeling aside. "It is done, Mohan-bhai," he said, the words more for himself than for his assistant. "We won't speak of it again."

The assistant's door had been damaged in the morning's madness, but he closed it as far as it would go. He considered sleeping upstairs, but he instead took a bedroll and blanket and settled himself with the men, choosing a spot farthest away from the washroom. When the pots proved to be silent, he did not want to seem as if he had distorted the truth. He would be a neutral observer, an ordinary person who'd experienced something extraordinary.

All these months, he'd avoided thinking about why Sagar had chosen pots to manifest himself in. He thought of the pot shard that had pierced his back. Fragments scattered on Sagar's funeral pyre. Other fragments, long ago, scattered at his feet. His hand rose to his eyebrow, massaging the skin. That memory, long suppressed, pulled itself loose, unfurled before him.

The boys had shared a chore since they were old enough to perform errands on their own: filling the two water pots at the village well each day. Sagar and Pramesh took the clay vessels from their corner in the kitchen, and together they walked to the well at the center of their village. Young girls, sometimes including Jaya, congregated around the well, their own earthenware pots gripped against their waists or balanced on their heads in miniature imitations of their mothers or aunts or grand-mothers. "Look at the Prasad boys," they sang out at Sagar and Pramesh's approach. "Are they *boys*?" one would say. "But they are acting like *girls*!"

Red-faced, shuffling, the cousins would approach the well and fill the pots as quickly as they could. Arms wrapped around their quivering loads, they made their escape, trudging away as fast as their small legs could carry them. "Such a heavy load for a boy—shall one of us help?" the girls would cry out in parting. Pramesh and Sagar would feel the blood rise to their necks and ears until they were out of sight of those giggling girls. At least, they each felt but did not say, they did not have to perform the task alone.

But then their mothers went to bed one night and were seemingly gone the next, the illness made its rounds in the village before moving on, and Pramesh, his breaths still short and labored, watched from the window as Sagar trudged off alone, hauling first one water pot, then returning for the other and repeating his journey.

"Did they say anything to you?" he always asked when Sagar returned and flopped down on his mat on the other side of the room.

"No one said anything. The girls pretend I am not there."

Pramesh did not believe him, and each day he watched with increas-ing guilt as Sagar made the two trips. Sometimes, he tired long before Sagar came home and had to lie down again. With each day, however, he strengthened. Soon he was waiting at the door with one pot in his lap, ready to hand it off to his cousin as Sagar traded the full pot for the empty.

All this time, his father and Sagar's were either lost in a drunken blackout or off somewhere, anywhere but the house that echoed with the absence of their wives and the presence of their widowed sister. One day, Sagar's father woke and stumbled to the back veranda, where he spied Pramesh waiting, hugging the empty pot to his hollow chest, his breaths still hot and hoarse. Pramesh felt his uncle staring at him, and he tried to keep still and make himself smaller than the fever had already made him. Finally, he heard the man laugh, and then he left.

"What did they say?" Pramesh asked when Sagar came back and reached for the empty pot. "The girls?"

"You are like an old woman, asking that question over and over," Sagar said. Pramesh *felt* like an old woman, or at least like an elderly person whose body is as useless as a puppet with broken strings. Sagar saw his face. "Nothing," he said as he turned back for his second trip. "They always say nothing."

"At least Jaya isn't here," Pramesh said. "You don't have to worry about her seeing you." Her parents forbade her from visiting that summer, lest she catch the same fever. Pramesh didn't say so, but he missed her chatter. He thought Sagar missed her too.

The next day, Pramesh was again waiting on the back veranda. This time, he recognized his father's footsteps behind him, and he froze and shrank within himself. Here, at least, was the one vestige of his old life that remained unchanged: fear was his and Sagar's old friend, and the fever had not driven it away.

"Sitting, all day? While the other one does the work?" Pramesh knew better than to say anything. His heart drummed a manic beat in his chest. Sweat beaded his brow. "Sitting," his father said again. "Such idleness, when we give you food, when you have clothes? When after all this, you . . . *you.* . . ."

You are the one still alive. Pramesh completed the sentence in his head. His father's words were garbled and halting and a sickening stench emanated from his person. He saw a small form walking toward the house, Sagar returning, and his heart lifted. He willed his father to grow bored, but the man did not leave. Sagar came closer to the house, and he kept his eyes on Pramesh until soon he was setting the full pot down on the veranda and taking the empty. But Pramesh's father was quicker.

"Take it," he commanded, thrusting the pot at Pramesh. "Take it to the well and fill it. You have rested long enough; you are no weaker than this one."

Pramesh had no choice. He grasped the pot, cool to the touch. He avoided his father's eyes. "I can do it," Sagar protested.

"Yes, he can do it," Sagar's father said, suddenly emerging from whatever dark corner of the house he'd used to sleep off his delirium. His face had an amused expression. He laughed and disappeared back into the house.

"Go," Pramesh's father said, ignoring them all.

And so Pramesh began to walk, and he soon heard two pairs of footsteps behind him: one loud and unsteady, the other quick and light. He concentrated on this second pair, Sagar's, and felt the rhythm match his own ragged breaths. Everything ached. His legs felt like the bones had dissolved and left nothing to hold up the flesh surrounding them. But he could not stop. He knew the price of stopping.

Halfway to the well, he collapsed and vomited. His head was bursting; his limbs burned. He sat on the bare earth, still clutching the pot, while Sagar hovered near him and his father stood behind him, saying nothing, offering no reprieve. When his cousin tried to take the empty pot, the man slapped the boy away. Pramesh got up again and wobbled, light-headed, but he set one foot in front of the other.

They arrived at the well. Small comfort that Sagar was right: the girls were still there, waiting, but they turned their heads and hid their mouths behind their hands, retreating to a nearby tree and pretending not to watch. At that moment, Pramesh wished they would say something, anything, to break the silence. Somehow, he hooked the pot to the rope; somehow, he lowered the pot into the watery depths. And then he pulled, and the weight below was too much, and he was gasping as he held onto the rope, in danger of being dragged down after the pot.

Sagar was there to grab the rope, to allow Pramesh to sink to the ground while he pulled up with practiced hands and retrieved the full pot. They both waited, fear sour on their tongues, for Pramesh's father to again swat Sagar away. But he said nothing and only watched the two boys with eyes that did not seem to see. Sagar unhooked the pot and began to lift it to his head.

"Take it," Pramesh's father said. The disgust in his voice sounded all the way to the girls by their tree, and they huddled closer to each other, eyes flicking from the well to each other. "*Take it*," he said again, and the fear in Pramesh's stomach exploded into a poison that washed over his insides. His trembling hands, slick with sweat, took the pot from Sagar. The weight was incredible. He tried to bend and create a perch on his head for his cousin to set the pot upon. He could not do it. He instead grasped the vessel, his arms too short to go all the way around, and he struggled to stand. Nausea overcame him, and he had a distinct sensation of fading, as if he were an old chalk outline like the ones he and Sagar sketched in the dirt of their front yard, sometimes with Jaya, and then ran their fingers through, blurring the shapes.

Left to himself, he could not have walked more than five paces without collapsing with his burden. Sagar could see that, and he tried to pull the pot from his cousin's hands. Pramesh would not let go. He observed his father's eyes and saw, beneath the many layers of drunken fog, a spark of revulsion. In those seconds, he was determined to do this impossible thing, to carry this pot all the way home without losing a single drop. But Sagar's temper broke. He grabbed for the pot again, and in the struggle the pot slipped and the clay shattered into several large pieces at their drenched feet.

A large shard bounced off the ground and landed at Pramesh's father's feet, like an offering of appeasement. He bent to pick it up. There was genuine curiosity in his face as he examined it, as if he had forgotten why he was even there. He looked up at the boys staring at him, at the well, and then at the audience of girls. And then, with a speed that belied his befuddlement, he flung the sharp piece of pottery straight at the boys' heads.

If Pramesh had been quicker, could he have stepped in front of his cousin or reached a hand out to shield them both? If he had been stronger, could he have pushed Sagar out of the way and taken his place? If he had been anything than what he was at that moment, would that have been enough? Sagar stumbled back, lost his footing, and fell. The sharpest part of the clay buried itself into Sagar's right eyebrow, cleaving it in two. He reached up and knocked it away, and then the blood poured like rain. Tears, which Sagar had once shed only at night, sprung from his eyes and coated his cheeks; sobs gurgled out of him, chest heaving as he tried to breathe. There was a jingle of anklets, urgent on the packed earth, and the sound faded and then returned. One of the girls had run for her mother, who swooped over Sagar and held the end of her sari to his head while she led him to her home to be tended to, Pramesh following. Just before they all disappeared into the woman's house, he turned to see where his father was. The man had not even waited to see which house the boys entered. His back was turned, small puffs of dust springing up beneath his steps.

The village doctor set careful stitches into the skin and closed the gash. When the boys returned home late that night, the stitched wound swollen and angry on Sagar's forehead, their aunt seemed shaken, and her eyes were lit with a fire Pramesh had never seen before. But she said nothing. When the boys sat down to eat across from the Elders, Pramesh's father stared at his food, his face hard. But Sagar's father took one look at his son and barked out a laugh. He slapped his brother's back, the gesture as devoid of camaraderie as his mocking voice.

It took years for Pramesh to understand that moment, years to see the meaning behind the cruelty. Years to realize that the laugh was the same as his uncle saying, *See? My boy even takes a beating better than yours.*

The hours ticked by. Some of the men dozed, woke, forgot where they were and what their errand was, then dozed again. Some remained awake, flicking matches or twigs between their fingers, staring up into the night sky. Some fell into dreamless sleep, as if they were in their own homes. Pramesh stayed awake out of habit. More memories visited him. He gazed at the washroom, and in the blackness behind the open door he saw two boys, twins.

Sagar and Pramesh, gathering fallen peepal leaves and giggling as they held them to their lips and blew, each trying to push their leaves further in flight than the other.

Midnight came and went.

Sagar, coming home with the day's lesson and then scowling when he saw Pramesh was already months ahead on his own time.

An hour into the new day.

Pramesh and Sagar marking out the new field boundaries, and Sagar scolding Pramesh for paying more attention to daydreams than work.

Minutes until the fatal hour. The men were all up now, shaken awake by their neighbors or the general hum of noise. Dev and Loknath had gathered by their door, and even Narinder was alert.

"Two hours past midnight, wasn't it? Two hours past?"

The seconds ticked by, and the hour arrived. Pramesh held his breath.

"Where is it? Where is the sound?"

The washroom was silent. The pots were still.

"The washroom, you said?"

"Two hours past?"

"Quiet, all of you! Perhaps it is happening. Perhaps we are not listening hard enough."

The minutes died away. Somewhere in the bhavan, water dripped. The men leaned forward, breathing as one, straining to see and hear what they'd devoted the day and night to.

"Is this a game? I hear nothing."

"That tapping? Is that it?"

Narinder stepped into the moonlight. He did not smile or frown. "I told you that the ghost moved on. You can see it is so. You have your proof, men of Kashi. Now what will you do?"

These men had already argued with him once that day, but none had the stomach to argue with a priest twice. The crowd, so filled with purpose just hours ago, felt their energy drain. They had sought something special; coming to terms with the mundane was a slow and difficult process.

Narinder's voice should have been the final word. A different voice, however, changed everything.

"The doctor, has he left? Is he still here?" Shobha stood in the kitchen doorway, the curtain shoved aside with one trembling hand. She had not bothered to cover her head, and she repeated the question, voice betraying the slightest quaver, eyes looking everywhere. She did not seem to care that the men either stared openly or looked away and smiled among themselves, embarrassed at her lack of modesty. Pramesh stood and found her eyes, and a chill rippled across his skin. "She is almost completely still. The fever is worse. She is so hot to the touch! I don't know what to do."

The doctor was still there, and both he and the manager pushed forward through the men. "Rani?"

Shobha nodded. She breathed her daughter's name into the air. "Rani."

The voice that responded was low at first, grumbling, but soon it grew louder, sending vibrations through the floor that hummed through every person's body, a sound felt before it was heard, like thunder or an ocean churning, building in fervor and intensity until at last, from the depths of the washroom, the pots erupted with the noise that the men had all been waiting to hear.

She had wanted something for as long as she could remember. Something she could not articulate or even understand.

At night, her feet led her. When she woke, she wondered what her heart had yearned after, but no one would tell her. In the morning, she picked the stones from her bare soles and searched her heart to see if the need was gone, if her wanderings had been satisfied. She assumed that was why she walked in her sleep: to seek the thing she could not identify while awake. Nothing changed; the sun set; she left her bed and searched anew; she returned and awoke and still the hole remained. Sometimes her mind would slide into a waking dream, and she thought she remembered this thing that was so vital, so necessary to her being. A thing from a very long time ago.

A family? No: she had a family, parents and siblings, a full childhood but for the emptiness that followed her everywhere, that she understood she would have to one day fill. Marriage? She expected this to be the answer, and yet felt no different the day after, a month later. This man who was to be one half of her soul was the piece she tried to fit into that hole, that want, but he would not go.

When her belly swelled, she remained in her bed through the night. A child, she decided. She'd been waiting for a child, and she was relieved to know that the hole—a gaping maw that grew bigger and deeper, that seemed to suck at her insides like an insatiable whirlpool—would be filled. The weight of the one she carried would drive her feet into this life, this world, like an iron post pounded deep into the ground.

But then the child died, and the hole widened to a chasm. How would she fill it now? The child hadn't been the answer. What need was there to try for another? She pushed away her husband, pushed away her life, always searching, compelled to wander, unable to find relief.

One night, she woke and found herself on the ghats. This had never happened; always she'd slept through the paces of her feet. She felt the chilled night air on her face, felt the river open itself before her. Despite the black ink of night, she followed the smooth currents with her eyes. She looked closer. There was something new there, or perhaps it was something old, something she'd never bothered to notice.

Each drop of water followed the next, jostling against its brethren, chasing after some unnamed goal. All of them, intent on something, traveling from such far-off places, some reaching their destination, some not.

That was it. She was like those droplets. She had been pulled along by this thing, this need, for many lifetimes. And so had everyone else around her—they simply didn't know it as she did. If she did not find the answer now, she would find it in the next life, and if not then, with the one after. On and on, the hole would follow her. But there was also this: She was bound to fill it, one day.

The relief was immense. She'd comprehended something at last, and that was enough solace to bring a smile to her lips. She was ill-suited to this life, but she felt she only had to wait. She would go back home, play her part as assigned, run out the hours and years on her clock. Her joy sent her running up the steps, then back down again, the light jingle of her anklets sending sparks of happiness into her heart. She repeated the steps, a dance on the stone. The river caught her eye. Back down she ran, then further still to touch her feet to the water, to show the river she understood, her toes reaching to feel the cool the wet the—

PART V

39

All of Kashi swelled with one new thing.

In the apartments above the chaat-wallah's establishment: "Wrap him in many blankets. And if anyone asks, tell him the doctors have advised us to get him into the air."

At the top of the old Singh bungalow: "Wait until we come back to tell the Kapurs. The place is filling up. We must make sure there is a spot for Dhani."

Behind the closed doors of a fabric shop: "Yes, I saw it with my own eyes. I *heard* it as well. The stories are true. It is the miracle we prayed for. We mustn't delay."

For a week, the building contained those who came, but then a newspaper featured a story about this former Death Bhavan turned Life Bhavan. The article included a detailed account of the local legend of Magadha and the tragic consequences for all the men who had gone there, seeking the Bearer. It ended with a quote from the prominent ghaatiyaa Kishore Chandne, whose praise of the bhavan's newfound properties ended with an endorsement: "Why chance a journey to Magadha when the dying can come and find new life here?"

This was all the revenge the ghaatiyaa took on Pramesh, but it was enough.

People came from everywhere; the rooms filled, the walkway gave refuge to squatters, and in the courtyard people spread out throws or used their clasped palms as pillows. Mohan's room and Pramesh's office became prime territory snatched up by two families who always left someone to guard the space lest others attempt to poach the rooms.

Shobha's kitchen, once protected and organized with such pride, was raided for its pans and pots and spices. The upstairs bedroom was the jewel of the place, hotly discussed, but no one managed to pick the lock, a testament to the new key plate from Thakorlal. Banarasis mixed with strangers to the city, and together these folk shared the stories of all the other places they had tried before hearing of the bhavan and its miraculous healing properties.

"The linga outside of that village? Yes, I have been there. Also the banyan tree where you tie the red fabric."

"Holy water mixed with honey. Every day, for ten days. And it did nothing, nothing."

"He said she would have to sleep in the same room with him, and his presence would leech out the illness. But our only daughter, in the same room as this baba? He took us for fools, so when we heard of this place—"

In the beginning, Pramesh had tried to reason with them. "You must understand, there is no more room. We have people even where no people should be, two families in every room, and the entire courtyard occupied."

"There is *always* room," whoever was at the doorway huffed, and shoved past Pramesh with no further regard for the manager's authority. Pramesh allowed each by. What else could he do? What difference could one more make?

The bhavan was a mass of people. There was relief during the day, when some folk left to procure supplies or take the air, but during the night everyone sprawled out on blankets across every available bit of space, creating a carpet of people stretching from the open entryway to the priests' quarters. Only the washroom remained empty, out of fear that human interference might dampen the specter's power. They gave the pots a wide swath of space even as they sent their injured, ill, and dying, their stricken, cursed, and feeble folk into this bhavan that promised to bring those loved ones back to a state closer to living than dead. Each day, they bickered and prayed and cooked and prayed and ate and prayed. At night, they waited for the hour when the ghost would make its presence known. After that initial miss on the day the mob broke down the gates, the pots returned to sounding at two hours past midnight.

Narinder had not exited his section of the priests' quarters since that night. Sheetal had barricaded himself in his room, and Dev had joined him to ensure that no one displaced the boy's father, the only man who rightfully should have been there. Mohan, who'd made the mistake of leaving his room one night only to return to a space occupied with two entire families who ignored him completely and bickered over his bed and steel cabinet, had joined the priests in their already cramped quarters. Had Pramesh the time to think over that first day's events, he would have felt his failure. As it was, another worry occupied him.

Rani lay on the upstairs bed, listless for many days now. The fever would not abate.

Shobha felt as if she were in the worst kind of prison, confined to a single stuffy room in her own home, with her only child beset with an illness so quick and mysterious that she felt truly terrified. The doctor had come and gone, careful to close the door behind him each time.

"Nothing to do but wait," he said with unsettling frankness. Shobha held her tongue even as her heart screamed out against this passivity. She tried to lower Rani's temperature with cool cloths that she kept soaking in a nearby basin, and she waited. She looked for signs that the girl was opening her eyes, whimpering, reaching for her, and she waited. At intervals, she parted the tiny lips and forced coconut water or a paste of jaggery mixed with water into her daughter's mouth, and she waited. She waited for this illness, which had come about like a curse, to detach itself and land elsewhere, away from her home.

"There is nowhere else I can take her," Pramesh said one night. "That doctor is the best in the city—you know this. What can we do but wait?"

"Wait for what?" Shobha asked, her voice becoming higher with each word. Downstairs, the sharp-eared women sitting below shushed their children, hoping a quarrel meant that the coveted upstairs bedroom might soon be empty. "I have a mob of people in my home, all convinced that this ghost downstairs will bring their loved one back to life, yet my daughter falls ill on the day that same ghost was supposed to be expelled. What are we waiting for? What reason is good enough?"

"What are you saying?"

"You know what I mean—this is no usual illness. It is the ghost—there is no other explanation. Why was he here, why does he still linger? What did he want when he came to see you?"

Pramesh ran his hands up to his temples, pulled at his hair. "I've told you. He was ill; he came to see me. There is no other mystery—and even if there were, who would we ask? I've spoken to everyone."

Shobha went to her almirah, her nerves on fire. "You are my husband, and I will not go against you," she said. "But you did not ask everyone."

She handed him a letter.

> *There was a letter someone sent. A letter asking about me.*
> *I am here. I am well.*
> *But when will he be here? My husband's brother.*
> *He said he would come.*
> *We are waiting. Write soon.*

Pramesh flipped the page over, flipped it back and read it again. He faced his wife. "How did you get this?"

"I wrote. Many weeks ago, when all of this began." Pramesh stared at her. Shobha twisted the end of her sari and summoned her courage. "I wanted to find out what had happened to her. You'd never told me anything of her before. But I'd heard things, that time we went to the village. Things that match the story your cousin told you." Still Pramesh was silent. "I thought perhaps someone in her family would answer, but *she* sent me that. I didn't know what to think. Those words—read them!" She watched Pramesh look at the paper again. His face was inscrutable. "I wrote her again, asking her to tell me what happened. And I got this only some days ago." She shook out the pieces of letter onto the bed and moved them into place with her fingers so Pramesh could see.

He turned away without reading them. "We told her people about Sagar-bhai, we gave them the land—they had a chance to ask about him,

THE CITY OF GOOD DEATH

to show me they understood everything he had done for them—for *her*. They said nothing. Why would you write to her?"

"But look," Shobha said, trying to pull him back over to the bed. "She calls me her sister. And she was expecting a visit from you. Why?"

Pramesh shook his head. "I don't know. How do you know it was not them talking, telling her what to write? Or if they were the ones to fix some idea in her head?"

She waited for him to say something else, to deign to look at those paper scraps, her heart beating furiously, but he remained stubbornly still and silent, and anger rose within her. "How can you understand what a woman thinks?"

"What?"

"She was married for almost ten years—as long as you and I. She is not the same woman who did whatever her elders told her to all those years ago—you don't know what she is. For her own reasons she decided to write to me. There's pain in this letter—can't you see it? She is expecting you. She must know something; she'll at least understand what your cousin was doing here. Even if her elders put her up to it—why does that matter? Why won't you go?"

He tossed the letter at the bed, and it floated gently to the edge and slipped off to the floor. "We went there once, all those years ago. It was a mistake. I've regretted it ever since. I vowed I would never go back again."

"Why not?" He said nothing, and Shobha almost sobbed out with frustration. "Why can't you just speak of it? What happened then? Why did they refuse to meet me? What did they say to you?" Shobha sank to sit on the bed, to curl herself up next to Rani, her eyes squeezed shut, her hand light on the child's head. She heard her husband walk to the end of the bed, pick up the letter, and sit down near her feet. After a moment he laid a hand on her skin, below the anklets.

"You weren't there to hear any of it," he said, softly. "I was always thankful for that." Her eyes fluttered open and found his. He looked away. And then he began.

40

A week after the wedding, Pramesh was making the rounds of the bhavan rooms when he stopped in the kitchen to check on Dharam. The old manager sat on a bare rope bed, a wool hat on his head and a shawl around his shoulders, and he beckoned to Pramesh to come in.

"How long has it been since you've returned to see your people?" A shuddering cough gripped him, and his entire body shook until he mastered himself. "A year?" he continued, clearing his throat in a phlegmy growl.

His blunt way of asking, as if they were already mid-conversation, made Pramesh smile. "You have kept me busy, ji."

"Then you should visit them. Now—with your new wife. It's only proper." The man had an urgency in his voice that Pramesh recognized. Anything said in that tone was not a request, but a command.

"If you wish," he said. "But perhaps I should go on my own. It's been so long. And they aren't expecting me to bring along a bride." He was still in disbelief over his newly married state, the fact that Shobha had said yes.

But Dharam would not be dissuaded, even as another coughing fit overtook him. His body shook with such violence that Pramesh grabbed a pillow and bolster and set them firmly at the manager's side to give him something to hold onto. Gripping a pillow to his chest, Dharam fixed Pramesh with a penetrating stare.

"Is it their fault they don't know? You married without obtaining their permission. You made that choice, didn't you?" Pramesh opened his mouth to protest, but Dharam raised his hand. His voice was gravelly, made no better when he cleared his throat. "It was necessary—you did it for me, to humor an old sick man, and I am grateful. But there are still consequences from your action. You cannot run away from them. Anyway, what are you afraid might happen?"

"My cousin will welcome her, no doubt," Pramesh answered carefully. "My aunt as well, in her own way. She won't say much, but that isn't a problem with your daughter." He attempted a smile, but it dissolved at the thought of the two he did not mention.

"Your father and uncle?" the old manager prompted. "Have they written to you at all while you've been here? Have you written them?"

A chill passed over Pramesh. He rubbed his arms; his hand drifted up to his eyebrow. "I ask about them in each letter. I've written to my aunt. She conveys whatever she'd like to say to my cousin. If they—my father, my uncle—had anything to say, they haven't passed it along to Sagar-bhai."

Dharam looked out the window. "Well. You cannot avoid them. No matter what they were, what happened, they are your elders. What you should do," he said, turning to face Pramesh, "is focus on your cousin, your aunt. Think of this as a visit for them—*they* are your family. My daughter should meet them, get their blessing. But you must still try with your uncle and father. You've been away a year. You don't know what that time can do to a father missing his son, how one can change."

There was no refusing the old manager. "Ji," Pramesh said.

He felt Shobha's anticipation as he waited with her on the train platform, the way she constantly looked down to make sure her bag was still there, her eyes flickering whenever it seemed like the train might be approaching, hands moving up to tuck away any hairs that escaped the coiled knot at her neck. Watching her, Pramesh allowed himself to forget his fears and to feel her excitement. She was wearing a new sari, sky-blue printed with small yellow flowers, arms stacked with her wedding bangles, a smile lifting her mouth and lighting her eyes.

He wanted to tell her so many things, stories of Sagar and the other people in his village, yet here on the platform, surrounded by passengers and porters, he was stymied by shyness. Strange, that it was easier to talk to her at night when it was just the two of them alone together, her face turned toward him and her breath warming his skin.

She caught him looking at her, and the pink that rose to his cheeks was mirrored in her own. She looked down, mouth twitching in a suppressed laugh. "Do you put your right foot first?" she asked softly. "When getting on the train?"

"I'm not sure." Pramesh tilted his head in her direction so he could better hear her in the bustling space. "I never thought about it."

"It makes for an auspicious trip, Bapa said. That, and saying the great God's name."

"Easy enough to do," he said. "We'll both do it, once the train comes." He was rewarded with another smile, his wife gracefully dipping her chin in agreement, and when the train arrived, he had her get on first, and he copied her movements exactly.

On the farmer's cart, Hardev, Champa-maasi's husband, regaled Pramesh with tales of Sagar's experiments in planting, in irrigation methods, in going around to all the different farmers for cuttings and seeds and advice. The air was filled with the light perfume of earth and the soft plodding of the bullocks leading them along, the bells around their necks punctuating their steps with a full and clear sound. "How is everyone at home?" Pramesh asked once the farmer paused to take a breath from his chatter.

The farmer clicked his tongue between his teeth. "Things don't always change when you leave a place," he said after a pause. "Some things, some places, remain exactly as they were ten years before. And they will continue to be the same in another ten, twenty, thirty years. It's like a furrow in a field. Once you are in that line, you cannot get out."

Pramesh felt the slightest tightening around his heart, a shallowness in his breathing. A light chime sounded behind him as Shobha repositioned her legs from where she sat in the back of the cart, her anklets like a cheery rejoinder to the bullocks' bells. And the band around his heart pulled tighter.

"My wife speaks of both you cousins often, and with fondness," Hardev said. "She would welcome you, if you'd like to visit the house first."

He spoke easily, as if this were the expected thing, for a man to bring his new wife straight to a neighbor's house after a long journey to the husband's childhood home. Pramesh bit his lip, eyes on the slow-moving ground beneath him, hands gripping the seat of the cart.

"Your wife must be tired as well. She can rest there. I can take you on myself. And then, when you return, you can take her back with you, or I will bring her. Later. If you wish."

So he'd done it. And though he'd lacked the courage to linger for more than a second on his wife's eyes as he left her in a place they hadn't intended to visit, as he neared his old home, he knew he'd done the right thing. Because there, dead drunk, was his uncle, asleep on one of the rope beds.

His snores were loud and he mumbled in his sleep. Once, he'd commanded the boys to do squats in the backyard, their fingers grasping their earlobes. Up and down they'd pumped their legs, over and over again, fifty times, sixty, while the man watched. When they slowed or stopped, unable to lever fully up, chests heaving, muscles burning, tears pricking the backs of their eyes, Sagar's father had been there to whip their legs with a tree branch, white slashes soon turning into red welts on their skin. When he walked away, releasing them, both boys had collapsed in the dirt, gnats buzzing around their sweaty heads. What had they done to anger him so? Pramesh wondered. What could a child do to a fully grown man that warranted such a punishment?

Now that same man seemed shrunk to half his size. Drool pooled on his sleeve as he slept. He held one hand, shiny and pink with the bonfire scar, curled near his chin, the gesture giving him the appearance of a sleeping infant.

Pramesh walked in, hoping Sagar would be inside. In the front room rarely used when Pramesh was a child, his father sat.

The man stared at him, dark shadows cupping his eyes, liver spots dotting his temples and throat. "A wife, they say. You have come here bringing a wife."

Pramesh swallowed. He'd forgotten how quickly news could travel, especially when you least wanted it to. "She is with Champa-maasi. I thought she should rest before—"

"We wrote you. And yet you deliberately defied my wishes. Didn't even think to tell us what you'd done. That idiot Nattu's grandnephew saw you getting off the train—I had to hear it from him."

Strange, to feel that fear, the old sadness, once again glaze over his heart, drip into his stomach. How much lighter he'd become in Kashi. And if this was how it felt to escape and return, what about Sagar? Had Sagar ever known life without that weight?

"I don't know what you mean," he said, slow and intentional with each word.

"You were never the quickest one. Among other things," his father replied. He was skinnier, with much less weight on his tall frame, and his hands, Pramesh noticed, betrayed the slightest of tremors as he filled a clouded glass with the brown liquid whose scent Pramesh recognized all too well. His voice had a quaver in it, not of old age and certainly not of feeling for his son, but of disdain. "What did you think you might gain, coming back here? When you left us as you did? When you threw away the chance that was never yours to take?"

A blessing, was on the tip of Pramesh's tongue. Shobha wanted the blessing, the chance to touch his father's feet and brush the dust on her forehead, to greet him just as she might greet her own father, because both men now occupied the same place in her heart. She was determined in this idea, this fantasy. And, bolstered by Dharam's conviction that a person could change, Pramesh had done nothing to tell her otherwise. Their marriage a week old, and he'd been the one to commit the first betrayal. He swallowed, thinking of her waiting for him.

Dharam's voice rang in his thoughts. *You still must try.* "Will you meet her?" Pramesh asked.

"Meet her? Why? You are no one. Why would I meet the wife of no one?" The old man didn't laugh, didn't raise his voice. He talked as if he were discussing whether or not it might rain. A chill rolled across Pramesh's skin.

The glass was already half empty, and his father downed the rest in a single gulp. "Better for me to meet this father of hers. Clever fucker. Getting to keep both the daughter *and* the son in his home." He replenished his drink, missed the table when he set the bottle down, and glass shattered, Pramesh flinching at the sound. "What of the dowry?" that man continued, as liquid pooled at his feet. "Did you think to tell them, or were you so besotted that you went into it thinking only of what you'd get to do to her in the night? Is your father-in-law both a fucker *and* a thief?"

Pramesh struggled to reply, but his tongue was clay in his mouth, his thoughts frenzied, his anger incandescent. He stretched his fingers to keep them from curling into fists, and when that did not work he pressed his arms flat against his sides. *Not like us*, he repeated to himself. He would not be like this man sitting before him.

His father barked out a laugh. "Yes. I thought so."

"The temple," Pramesh said, words rushing out with all the contempt he could muster. "He asked me what I would have. I said nothing. He gave it all to the Mother's temple. And he paid to feed anyone who came to the bhavan that day."

"So he decides how to use my money—I should thank him for that? *Thank you, thank you, dearest fucker father-in-law, thank you for showing Rama what a thief you are at my expense,*" he said mockingly.

Had he always been this cruel? Had he talked to the Mothers this way? Or had that ugliness festered in this man, lying dormant while Pramesh was in his home, under his control, becoming inflamed once his son showed he was capable of defying him?

"You have disobeyed me this second time," his father said, draining his glass. "Did you think about how we would look, what people would say? Only a wretch marries without his father's blessing. You have dragged us down into the mud—and here is the most surprising thing—you returned! Why? Did you think we would welcome you and that thief's daughter with marigolds, with sweets?"

And then he rose with the jerky movements of one who is sure of his actions, only to find himself unbalanced, the world turning suddenly, and when Pramesh reached out with the instinct of a son, catching his father's arm before he fell, the old man wrenched away, righted himself, and continued on his own through the hall and out the back door.

What had he meant when he said *the second time*?

His entire body was frozen, every muscle clenched. His hands ached from being squeezed into tight fists, palms branded with red half-moons from where his nails had bitten into the skin. The only thing stopping him from striking that man was his and Sagar's childhood refrain. He wouldn't be like his father, wouldn't succumb to the instinct of violence. He would be himself, the person he'd discovered only recently during his months in Kashi.

A hand touched his elbow, and he jumped. His aunt had come up behind him. Likely she'd heard every word from her usual spot in the kitchen. "Bua," he said. When he knelt to touch her feet she caught him and wrapped him in her arms. Slowly, he relaxed, and a small sob escaped his throat. He bit back the rest, gritting his teeth.

She released him, led him to the kitchen. "They had picked a bride for you," she said softly. She handed him a cup of chai. "A girl from the next village. He wrote to tell you to come home for the wedding."

"When?"

"Months ago. And with no reply from you, they assumed that was your answer. To deny them."

"I never received it."

Her eyes lingered on him for a moment, and then she set to peeling ginger and chopping it into tiny bits. When he finished his chai, she took the cup from him. "He was visiting someone. But he should return soon. He'll come by the back way."

Sagar. Pramesh stood to leave, paused at the back door. "Who was the bride?" he asked.

She kept her eyes on her work. "If you knew, and if the letter had come, would you have done something differently?" He understood. What could it matter who the bride was? He had a wife, and even if he'd received that letter, he would have defied its instructions outright. They both knew this. They both knew any business of his father's, his uncle's, that concerned him or Sagar was business bound to end badly.

Out back, he was mercifully alone. He paced the yard, grew impatient, then decided to walk through the fields and toward the old prayer tree. He did not want to meet Sagar like this, blood frenzied. As he walked his anger quieted to a hum, faint but tolerable. The path was as familiar to him as his old home. As he approached the tree a cool breeze wafted his way, and he breathed in deeply. He could still pinpoint exactly which of the red strips of cloth and holy string had been tied by his mother's hands, his aunt's, his own—or so he liked to think. Looking at the tree, the only thing that matched his memory in size and appearance, he felt melancholy. The tree was holy, his mother had said, because it was the earthly body for a great holy man. How many hundreds of years had that soul been trapped, condemned to the near eternal life of a tree? How many more pieces of string and cloth would join the others, how many desperate pleas for some relief in this life on Earth would that being hear before finally being freed?

"I knew it, Bhaiya. I knew that there was no other place you would be."

Sagar stood to one side, eyeing Pramesh and frowning, and then his frown broke into a wide smile and he enveloped Pramesh in a hug that made the breath leave his body, slapping his back until he wheezed with laughter, his entire body humming with a welcome feeling: delight.

"Bua said you were out back, wandering. Gone just a year; already managing a death hostel and *married*! So much for that education you were so desperate for, Bhaiya!" he laughed. "Where is my new sister? Where is your wife?"

"Not managing, assisting, assisting," Pramesh hastened to say.

But Sagar was unstoppable. "Everyone is talking about it. Why didn't you bring her straight here? And why didn't you tell me you were coming?" He chattered on, and for a moment Pramesh forgot about his father's words. Shobha had wanted a blessing. She would get something better; she would get a meeting with the one who knew him better than anyone.

"She is eager to know you," Pramesh said, the words bubbling forth. "She's brought something for you as well—a surprise; I heard her wake early to make it for you."

"You could have warned me, at least," Sagar said, suddenly slapping Pramesh's arm with a vigor that made his skin tingle. "How will it look, my new sister feeding me, and I have no present to give her in return? You aren't making me look very good, Bhaiya. Tell me: what is she like?"

"Later, later," Pramesh said. "We have bigger plans to make. You haven't got an excuse now—what about Jaya? You never wrote to me about her. Oh, Bhaiya—too shy to put your heavenly love into words? You didn't need to try hard; the lyrics from any film song would have done nicely," he teased, sounding and feeling like his teenage self. But perhaps he was out of practice; Sagar turned to the well-worn path that would lead them back to the house.

"Come," he said. "Bua will be wondering where we are."

The walk was the same, the voice, the way he spoke. But something was different. Pramesh watched his cousin's back as he led the way, glanced at him from the corner of his eye when he sped up to walk at his side. Always impetuous, always full of mischief—and then he saw it. A new seriousness fixing the shoulders, creasing the brow. He, too, had changed in that year apart.

An unfamiliar silence inserted itself between them as they walked, until Sagar broke it. "How did you find the Elders?"

His anger reasserted itself. "It isn't worth repeating," he said. Telling the story, he thought, would only solidify the memory and make it stronger, but something slipped out before he could help himself. "I am no one, apparently. They refused to meet her." He blushed, unable to say Shobha's name in front of Sagar.

"I wish I'd known you were coming, Bhai. Although you walked into it, didn't you, coming here knowing that they'd arranged another match—"

"I didn't know. Bua said they sent a letter—I never got it."

Sagar stopped and looked at Pramesh. "So you didn't do it on purpose? To spite them?"

"What?"

"Get married, Bhai. Why else would it be so speedy, and no notice?"

"Her father is ill," Pramesh explained. "He caught a cold, it spread to his chest—he was afraid. He did not want to leave her unprotected."

"Gallant of you," Sagar said with a small and strange laugh, his voice carrying a slight edge.

Pramesh blinked. "She wasn't forced into it, Bhai. I never thought she'd have me. . . . It was the shock of my life when Dharam-ji told me she'd accepted."

"No, no, you are right, Bhaiya," Sagar said, and the edge was gone, his face contrite. "I meant nothing by it. Truly." A few paces later: "I thought it was intentional. Getting married, knowing they had picked someone else for you. A way to show them how little they mattered to you. Their games, their deals. I felt happy, thinking that." He picked up a pebble, tossed it with one hand and caught it, flung it into a nearby ditch. "But it doesn't matter how it happened. The point is you did the right thing—all of it. Leaving, making a new life, marrying as you wished."

Pramesh gripped his cousin's shoulder. "I won't bring her to this house, not after today. You will have to come with me to see her." Sagar reached up, patted his hand.

They walked the familiar soil, and Pramesh breathed in the scents of rain-washed mud, new green leaf, the sweetness of a distant flower. "Who was to be the bride?" he asked, more to fill the silence that once again filled the space between them.

"A girl named Kamna."

Pramesh tilted his ear toward Sagar. "Well-known?"

"In a way—not a good way, Bhaiya. They move frequently, this family, or so everyone says. The stories only started a few months ago, when they moved one village over; everyone seems to know some version. Something about the girl. I never met any of them. I was traveling everywhere, talking to any farmer who would have me. I had no idea what the Elders were doing until Bapa came home one day and told Bua to begin to prepare."

"What do they say about the girl?" Pramesh asked, idly. His thoughts wandered to Shobha. The longer he tarried here, the longer she would sit waiting with people she did not know.

"Depends on who you ask," Sagar said. "Most of the stories say she is a runaway, has been since she was a child. Which is why her people are so keen to get her married. Another story says there was a man, someone she bewitched." He snorted, looking over at Pramesh. "The fellow died, apparently. So that's another mark against her. Unlucky; poor thing."

"Rama," Pramesh murmured. And then he realized something. "A runaway," he said. He stopped and pulled on Sagar's elbow. "Don't you see? *I* was a runaway to them." A soft laugh of disbelief left his mouth.

"Their idea of a perfect match," Sagar said, grim. "Or whatever new bet they'd made. Who knows, Bhaiya? It's sickness, what they have, in their minds. It's not something worth trying to understand."

Pramesh felt the old closeness click back into place. It helped to think of the thing that had twisted the Elders as a sickness. A sickness was not inherent. It could not be passed down, not always. "I hope she finds peace," he said as the house came into view. "She's not the only one with a story on her name. Think about what they must say about us."

Sagar looked at him sharply, then relaxed. "You say my sister is with Champa-maasi now?" he asked, and Pramesh wagged his chin. "Of all the places to leave her, Bhai," Sagar laughed loudly. "That Divya will talk her ear off. *And* tell every single story she remembers about you! The well—remember the well?"

The smile on Pramesh's face faltered. He suddenly felt tired. The journey, he thought. He'd been up since the early morning hours, hadn't slept on the train. He rubbed his eyebrow. All he heard was his father's voice, the poison words finding their way into his thoughts. *You are no one. Did you think we'd welcome that thief's daughter?* The sight of the house growing closer made him nauseous. "Why don't you come with me?" he burst out.

Sagar turned to look at him. "I am, Bhaiya; I am—we'll just fetch Bua and—"

"No, I mean to Kashi. You said so earlier; you said it was good I left, made my own life. Why must you be the one to stay here?"

"And do what? Work at the death hostel?" Sagar wrinkled his nose. "Bhaiya—"

"How can you live with them like this? Alone? I left; you can as well. With Jaya—think of it; you can't bring her here, to live with *them*. But if we were together in the same city, our wives as friends, and our children—"

A noise, a low wail, reached them. Sagar quickened his feet toward the house, Pramesh following. The wail turned into a keening moan. It sounded wrong, pain like he'd never heard before. They rounded the corner, and on the porch, Sagar's father lay, weeping.

Pramesh stopped short. He had never seen the man cry, had never imagined him capable of such a thing. The sound was that of a wounded animal. Sagar's father lay on his side on the sagging rope bed, hands clasped to his chest, his open mouth reeking, several teeth missing. Sagar mounted the steps, unhurried, knelt at his father's side, laid a hand on the man's shoulder, and shook him gently. "Bapa, wake. Wake; you are dreaming."

And so he was. Eyes closed, wetness seeping out between the lids, sorrowful keening and spittle dripping out of his mouth, Sagar's father shook on his bed until the gentle pressure of his son's hand woke him. He saw Pramesh first, watching him from the distance of the ground below the veranda. He whimpered, and then seeing Sagar, he clutched at him, grabbing his hand, his sleeve, pulling the man to him in a clumsy awkward embrace, still weeping the shaky sobs of a newborn who doesn't know if it is dreaming or awake. Sagar held himself stiffly, eyes and mouth frozen in a neutral look, as if he were handling a bundle of sugar cane rather than a person. The man continued to hold him in his grip, moaning in half-formed sobs.

Pramesh moved to the veranda, not knowing what to do. The man grew more agitated, and Sagar spoke over him. "Bhaiya—go. Go back to my sister, and tell her I will visit in the morning. I will bring Bua. I have to do the morning work first, but I will come."

"But—"

"There's no point in you waiting here. He could go on for another hour before it wears off and he remembers himself." Sagar rose, disengaging his father's arms. His father continued to whimper. Sagar again laid his hand on the man's shoulder, and when he looked at Pramesh, his eyes made plain that he had dealt with this before.

Pramesh turned, heart torn between leaving Sagar on his own and leaving Shobha for longer than he already had. And then he thought of something. "Does my father do this as well?"

"Not this," Sagar said. He didn't elaborate, but his tone made it plain that the vitriol that man had spewed earlier was not uncommon. "Don't keep her waiting, Bhaiya."

Pramesh had been gone for a year. He'd left, he'd created a new life, had even embarked on starting a new family. Who did Sagar have to help him? How often did he cope with such outbursts? How could he stomach it, the quavering plea for affection from the same man who had once stood over both of them doing their endless squats while they clutched their earlobes, wrenching them up by the hair when their legs burned and wobbled with exhaustion, and then giving them both a final box on the ears when they stayed squatting, crying, unable to continue?

"You will come?" Pramesh said, still unwilling to tear himself away.

Sagar waved his hand at Pramesh, bidding him to go, eyes on his father. Pramesh turned for the farmer's home, the path before him familiar and yet strange, like the house he was leaving behind.

As eager as he was to see Shobha, he could not outpace the sun, and by the time he entered the house the family was busy with preparations for the evening meal. He saw a glimpse of his wife, mixing something in a bowl amid the gaggle of women preparing the meal, but someone handed him a glass of water and he was pushed to the backyard to talk to the men.

Hardev, his sons, and sons-in-law were all gathered in a circle beneath a tree, seated on low rope beds. None asked where Sagar was, nor did they question whether Pramesh and his wife would spend the night in their house.

"I had to leave him suddenly, but he said he would bring Bua in the morning," he explained, unprompted.

"Splendid—you'll have the whole day together," Hardev said, as if it were totally normal for Pramesh and his new bride to stay at a neighbor's house while his familial home was nearby.

As Pramesh partook in the conversation, fixing a false smile on his lips, he marveled at his incredible foolishness. To be so blind to this thing that everyone else knew. The Prasad family, the talk of the village all those years ago, and still so now. And he had stumbled right into their pity. Worse, he had brought Shobha along, to share in the humiliation of his family. He thought of the other girl, the wedding his father had been so intent upon. Should he tell his wife? Or leave it among the rest of his family stories he never shared?

The question was answered for him: there was no opportunity to speak with her in the midst of a large family like this one, women all clustered at one end and men at another. When the meal was served, he got his first full sight of Shobha since he'd left her, her delicate wrists jangling with her new bridal bangles as she dipped a ladle into the dish she carried and served the men one after another. The other women followed behind with roti, water, other dishes, and Pramesh followed her with his eyes as she came closer. And then she filled his plate and moved on to the next man, with not even a quick look in his direction.

Stretched out that night alongside the other men, the house filled with the sounds of sleep from within and singing insects from outside, Pramesh tried to sleep. He had wanted so badly to talk to his wife, to explain that Sagar would come in the morning, bringing their aunt. Shobha would finally get to meet him, and he and Bua would be enough family to make up for the lack of the others. They would have to be. Thinking this, he fell asleep.

In the morning, he saw his chance.

"Come into the fields, have a look, nah?" Hardev said when it was still dark, as he prepared to follow his sons out on their morning rounds.

Pramesh declined. "Sagar will be coming, and I want to be here when he arrives."

"Ah, perhaps I should wait for him myself—I should have realized I was talking to the wrong Prasad when I mentioned the fields," Hardev said, laughing. He clapped Pramesh on the back and left after finishing his chai. Pramesh walked to the front of the house, eyes on the road, looking for that familiar form and gait. It was early, the sun just barely cresting the horizon, but one never knew with Sagar. More likely he would be late. After a time he gave up and walked to the back, and there, like a miracle, was Shobha, hunched in the yard and washing the dishes from that morning.

He suddenly felt shy, seeing her on her own, as if he were spying a glimpse of the bhavan manager's daughter delivering something to her father. He stepped as close to her as he dared and squatted down, worrying the grass with his fingers. She was the one to break the silence.

"You shouldn't be here—it won't look right."

He glanced at the open back door, but they were safe; no one was looking for them yet. Her voice was not welcoming. He made a joke about never being able to be alone with her, but it fell flat. Everything about this trip had been a horrible mistake. He could feel her looking at him, and her voice was softer, gentler this time. "A year, at least, before a married couple can be trusted to be alone together without folk talking. Depending on the place."

"We are lost, then," he said, and this time he mustered a real smile. What could he tell her? How could he explain that his childhood home held a pair of men he'd no sooner want his wife to meet than a rabid dog? That the blessing she wanted was an impossibility? He dusted his hands and worried at his eyebrow, almost wishing for a headache so he'd have the excuse of lying down, shutting himself away from this place he'd grown up in.

In the years to come, Pramesh would learn that his wife could speak of certain things with an ease unknown to him; she could breach the high walls of his silence and go straight to his deepest fear or worry and pull it out of him with a single tug. When she did it there, in the backyard of the farmer's house, he was struck dumb.

"There was talk that I heard yesterday. About your elders picking someone else for you to marry," she said. Her voice was calm and even and she continued to scrub each dirty dish with ash before rinsing it clean. "Is that why you left me here? Is that why you haven't taken me back to your home?"

She was brave to ask that. But there was a slight quaver in her voice at the end, a tremor that sliced Pramesh's heart. Of course that news had reached her ears, especially when she spent all day in the company of women. But worse than that: she had sat with that fact in her head all the previous day and all last night. Sitting in a stranger's house when she should have been sitting in his; eating their food when she should have feasted on Bua's cooking; talking to Champa-maasi's family when she should have been welcomed by the Elders and Sagar. And it had hurt her.

He'd betrayed her once by bringing her to this place. He would not lie to her as well. "It was a surprise to me. My father told me when I reached the house."

They both stood at the same time. "Something happened," she said.

He didn't want to tell her, because he didn't want to remember. Nothing good could come from passing around that pain. "Sagar is coming. He is so eager to meet you—he was scolding me because I hadn't written in advance and he has nothing to give you. And he is bringing Bua."

"And your father and uncle? Why aren't we going to your home to meet them there?"

He didn't know what to say. "It was supposed to be different," he said at length. Her eyes caught his, and he felt the warm comfort of that gaze. "A whole year away, and nothing changed. They will never change."

"Pramesh-bhaiya!" Divya came out, a girl he remembered from his and Sagar's childhood trips to the well, her mother following. They exclaimed over Shobha, took the dishes from her, asked him about lunch, told him it was no trouble that Sagar and Bua would be arriving later. Champa-maasi wrapped her arm around his waist and pulled him toward the house. He glanced behind at Shobha just before they entered the house, to let her know that even if he wasn't at her side, he was with her.

The hours passed slowly. He paced from the house to the road, then to the backyard, then back inside. Shobha had set herself to making pura, and his heart lifted a bit smelling the buttery sweet batter hit the pan, imagining Sagar's relish in eating food made by his wife's hand.

"He was always late as a child," Champa-maasi said as Pramesh entered the house after yet another round outside. He saw Shobha say something to the women, and they began to serve the midday meal, and he took himself outside yet again, irritation prickling his veins. They should have had the day to spend together. Where was he?

He quickly ate the food Shobha brought him, tasting nothing, ears alert for Sagar's step. As Champa-maasi milled about, readying the afternoon's chai, he decided he could wait no longer. "I will fetch him," he told his wife, where she sat in the kitchen with the stack of uneaten pura wrapped in cloth. "Likely he got caught up in something and lost the time."

She followed him outside, asking to come with him, but he kept walking. "I won't be long."

He walked quickly, dust blooming from his sandals as he walked the dry dirt road. What if both his father and uncle had an episode at the same time, one sobbing and pleading for Sagar, the other spouting curses and insults? Cutting across a field, halfway to the house, he saw the familiar gait coming toward him in matching haste, and he felt both relief and annoyance. Sagar was alone. His cousin spotted him, raised his hand in greeting, and ran lightly to meet Pramesh.

"Sorry, Bhaiya," he said. "It was on my mind all morning but I got tangled in something else."

"She was waiting," Pramesh said, sharper than he intended. "As was I. Where is Bua?"

"She was tired," Sagar said.

There was something odd in his manner, a glint in his eye that Pramesh did not recognize. He pushed away his disappointment. "Did something happen at home? What were you doing?"

"Nothing happened; I forgot the time," Sagar said.

"Fine," Pramesh snapped. "Will you keep your sister waiting even longer, or will we go?"

"Lead the way." Sagar's tone was clipped, his face set. Pramesh began walking, wondering how to improve the mood before they reached Shobha. But as he walked, he grew more and more irritated, until he stopped.

"This thing you say you were tangled in," he said, rounding on Sagar. "What was it? What was so important?"

"We shouldn't talk of it now," Sagar said. "As you say, she is waiting. . . ."

He began to walk, but Pramesh stepped in front of him, placed his hand on his cousin's chest.

"Where were you? Why won't you tell me?"

For a moment, he thought Sagar was ready to strike him. But his cousin merely stepped away from his hand, turned back in the direction he'd come from, turned again to face Pramesh. "I went to speak to her family. The girl's." His gaze flicked up and met Pramesh's eyes. "I'd been thinking about it for a while. All those months going by, no answer from you. The Elders pretended like the agreement was still on, but the girl's family realized soon enough. They felt cheated," Sagar explained. "They had an understanding with the Elders, expecting a husband for her. It wasn't fair to assume they would just let everything go—you on your way to Kashi, me here with the Elders, both of us living our lives while they still had an unmarried daughter."

The words filtered into Pramesh's brain slowly. "Bhaiya. . . ."

"It wasn't right, what we did to them. So I agreed. I said I would marry her in your place."

Pramesh felt himself sway, the field and Sagar all tilting then righting themselves. "You can't do this," he said, his own voice sounding far way. His senses felt muted, as if his ears were stuffed with cotton. He remembered something. "What about Jaya?" The words burst out of him. "Would you really abandon her, just for the chance to placate the Elders?"

"I am abandoning no one," Sagar said sharply. He squeezed his eyes shut, opened them. "She is married."

Pramesh stared. "When?"

"A month after you left."

"You never said—you didn't write a word—"

"What would you have done, if I had?" Sagar shot back. "You would have returned, immediately. You would have tried to fix it. And you would have humiliated us even more than the Elders already had. Too late, Bhaiya, it was too late. They destroyed any chance there was. Every family has their limits—what man will let his daughter live in the house of someone who has insulted him the way that those two are capable of?"

All those letters, with Sagar talking of himself, of farming, giving news from the village, and Pramesh writing whatever nonsense he'd sent in return. Asking about Jaya again and again. Those letters he'd waited so eagerly for, that he read repeatedly until the paper grew soft from his hands—none of it had been true. "What happened?"

"It isn't worth saying."

"I want to know." He stepped closer to Sagar, as if his proximity might pull the words out of his cousin. Sagar stared at the ground, jaw working.

"After you left . . . they were furious. First they fought with each other, saying they'd agreed to send me, and that your father had reneged on the bet. For hours, it lasted. Then came the drink, and they were quiet." He pushed his palm up his forehead, back over his hairline. "They were quiet the next day. And the next. I had to go with Nitin the day after; he'd promised me a look at his brother-in-law's farm. That's when they decided to do it." He scratched his throat. "They waited for a day when everyone would be at Jaya's grandparents' house—her parents, her aunts and uncles, her cousins. They paid the whole family a visit, as if they were just dropping by for chai. They began talking as if they really were there to discuss a match between the families. Only instead . . . instead. . . ."

Sagar's shoulders drooped, defeat on his face. Pramesh had never seen his cousin look that way, even during the Elders' most violent rages.

"They held nothing back—every time they felt slighted by Jaya's grandparents, all invented things, none of it real. Every petty thought and jealousy. And they spoke every possible insult—questioning her family's line, their blood. By the time the Elders left. . . . It was lucky I didn't meet any of her cousins on my way home." Sagar said.

Pramesh could imagine it. A torrent of insults, spit one after the other, ugly thoughts erupting in uglier words, every blackness in the Elders' characters fully revealed. If the village was unsure about the quality of the Prasad family, the Elders would have smashed any last doubt in that meeting. Theirs was a family not just to stay away from—it was one to run from. And that included the Prasad cousins.

"Where is she now?"

"Far." Sagar looked at the ground, arms hugged to his chest, and gave a sad little laugh. "They took her away immediately, arranged a match with someone else. She married a university man after all. He took her to Agra."

"Did you get to speak to her? Before she left, before the wedding?"

Sagar toed the ground with his sandal, creating a divot and building up a small hillock of dirt that powdered his toes, saying nothing. Pramesh wished that the impression Sagar was making in the ground would widen just large enough for him to lose himself in, for him to escape from this feeling of crushing guilt, the sickness rising in his throat. He opened his mouth, but nothing came out. He reached out, and Sagar stepped back.

"It's done, Bhaiya. She is happy. Her eldest cousin made sure I knew that—along with every other detail of what the Elders said."

"He never liked either of us," Pramesh said, remembering that boy—now a man—spitting at his feet. *Nothing but the son of a drunk.*

Sagar waved his hands. "I was grateful that he told me. He owed me nothing after what happened that day. Leave it. Leave her."

But Pramesh couldn't. He kept thinking of his first weeks in the city, his dazed happiness as he walked the narrow lanes, exploring every turn, sitting on the ghat and daydreaming about what it would be like to create a life for himself there. And all the while, Sagar's future had combusted, the Elders' wrath like a lit match held to a butterfly. "Even if it is too late for her, it isn't a reason for *this*, this other madness you've agreed to. I'm sorry for the girl, but we owe them nothing."

"We do owe them something," Sagar said, his tone weary. "There was a dowry."

Pramesh swallowed. "How much?"

"Sizable." Sagar laughed, bitter. "Surprising, that they'd have so much money. But remember the man I told you about, the man who everyone said died because the girl bewitched him? They say the money was from his family. Bhaiya, the story—"

"Just give it back," Pramesh said. "It wouldn't be the first time for such a thing to happen. Blame me; tell them the fault is all mine; tell them I willfully defied the Elders."

Sagar made a sound of impatience. "Do you really believe that the Elders would keep the money safe for all that time? Wait until the marriage was official before they touched it?"

Pramesh's heart sank. "All of it?"

"There were loans on the land, Bhaiya. We weren't living on soil that was ours. They never told us—I found out from Hardev-maasad."

Too many things; too much pain Sagar had hidden from him. Pramesh's thoughts scrambled to keep up. "We can repay it."

"This isn't just about the land, the money. It's not the only reason to do this; it's—"

"No. We can repay it. I'll borrow what I can from Dharam-ji, and you'll come back with me to Kashi; we'll find you a posting somewhere; we'll—"

"No." Sagar held his hand up. "I gave them my word. The date is set. And I already told Bua and the Elders."

Pramesh froze. There was something so final in Sagar's voice, the old stubbornness and steel from before returning.

"They aren't what you think—" Sagar began, but Pramesh cut him off.

"This is not your problem—it's of the Elders' making; let them fix it. And this girl's family sounds no better —willing to sell their daughter to whoever names the right price. What did they say to you? How can you entangle yourself with a family like that? Isn't the one waiting for you at home bad enough?"

"It isn't like that! You said you felt sorry for her," Sagar countered. "I was watching you yesterday. You felt pity for her—it was in your face. Even if her family is what you say, it means she's *just like us*. Remember? She knows, Bhaiya. She will understand what we went through."

"You knew you were going to do it?" Pramesh's heart juddered. "You said you were watching me—this is something you planned on doing, then?"

"An idea." Sagar half threw up his hands, paced a few steps and turned. "It was only an idea. I wasn't sure they'd agree. But if you'd only listen to what they told me, only—"

"They told you a fairy tale, Bhaiya," Pramesh said. "You were never one for such stories, and yet you believe one now?" He was breathing heavily, as if he'd run a great distance. "They are taking advantage of you, and you are letting them. Why must you always walk where you are never meant to go?"

"And what of our story? What of what everyone says about us? I was visiting with every family, seeing what I could learn from those farmers, but I also wanted to know where I stood with them. And do you know what I found out?" Pramesh watched Sagar pace back and forth, his feet pounding a rut into the dirt. "I began talking to them, really talking to them—not like a boy going to his aunt's house, but like a man talking to his neighbors. And then I could see it. What they really thought of us. Pity, and disgust, and curiosity. *Are these Prasad cousins like their fathers or they like their mothers?*"

Pramesh waved his hands. "They will say what they say, it isn't—"

"Listen to me, Bhaiya," Sagar said. "I wanted to know how damaged we were, how people saw us. Now I know—and I am going to fix it. I won't run away for a new life. The one I have now is good enough for me, and so is the Prasad name. And I will make everyone here realize that. That we are people of quality—we aren't the Elders. Our word means something."

Pramesh listened to Sagar's voice rise and spit out the words in rapid bursts and watched his feet move back and forth in tight paces, feeling his anger increase with every one of his cousin's steps. "Is *that* the knife they are holding over you? That they will smear our name unless you give yourself to them? Who cares what they think? And if you *really* care, why then are you marrying her, joining this family? You aren't saving anyone by doing this—worse, you are dragging yourself down. Whatever she's done, her story, her family's story, all of it will drag you into the mud."

He was echoing his father, but in this case he knew he was right: whatever Sagar thought he was doing would miss the mark, curving back around to strike him instead.

"Fine," Sagar spat back. "I don't want your blessing, Bhaiya, and I won't wait for it. And why would you think that I need your permission to do anything?" His eyes bore into Pramesh. "*You* walked away; you didn't even look back as the train pulled away. Do you know what it was like when you left? Like I was living in a house of silence, of ghosts. You ran off, pushed me from your mind, started a new life. Why are you pulling me back from mine?"

Pramesh felt winded. "You made me promise," he stumbled, "*You* told me not to look back." His mind flew back to that day, the train, trying to recall Sagar's words. Had he misremembered?

"You keep begging me to join you, to run away like you did. Can't you see how selfish it is? Not once have I asked *you* to stay here with me. Do you know why?"

"Because there is nothing left here, for either of us. And if you remain, they will destroy you; you will be eaten from the inside. Even now you are a pawn, playing right into their hands, fulfilling a contract they had no right to make with that girl's family. No different than the children we once were, accepting whatever punishment they doled out. It won't end well. And when it all falls apart, what will you do?"

Fury filled Sagar's eyes. "And what about you? You went there to take my place at the university, didn't you? Did you ever meet that head of sciences? Did you attend a single class? Or did you hide yourself in that hostel from the first day? Doing what—watching people die? They aren't even your own blood. Don't forget—you weren't there for the Mothers' deaths. *I* was. It doesn't matter how many other mothers you see die. It will never match what I had to see, alone."

Pramesh listened, unable to respond, feeling the blood pounding in his ears.

"You see, Bhaiya. You aren't the only one with things to say about the other's life."

When Pramesh found his tongue, the sound from his mouth was neither a laugh nor a sob but something in between. "Is it my fault I knew nothing of how you felt? You lied to me, Bhaiya. Everything you said, everything you wrote—none of it was true." His lips trembled. He felt he might shatter at the slightest touch.

"What good would the truth have done you? You've never had the courage to do the thing that has to be done. Even back then, if only you'd had the stomach to tell the Elders to their faces that you would take my place . . . I had to do it for you. *I* had to give you permission.

And remember this: I never interfered with what you did after. When you shunned the university, when you surrounded yourself with dying folk in that forsaken hostel—I said nothing. Even when I thought you were wrong, being foolish, I never interfered. And I see you still need my permission. So be it: I release you from any obligation you have to this family. Go, go to your life in Kashi. Go to your bhavan. Go to your wife."

The words were like stones, each larger than the last, Sagar throwing with such precision that Pramesh no longer felt pain. He was numb. He squeezed his eyes shut. Just a year ago, he and Sagar had been in their childhood bedroom, where Sagar had made a decision for him, one that he'd accepted. When he spoke, he said each word clearly and slowly, to be sure that Sagar understood what he was saying.

"One word from you, Bhaiya, and I will go. But you must think carefully before you speak."

Sagar did not flinch; he did not hesitate. His voice was perfectly controlled, and he met Pramesh's gaze with his own determined one. "Bhaiya," he said. "Go."

And then, as if he did not trust Pramesh to do the same unless he did so first, he turned abruptly, striding back in the direction of the house. Pramesh stared at his cousin's back, heart galloping, sorrow and anger fusing into a hardened mass at his center. With every step that his cousin moved further away, Pramesh felt something diminish within himself, some essential part that existed only in conjunction with Sagar. He was desperate for his cousin to look back, just once. But a louder voice in his head told him to move his legs, walk in the opposite direction just as fast as Sagar was moving. To help his cousin in this decision he'd made, to widen the distance between them, make it a gaping chasm, and to move as far away from the pain that this life in the village had only ever caused him. To leave that old life—everyone, and everything—behind.

Once he began, he walked with purpose. And he did not look back.

41

Pramesh kept his eyes on the window with its unchanging view, clear blue sky, the barest glimpse of the neighboring building terraces from where he sat. Shobha held his hand.

"Your father and uncle. . . ." She started and stopped. "Such a thing to keep from me." She leaned her face into his shoulder, reaching her arms around him, and he allowed himself to be held. He felt like a hollow shell, emptied of everything that he was and had been.

"They died long ago," she said. "They are gone—they were the past. Whatever they thought then, whatever they did to you and your cousin— they were wrong."

"I should have gone back to him," Pramesh said. "I was older. It was my responsibility, even if we'd fought. I should have tried harder to talk to him." Shobha squeezed him gently.

"Perhaps. But would he have let you?"

"I don't know. I'll never know."

She released him. "On the train platform. You asked me about not looking back, about whether I believed in it."

The end of her sari brushed his hand, and he grasped that cloth, smoothing it between his fingers. "Yes."

"And I said yes. I believed it then." Gently, she held his chin between her fingers. She turned him to look at her. And then she forced him to look at Rani. "She is all that matters. It's not looking back if you do it for her. Please."

The exorcism had failed, the transfer of land, tripindi shraddha— nothing had worked to dislodge the spirit from the washroom. Shobha was right. There was nothing left to try but to ask that woman. She'd never entered his thoughts, never even seemed like a whole person, only a character in the stories he'd heard about her.

"What if she isn't there? What if she refuses to speak to me?"

"She's asked for you," Shobha reminded him.

He turned back to look at Rani again. He touched her foot. She did not stir; her skin was so hot that he almost lifted his hand away. Her tiny chest rose and sank in shallow breaths. "If only you could come as well, and Rani with you. If only. . . ."

He did not continue. He thought of those scraps of letters. *Your sister, your friend. . . .* Kamna might refuse to talk to Pramesh, but she could not refuse to speak to Shobha. But bringing Rani, or Shobha leaving her, was impossible.

"You must try your best with her," she said, her hand on their daughter's burning forehead.

Pramesh rocked his chin slowly. "In the morning, then." He rose and stepped to the door. His eyes caught on the lime garland. "Do you—did you think that she . . . ?"

Shobha made a helpless gesture. "I don't know what to think. But you'll go. And you will ask."

⚬

Shobha could not find sleep as the hours ticked by and Rani's breaths labored, hot and harsh. As he'd done every night since the hopeful multitudes came and Rani fell ill, Pramesh slept with his body stretched across the doorway of the family quarters, while Shobha slept upstairs with her daughter in the bed beside her. Throughout the illness, Rani had suffered a fevered sleep that kept her tiny body still, but now a coughing fit shook her. Shobha rose and poured a glass of water from the clay pot on the bedside table. She helped the girl sit and held the cup to her mouth. For a moment, Rani was quiet, but another fit overtook her, and then a darkness left her lips that Shobha recognized even in the blackness of the room.

Blood. Blood in spots on the pillow, and blood flecking the girl's mouth. She put her fingers to the wetness on her daughter's lips and smelled it, and the certainty of that wet metallic scent, like coins discarded in a puddle, filled her heart with fear.

And then the pots rang out.

The pots. All these months, something had pushed Rani's blood to the point of fever and back to the depths of chills; something had moved blood to spill with abandon from mysterious cuts and had painted the girl with purple-blue bruises. What else but the pots? And she felt a chill wash over her. During that first exorcism, when an insect had feasted on Rani's blood and Pramesh had killed it . . . when their daughter's blood had stained his hands and the ghost refused to leave. She now saw what she had been blind to before: not a nazar from Kamna, but blood like some hideous rope wrapping around the girl's throat and leading to the washroom. Each time the pots called out, the ghost tugged on that rope, and the girl suffered.

She was aware that the women in her kitchen nudged each other awake and probed her with eager glances as she came down the stairs; that her husband sat up and followed her; that the strangers crowding the walkway perimeter and courtyard stared at her, some openmouthed, others greedy-eyed, as she strode through their midst with her head bare and face in full view. She ignored their shouts as she entered the wash-room, a place they'd deemed holy and therefore off-limits. She closed the door behind her and turned to face the noise that had haunted the bhavan for months. "He is going," she said. "Whatever it is you need, whatever you wanted before you died, he is going tomorrow to find her. He will set it right."

She'd never before come to the washroom. She'd never seen the pots thrash about, never felt their cold brass shock her toes as the vessels rolled toward her. With the door closed, the hollow wail of the ghost was excruciating, as if someone had pulled the nails out of her fingers or filled her chest with ice. She had to remind herself that this being was once attached to her husband, and therefore to her; that Sagar had been a man made of flesh with a heart and a mind and a life that he'd been unable to live to completion. If she could imagine a man's voice in place of that cold metallic wail, then she could hear the pain in that sound, a longing for something out of the ghost's reach, a sadness that touched Shobha's heart even as the maternal anger she felt toward this specter gave her courage to speak into the damp night. "Whatever has passed, whatever has happened—can it truly be worth *her life*?"

The pots were still. But as she took a step backward, the unearthly screech recommenced. "What is it?" she asked, feeling ridiculous and desperate as she spoke to the empty room and her invisible conversation partner. "What could you possibly want?"

The pots wailed ever louder and longer. And then each pot tumbled toward Shobha so that she was encircled by a ring of the haunted vessels, and the sound emanating from each rose up and over her in a cage of despair and anger that she could neither understand nor escape. "He is going," she kept repeating. "He is leaving in the morning; your brother is going!" Louder they wailed; closer they came. She felt as if the living soul in her body would suffocate in the unnatural presence of this shadow.

And then she understood. "I will go with him. I will speak to her, and she will listen to me. I know she will." The pots were still. Her body moved of its own accord. Out of the washroom, past the leering men and her own husband, away from the women who regarded her with narrow eyes as she fled up the stairs. She scooped her daughter up and ran back down, Pramesh behind her as she sidestepped the crowd occupying the court-yard and walkway. Out of the bhavan, the lane felt strange in the dark, but she did not have far to go. Her daughter felt weightless in her arms as she mounted the three steps up to the Mistrys' veranda and pounded at the door, oblivious to the neighbors now looking out their windows.

Mr. Mistry answered the door, took one incredulous look at the bhavan mistress and Pramesh behind her, and went to fetch his wife. Mrs. Mistry came down directly, and whatever anger and hurt and mortification that may have been jockeying within her during the previous days melted away at the sight of Shobha standing in her doorway, a limp Rani in her arms.

"Maasi," Shobha said. Her voice quivered with pain. "Maasi," Shobha said again, her voice now a whisper. "I need you."

42

One bit of good fortune came out of Mohan's becoming the temporary manager of Shankarbhavan: his nighttime visits ceased. This wasn't because of a change in diet, or an aftereffect of his blurry night on the ghat, the details of which he still could not completely recall. Rather, the sudden onset of responsibility, of worry over Rani's worsening condition, of trying to make quick decisions in the face of people who did not belong in the bhavan—all of this conspired to create a perpetual ball of anxiety that resided in Mohan's stomach. Instead of manic twitches and cramps, he felt the round weight of worry weigh him down wherever he went.

"Pramesh-ji," he had pleaded with the manager, "I am not the man you need. You should not put the bhavan in my hands."

"There is no other man, Mohan-bhai. You have never lied to me. We know that I cannot say that for myself."

And there it was. With that long-awaited admission, Mohan felt his heart swell. He tried to dwell on that single truth when he felt overwhelmed, which was often. As it turned out, Mohan was exactly the right man for the job, although the reason for this was something neither he nor Pramesh anticipated.

"There he goes," various men and women whispered when they spotted the assistant. They stopped bickering and moved aside wherever he walked. When he spoke, all chatter ceased. They all tilted their ears in his direction, even if he was only telling Dev that the weather was unusually cool. He'd acquired almost instantaneous respect from these hopeful travelers, who passed the knowledge among themselves that *this* was the man, the proof of what this bhavan and its washroom spirit were capable of. To them, Mohan was not the proxy manager. He was the Dead Man Come to Life.

"How quickly did it happen?" men asked him. "Was it an immediate thing, an immediate feeling?"

"What was the nature of your illness?"

"How long were you dead for?"

"Where exactly were you when you came to life?"

"Were the pots banging when it happened? What was the cadence, exactly? Fast, slow? Do you suppose it makes a difference?"

They treated Mohan like a holy man or a movie actor. Eyes followed him wherever he went. Once ridiculed for something he had not done, Mohan now found himself praised for something else he did not do.

Mrs. Mistry sent over meals. Mohan ate with the priests and with Sheetal, united in their fellow feeling of false occupation. Sheetal endured dark glares from the crowds waiting outside, who felt that his father had already benefited from what the washroom specter could offer. "He is alive, isn't he? Why take up space here? Take the man home!"

As for the washroom, the pots acquired renewed vigor with Pramesh's departure. Once they began each night, the banging continued until the sun touched the open courtyard. During that time, the more zealous guests engaged in loud bhajans or threw flowers and rice and holy water into the washroom, hoping the specter might notice their attentions and home in on their loved one. Sleep in those hours was impossible both in and near the bhavan.

Every morning, Mohan rose from his cramped space between the priests' neatly lined beds and steeled himself for what always happened first thing. A crowd of people awaited his entry to the courtyard, all descending upon him with the same angry plea. *Why are they not better? What must we do to appease the ghost? Why isn't it working?*

"Friends, please. Anger will achieve nothing with this ghost, believe me. As I once told other families who stayed with us at Shankarbhavan, no one can tell when death comes. So it must stand to reason that no one can tell when *life* comes, yes? Isn't it so?"

What to tell these people? Mohan did the best he could. His years of negotiating with the Doms, of making shopkeepers smile even as he bargained for a lower price, of making friends with every stranger he met, all gave a kind of varnish to his person that made others instantly trust him. And while Mohan couldn't help with the question of life, he could and did help with living. He gave advice on the best markets to visit, directed women to the safest and cleanest ghats, even hailed rickshaws to the train station for those few who gave up and wished to return home.

With every passing hour, more and more people crammed into the building. Soon they were spilling out of the hole where the gates had once stood and crowding into the alley between the bhavan and Mrs. Mistry's house. Mrs. Chalwah could have easily seen them from her usual window perch, but she had been in her bed for many days. She received reports from her daughter-in-law, who'd taken on a new respect for her husband's mother since the circle officer's visit. "So many people, Ma. And at night, the racket! I don't know how you sleep through it. They all get up and rush in once the washroom gets especially loud. A sea of people, hai Rama." The old woman said nothing. As the younger one took back the untouched dinner thali, or the still full cup of chai, she often cast a wistful thought toward the bhavan just across the street. After all, Ma was doing poorly. She'd never given much thought to her mother-in-law before, thinking her a simple and submissive old woman. But now, if the stories about the bhavan giving life were true. . . .

As for the hopeful people who came from places far south and west and north and east, who traveled days or took a short train ride over— they shared the commonality of illness. What always differed, however, was the story that lay behind it, and that was how these folk passed the hours between each bout of sound from the washroom.

"My sister lives in that village; perhaps you know her?"

"That was how our Ravi became ill! They closed the well up the very next day."

"Well, she was born in this position, but all the doctors said she would die very soon after and look, she is now in her sixth year! But always suffering, always in pain."

"Brain fever, they said. He was so bright, first in class, bound for university, and then in one week he was in bed and everything changed."

"Did you happen to try. . . ."

So many people, so many illnesses, so many stories. So much sadness, and yet so much hope! Mohan tried very hard to keep them all straight, but the sheer volume of people made the task impossible. The new tenants coming to the bhavan were just like the former guests in that they, too, were dying, but these folk all aspired for an end to their story that would match that of the weaver who had left so long ago. However, they forgot one crucial detail of the weaver's tale. Out of the sick and the young and injured, out of the brain-addled and disabled, out of the ones who were skin on bone and the ones who'd ballooned so large that no single room could comfortably accommodate them—out of all these ailing men and women, youths and children, none of them realized the missing detail that made their stories different from the weaver's.

None of them had actually died.

43

On the first day of their journey the engine broke down, and Shobha and Pramesh waited on the tracks with the rest of the passengers as the engineers clanked with their hammers and ran back and forth between the cars. They tried to sleep that night in the carriage, their thoughts overwhelmed with worry for Rani, and late the next morning they heard the rumble of the replacement engine. Several hours later they disembarked in a cloud of dust whipped up by a sudden wind, Shobha holding the end of her sari to her mouth, Pramesh shielding his eyes as he led the way. It was late afternoon, and they walked until Pramesh was able to hail a farmer, a man he'd never seen before, rattling toward them in a bullock cart.

"Can you drop us close to the old Prasad house?" he asked.

"The Prasads!" the man exclaimed. "Relatives of yours?"

"How were the rains for you this season?" Pramesh asked in reply, diverting the farmer's attention, and the man talked of too much rain, then not enough. Pramesh looked toward the fields, felt the sun warm his face while a deep melancholy settled over him.

"What is it?" Shobha asked, worried, her voice low enough to settle beneath the farmer's ongoing monologue. Pramesh touched his hand to hers, the farmer lost in his own story.

⁙

The cart came to a creaking stop. Pramesh helped Shobha down and they bid goodbye to the farmer, who refused the payment the manager tried to press on him. As the cart pulled away, Pramesh fumbled with his bag and kept his eyes lowered, leading the way to his childhood home. Shobha imagined him as a boy, running around in play, and then she forced herself to imagine that same boy, this time running from his father, not quite fast enough to escape. She shuddered. Pramesh pointed to the peepal tree still standing in front. "The tree has barely grown at all. I would have thought it at least twice this height by now."

Shobha pulled the end of her sari over her head as she followed her husband. "You are older," she said. "The things our childhood selves saw as large rarely remain so."

She felt a pain in the center of her chest where she imagined an invisible thread had frayed between her and Rani when she'd left the city. Mrs. Mistry had taken the child in hand, applying cold compresses to Rani's arms and legs while yelling for her daughter-in-law to fetch several spice mixtures. "Nothing to worry over," the older woman had said to Shobha, as if Rani had only a sniffling nose or a scratched elbow. "Of course you must go. You have written to her." She switched out the cold cloths and rubbed a cooling turmeric paste on Rani's stomach and limbs. "She will see you as a friend, as someone safe. She will tell the real story to you, and only you."

What if Kamna was not there? Shobha thought now as she stared at the far-reaching fields and breathed in deep the scent of earth and dust that sifted upward from her footsteps. She could still feel the heat coming off her daughter, the child's skin so hot that Shobha had wondered how the little body could withstand it. She looked up at the house, at the place where her husband had come into being. She would not leave this place until she found Kamna and listened to whatever thing the ghost wanted her to hear.

Near the peepal tree, with his hands on the smooth bark, Pramesh held himself still, listening to the sounds of leaves moving with the breeze, of birds calling. Nothing about this place seemed changed, even the dread it invoked in him. The feeling grew more pronounced as he faced the house.

"Hello?" Pramesh called out from the front. He felt ridiculous, calling for permission to enter the house he had once freely roamed. Shobha stood beside him, peering beneath the veil of her sari at the open front door. They saw no one, and no sounds reached them from the inside. He walked to the open door and knocked on the frame. When no one came, he hesitated at the door, and then he took a step inside and stopped.

"What is it?" Shobha peered around his shoulder and breathed out a small exclamation. A small photograph wreathed in fresh flowers hung on the wall to their right. The picture was not a traditional funeral pose showing torso and face, with solemn eyes and flat mouth. Sagar seemed alive in this picture—he stood smiling in what looked like the shadow of the peepal tree in the front yard. His sleeves were rolled up and his arms crossed, one foot cocked back with his toes pushed to the ground while the other stood flat and steady. Pramesh looked into a face exactly like his own and felt the pit in his stomach deepen.

He observed the rest of the room. There was a worn bolster where his mother had sat with her sewing. Sagar's mother had used that basket in the corner for newspapers and other reading material. A line of cushions sat beneath Sagar's picture. He remembered the sun hitting that spot in the afternoons, his mother's hand on his cheek waking him from a nap. Then he remembered a different nap, one in this same room. After the Mothers died, he'd curled up next to the bolster, trying to catch some last trace of scent from either of those women. He'd fallen asleep, only to wake to Sagar's father grabbing him by an earlobe and wrenching him upward. The bruises on his face had taken days to fade.

He recalled the anger in that man's touch, the agonizing anticipation of each blow, as familiar now as twenty years prior. His breath felt sluggish in his lungs. He moved away from the door and sat down on the front stoop, unable to venture in further. He held his head in his hands, and then felt his wife's hand on his shoulder. "Remember why we are here," she said. "Remember Rani." He forced his thoughts toward a different terror: his daughter's aching breaths, her listless form when they'd left her. After some moments, he stood and led the way into the house.

They walked to the back. The kitchen was small and clean, with a tidy hearth and earthenware pots and jugs lining the walls. Like the front room, this one was neat and organized, not a stray speck of dust; all evidence of a comfortable and well-cared-for home.

The door from the kitchen to the back was open, and they stepped outside. Pramesh peered into the distance, taking in the fields and the trees, remembering Sagar's sturdy form as he walked back and forth with those water pots. Even the day after his injury, he had continued to make the trip alone until Pramesh was strong enough to join him.

"There is no one here," Shobha said. The disappointment was heavy in her voice.

"Perhaps they are away," Pramesh replied. His eyes remained on the fields, the image of Sagar burned into his memory so that the boy he remembered trudged toward him even now through the tall grasses. He rubbed his eyebrow and turned back to the house, this place that seemed so familiar and yet so strange, like a place he had visited in a dream. They could walk to the center of the village to see if any of the old neighbors were around, loath as he was for anyone else know he was here. It was probably safest to go to Champa-maasi's. He shifted his bag in his hands.

"Wait," Shobha said. Her hand grasped his elbow, a mixture of fear and hope in her eyes. He followed her gaze back to the fields. There was that imagined version of Sagar again, still walking toward him, clay pot in hand.

And a woman, walking with an elderly man at her side. An uncertain beat began to sound in Pramesh's chest, while Shobha gripped his arm tighter. At the edge of the field, those others spotted the manager and his wife, and they stopped. The woman looked as if she might faint. But the old man whispered something to her, and the color came back into her face.

And then a boy came bounding out of the fields and thrust some long grass stems and limp flowers into the woman's hands. The child turned to the house and noticed Pramesh and Shobha standing on the back veranda. His eyes widened. Pramesh noted the trim body, the long arms and legs and the boy's large head overrun with thick black hair.

The boy remained where he was, gaze fixed, until a smile broke across his face, radiant. He turned back to the adults behind him. "He is here!" the child cried out, his tone triumphant. "Pramesh-taya is here!"

44

Pramesh could not take his eyes off the boy, this child version of his cousin. His heart seemed to expand in his chest until he felt he could not breathe. He sipped at the water that Kamna brought to him and Shobha in the front room. The boy—Kavi—lingered first on a bolster near Pramesh, then at his grandfather's knee, then leaned against his mother when she returned from the kitchen and sat next to Shobha. So like Sagar! The movements, the smile, the entire manner about him. And his eyes—there was a light in the child's eyes that Pramesh had only ever seen in one other person's. "How old?" he asked.

"Seven." Kamna smoothed her son's hair and he batted her hand away, his smile wide, his eyes darting everywhere even as he snuck glances at the manager.

"A son . . . *his* son." Pramesh swallowed. "I never imagined it."

"That was the reason he left this place—to tell you. What did he say when you saw him?"

The manager tried to return Kamna's gaze, but he could not. He looked to her father and then to the boy, who continued to stare at him with wide eyes. The old man stood and beckoned to the child. Once the boy was out of hearing, Pramesh summoned his courage. "He made it to the hostel. But there was . . . a mistake. He died before I ever saw him."

He told the story, starting with Sagar being led to the wrong hostel, then being turned away at the gate, his walk around Kashi, his body in the boat, the botched funeral rites, the nighttime washroom disturbances, and ending with the ailing and decrepit guests who refused to die and the weaver who came back to life. As he talked, he kept his eyes on the scene just outside the open doorway, on the child who ran about outside. But when he spoke of the ghost that lingered, he shut his eyes, unable to face either his cousin's child or his wife.

Kamna's eyes were bright and wet, but the tears did not fall to her cheeks. "I asked him to tell you earlier. When Kavi was born, his every birthday. . . . Many times, I told your cousin to write to you. He meant to, but he could never finish the letter. The days flew by, the months became years."

Kamna looked at the tree through the open front door as she talked. She spoke carefully, choosing every word as if she were picking through lentils in a sifting basket. "He thought then, as we all did, that there would always be time." Her face was tight and tired. She opened her mouth to speak again but instead a low sigh escaped her lips. Shobha reached out, hesitant at first, and then touched the woman's fingers lightly. Kamna met her eyes with a small smile. "When the sickness came, it struck so many of us, our neighbors, my family. Many got better, but he never did. I could tell. He stopped running races with our son; he returned earlier from the fields and had to lie down for whole afternoons. Food always remained on his plate. And then I became ill—"

"You were ill?" Pramesh asked.

"Yes. The same awful fever, the same sickness. He was afraid that we would both die and you would never know about our son. He wrote, but he did not send the letter. So foolish. Even when I said I would mail it myself. . . ." She made a weak sound of impatience and rubbed her temple, bangles softly jangling. "He thought for many days, and then he came to me with his decision: too much time had passed for a letter to suffice, he said. He wanted to tell you himself. He seemed weaker every day, and my father discouraged him, but you know how he was; he had decided. He had to see you; he wanted so badly for you to hear about our son from his lips."

The manager thought of Sagar enduring the journey to Kashi, walking through the streets, body burning with fever, limbs limp and aching. He must have been in agony. And yet he'd pushed on—of course he had, with the thought of his son driving him. Pramesh watched the boy running outside, the old man sitting on a rope bed and shouting things at him. "Jump! Run to that tree! Throw that stone as high as you can!" The boy obeyed, giggling when his grandfather's commands overlapped and he had to do two things at once.

"He was so ill. I begged him not to go," Kamna said. She looked at Pramesh and Shobha and her gaze was defiant, but then it softened. "I think I knew he would not come back. I felt it, somehow. Such bad dreams. He laughed when I tried to tell him. He would not let the idea go. He wouldn't be happy any other way, so I finally relented. I did every puja I could think of; I made him sit so I could remove any nazar. And he left." Her voice was faint now. "I never doubted him. When he decided on something, it was always done, no matter how impossible. But when we received your letter—I knew, even before then. It was a feeling."

Shobha reached her hand toward Pramesh's bag and undid the clasp. She reached inside and brought out a full glass bottle, which she handed to Kamna. "The river," she said. "He meant to fill it and bring it back to you, didn't he? For you and the child; for your illness."

Kamna attempted a smile, but her lips quivered beneath her full eyes. Her sadness pierced Pramesh's heart, and he looked away. "I asked him for it," she said. "He laughed; he never believed in such things. But he never denied me anything, nor our son."

They sat in silence, listening to the old man and the young boy play outside. Shobha spoke up. "I am sorry," she said. "We arrived here without an invitation or sending word."

Kamna looked surprised. "You hardly need an invitation to your own home. And you forget: we have been expecting you for many months now, even before I wrote you that letter."

"But I never wrote to say we were coming, and your letter arrived damaged; I could not read it." Shobha reached her hand back into Pramesh's bag and pulled out the envelope of scraps as proof.

"Still, I knew you were coming. He promised me right before he left."

"What do you mean?" Pramesh asked.

Kamna set the bottle down and took Shobha's hand in both of her own and spoke as if she were stating something obvious. "He said you would come to us." The words came back to Shobha: *When will he be here? He said he would come.* "He was certain," Kamna continued. "Always, always, he said you would come."

Kamna and Shobha retired to the kitchen to fix the evening meal, and Pramesh ventured outside to the veranda to watch the old man and Kavi. The boy stopped playing as soon as he saw the manager and clung close to his grandfather, stealing glances and smiling at Pramesh. He seemed smitten, and did not leave until his grandfather pushed him toward the front door and bade him to go to his mother. The old man then beckoned Pramesh to the two rope beds sitting at angles from each other on the veranda. The sun had dipped down the horizon, and the air sounded with the pleasant rustle of birds nesting for the night and insects beginning their evening reverie.

"I don't believe you know much about my family," the old man said. He pointed to himself. "Om. My wife passed just a few years ago. And we have only one daughter, our Kamna-beti. And you—your wife is Shobha. Children?"

"A daughter. Rani—younger than Kavi."

"A daughter." Om smiled. "Your cousin wondered, especially after Kavi came. Nothing lovelier. Sons are headstrong, my wife used to say. Daughters are stubborn, but their hearts are bigger. Or so I've always thought." He was quite at ease across from Pramesh, humming a low song beneath his breath.

"The land—I trust that you had no troubles with the ownership?" Pramesh stumbled over the words, but he wanted there to be no question about the motives for his visit.

"None." Om drew his hands over his hair, which was silver and cut short but still full. His face was clean-shaven and his body was slight with a sculpted softness to it, the evidence of a man once wiry and strong whose muscles had stretched and relaxed with age. "We did not expect it. I thought perhaps that was your way of settling things. And it secured the boy's future. I was grateful."

"Of course. I am glad of it."

"We thought—*I* thought—that you knew about the boy, and that you still chose not to visit. That your feelings prevented you from coming here. I misjudged you." The old man's gaze never flinched.

Pramesh hunched on the bed, legs crossed. "I think, perhaps, that fault is mine."

"You were not happy with the marriage," Om said. "You were not happy with the family he chose to marry into. With *me*." When Pramesh demurred, the old man continued, "I never blamed you for this. But humor me: tell me the story you know."

"I never believed the gossip," Pramesh said. "I admit: I doubted your motives. But the stories about her always seemed too outlandish, too cruel. . . ."

"Ah. But you felt I had sold her, perhaps?" Om peered closely at Pramesh, who blushed. "Yes." The old man wagged his chin to himself. "Tell me the stories, whether you believed them or not. Perhaps then I can explain to you."

He was earnest, and so Pramesh told the story. There was no embellishment, no room for anything but what he remembered Sagar telling him. He was quick in explaining Kamna's reputation for running away, of her dalliance with the wealthy man, encouraged by her parents, who later spurned her. Of the money Om had extracted from that man's family, of the man's later death and the family's forced peripatetic existence from then on, no village content to have people of that sort take up residence for too long. Of the other men she was said to have met. The words gave him no pleasure, and when he finished, he expected the old man to be defiant and defensive at this rehashing of his family's past.

"That is all?" Om asked. He seemed more weary than angry.

"What do you mean?"

"It is only that some versions go a different way. In some versions, she is the one to spurn the man, break his heart. In some versions, they have her with child—in others, she is assumed barren, because they say she has been with so many men. We'd hear all the stories from our neighbors. *We've heard*—that was the way they'd always begin. Never mind that they could have gotten the truth from me at any time. They were content with others' tales."

There was no emotion in Om's voice; he talked as if this painful history was someone else's to bear, and yet Pramesh could see the control in the old man's eyes, the years of indifference he'd had to practice to come to his present state. "Only one man ever asked for the truth, and so only one man ever received it. He came to my home, drank my wife's chai, and had the courage to ask me what had really happened. I had a clear conscience when I gave him my daughter. And your Sagar, *our* Sagar, had a clear heart when he took her from me."

As the old man took possession of Sagar with his words, the sensation Pramesh felt was like a cool cloth applied to his face on a hot day.

"I would like to tell you what I told him, if you have the patience."

Pramesh nodded.

"My daughter was indeed a bit of a runaway, but she did so with the full permission and knowledge of her parents. She was always happiest when she was by herself, walking among the fields or near the stream that ran near our home. When she was younger, very young, folk laughed and said she was led by fairies. A blessed girl, they said, who could see things that others could not. Funny, how folk accept that a child might have an eye to another world but a grown woman may not. When the girl became older, the same people forgot about the fairies and instead called her lazy. They said a girl who ran when there was work to be done was a girl not worth the food her family fed her. They called her slow, dim-witted, and worse.

"None asked us even once for the truth about her. I would have told them of a girl who was shy and quiet, and her mother would have spoken of a girl who finished all the housework while everyone else slept, who nursed both parents and neighbors when they fell ill with summer fever. Yes, this girl would often disappear, would go for long walks and sit on her own, but her mind was sound and her heart was patient.

"Around that time, we had some bad luck. Some land that my family had been farming for decades from a neighboring family produced a poor harvest. When that patriarch came to visit me, I thought he wanted to discuss the fields. Instead, he wished to discuss my daughter. Like everyone else in the village, it seems, he had heard some story about her. But he wanted to take that worry away from me, he said. He was coming to ask for my daughter's hand for his son. The son, it turned out, had come upon her during one of her walks. He'd fallen in love with her and could not be dissuaded.

"I'm ashamed to admit that I was happy with this news. I thought she would be comfortable there, that the stories about her would stop once she was married into a powerful family who could control gossip as well as they controlled their land. But my daughter refused to marry him. I was angry; I felt she'd taken advantage of the freedom she enjoyed for so many years. I declared that she would marry him regardless.

"She diminished in the days that followed. The boy and his mother visited a few times, and she sat still and lifeless as a bit of wood. During the last visit, she would not leave the back room, and I . . ." Om paused. "I told her if she did not come, I would drag her there. So she came." He was silent for a long while. Pramesh realized the old man was trying to compose himself. Wetness shone in his eyes.

"Her mother was the one who pulled it out of her. That man . . . that man I'd made her sit next to . . . he hadn't just followed her around." The words stuck in Om's throat. His jaw worked. He looked away and wiped his palm across his eyes.

Pramesh felt his breath stop. He knew what Om could not say. "Rama," he whispered. "Oh, Rama."

Om took a deep breath. "I called off the marriage. They were furious. My daughter was no longer clean, they said; didn't I realize that she would never get a chance like this again?

"But I had heard stories of my own by that time. My daughter wasn't the only one, apparently, who had caught this boy's eye. I went to every house in the village, every house with a daughter. Some of them agreed with me but were too afraid to do anything. Some of them simply called me a doddering old man. Some of them said it was nothing new, these things happen. Many of them refused to open the door to me.

"The family heard what I was trying to do. And in revenge, they took back those acres of fields that my family had farmed for years. They used the excuse that I had been unable to reap a satisfactory crop that season and perhaps they needed to find a man with more industry than myself. I thought that was the end of it, but small-minded men think deep when they have an insult to avenge.

"The stories spread slowly at first, but a month after the broken engagement, everyone had that family's poison on their lips. My daughter, they said, had taken to chasing after men in her wanderings." Om's voice shook with anger. Pramesh tried to tell him he need not continue, but the old man held his hand up. "They said she'd bewitched the wealthy boy, and thankfully the family had made their son see the error of his ways, but the warning was out: my daughter was shameless and would be the misfortune of any man associated with her.

"That was just the beginning. My wife could not even go to the well after that without some woman spitting in her water pots. Children chased after my daughter, throwing stones, pulling her sari, the boys betting who could pull it off. We had to leave—there was no other way.

"In the beginning, when we settled in a new place we were left alone. But always the stories would float after us, carried by someone's visiting relative, and then the jeering would start, the shunning, the refusal to sell us things in the market. We grew to recognize the signs. None of the people in any of the places we lived ever took the time to know us. For them, the stories were enough; they served as truth.

"My wife decided that we had to find a husband for our daughter— that the stories would never stop until we did. But if we couldn't find a place to live, how were we going to find a suitable boy? We spoke to a traveling matchmaker, and he was honest in naming our prospects. He told us of a family living in the next village over. Both I and the girl's mother should have been happy for the chance for our daughter to live so close to us, but just as folk had told stories about our daughter, so had we heard stories about that prospective boy's family. And the stories, which we believed as truth, were not good. You must know what I speak of."

"Yes. But tell me anyway." The old man hesitated. Pramesh sensed that he was trying to be delicate. "I knew what was said from my own perspective. I want to hear what everyone else would have been thinking. Please."

And so the old man told the story of the Prasads: how the two brothers had been spendthrifts partial to drink, fortunate only in their choice of wives, who'd come with sizable dowries; how they'd gambled away their land and neglected their children after those two women died; how the remaining money paid for liquor; how the two boys, the cousins, mere children, were always skinny, always decorated with bruises; how the men seemed to see their offspring as commodities or obstructions; how only the widowed aunt seemed to have a shred of feeling for the children. And how the saving virtue of those boys had been their devotion to each other until the older one abandoned his cousin and his family in a single impetuous step.

"I had no idea if you and your cousin had also inherited that same dark character as your father and uncle, but there was no other choice. We had only the word of the matchmaker to go on, and while he spoke bluntly of the family, he felt the boys were different. I agreed only because I thought that Kashi was a place big enough, where she might make a life for herself that was free of haunting tales. But weeks went by, with no wedding date set. I knew something was wrong; your elders sent no answers to my letters; they refused to meet me. I didn't know what to do. We were not in a position to ask or demand for things. You must know how it was; we were the family whom others told stories about. We were not allowed that privilege ourselves."

"There was a dowry, I thought," Pramesh said slowly. He was so unsure of what was true and what was false, but the old man's eyes prompted him to continue. "Sagar-bhai said that you all had received money from that wealthy family to stay quiet, and you gave it to us as part of the marriage contract. And the Elders spent it. He was so worried over the family name—what people would say if our family reneged on the agreement. What you would say about us."

"There was a dowry. But every penny of it had been saved by my wife. Each month since our marriage I gave her money for the household expenses, and she set aside a portion of it for our daughter. We never touched that money. It was not ours." He shifted on the rope bed. "You may not believe me, but I never approached your cousin about my daughter. I had bid farewell to both the dowry and the marriage offer by then. Our future was precarious: I didn't know how much longer we could stay in that village, or what would happen to my daughter when I was gone. I felt I had failed as a father. I had tried to make her happy by giving her one thing: freedom. And yet that very act seemed to guarantee that she would never be happy in adulthood. Still, I never asked your cousin to do what he did.

"You grew up with him; there was a time when you knew him better than anyone, and perhaps in a way you still do. But there is one thing you still do not understand. That day he met with me and my wife, he sat as close to me as you sit now. We made a bargain—he would trade me an honest story of his life for an honest account of my daughter's.

"I heard from his lips that your departure was no premeditated selfish act. He made it plain that you left because of him and *only* because of him. I told him the story of my family in exchange. He did not take long to make his decision. He married her because he wanted to." Here, the old man set his legs to the floor and left Pramesh for a moment. When he returned, he held the picture of Sagar that Pramesh had stared at for so long. "Look," the old man said. "This was taken a year after their marriage. Look at his face, and tell me if you feel I've told a falsehood."

Pramesh looked at his cousin, at the relaxed pose, the smile, which he realized was the reason the photo had transfixed him to begin with: the smile was genuine. He had not seen that expression on Sagar's face in so long, neither in reality nor in memory. "He was happy with her," Pramesh said, and as he spoke the words, he realized he believed them. "They were happy together."

"Yes. They were happy, despite their pasts. Despite every story told about my daughter, and every injury your cousin sustained." He looked at Pramesh intently. "He said it was worse for you." Pramesh's breath caught. "He said you often took more beatings than he did. That you stood up for him and took his place many times when your elders focused their wrath on him."

Pramesh pressed his hands together, staring at his feet. He could not think. "I seem to remember him doing that for me more than the opposite."

"With his accident, perhaps." The old man reached for his own wrinkled forehead. Pramesh nodded, surprised that the man knew the story. "He said you suffered over that wound more than he did. Tell me: do you remember the things he did for you?"

"Always."

"And he, on the other hand, only remembered what you did for him. He spoke of you often—to my daughter, to me, and to the child. Do you not wonder how the child recognized you so quickly when his mother and I were struck dumb in the field, thinking that a ghost had come to visit us? He knows you as more than just his uncle. You were his father's brother, his best friend, his partner in every adventure. You are the hero in every story your cousin ever told, the cornerstone of his past."

"But he has never seen my face until today."

"That matters not. Don't you understand? To the boy, you are proof that every story his father told him was true."

"What stories?" Pramesh could only remember the same scenes, the same horrors. He could not imagine Sagar passing down such a black inheritance to his son.

"Ask him," the old man said. He got up again, this time resting his hand on Pramesh's shoulder as he passed. "He knows all the tales by heart. Not all the memories were bad. Ask the boy, and perhaps he will help you remember."

∴

Shobha stole glances at Kamna as they pinched out balls of dough and rolled them out. She saw a woman of about her height, black hair coiled into a bun at her neck, just two gold bangles on each wrist, a simple white sari without adornment. This was the woman she had feared for the last ten years—but also the same woman who had called her sister and friend.

They did not speak at first and instead allowed the work of their hands to fill the silence: the rhythm of the knobby pin rolling over the uneven board, the slap of the dough round on the dry metal tava, the soft exhalation as the round puffed up on the fire.

"Must you go in the morning?" Kamna asked.

Shobha thought of Rani, sick and far from her, and felt the great aching lack that had pulsed within her since they'd left. "We came in a great hurry," she said. "Our daughter was very ill when we left. I cannot be away from her for long."

Kamna listened as she described the illness, and then she got up and took a powder from a tin canister, twisted it up in a bit of cloth, and handed it to Shobha.

"Have her hold this to her nose. It will help her breathe better."

Shobha took the packet, murmuring her thanks, and looked at it, now thinking again of those insinuations of black magic, of witchcraft.

Kamna laughed softly. "Roasted and crushed fennel seeds. Nothing more."

"Forgive me," Shobha stumbled. Kamna continued to roll balls of dough between her palms, going at a rate that far outpaced Shobha's hand with the rolling pin. "I knew nothing of you. I still know nothing."

Kamna shifted to the side, procured another rolling pin and board, and began to flatten roti alongside Shobha. "My mother and I used to do this in the kitchen together. No matter where we lived. It made it seem like a home, wherever we went—for us to roll roti together."

Shobha thought of her own mother. She used to fry onion pakora, Shobha's favorite, and she'd laugh as she fished the fritters out of hot oil, dodging Shobha's fingers as she tried to steal one before it cooled. "Has it been long since she passed?"

"Five years," Kamna said, her rolling pin continuing its smooth back and forth.

"Twelve," Shobha said softly.

Kamna looked up. "It's difficult." She slapped a round of dough on the tava. "Losing her made me terrified of losing them all. Especially when the sickness came. For a while, after Kavi's father—your brother—became ill, Kavi also had the signs."

Shobha wondered at this sudden acquisition of a brother, a sister, all in a single day.

"Even now," Kamna continued, "when he wheezes or slows while playing, I worry that the sickness is still there, lingering. I cannot sleep at night sometimes."

"Does he talk of his father?"

"At times." Kamna wiped her forehead with the end of her sari and turned her attention back to the tava. "He knew his father was ill. They were very close. It hasn't been easy. He is so young—they should have had many more years together. He talks to me, sometimes, when we go out for walks. When we 'run away,' as I call it." A smile curled the edge of her mouth.

"Do you do it often?"

"Running away, you mean?" Kamna smiled. "I do. Kavi's father sometimes came with me, you know. And now my son comes in his father's place."

"And what do you think of?" Shobha could not bring herself to look at Kamna. The question was presumptuous; she was ashamed at her brashness. For a while, Kamna did not speak. "Forgive me; I should not have."

"There is no need for an apology between sisters," Kamna said. Again, Shobha marveled at the ease with which this woman had gathered herself and Pramesh into her speech. "In my home village—everything. I had questions about everything, the things I read in books, the life I saw in the village, the land that I walked over every day. So many questions, and not many to talk to, and so I walked alone and talked to myself. But then, something happened."

She turned suddenly, using her fingers to lift the roti from the hot tava and flip it, but she dropped it. She paused, took a deep breath, and tried again, this time flipping it perfectly.

"I don't want to speak of it. But after that, we left the village. And I did not walk on my own again for a very long time."

Shobha had been watching her carefully. She thought back to Pramesh telling her Sagar's story, of how Kamna had apparently met a wealthy man's son who wanted to marry her, and how they'd had to leave the village soon after. She watched the woman across from her, her hands betraying the slightest trembling. She quietly took up another ball of dough, as did Kamna, and they rolled together in silence until that woman softly spoke again.

"After I married, and especially after Kavi came, the world seemed a bit simpler. I had Kavi's father to talk to. He told me so much about his cousin, his twin as he called him. And he told the same stories to Kavi as well—always about his uncle. But he and I also talked about you."

Shobha's rolling pin slipped on the board. She looked up to meet Kamna's eyes.

"I'd heard all about my husband's brother, you see. I could picture him in my mind; I knew exactly the kind of man he was. But we knew nothing of *you*. And so we talked of what we thought you were like, the wife my husband wanted his brother to have."

The heat rose to Shobha's face. She looked down at the rolling pin and saw it shaking slightly. And then a hand was on hers, and she looked up to see Kamna intent upon the ground, unable to meet Shobha's eyes. "Shobha-behan, everything my husband said about what his brother needed most—there is no difference between that dream and you. Truly."

"You know me so little," Shobha said after a time.

"I know that you knew nothing of me, yet you took the time to write to ask about where I was and what had become of me. You called me your sister and your friend; you left your sick child in someone else's care just so you could bring my brother here to see me, to meet his nephew."

"That was my husband's choice," Shobha protested.

"Yes, but I know you must have persuaded him. You must not forget: I was married to his brother for almost ten years. I know those two men have a stubbornness and pride that even the great God cannot move. But a wife can. You and I.

"I knew my husband's brother would come, even if I was afraid of that moment. I know he did not approve of the match, of my family. I didn't know if he cared about his cousin's widow. But I knew you did, from your letters." She said all of this with a tone that spoke of facts. She was so sure of herself, of the place that Shobha and Pramesh held in her family. Such thinking was not the work of days or even months: Kamna must have set aside a room in her heart for the two of them, and for any children they may have had, for a very long time.

"I wanted so badly to meet him," Shobha said. "I thought about nothing else for the entire train ride. And oh! I made pura for him—twice! I knew it was his favorite food; I wanted to impress him." She stopped, looking at Kamna, who had suddenly covered her mouth with her hand, looking like a schoolgirl who'd just heard a delicious new joke.

"If you only knew!" she said, laughing, "We tried so many times to guess between us what you had brought for him! He knew from his brother you'd done something. I *told* him it must have been pura. All these years, he would have been so mad to know I was right." She laughed, a full peal as pure as the tone of a bell. Shobha broke into a smile.

They finished the roti and Kavi walked in, setting himself down next to Shobha with an ease that warmed her and made the hollow in her heart ache for Rani. Kamna handed a jar to her, and when she looked inside and smelled the sweetness within, she smiled. She scooped out a chunk of jaggery and placed it in the boy's palm. "For you," she said, smoothing the child's hair. "For being especially good today."

⚶

After the evening meal, Pramesh wandered out the back door. Even as the sun set, he continued to stand there. And as the sky darkened and the chorus of insects rose, he felt a small hand on his own, and he looked down to see the boy, Kavi, beckoning him to come inside.

"Taya, will you tell me a story?" He gestured at the back of the house, where the manager saw the old man waiting near the door. "Nana said

399

you would, if I asked. He said you know different stories from the ones Bapa told."

"I don't think I can remember any," he said. "I don't think I have the same memory that your bapa had." The child released Pramesh's hand but remained standing there. Pramesh breathed out and looked at the fields, at Sagar's land. He had accused Sagar of lying to him, yet he knew Sagar would have only told the boy the truth, just as he had only told Pramesh parts of it, to protect him. He thought of what Kamna's father had said to him about remembering. "Perhaps," he said, turning back to Kavi, "if you tell me a story first, I might be able to tell you one back, nah?" He held his hand out to the child to take again.

"I can tell you about the girls at the well," Kavi said. "And how they used to laugh at you, and the trick you and Bapa played to get them to stop!"

The girls, the well. . . . The child's words created a hazy picture in Pramesh's mind: of Sagar filling the pots and then handing Pramesh a pocketknife to cut the well rope with, of the girls laughing at them and then shrieking as the pot they sent down the well plummeted to the bottom, the weight snapping the frayed rope.

"Yes," Pramesh said, leading the boy back to the house. "Tell me that story first. And then tell me the others."

45

What power did a holy man have? The question occupied Narinder's thoughts as he sat in the corner of the priests' quarters with his prayer beads. The mantras had been replaced by circling thoughts. Ever since that failed tripindi shraddha, the gates in his mind had collapsed, like the ones formerly protecting the bhavan. All the hidden fears and doubts that he'd always kept at bay now crept in and drowned out the holy words he'd fed his mind on for so long.

And the bhavan, that place of refuge that his soul thrived in, now wearied him. His heart felt smothered at the sight of the open hole where the gate once was, of the people sleeping outside in bedrolls on the street, of those crowds standing two men deep, trying to look over each other's shoulders for open room where none existed. In the few days that the manager and his wife had been gone, a constant stream of people had flowed into the building.

He closed his eyes and felt for his prayer beads. He grasped one wooden bead between his thumb and forefinger, ready to push it aside for the next, when he felt Mohan at his side. "Something has happened," the assistant said with cautious quiet. Indeed, the entire bhavan, which had taken on the atmosphere of a raucous tree of monkeys or a common guesthouse, was still. Narinder followed the assistant out of the room and found all eyes focused on a family who'd overtaken the center of the courtyard.

"Dead," Mohan said. "Their young man, the son. Just some minutes ago. Loknath checked as well, after I confirmed it." He spoke the last sentence with loud deliberation.

Narinder squeezed the assistant's shoulder and strode forward. He leaned down and checked the man's wrist. The veins were slack; the hand he held to the young man's nose came away cold. "Dev," he called, and the younger priest poked his head out of Sheetal's room, where he'd kept up a constant stream of mantras at the feet of the boy's still lingering father. Without asking, he fetched the things that Narinder would need. The family cried silently. The women covered their faces while the men sat on their haunches and rocked back and forth in a listless rhythm. The man was young, barely nineteen. He'd arrived with a large and bulbous lump beneath his jaw that made it impossible for him to eat. His mother and aunt had spoon-fed him lentils cooked to a melting softness and fruits mashed into pulp. The pain must have been terrible; his body was emaciated and he'd moaned when anything touched his skin.

Narinder emerged from the priests' quarters with his prayer beads and a brass lota of river water. He stood over the body, ready to pronounce the mantras and sprinkle the corpse with water. "Om—"

A piercing shriek interrupted him. One of the crying women moved to cover the body with hers, her arms creating a protective barrier between the dead man and Narinder. "You will not!" she sobbed. "We have come so far, you will not take his last chance from him!" A fistful of holy water dripped from Narinder's upraised hand, and one of the surrounding men quickly moved the dead man's leg away from the falling drops. The water fell to the ground, and Narinder took an instinctive step back to avoid stepping on that holy substance.

"Narinder-ji knows the proper way to send the soul onward," Mohan intervened. He knelt next to the man's father. "You must let him continue so that your son receives a proper end."

"No one is to touch my son. No one, you hear?" The man threw Mohan's hand from his shoulder. His mustache bristled; his eyes scanned the crowd with a crazed paranoia. He pushed his clinging wife aside and gathered his son in his arms. All eyes followed him as he walked with the withered body toward the washroom. Just inside, he laid the body down with care. He straightened the limbs, stroked the disfigured cheek. He squatted next to his son and glared outward.

Narinder released the water in his fist back into the brass lota. He curled his prayer beads around his hands and returned to the priests' quarters, Mohan following behind. "Narinder-ji, don't listen to them. Complete the rites as you always do. They are country people; they must not realize how these things go." Narinder said nothing. The assistant lingered at the door before turning back to the full room. They both knew that neither of them had any purpose there. The man did not want death rites for his son. He wanted what the washroom could give him. He was waiting for the pots to sing.

"There is something bothering you," Bhut's wife said. The circle officer had been silent for many days. He occasionally went to his office, but mostly he stayed sitting in the kitchen with his wife and sisters.

His sisters had tolerated this for a day, but soon the older one could not hold her tongue. "A man in the kitchen with the women. In his uniform, no less. Or perhaps I am wrong; *is* it truly a man? Or perhaps still a boy, even after all these years?" She had been sifting through a pan of black lentils as she spoke, and the tray was almost free of stones and ready for soaking, but it never got its chance. Bhut rose, ripped the pan from her hands, and threw it across the room. He then resumed his seat on a stool. His sister sat frozen, palms still upright from holding the pan. Then she lowered her hands and seemed to shrink within herself. She did not look at Bhut, nor did her sister.

"Did you know?" he asked. The question had been burning him from the inside for days. "Did you know she walked in her sleep? Did she do it before she was married, when we were children?"

Neither of his sisters blinked; neither moved. A slow and deathly sigh escaped from his second sister. His older sister's mouth quivered. Two tears left her eyes and ran rivulets down her cheeks to the corners of her mouth. "We always thought she would grow out of it," she whispered. "Ma, Bapa . . . they thought marriage. . . ." Her voice faded, and she squeezed her eyes shut.

That was all the answer Bhut needed.

His wife knew the signs, and she kept out of his way and warned their children to stay clear of their father. He would not receive any of his deputies, who'd come to the house several times and who reported back to the station that the man was ill and would not be back for some days. Formerly a restless man, Bhut now remained still. His mind, however, was active. He thought only of Mrs. Chalwah's story. And the part that troubled him, the thing he could not figure out, was how was it possible that after all these years, when he laid her version on top of the version he'd always known to be correct and connected the joints between where his story ended and hers began; how was it that those two versions fit together perfectly, as if both were equally true?

46

The hours ticked by. Children tossed in their beds. Men rubbed bloodshot eyes. Women rolled prayer beads between their fingers and recited the mantras over and over. Night fell. The hours passed; the children still tossed; men stared sightless at the walls; women trembled and prayed.

Midnight struck. The man sitting at the washroom door adjusted the shawl he'd flung around his shoulders. He'd spread a blanket across his son's shrunken chest. His own mind was blank. Two hours remained.

Bhut had not intended to come to Magadha. He had not intended to go anywhere, in fact, but the combination of a still body and racing mind had driven him mad over the past few days. His family avoided him; even his youngest daughter, his favorite, had flinched when her hand accidentally brushed his during the evening meal. The sight of his sisters disgusted him. His house felt filled with a poisonous air that took him many hours of thinking to identify.

Lies. The house—once his childhood home, now his adult dwelling— was full of lies. He smelled it in the bedding, in his clothes, on the cotton towel his wife brought for him to dry his hands on. The sisters reeked. Even the food stank of lies, so much so that he'd spit out a mouthful of eggplant and roti during the evening meal, right on the brass thali with the rest of his uneaten dinner. In that moment, even his wife seemed terrified of him. Her hands trembled when she brought the brass lota that he demanded; she looked away as he gargled and spat out the window to rid the taste from his mouth. The action was useless: the water carried the same stink, as did all the vessels in the house.

That was when he'd left. He stopped at the first chaat stand he saw and ordered two bowlfuls, neither of which carried the smell. He ate quickly, only to fill the aching cavern of his stomach. Then, he walked. "Officer-sahib! Oh, Officer-sahib!" Someone spotted him, but Bhut ignored the call. He walked for hours, the low ache in his knee fast growing into a burning throb, then a sharp pain that felt like glass scraping the bone. Still he pushed on, his footsteps leading the way as night fell and blackness blinded him. By the time his legs brought him to the ghats and down to the river, the hour was late.

He knew why he was here. Menaka—his Mini—had taken her last steps here, had danced on this ghat. What was she thinking? What Hari had she been so eager to see? He thought of her body, sprawled out on the stone. He stretched out on the ledge to see how it must have felt, groaning as he straightened his legs, unmindful of the straggling folk who tittered at him. Had she lost all feeling by then? Had her soul fled instantly, or was it instead a slow and dreadful pull from the body?

The cold seeped up from the hard surface and pierced his skin. His skull ached. Sleep came slowly, but it came. Once, in his dream, he thought someone was yelling at him. *Bhut-sahib, get up! Bhut-sahib, you must not rest here!* But when he woke, the sky was black, the stars had been blotted out, and he was alone. Mini was not here; this was the spot where her soul had fled, and in spite of the stories that warned otherwise, she had not returned.

But the land of ghosts waited on the other side of the river.

It was hard work moving against the grain of the current, and the boat traveled a diagonal path. His arms pumped, his heart heaved; several times he had to stop, and then the river carried the boat further downstream, further down Magadha's shore. At last, the boat bumped up against the cursed place. He stepped onto the hard sand searching for—what? He did not know.

Mini-behan, your little brother has come. Chhoto-bhai has come. He was searching not for a thing, but for the spirit of a person who had lived, because for what other reason do you come to Magadha? *Mini-behan—why did you never tell me?*

He remembered her sitting in his room. She shared a space with their other sisters, but those two often squabbled, and in those times Mini sought him out. He would sit at his desk, drawing with the colored pencils their father had given him. She would sit on his bed and run her slim fingers over the thick braid of her hair. Her eyes were always on something he could not see. "Did you know," she'd say, looking away from the window or waking from her dream, "that a dog visits the house two lanes over sometimes, and every time he visits, someone in that house falls ill?"

"How do you know that?"

She laughed, a laugh of pure amusement, pure joy. "You will be smarter than me, one day, Chhoto-bhai," she said as she returned her eyes to the world outside the window. "But not today, not yet."

Mini-behan, who was this Hari? "When you marry, will I still see you? Will you visit?"

"Every day, Chhoto-bhai. Even in your dreams, you will see me." She seemed to him then the most marvelous thing in the world; this girl, this dreaming woman who was his sister.

Mini-behan, you lied. I never see you. I look and look, but you never come.

The night blended in with the river, and the sacred city across the water made a strip of light between the two blacknesses. They'd dressed her as a bride and given her to a man; they'd dressed her as a bride again and given her to the Ganges. What was the difference? Everyone seemed to know what happened to a person dying a *good* death in Kashi. No one would say what happened to his sister.

"Mini-behan," he said, his voice cracked, his breathing labored, his chest tight. "Where are you?"

The night made no reply.

***

Not much time remained. The steps to the ground level of the house were much steeper than Mrs. Chalwah remembered, the concrete hard and unforgiving. No matter. She had given up comfort long ago. She gingerly bent her knees and sat on the topmost step, rested, then moved forward and down until she hit the next step. The shock of movement vibrated through her body. She had learned to navigate staircases in this way when she was a child. Then, she'd used the same method to go up the staircase; now, she was going down, in one of the last acts she would take. There was satisfaction in such symmetry.

She did not know how long it took to reach the bottom, but no one in the house woke. On the ground floor, the old woman breathed out the great God's name and tried to stand. With the wall's support, she managed it, her back curved forward.

Once standing, she walked in a shuffling gait, her steps slow enough to be quiet, her hand on the door equally silent. In the street, the night air enveloped her, and she breathed in deeply. The smell was different from what she could glean sitting by the open window, but it was also familiar. It smelled of That Night: dark and rich with dirt and river and stone, but tinged sweet with the perfume of some evening flower.

The journey was slow, but she enjoyed it. The world seemed to her reborn, though she could hardly see for the dark and her own diminishing eyesight. She crossed lanes she'd journeyed through as a child, a schoolgirl, a maiden, then a married woman. The ribbons her mother had tied on her braids came from a stall that once lingered down that side street. Her father had worked as an office clerk in a building a few lanes over. She remembered seeing him walking home, his stride so familiar that she could pick him out from a crowd of men when she watched from an upstairs window. There was the neighbor's house where her future husband had first seen her; she'd carried her older son to that shop over there for his school uniform. Every Diwali she'd bought boxes of sweets from the shop that she now passed, and she brushed her fingers against the windows as if to conjure up that time, those smells, the happy crackle of butter paper, the sweets tucked into boxes like an array of sugar-soaked jewels.

Onward, to places she had rarely traveled. In the pitch-dark of an alley she tripped over some discarded boxes, and when she leaned against the wall for support her sari was instantly wet and cold, soaked through with whatever foul liquid the building was awash in. Her head ached. She was chilled and could no longer understand the scents she took in or the sights before her eyes. But she continued; she knew she was nearing her destination.

At last, she arrived. Everything was as they said it would be: the soil felt different beneath her feet, the air was thinner in her lungs. She found a spot of earth and crumpled slowly to the ground, like an oil wick depleted of all its fire.

She had always maintained that she was a fair woman. Even in those beginning days after it happened, when women would see her and turn away, when schoolchildren would run alongside her and sing awful songs in their high-pitched voices, through all of this she remained firm in the person she was. Things had occurred in her life that had not been within her control, and she had done the best she could.

This, at least, was something she could control. This death, this end. She knew what she wanted. All those years of watching the bhavan—she'd envied those folk who filed into the building and died their good deaths, never to return. She could not allow herself that same, exalted fate. The act of unburdening herself to the circle officer had cleared the path for her. Perhaps she had wronged Menaka—she did not know, and it was not for her to decide. If she had, at least now that girl would have a chance at balancing the scales. That was why she had been so careful with the spot she'd chosen, careful about where her skin touched the ground. Every part of her lay outside the holy city. Outside of Kashi, Mrs. Chalwah ensured that she would die and come back. Outside of Kashi, she submitted herself to whatever fate in rebirth the laws of karma promised. And if fate decided to reincarnate her in a position that helped Menaka avenge herself, so be it. Perhaps Kashi would be hers in the life after that. Perhaps not.

Menaka had died dancing. And here *she* was, an old woman on her belly, crawling toward death, begging for the end to come. It would not be long now. Her eyes were closed, her ear flush against the ground. The cold seeped into her clothes, into her bones. A breeze passed over her, the air silent. All those years ago, who had Menaka been singing after?

Hari, Hari. *Menaka, did you find your Hari?* She thought. *Did he finally come for you?* She pressed herself closer to the ground. Her body was numb. She tried to hold onto her thoughts, tried to focus on the great God, but only one thought circled her mind, her last in this life: *Menaka, send your Hari to me. Please.*

"Is it time yet?"

"Three minutes, by my watch."

Everyone was alert; the children leaned in with drowsy anticipation, women sat with straight backs. The dead man's father clasped one of his son's hands to his chest; the mother held the other to her cheek. They both had palms to the man's heart, to his face.

They knew what the pots sounded like; they knew the exact moment those vessels would begin to roll and clatter; they knew the consistency with which the spirit spoke. A man with a watch took his place by the washroom door as unofficial timekeeper, and when the last seconds ticked by, he held his wrist up. The watch hands reached the new hour.

Silence.

The mother began to pray. She pressed her son's hand to her breast and rocked back and forth, the Mahadev mantra emitting from trembling lips, her voice loud and ragged. The priests stared at the floor or their prayer beads, and they, too, waited for that familiar sound that had haunted them for many months.

The pots said nothing.

"Narinder-ji?" Mohan asked. The old priest shook his head and kept his eyes to the ground. The mother's chanting grew louder, wilder. Her husband joined her, but his voice was heavy with tears, his words labored and two syllables behind his wife's. The crowd murmured; men gathered round the timekeeper to ensure he'd gotten the hour correct. "Narinder-ji?" Mohan tried again.

No one seemed willing to make a pronouncement. Five minutes passed. Ten. The mother continued chanting, her breath dying away and rising again, the words flickering like a wet candle wick. The father had stopped entirely. His face was buried in his son's chest, the body now wet with the man's tears. A quarter hour died as people waited for the washroom spirit to assert itself. The mother took a long breath and sighed out the last words of the mantra. All eyes looked to her, then at each other.

"Narinder-ji?" Mohan could not bring himself to ask the full question.

"Wait," Narinder whispered. The mother brought her son's hand up to her cheek and squeezed it with both of her own. Then she screamed, a terrible piercing wail that tore through the bhavan with the force of a gale. Her sobs engulfed the entire place; every room and inch of floor, every ear heard those sounds and trembled before the woman's grief. The crowd granted her silence at first, but they could not hold themselves for long. Men and women in the courtyard and the surrounding rooms, in Mohan's bed and beneath Pramesh's desk, in Shobha's kitchen and on the staircase and outside the bedroom door that no one had been able to break through—all of them erupted in waves of talk, calm at first, then urgent, then frenzied, until the entire bhavan was a hive of sound.

One corner of the hostel, however, kept its silence. In this corner, in a room that had known only one pair of occupants, an old man long watched over by his son eased himself up in a single decisive motion. The eyes that had held a vacant gaze toward the ceiling now looked out the small window, at the cobwebbed corners of the walls and the chipped green paint flaking near the door, into the face of the boy who was now a man, watching him with wide, fearful eyes. Months had passed since this old man and his son had entered this room, this bhavan. Dev, who'd been reading aloud from a holy book in one corner in a steady tongue through mobs and ghosts and dead men come to life, stopped.

"Bapa?" Sheetal grasped after his father's hand. The old hand grabbed the young one and squeezed hard and long.

"Well," the man said. He paused as if the syllable was all that was needed to sum up his mind's long absence from the world. "Well," he said again.

"Bapa?"

"Well, I am going," he said.

In the next instant, true to his word, he was gone.

47

During her first night in her in-laws' home, her husband's birthplace, her true bridal dwelling, Shobha slept free from the company of dreams and her own anxieties. The next morning, she sat with Kamna on the smooth kitchen floor, both women looking through the back door and watching Pramesh playing with Kavi outside. The boy held a cricket bat, his face scrunched in concentration, and as the old man yelled out encouragement and advice, Pramesh bowled and Kavi batted.

Last night, Pramesh had repeated everything the old man had told him, confirming what Shobha had feared. Shame at what she had thought and done filled her. She did not know how to ask for forgiveness. Mrs. Mistry had said that the rooms in the heart are there; one only had to fill them. She looked out the backyard at Kavi, who had allowed Pramesh to hoist him up and gallop around the yard. The child had a thin twig in his hand, and he pretended to whip Pramesh with it to make him go faster. "You must beat him very hard," the old man said from his perch on the rope bed. "Old horses require much beating, child. They refuse to learn otherwise."

Her husband, Shobha could see, was smiling. She wondered about his heart. Did he have those same rooms already built, waiting to be occupied? Or did he have to create them anew for this moment that he never could have anticipated? "I am glad we came," she said.

"If you would come again," Kamna began. "With Rani, once she is well. The journey is far, I know. But if you *could* come again. . . ."

"We will," Shobha said.

Outside, Pramesh stooped so that Kavi could slip from his back, and he walked to the old man and sat down on the rope bed next to him.

"Tired, yes?"

"I suppose we had just as much energy when we were children," Pramesh answered.

"It is natural that the younger folks can tolerate more. When you know nothing, you risk more of yourself. That takes energy, nah?"

Pramesh nodded. He still felt wonder at this boy, this son of Sagar's who knew his childhood better than he did. "We must leave soon—the train keeps to the same schedule, I think," he said after some time.

"As you should. Your daughter and your bhavan need you."

"Will you visit?"

"No. I am too old for such a journey. Perhaps you may persuade my daughter—she would do it, for the boy's sake. Not now, but later, when he is a few years older."

"But you will have to come, eventually. You know what the city can give you."

The old man shook his head. He had a long spike of grass in his mouth that he chewed on. "Not for me. Not in this lifetime. My life has trundled along in a simple kind of direction. Not easy, mind you, but simple. And though it is tempting to make an end in your Kashi, it seems to me not right to suddenly veer from one path onto another. I would much rather see this one through to the end, no matter where the next life will take me."

"And Sagar? What did Sagar want?" The question was painful for Pramesh to ask. He had no idea what his cousin had wanted in death.

"You mean did he want what Kashi could give him? Can any man tell what another man really wants for his end? I know as much as you do. But I am certain of this: all he ever wanted was to see you and tell you about the boy. Simple wishes, but enough for a dying man to journey into a strange city in hopes of meeting you."

"He never did see me, though. He died without fulfilling that last wish."

"Perhaps. Or perhaps not. You are sitting here, among the trees of your childhood where the two of you played. You have eaten his wife's food; you have carried his son upon your back. You slept where he once rested his head. He may not have physically seen you, but you have as good as gathered all the remaining parts of his existence in your arms and held tight. Many people could do worse."

The boy Kavi, who had been lying on his stomach in the shade of a tree and counting ants as they walked up the trunk, rose and gestured to his uncle. "Taya, come look!" he shouted.

"We can see you from here," the old man bellowed. "Give your Taya a chance to catch his breath. He is an old man like me. Go bother your mother and aunt; they are young still, nah?" The child ran giggling through the door. The two men sat and felt the breeze rustling through the tree and onto their faces. The old man handed Pramesh a long stem of grass. Pramesh bit down and tasted a sweet and sharp greenness that he thought he remembered.

"This is how it could have been," Pramesh said after a time. The old man clapped his back in a sudden hearty gesture.

"Different paths. The time for that version of the story is past. Think instead on another version. Think instead that this is how it could *be*."

"Mittu, fetch that green coconut your grandfather just bought and ask him to crack it open. Get him to pour the water into a glass and bring it up for Rani. Can you do that?" The boy ran downstairs to do his grandmother's bidding. Mrs. Mistry knew her grandchildren all loved her, but Mittu did not move so fast because of his affection for his grandmother. He had a soft spot for Rani, and the boy had hovered at the girl's door and sometimes next to her bed until a wandering adult pulled him out by the ear and scolded him in the muffled quiet of a bedroom.

Mittu was not the only one—the entire household, which usually operated on a system of bickering and making up, had molded itself around the little girl. The child was doing better. Mrs. Mistry had sat up nights, trading sleep with her daughter-in-law in shifts. The girl had become hotter and hotter, her breaths shallower, her body so still. The two women had soaked cloths in water and placed them on the girl's body to bring the fever down. At one point, they were constantly shifting the cloths, which seemed to dry as soon as they touched the girl's skin. The doctor, who Mrs. Mistry viewed through skeptical eyes, had no better solution. "The turn will come soon," he said with useless authority.

"Turn for what?" Mrs. Mistry had demanded.

"That remains to be seen," the gentleman replied.

The turn *had* come, late that night, two days after the girl's parents had left for the manager's home village. The room was dark and Mrs. Mistry had dozed off. At first, she missed the girl's breaths becoming deeper and fuller. She realized the change when she woke with a sudden start and began to once again switch out the cloths. They were no longer hot; they were simply warm, and when an hour had passed, they became cool. After another half hour, Mrs. Mistry removed them completely.

The girl's eyes opened by the time the sun came up. She was sitting up an hour later and eating the rice and milk that Mrs. Mistry fed her with a spoon.

By the afternoon, she was well enough to have the other children come in and read to her. By the next day, the older girls were able to braid her hair and act out a play for her in the room. That afternoon, Mrs. Mistry felt the girl was well enough to be out of her bed, but decided against it. Mittu was in the room, pulling at Rani's hand.

"Leave her be," Mrs. Mistry said as she pushed her grandson out with a gentle shove on his shoulder, and the boy disappeared down the hall. When she turned, she saw that the girl had slipped off the bed. "Back into bed with you," Mrs. Mistry said, and she tried to lift the girl away from the door. For a moment, Rani relented and allowed the older woman to tuck her in. Ensconced in a chair beside the child, Mrs. Mistry was about to take up her lacework when Mittu returned.

"Yes, I heard you, what is it?" the boy asked from the hall. Rani pushed the blanket away and shoved off the bed; small feet pattered across the floor.

"Mittu, what nonsense are you spouting, didn't I say to leave her be?"

"Yes, but she *called* me, Dadi!"

"Don't tell lies, child. Shall I call your Dada? He's just in the other room and he is not afraid of giving out punishment."

"She *did* say it, Dadi. She told me to wait, so here I am. It isn't my fault you didn't hear."

Mrs. Mistry looked from one child's face to the other. Rani had Mittu's hand in hers; she smiled at the boy and tugged him toward the terrace. "All right then. Away with both of you. But only for a little bit, and don't you dare wear her out, do you hear? Ey, Mittu, I said, *did you hear?*"

The children bolted for the terrace. "We heard you; we heard you," came an impatient cry from the stairs.

48

Stretched out on the ghats in his usual place, Maharaj slept the dreamless sleep he'd always had since That Day. He woke once in the middle of the night, turned over and pointed his face toward the river, and fell back asleep. He'd had plenty from Thakorlal, who'd paid him to fold paper into envelopes and glue down the seams. The man had been stingy with the payment, but Maharaj had surprised him with the speed of his work, the steadiness of his hands, the straight seams and crisp folds he created on envelope after envelope. At the end of the job he received a few extra coins, most of which went to back to Thakorlal.

Despite all the home brew, when he woke his head was clear. The light was still dim; the sun had only just begun to rise. He rubbed his eyes and sat up, and then he realized he was not alone. A woman and her companion sat below him on the second to last step of the ghat where the stone dipped into the river. Her hair was dark and piled atop her head; her clothing was rough and she wore no ornaments, but she was beautiful with luminescent skin and dark eyes that he felt he had seen before. She took no notice of him. Another man's head lay in her lap, his body stretched out on the stone. The woman touched the man's brow, and then she looked at her companion. Maharaj was surprised he hadn't noticed that person first. He had an animal skin slung around his shoulders, and strings of prayer beads snaked around his powerful arms. His hair was matted and wild. He knelt by the woman as if to whisper something to her, but he bent lower still and whispered something into the supine man's ear. Maharaj strained to hear the words, but he felt as if all the sound in the world had been muted. The ghat was quiet.

The sleeping man lifted his head from the woman's lap and stood. He was tall and lanky, with long arms and legs and a mustache that sat beneath his hawk-like nose and large clear eyes. When he turned away from the couple Maharaj saw it—a white flash of a scar on the man's forehead, a split in the eyebrow. The man took a step forward, and was gone. Maharaj blinked. And then he saw that the wild-haired man bore a trident in his hand. He grasped the woman's hand and turned, and when Maharaj blinked again the sun was further up in the sky and he was alone on the ghat.

Maharaj shook his head, rubbed his eyes. He sat on the steps for a while and thought. He'd never breathed a word of what he'd seen That Day on Magadha, the day he'd gone to seek the Bearer. He would say nothing about what he'd just seen now. Both stories were boons from the universe, meant for him only, and he would keep silent about both, always. Some gifts, he knew, could not be shared. Some gifts could be given only once, to stay with the receiver forever, until the memory of the gift, of that life, faded when death came.

He sat there for some time. Eventually, people joined him. He felt their disgusted looks, the prayers they spat in his direction to ward off the evil eye that he surely carried.

"Thieves! My boat is gone!"

"Raman, you idiot, why can't you secure your boat like everyone else?"

"Ask that Maharaj over there what happened to it. Ey, Maharaj! Where is this duffer's boat?"

He scraped the last remaining coins from his pocket and shook them in his hands. He stood and stared down at his palms. "Magadha," he said.

"What's the fool talking of now?"

"No, he is right. Look, look there, isn't that it?"

"So far down shore! Ey, Maharaj, who took it?"

The drunk threw his hands upward, palms out. "Not I, Bhaiya." He walked up the steps. At the head of the ghats, a child waited. "Where is your ma?" Maharaj asked. The child did not answer. She looked back at him with woeful eyes. Maharaj thought a moment. He held out his hand and the girl cupped her palms beneath his fingers. He dropped the coins into this cup. "Spend it on sweets," he said. "Spend it on ribbons, on a doll." The child ran off, the coins making a dull jangle in her hot fists. "Spend it on life," Maharaj said to himself, and he disappeared down the adjoining alley.

⚬

"Push that way, Bhaiya, pull up to the left."

"How many times have I said Raman is a simpleton? His poor mother."

"There, just there, yes, pull up onto the sand."

"You get out, Bhaiya."

"Fine, I will be the brave man. You stay there. Don't leave, you hear! Wait for me to push off first."

"Anything in the boat?"

"Nothing. Where do you suppose this thief went?"

"Not far. Shall I wait for you?"

"You mean wait while *I* walk around Magadha, looking for this fellow?"

"I will be right here."

"Your mother raised a coward, you hear?"

The boatman flicked his hand at him and remained seated while his companion trudged off on the sand. He spread his knees wide and released a comfortable belch. He'd made sure to moor only half of his boat on the sand. The other half, the half he sat in, bobbed in the water apart from this cursed land.

"Bhaiya!"

"Well? What is it?"

"Bhaiya, this way, this way!"

"Can't you simply tell me?" He waited for a single disgusted minute, then cursed. He crawled over the seating slats to the bow, muttered a quick prayer, and touched his feet to the white sands. He pulled his boat up higher onto the shore out of the current's drift, and then he ran down to where his companion stood waving and yelling, his voice high and shrill.

The anklets were still in Bhut's hand when they found him. The fingers had curled so tight in rigor mortis that the chains did not sing nor weep—they did not make a single sound as they moved the body from shore to boat to shore again.

Halfway across the city, a different search party came upon a different body. They found it just one step outside the city, carefully aligned so that not a single toe brushed the boundary into Kashi. The men were silent as they lifted Mrs. Chalwah's light frame onto a bier. They said nothing as they carried her home, where her son and daughter-in-law waited. No one spoke about her past, or her family, or her disappearance from the world in her later years. No one spoke of that story from so long ago. In the end, what they said about her, what they would always say about her, was that she died with her eyes open.

49

Footsteps shuffled outside the hole in the bhavan where the gates had been, hesitated, and then shuffled back to the entrance. The bhavan was empty, and every noise echoed. With Sheetal's father newly cremated, not a single dying guest remained.

News of the bhavan transforming into a House of Life had traveled with the quickness of a thieving monkey, but news of the bhavan coming back to what it used to be, a House of Death, was much slower to make the rounds. Mohan had tried. He'd been around to all his connections to ask them to pass the news. He'd even tried to contact the newspaperman who'd written the story that had brought such masses of people to the city in the first place. That man had demurred at first, but he relented in printing a small retraction that fell on the last page of the paper in type that Mohan had to hold close to his eyes to see.

Pramesh did not worry about this much. "They will find out soon enough, Mohan-bhai. Patience, that's all we need." He and Shobha had returned after being away for three days. They'd walked straight from the train station to Mrs. Mistry's house to fetch Rani, and then the three walked over to the bhavan, which was much changed from the building they'd left behind. Furniture had been damaged or stolen outright. Doors rested on bent hinges, moldering flowers and dried rice littered the stone walkway, foodstuffs and clothing forgotten in the haste of departure attracted mice and rats, which scurried about in the open. Shobha's kitchen had been raided entirely—even the leftover wood perched in the grate was gone. Only the contents of the upstairs bedroom remained intact: Thakorlal's key plate had stood strong.

"You cannot stay here," Mrs. Mistry pronounced upon visiting a day later to check up on her young charge. "She has only just recovered! Do you wish her to be ill again?" That was how Shobha and Rani came to stay with Mrs. Mistry. The men, Pramesh included, remained behind to assess the damage and begin repairs. Though he slept in his office, the manager spent most of his days outside the bhavan, speaking to workmen and inquiring about new furniture for the rooms.

In the interim, folk who still did not know that the bhavan was once again a death hostel became Mohan's responsibility. Now, hearing the shuffling outside, he straightened his cuffs and smoothed his hair with his hands, intent on matching the bhavan's reputation as a holy, clean place. A man waited at the entrance, a bundle of clothing on his back. "Is this Shankarbhavan?" he asked.

"It is," Mohan said, preparing himself to make the same explanation he'd already given twice that morning. "Listen, Bhai, the thing is—"

"For the dying?" the man said.

"What? Yes, for the dying." Mohan peered past the man into the empty lane.

"Do you always make people wait? That room over there, is it empty?" The man strode ahead. "This one," he said, gesturing with his chin at it, empty though it was, with no rope bed, not even the peeling list of instructions and rules for the bhavan. "I came ahead of my family," the man explained. "My brother is bringing her. My mother. And also my wife, my brother's wife, my children, grandchildren. . . ." He peered at the scene behind Mohan, the empty courtyard, his voice echoing against the walls. "You're sure this is the right place? The death bhavan?"

"What else could it be?" Mohan said. And he hastened to get the register from the office while the man unloaded his bundle and went into the lane to wait for the rest of his party.

50

"I will be back in an hour," Pramesh said, scooping up Rani in his arms, swinging her back and forth. He put her back down as Shobha approached with a glass of milk. Shobha stood over her daughter until the liquid had all disappeared down Rani's throat. She'd never had frequent cause to scold her daughter before, but alongside Rani's health an impish quality had emerged. She'd taken to hiding in the bhavan's many crevices and shadowy corners whenever her mother required her. Once, in a panic, Shobha had spent a half hour searching for the girl before finding her in room No. 5, empty since Sheetal had left it behind. He'd returned to his family farm, having completed his father's rites and spent the mourning period at the bhavan, every step completed perfectly under Narinder's instruction, the skull cracked on the first try. Rani had only smiled and proceeded to hide beneath the bed until Dev coaxed her out for Shobha.

"Going for a walk?" Shobha asked.

"A short one. To the ghats," Pramesh answered. "And then I will take her out in the lanes. There is a chaat stand that I've wanted to try."

"Don't mention that to Mrs. Mistry. Full of germs, the dangers of street food, she'd say."

"Strange; I'm sure I saw Mr. Mistry there some days ago."

"He would not be the first husband to keep something from his wife," Shobha said, and she turned away, Rani following, before Pramesh could reply.

Out of the gate, he looked up reflexively, hand raised in habitual greeting. The shutters on Mrs. Chalwah's window were closed, and he dropped his hand, moving on.

The streets were crowded. The air was festive but tense, everyone intent on some mission. Pramesh walked through narrow lanes, where children trailed each other with purpose, dogs trotted past fresh garbage piled in the alleys, and older women waved their hands when their neighbors tried to flag them down for gossip and instead continued with hobbled steps, holding market bags tight.

Out into the open air at a crossroads came competing sounds: radios spewing music and static in equal proportion, men scolding their wives who scolded their children who scolded their siblings, old folk who moaned at the windows in hopes that someone might hear them, unlike their families who'd long ago stopped up their ears to the sound.

Up the sloping path, past crooked doorways, folk sat ensconced on verandas high above the street, their faces like the statues hidden in temples across the city. Waving tree branches mingled with tangled power lines; monkeys scaled thick black electrical wires with the skill passed on by ancestors who rappelled down vines and across treetops. The air grew thick with incense and the warmth of human bodies, and the walls fell away to reveal the sigh of open sky and wide flowing river.

Pramesh sat at the foot of the ghats, his back to the sound and the crowds, his eyes straight ahead. He spied the skinny man with the spare stubble lighting a beedi with trembling fingers, the man he remembered to be Raman, the blubbering boatman who had helped bring Mohan back into the bhavan. There, under Raman's tight but nervous watch, was the man's boat: twice exorcized, the second ritual completed most recently after the vessel returned carrying the circle officer's body.

That was the boat that Sagar had taken; the boat he'd chosen under the guidance of the desk boy at the false Shankarbhavan, the boat he'd pushed off into the river. The boat where Sagar's life had come to an end. Pramesh had walked every step that Sagar had walked in the city, visited every place his cousin had wandered—except one.

"Ah, Bhai, you mustn't take that fool's boat, don't you know the stories?"

"Bhai, my vessel is just a few steps away and you'll see it's recently been blessed; surely you'd rather travel with me?"

Pramesh stood before Raman, who looked back at him with anxious eyes and hands that trembled with the slim weight of the beedi wedged between his fingers. "Raman-bhai. No other boat will do. Will you take me?"

The journey did not take long. Raman guided the boat with precision to the spot Pramesh had specified: the middle of the river, the halfway point between cursed sand and holy land. Whatever other men may have said about the boatman, he was a reliable captain for his beleaguered craft. He kept the boat steady when it seemed to drift, and he had the sense to keep his thoughts hidden regarding the nature of Pramesh's trip.

The city was beautiful from this distance; the buildings glowed with the sun's light and the entire panorama seemed immovable. What had Sagar seen? Had he looked only to his goal, to the river, to the infinite blackness that cradled the boat in liquid hope?

There were things Pramesh knew and things he did not, things he'd seen and things he could not imagine. He could picture Sagar with the clarity of his own image in the mirror. He saw him disembarking from the train, running into the tout, walking with weak purpose after chatting with the boy at the false Shankarbhavan. He saw him charm Thakorlal into giving him a glass bottle and then resume his wandering, perhaps taking a circuitous route through the lanes. He sought out the boy at the hostel, walked to Shankarbhavan, was denied at the gate. Peered through the iron bars, hoping for a glimpse, then turned away. Walked the city, following a young boy, slept a feverish sleep on the ghats, and woke. Built up his courage, his belief, and was persuaded to take a boat by himself into the river, to dip from that holy water at the place where sacred met cursed. And then what? Did his body give out in the boat? Did he slip as he leaned over, trying to reach that elusive nectar? Did he tie the anchor rope around his arm with purpose, knowing that his end was near and choosing to seize the moment himself?

Pramesh would never know. That pain of ignorance would remain with him forever until his own good death many years later; the twinge in his heart would remind him that his cousin's story was short and blurred in a way that he did not deserve.

He focused on the early afternoon sun against the river, the spots that sparkled with white pricks of light. The light shifted and bobbed with the water, refracted and broke apart and came back together with the current's movement. The river would flow, the sun would rise and fall over the city; he and Shobha would grow old; his child and Sagar's would create their own lives; the light would continue this dance for time immemorial. Always apart, always together. Pot broken, relationship finished.

Not finished, Bhaiya. Never finished.

He could imagine Sagar's death, or he could imagine Sagar's life, the parts he had missed, the parts he did not know. Sagar holding a newborn Kavi in his arms. Sagar tending to his fields. Sagar running through the small grove of trees behind the house with Kavi on his back, Kamna watching from the kitchen and laughing at them both. A good death, a bad death; in the years to come Pramesh would never discover an answer that satisfied him, but in those moments his mind turned toward the one thing he knew to be true.

The life, he was certain, had been good.

END

AUTHOR'S NOTE

Though the death hostels of Banaras are very real, Shankarbhavan is a place of fiction. Similarly, the tale of Yamraj and Magadha has no direct basis in scripture or in epic, nor is it part of the storyscape of Banaras. Any other deviation in geography, custom, and language concerning the city or the hostels is entirely my own.

While I chose to write about characters who have Hindu beliefs, Banaras—like the entirety of India—is home to significant populations of people who practice other faiths. Muslims, Buddhists, Sikhs, Jains, Christians, and more have all lived in the city, some with families that go back generations.

Many thanks to Amrut Champaneri, Nila Champaneri, and Ranjani Murali for their patience and generosity in conversation, and to the following: *End Time City*, by Michael Ackerman; *Banaras: City of Light*, by Diana L. Eck; *Forest of Bliss*, directed by Robert Gardner; *Dying the Good Death*, by Christopher Justice; *Benares Seen from Within*, by Richard Lannoy; and *Death in Banaras*, by Jonathan Parry.

—PRIYANKA CHAMPANERI, NOVEMBER 2020

ACKNOWLEDGMENTS

With gratitude to the following:

Courtney Angela Brkic, for walking every single step of this decade-plus journey with me.

Leigh Feldman, who loved this book on the first read and never stopped loving it.

Téa Obreht and Ilan Stavans, for the Restless Books Prize for New Immigrant Writing, and for opening the door.

Nathan Rostron, for guiding every aspect of this book's publication with such enthusiasm and care. I waited a long time for the right editor to find this book. It was worth the wait.

Alison Gore, for plucking these pages out of the submission pile, Christine Pardue, for being the best promotional and publicity partner in crime, and everyone at Restless Books, for their dedication and love for stories from every place, every voice.

Manasi Subramaniam, and everyone at Penguin Random House India, for giving this book a second home and life in India.

Susan Richards Shreve and Mary Kay Zuravleff, for the right words at the right time.

Courtney, Susan, the late Alan Cheuse, Stephen Goodwin, Helon Habila, Bill Miller, Kyoko Mori, and the rest of the MFA faculty at George Mason University, for the thesis fellowship. And Alok Yadav, for that early and perceptive reading.

The Virginia Center for the Creative Arts, for providing me with the ideal working environment on multiple occasions.

Fairfax County Public Libraries in Virginia, whose halls I have wandered since I was five years old.

George Mason University, for educating, employing, and making space for me for almost two decades.

Katie Burgess, steady anchor in the stormiest of seas.

Lisa Carey, for treating me like a writer before she'd read a single word.

Chris Freas, for sending me that email all those years ago.

Collin Grabarek, for reading every single line of that early draft (twice!) and for astute insights each time (same to CAB, LC, AK, EEM, RM, TR, and SW).

Alissa Karton, eternal ally in weather foul and fair, and Gary Karton, the first writer I ever met and still the most generous.

Elizabeth MacBride, Alyson Foster, and Shabnam Bozzelli, for fellowship in this writing life.

Ilana Masad, for being the reader of my dreams.

Bobbie Merritt, Marylou Holly, and Brian Selinsky, for the Mason Staff Study Grant.

Elizabeth Eshelman Moes, for always getting it, for always getting me.

Ranjani Murali, whose friendship and enthusiasm know no bounds.

Lorrie and Mouse Neumeister, and Louise Murray, dear friends and open hearts.

Timothy Rowe, for always assuring me that I am "crushing it," and to the memory of Mikel Sarah Lambert Rowe, whose kind words in those early days remain a bright light.

Laura E. Scott, for being the first person who thought I could.

Christina Nienaber Shotwell, generous with her trust and a singular memory.

Kim Sneed, for asking, for listening.

Susan Woodruff, for bringing the rains.

Shivam Champaneri, best of brothers, best of friends, and a pretty good reader (and snack maker) as well. Thank you for feeding me, for listening to my "great" ideas, and for asking the most important question of all.

Amrut Champaneri, for coaxing roots down into alien soil, for the thousand sacrifices and indignities and suppressions endured—all to ensure that the family tree would flourish, all so that your children might sit in the branches and dream. For embodying the life of the mind. For never, ever, ever giving up.

Nila Champaneri, for loving stories and for sharing that love, for reminding me of the virtues of the tortoise and the bird's eye, for teaching me all the things that matter most, and for everlasting patience with the butterfly. Darling Buh, softness made steel, fierce mother heart.

Thank you.

READING GROUP
DISCUSSION QUESTIONS

1. In *The City of Good Death*, what does it mean to die "a good death"? What does dying a good death look like in your culture or faith tradition?

2. Both Pramesh and Bhut have traumatic pasts that shape the men that they grow up to be in profound ways. How do their pasts inform the choices they make as adults? How are the two men similar? How are they different?

3. Maharaj originally appears to be something of a vagabond, but is later revealed to have a history closely tied to the city. Did your feelings about him change from the beginning of the book to the end?

4. The idea of not looking back is important for how Hindus process death; it's a literal component of Hindu funeral rites. What role does memory play in Pramesh's life and his grieving?

5. When the violent clanging of pots haunts the bhavan after Pramesh's mourning period, he reflects that, had Shobha performed the funeral rites, she would not have looked back like Pramesh did. Considering the established gender roles in the novel, how would the story have been different if Pramesh's story had been told from a woman's perspective?

6. Mrs. Chalwah makes a very specific choice about her death in terms of where, when, and how. What drives her decision? Do you agree with what she does?

7. Shobha feels threatened by Kamna because Kamna was the first choice of bride for Pramesh. Is Shobha justified in her insecurity? How might you have acted in her place?

READING GROUP DISCUSSION QUESTIONS

8. Whose story did you enjoy the most? Were there any characters you wanted to know more about?

9. A central theme of things being more than what they appear to be runs throughout the novel. Discuss the plot lines or characters where this was most apparent to you. Whose story surprised you the most?

10. Grieving is an incredibly social process in the novel. How does it compare to other literary depictions of grief that you've encountered? What about in your own life?

11. Has your idea of what it means to die a good death changed through the course of reading this novel?

AN INTERVIEW WITH
PRIYANKA CHAMPANERI
AND MALLIK THATIPALLI

MALLIK THATIPALLI: You have worked on this book for ten years. . . . Can you tell us about the process of writing the book, and your experiences?

PRIYANKA CHAMPANERI: Because I work a full-time day job, my writing is limited to a few hours in the evenings, but my process is also admittedly quite slow-going. I am an organic writer, meaning I don't work from outlines or have an idea of where the story will end. Writing for me is about that process of discovery—excavating who the characters are and what fears and motivations drive them, and then feeling my way into the story and following it to the end. Writing this way takes time, especially when I realize that scenes I'd been working on for months no longer work and I need to backtrack and start over. But when the writing is flowing, this process is also incredibly thrilling, because I get to experience the story unfolding in a way that I hope is very similar to a reader's experience in wanting to turn the pages to find out what happens next.

MT: How did the idea of setting a story in Kashi, and the premise of using the age-old belief that death in the city will free one of future births, come about?

PC: In between college and graduate school, one of my coworkers sent me a link to a Reuters article titled "At an Indian Hotel, Guests Check in to Die." That article was my introduction to the death hostels of Varanasi, and it piqued my interest immediately. I had grown up in a Hindu household and from an early age had been surrounded by

437

books of philosophy, Indian mythology, and fairy tales. The part of me that was firmly ensconced in that faith saw the death hostels as something necessary and practical, as ordinary as a rest stop along a highway.

But I'd also been born and raised in the US, in a culture more centered around a Judeo-Christian way of thought, and from that perspective I could understand how a death hostel could appear to be incredibly unique. That contradiction between necessity and novelty was immediately intriguing to me, but it's a very big leap to go from reading an article to deciding to write a book centered around that place. I set the idea aside for many years until I finally felt confident enough in my ability and the research I'd done to give the writing a try.

MT: What I found striking was the atmosphere of the city, its religious practices, and its narrow lanes . . . and you haven't even visited the city!

PC: While I have visited India previously as a tourist, I have not yet visited Varanasi. My lack of firsthand experience with the city was one of the biggest reasons I hesitated to start writing this book. But I was intensely interested in the city of Varanasi and the death hostels, and I began to read more about both just to satisfy my curiosity. The more I read, the deeper I fell into the rabbit hole of research. And then as the months went by, bits of dialogue started popping into my thoughts, as well as snippets of scenes. Slowly, a story began to grow within me.

I felt I knew this imagined version of the city quite intimately, and it was vivid enough, rich enough, for me to finally gain the confidence to begin to write. And I was also able to pull from other areas where I did have firsthand knowledge—my lifelong experience with Hinduism, and the intensely visual memories I'd stored away from my trips to India, all informed the book.

MT: Dying a good death is a significant part of Indian culture, and is an important constituent of the book. Though the book is about loss, it has an optimistic and uplifting tone about it . . .

PC: I wanted to approach death in as neutral a manner as possible, and that meant writing each death scene as if I were a bystander dutifully recording what I saw while keeping my own emotions out of the narration. My goal was to give the reader the freedom to approach the material and come away with their own feeling without the encumbrance of my perspective bogging them down. So in some instances it might be that the death was celebrated, while in others it's a grave loss that paralyzes—no matter who I was writing about, I surrendered to the characters and simply followed them around and wrote down their reactions.

And while certainly some of the characters experience paralysis because of grief, life does go on—so I was equally intent on showing these two things side by side.

MT: At the core of the book is a supernatural visit by a character which takes the story forward. How difficult was it to ensure that it blended with the idea of the book, without overpowering it?

PC: Among the things that influenced my writing were fairy tales. I still read such stories now whenever I'm feeling unmotivated or uninspired. One thing these stories have in common, no matter their provenance, is this easy coexistence of the spectacular with the everyday. For example, a woman goes on a journey and suddenly meets a talking fox who gives her advice and a magic charm, and the woman takes these and goes on her way. The question of why or how the fox is talking is never broached, it's just assumed that this is a thing that happens in this world.

I tried to take the same approach when writing about the supernatural in this novel. While the characters are certainly affected by the presence of this thing in their midst, they never express shock in a way that suggests such an occurrence is outside their realm of possibility. Their feeling is more one of coming to terms with this very unfortunate problem, and then subsequently moving toward a resolution.

The choice to have a ghost manifest its presence using a common household object, in probably the most practical room in a dwelling, was also intentional. I wasn't looking for this haunting to be overly dramatic or jarring, as you might expect in the horror genre. But it did have to be frightening and carry a sinister quality. And I tried to accomplish those things by taking a mundane object and then twisting it to do something it should never be doing, because what is more frightening than that? Anything that upends the reality to which you are accustomed is terrifying, because it makes you reassess all the other things you thought you knew to be true.

MT: The relationships in the book are at the heart of it: husband and wife; brother and brother; friends and neighbors . . .

PC: Very early on, I knew this book was going to be about two men who were cousins but had grown up essentially as brothers. Family relationships and dynamics are things I'm centrally preoccupied with as a writer, but I'm particularly attracted to sibling relationships.

Out of all the human connections a person has, via blood or via choice, a sibling is the one person who potentially has the privilege to see you from the earliest stage of your life and then experience all the subsequent stages alongside you, in real time. And as you get older, a sibling is the one person you can never completely hide from, because they saw you from your earliest days and have full knowledge of the arc of your growth as a person.

That unique knowledge can be either freeing or stifling. There is just so much to delve into—obligation, loyalty, the generosity it takes to let each other grow, the animosity that can develop when one refuses to let go. I'm not sure I'll ever tire of exploring that dynamic.

MT: The setting of the book is timeless, there is no clue as to when it is set. It can be any time in the last century (before mobile phones and the internet). Was it a conscious decision?

PC: I was intentionally unspecific regarding the time period of this book for a few different reasons, including the one you just mentioned— I wanted the reader to be able to see this story happening in any decade. Part of this was my own limitations—I did not want to be tied to a specific time and consequently have this book pinned to the historical events surrounding that time. But also, I was delighted to find in my research that one of the reasons Varanasi is said to have this effect of freeing a soul from the cycle of reincarnation is the notion that time simply does not exist in the city. I really seized on that idea and ran with it, initially out of necessity and convenience.

But as the years went by and I fell deeper into the story, I felt more confident about the decision because it seems truer to the ways in which we all live our lives—we're far more wrapped up in our own personal dramas than the larger events around us.

MT: I found the book to be labyrinthine with its store-well of stories. Ghosts, the ghats, and grief give each character a backstory. How difficult is it to achieve this while writing?

PC: The process of creating these stories individually was so much fun for me. It was also an effective diversion tactic, especially if I was stuck with the main narrative—I could choose to write a little side story, and in that way still be productive even if I couldn't figure out how to move the larger plot forward. And then, when I was able to get to a place of once again writing the main narrative, I had these additional seeds planted with these other stories that I could pick up and weave into the main story as I went along if the opportunity arose.

None of this was easy—it was an intense and laborious process. I'm often blind or willfully ignorant to what should stay and what should go. But I don't think I could have written this book if I'd known from the start how everything was going to fit together—it would have been too overwhelming.

MT: The book deals with Hinduism, in all its generous expanse. We live in a time when majoritarian forces have construed a narrow narrative of the religion. How do you view this dichotomy?

PC: Every religion has, at some point, been twisted to suit the interpretation of the loudest, most powerful voice in a room. This has been happening for thousands of years, and Hinduism is no exception.

From my own reading and experiences, I've found that there is so much richness to absorb and so much to be learned from every religion and belief system. And ultimately, spirituality is about the individual. No matter how loud or how powerful a voice might be, it's up to the listener to choose to absorb that rhetoric, or to instead walk away and trust in their own instincts and interpretation.

FIRST PUBLISHED IN FIRSTPOST, MAY 10, 2021

ABOUT THE AUTHOR

PRIYANKA CHAMPANERI received her MFA in creative writing from George Mason University and has been a fellow at the Virginia Center for the Creative Arts numerous times. *The City of Good Death* is her first novel.